THE REVENGE

OF THE SHADOW KING

GREY GRIFFINS BOOK 1

THE REVENGE

OF THE

SHADOW KING

Derek Benz
& J. S. Lewis

Orchard Books
NEW YORK
AN IMPRINT OF
SCHOLASTIC INC.

Library of Congress Cataloging-in-Publication Data
Benz, Derek. Lewis, J. S. The revenge of the Shadow King /
by Derek Benz and J. S. Lewis. — 1st ed.   p. cm.
"A Grey Griffins book." Summary: When Max Sumner and three
friends play a magical card game called Round Table, they realize
that it is up to them to prevent the wicked creatures of the cards
from destroying their town, indeed, their world.
ISBN 0-439-79574-5 (hardcover: reinforced lib. bdg.)
[1. Magic — Fiction. 2. Card games — Fiction. 3. Goblins — Fiction.]
I. Lewis, J. S. (Jon S.). II. Title. PZ7.B44795Rev 2006 . [Fic]—dc22
2005011976   10 9 8 7 6 5 4 3 2 1   06 07 08 09 10

Printed in the U. S. A.   23
Reinforced Binding for Library Use
First edition, March 2006
Text type set in 10.5-point Res Publica
Display type set in Skreech and Stinkymovement
Book design by Richard Amari

For Ioulia . . . my amazing wife and inspiration.
Thank you for sharing the light that you shine so brightly.
And for my grandparents, Bill and Jeanne Doughten,
for building a family that reaches for their dreams.
— Derek

To my wife, Kelly, for your beauty, sacrifice,
and unyielding love. And for my daughters, Bailey Anne
and Olivia, the enchanting pixies who make my heart sing.
— Jon

With eternal gratefulness, we would like to thank Nancy,
Lisa, and Ken for believing in us, breathing life into the
tiny town of Avalon, Minnesota.
— Derek and Jon

Very special thanks to
Mike Reynolds and Vito Consulting for your support and
dedication to the Grey Griffins. We are humbly in your debt.

Contents

THE Revenge

OF THE SHADOW KING

GREY
GRIFFINS
BOOK
1

PROLOGUE

Max Sumner peeked over his blanket, paralyzed by fear. Something was in his bedroom. Something in the darkness. Something bad.

His eyes peered into the web of night that draped his room in mysterious shadows. From beneath the familiar shape of his desk, which was strewn with comic books and trading cards, something was watching him. Max couldn't see it. But he could hear it breathing.

A flash of lightning illuminated the room, and for a brief moment Max saw something dark and sinister creeping toward him. Its skin was like coal, and instead of eyes, only cold empty sockets peered back. Step by step it inched closer. Max opened his mouth to scream, but no sound came. He tried to jump, but his legs wouldn't move.

Another lightning burst and the monster was next to Max, reaching its hungry fingers toward him.

Before Max could cry out, he was ripped from his sheets and thrown against his bedroom wall with a crash. He cried out as he felt the nails rip, the boards shatter, and the electrical cables snap. Like a rocket, he flew into the stormy night, three stories above the rain-slicked cobblestones far below. He never had a chance.

1

It's All in the Cards

AVALON, MINNESOTA, was a perfectly boring town. That is, it was both perfect and boring all at the same time. Every yard was beautifully manicured, and each garden was overgrown with flowers worthy of a blue ribbon at the county fair. It was also quite small. There was a single streetlight, one bank, a grocery store, and a one-screen movie house that was closed on Sundays. Parents let their children play outside after dark, and nobody ever locked a front door. In fact, Avalon was a town where every perfect day was just like the day before, and would be in turn just like the next. While this might seem refreshing to somebody from a bustling city filled with noisy cars, towering skyscrapers, traffic jams, and police sirens, to Grayson Maximillian Sumner III, or Max, as he preferred, Avalon's serenity was a perfect nightmare.

Like Avalon itself, there was little remarkable about Max—at least on the outside. He was tan from a summer spent back and forth from the beach to the baseball diamond, and his thick, brown hair, not short, but not long, had been bleached by the sun, giving it the appearance of corn silk. None of those qualities made him look out of the ordinary.

Yet if Max did have one special feature, it was his eyes. They were large and tended to change color with the weather, though most often they were a deep gray. Much to his embarrassment, little old ladies liked to point out just how beautiful those eyes were—and typically at the most inopportune times (like at the mall in front of his friends, who would tease him mercilessly later). But in a crowded schoolyard Max just didn't stand out.

At eleven years of age he was neither short nor tall, thick nor thin. He wasn't the fastest runner, couldn't hit the ball the farthest, and he lost as many arm wrestling matches as he won. But when teams were picked, he was never last, either. It was true, Max didn't stick out. Except for his money.

The Sumner family was rich. Not the kind of rich that meant he lived in a big fancy house (though he did), or that his father drove an Italian sports car (he had at least three). The Sumners were the kind of rich that meant they owned entire towns, megamalls, high-rise towers, and vast acreages of farmland all around the world. Real-estate investments had made the Sumners billionaires (rumor had it, many times over). Avalon, for the most part, was one such Sumner property.

But Max never cared too much about any of it. All that concerned him for the moment was that he was late. He glanced at his watch and frowned. Terribly late. Max zipped through Avalon's side streets on his bike en route to the Shoppe of Antiquities—the only place in town he found interesting, and the only place, it seemed, that hadn't changed since his parents' divorce.

The Sumner mansion seemed empty without his dad, even though Max's mom and baby sister were still there. But Annika Sumner hardly paid attention to her kids. There were simply too many activities for Avalon's leading socialite to be burdened with raising children, especially now that she was single. Besides, that's what Rosa, the children's nanny, was hired for.

Max had never felt so alone in all his life. And with summer vacation drawing to a close, he was getting even more depressed with thoughts of homework, and worse—having to talk about his parents' messy breakup to everyone at school. News of the divorce had made the local paper, of course. That's just how it was in a small town like Avalon, Minnesota. Privacy didn't exist. Especially when your name was Sumner.

The headlines talked about the enormous sum of money Max's mom received as a settlement, but money didn't read you bedtime stories or go on family picnics. It wasn't good at consoling you after a loss in Little League or at helping you with math homework. No, Max was starting to resent his family's money. His parents chased it like dogs after a mail truck, but he'd have traded every penny to have his parents back together. Max wasn't holding his breath, though.

Angry, he pedaled harder.

As the pavement raced beneath Max's tires in a blur, the vague memory of a horrible dream lingered, tugging at the corner of his mind. But whenever he tried to recall the details, it seemed to slip away.

Arriving at his destination, Max jumped off his bike and leaned it up against the wall as he walked under a faded sign that read SHOPPE OF ANTIQUITIES. It was a store that dealt in rare books, ancient mysteries, the occasional tourist trinket, and a vast array of collectibles. Some authentic. Some not.

Breezing through the creaky doorway, Max was immediately greeted by the aroma of musty books and sweet pipe tobacco as he stepped into the shadowy front room. A handful of stained-glass lamps offered meager light as Max's eyes slowly adjusted to the place he had come to know so well. All about lay a curious muddle of treasures. Ancient yellowed books were stuffed in every possible crevice, and curling maps were tacked to the walls.

Max wove through the clutter, ignoring the BEWARE OF DRAGONS sign that hung askew on the back wall. Disappearing through a low archway, he rushed up a flight of steps and grabbed hold of the knocker that hung on a heavy oaken door. As Max knocked, the sound echoed all about, filling his mind with visions of castles and knights.

"What's the password?" a nervous voice asked from the other side.

"Excalibur," Max replied. A series of locks clicked, slid, and unsnapped before the door slid slowly open.

"Hey, Ernie," Max offered, slipping in. "Am I late?"

"It's just me and Natalia so far," Ernie Tweeny explained, wearing ridiculously oversized black-rimmed glasses that perched crookedly on his face. He was chomping loudly on a chocolate bar that was sticking like brown goop to his once shiny braces. It was a wonder he wasn't as wide as he was tall, given his zealous consumption of sweets. Ernie was thin and dangerously uncoordinated, with a jumble of black hair that needed constant combing. His wardrobe choices were best described as eclectic, regularly consisting of argyle socks, plaid pants that were a bit too short, and a striped sweater a few sizes too big. Ernie was a self-admitted coward, spooked by everything from spiders to his own shadow, but despite it all he wasn't ashamed of who he was. To his credit, Ernie was incurably enthusiastic about everything, and a loyal friend. But though his quirky antics were good for a laugh, they were bad news for his asthma. And for all of that and more, Ernie was one of Max's best friends.

Behind Ernie perched Natalia Felicia Anastasia Romanov. In perfect posture, she sat at a hulking round table that filled the little room with the large picture window overlooking Main Street. "Hello, Grayson," she greeted him, using Max's formal name. Natalia loved formalities. If one wasn't required, she'd invent an occasion. She also loved detective work, particularly solving mysteries, spending a great deal of her time studying things like voice recognition and footprint patterns. She knew it had been Max coming up the stairs long before he knocked, and it was for that reason she didn't bother looking up from the stack of strange cards that lay neatly before her when he entered the room.

Natalia's snow-white face was painted with a light dusting of freckles, and her red hair, long and wiry, was pulled into two fierce-looking braids. Spunky was a word adults often used when describing her. But precocious might have fit her more aptly. Natalia was fearless, with a razor-sharp wit and a startlingly large vocabulary for an eleven-year-old. She was best known for her voracious reading habits, an obsessive love of unicorns, and having the finest detective mind in the whole school (admittedly, there was very little competition).

Two ugly mismatched chairs remained empty after Max and Ernie took their seats next to Natalia. One chair was a good deal larger than the other, which might have seemed odd, but for that matter, the entire room was rather odd. Strange symbols were painted across the peeling plaster of the brick wall, which also held numerous pictures and charts of mysterious places, creatures, and other things. In the corners were iron sconces, and the smoke from the candles crept across the dark tin ceiling like a nest of dizzy snakes. Some people might have called it cozy. Others might have called it cramped. But to Max, it somehow felt like home (at least more than his house did lately).

"So are you ready to play?" Ernie asked anxiously, thumbing through his own stack of cards, which were very much like Natalia's deck, apart from being in far worse condition and in no particular order whatsoever.

"I guess," Max answered, looking around. He was still trying to catch his breath, relieved he wasn't the last person to arrive. He hated being late for anything. That was one of the first lessons in business his father had taught him. You don't want to be too early for an appointment, but never, under any circumstances, were you to be late. Max had never had a business appointment, of course. And though he could imagine what one might be like, he was in no hurry to grow up. If only his father felt the same way.

However, the three friends weren't worried about business just then. Their thoughts were focused on the cards held in their hands. They belonged to the game called Round Table — an ancient game that was rumored to have been invented by King Arthur, and taught to only the most trusted and valiant boys and girls in the land (at least that's what it said on the box). Larger than a deck of traditional playing cards, in both scale and number, the cards were painted with all sorts of fascinating traps and spells as well as knights and monsters. The objective was to defeat your opponents' armies through strategy, strength of arms, and the luck of a pair of ten-sided dice called knucklebones. All three friends had their very own deck, which they had spent incalculable time collecting, building, and worrying over. Yet to them, the juiciest part of Round Table was the fact that as far as they knew, nobody else in the entire world (or at least in Avalon, Minnesota) played. It was their secret, and they liked it that way.

As Max slipped off his backpack and reached for his deck of cards, Olaf Iverson, whom everybody knew as "Iver," strode into the room in his immense black boots. The owner and proprietor of the Shoppe of Antiquities, Iver was rather tall, with sloping broad shoulders and a waistline not dissimilar to Santa Claus's. He was very distinguished, as one could tell by his silvery, waxed mustache and closely groomed beard. He was also very intelligent, speaking no less than twenty-seven languages, by his own account. Where he came from and what he had done before he had opened the Shoppe of Antiquities was always up for heated debate. But the kids loved him like an adopted grandfather, and he was the only adult who seemed to really understand them. Not to mention, his was the only store in the world where Round Table was sold.

"Good morning, Iver!" Ernie said, beaming.

"A good morning indeed? Well, I will take your word for it,

Master Tweeny," Iver responded in his deep rumbling voice. "But be careful. I did not ask for a good morning, and here you are wishing it to me all the same, whether I want it or not."

While Ernie was trying to puzzle out Iver's reply, Natalia laughed. She was the kind of girl who liked to pretend she knew things others didn't.

"And you, Natalia? What have you got there?" asked Iver.

"My new costume! Do you like it?" Natalia rose from her seat, showing off the elf outfit her mother had made for her, complete with green moccasins and a matching emerald dress and cape. Why she wore costumes to their games was anyone's guess. She said it helped her "get into character" — whatever that meant.

"You look like a tree frog," Ernie joked, feeling unusually brave. Normally, Natalia would have pinched him for the insult, but today she either didn't care or hadn't heard him. Instead, she spun around in obvious pride.

"Very pretty," Iver said with a brief clap, "but I'm afraid we have quite a quest ahead of us today, and we really must begin. No time for dawdling. Are the Grey Griffins ready?"

"But we're still missing a member of our team," Ernie, the smallest member of the Grey Griffins, pointed out. "I thought the rule was that we never leave anyone behind?"

Just then, panting heavily and caked with mud, Harley Davidson Eisenstein burst through the door. He was big, looking at least thirteen years old, even though he was only eleven, with a rough reputation to match. Intense eyes, the color of a blue storm, were hidden by shaggy chestnut hair, and the grease smudges on his sturdy jaw showed he had been working on his go-cart again. Harley tended to wear T-shirts with pictures of muscle cars and rock bands, and his old jeans were slightly tattered and fringed around the cuffs, covering his faded canvas sneakers. Girls thought he was gross because, among other things, his fingernails were always dirty and his knuckles were covered in warts. But Harley didn't much care for what other people thought.

"Ah, young Master Eisenstein . . . it appears you have joined us at last. Please, pull up a chair. But be quick about it, mind you," Iver said sternly.

"Sorry, Iver," Harley mumbled as he slumped into the last empty seat. Despite the commotion, Iver began to explain the tournament rules, set the time limit, and inspect everyone's knucklebones to ensure they met with his strict approval. Pulling out his own deck of cards, Harley turned to Max. "You won't believe what just happened. . . ."

"Where'd you get that card? It's awesome!" Ernie exclaimed, cutting off Harley midsentence.

"Ah yes," Iver said as he reached over and drew the card in question from Harley's stack. The old man studied the image intently, frowning as the wrinkles around his eyes formed great crevices. "Oberon . . ."

The room seemed to grow cold as the young friends quieted.

"Yes . . . ," Iver continued. "This is a rare card, but I don't recall giving it to you. Do you remember from whence it came?"

Harley shrugged.

"Well, in any event, I suggest you put it away and forget you have it."

"Why?" asked Ernie.

"Why indeed, Master Tweeny. Do you not know who Oberon is?"

Ernie looked at him with a blank expression, his jaw hanging as a bit of chocolate drool slid off his chin. Pop quizzes were not his thing.

"Oberon is the Shadow King. A rather menacing name that doesn't even begin to describe his more charming traits. Wise and terrible. Deadly and ruthless. He's the cruel and unimaginably powerful ruler of the Shadowlands of Faerie. Master Eisenstein, you hold a card that will give you a great advantage in this game, but at what cost? The card almost assures victory, but it has been known to betray the holder at the most inconvenient times."

"That's silly." Natalia waved her hand as if she were waving away a fly. "This is just a game. A card can't betray anyone."

"Young lady," Iver said, frowning. "You will have to learn that not everything is as simple as your Saturday morning cartoons. Taking this card for granted, or anything for that matter, could be your undoing—and the undoing of your friends. I certainly will not have you putting your friends in danger simply because you failed to recognize this simple lesson."

Natalia squirmed a bit under his stern gaze. But Max and Ernie scrambled from their chairs to huddle around Harley, each trying to get a closer look at Oberon's trading card. Wrapped in a cloak of darkness, the Shadow King's eyes glowed with malice beneath a deep hood as grasping fingers reached toward the four friends hungrily. It was a disturbing picture, and Max quickly wished he hadn't looked at it.

"He's freaky," Ernie said, chomping loudly on a second chocolate bar, though this one had peanuts.

"Quite so." Iver frowned. "But until we solve the puzzle of how this card found its way into your deck, why don't you put it away for now, eh, Harley? In the meantime, the rest of you will need to take your seats. We have a game to play, so let no cloud of darkness stand in our way."

"Before we begin, though, I must set the scene." Iver was a masterful storyteller, and his involvement as their Game Master added a depth to the game that made it almost seem real. "A twist, for this won't be a free-for-all today. No, today is different. Today you must fight together. An ancient evil has awakened, and darkness has spread across the land."

Iver looked into each of their eyes. "You four are all that stands between this army of darkness and the complete destruction of the world you love. Your armies, your magic, and your intelligence are your only tools. No one will be here to save you. And I must tell you, if you fight, you have very little chance of surviving. But if you don't take a stand, life as you know it will be changed forever."

The kids sat enraptured by Iver's tale. They'd never played as a team before, but that only made it all the more exciting.

"You have precisely ten seconds until they attack," Iver stated, pulling out his own stack of Round Table cards and laying them on the table. The cards were facedown, but they all suspected what lay on the other side. Goblins. Horrible, nasty, and smelly goblins. An army of them.

"What are we gonna do?" Ernie stuttered in fear.

"We fight," Max replied, pulling out his knucklebones.

"Excellent," Iver said with a smile. "Then it begins."

Round Table was played on an elaborate board that resembled an ancient, yellowed map that could hold up to four players, but could be expanded to accommodate six when two boards were attached. That was the case this day, for Iver was building his army of cards on the far end of the table, directly across from Natalia. The three boys flanked them, palms sweating as they awaited Iver's first move.

The odds seemingly stacked against him, Iver went first. The question was whether he would build his defenses or go straight for the attack. The Grey Griffins didn't have long to wait; Iver quickly flipped over several cards lined up before him, revealing a gruesome army: a horde of goblins, stony gargoyles, a snarling werewolf, and a creepy monster called a Slayer goblin. . . .

Max practically fell off his chair. The Slayer goblin! It looked exactly like the monster from his nightmare. But how?

Iver himself seemed a little surprised at the cards he had drawn, and for a long silent moment his brow furrowed in deep thought. Was it worry? Max couldn't tell. But whatever it was, it quickly passed, and Iver's attack was swift and vicious. "I challenge thee, Master Tweeny," Iver called out as he rolled his knucklebones—a beautiful pair of dice that seemed to be made of pure silver. Ernie countered with a roll of his own, but Iver's cast was higher, and before Ernie could even voice his disappointment, the old man removed Ernie's card from the battlefield. Then he turned to Max.

"The Slayer goblin attacks," Iver challenged. Max gulped as Iver shook his hand before casting the metallic knucklebones. An 85. A good roll. On top of that, each card (and in this case, each monster) had an attack value, making it stronger or weaker than the other card. A garden faerie might have a small attack value. A troll had a big one. The Slayer's attack value was even higher. And when Max saw Iver's roll, and combined it with the massive attack value, he bit his lip in frustration.

The Slayer would not be easy to defeat.

Max shut his eyes, remembering the horrible sound of the Slayer's claws scratching across the wood floor of his bedroom. Weakly, he let his own knucklebones fall from his hand. The first bone fell. A nine. That meant whatever his roll, it was in the nineties. He had a chance. But his heart skipped a beat as the second bone rolled off the table, skittering across the floor before resting next to Harley's foot.

"Well?" asked Ernie, the suspense more than he could handle. Max needed a roll of 94 to combine with his knight's fairly high defensive value to win. That meant . . .

"It's a three," Harley shouted as Natalia and Ernie cheered. A tie. He didn't win, but Max had survived, repelling the Slayer's attack. But the battle was far from over.

The game went back and forth, to and fro, as both sides took heavy casualties. Yet even though the Griffins outnumbered Iver's army four to one, and they should have defeated their old friend with little trouble, his cards were simply too powerful. And as daylight gave way to dusk, there was no definitive winner, and so Iver decided to suspend the game until next Saturday.

"You have all fought valiantly," he said with an approving smile.

"But you practically wiped me out," Ernie sighed, looking somberly at his depleted deck. "What do I have to play with next week? I almost lost every card I own."

"Me, too." Harley shook his head in disappointment.

"Indeed," Iver noted. "But winning was not today's goal. Only survival mattered." He then returned a stacked deck to each of the Griffins, much to their surprise. Usually, when a card was lost in battle, it was gone forever (or at least until it could be won back). Iver's gesture was generous to say the least. "What I'm most concerned with is that you have each learned something today."

"Learned?" Natalia asked with a frown, but greedily accepting her old cards back all the same. "What do you mean?"

"I mean exactly what I said, of course. You can think about it and tell me later, if you like. But now I must insist that you rush home to the dinners that are no doubt waiting for you."

The four kids were best friends. It had been that way since kindergarten, when they had found themselves united to protect Ernie from the school bully. Now, just a few years later, they were inseparable, with their very own secret society called the Order of the Grey Griffins. It had been Max's idea, and his father had encouraged it, even building them a vast clubhouse in the woods where they could meet. There were secret passwords (which Ernie never remembered), secret handshakes (which seemed to change on a daily basis), and even secret songs (which no one sang except Natalia).

"Where were you today?" Ernie asked Harley as they stepped through the door and into the fresh air.

"Me and my mom had to rush Roscoe to the vet," Harley said gravely. Roscoe was an enormous hunting dog that Harley had received for his sixth birthday. The dog was as big as a tank, ferocious as a lion, and had developed an unfortunate taste for postal workers and truck tires. But Harley loved him.

"What happened?" Natalia gasped, finally noticing several small cuts on Harley's forehead. "There's blood underneath your fingernails. What's going on?"

"Roscoe got in a fight with something out back behind our place," Harley explained. "I was outside working on my go-cart and Roscoe was chasing squirrels, when all of a sudden that stupid dog started growling and barking. The next thing I knew he was running out toward the trees."

"What was it?" asked Max.

"I'm not sure. By the time I got there, Roscoe was fighting with it in the bushes. But whatever it was, it was strong. And mean. It had Roscoe pinned to the ground." ·

"Roscoe?" Ernie gasped, thinking anything less than an elephant wouldn't stand a chance against Harley's giant canine.

"Yeah," answered Harley. "If I hadn't got there, I don't know what would've happened to him."

"What did it look like?" Natalia asked as they walked down the street, though not before stopping to pull out her *Book of Clues*—a pink spiraled tablet liberally decorated with unicorn stickers. She always took notes when trying to solve a mystery.

"It happened so fast I didn't get a very good look. But I know it was black. That's all I could see." Then Harley frowned. "Except . . ."

"Well?" prompted Natalia, pen in hand.

"I didn't see any eyes," Harley explained.

"What do you mean?"

"Well, you know how a raccoon or deer reflects light in their eyes, and you can see 'em from a mile away? Whatever I saw, its eyes didn't reflect anything when I put my flashlight on it."

"Hey, that sounds like that card in Iver's deck today," Ernie said, biting into a chocolate bar.

"Yeah," Natalia agreed. "The Slayer goblin."

"I actually have one of those cards," Harley recalled, pulling it out of his front pocket. "Here it is. Iver gave it to me before we took off."

"Slayers are the worst kind of goblins," Natalia read from the card as Max and Ernie moved in for a better look. "It says here that they're blind."

"Where're its eyes?" asked Ernie, studying the picture intently.

"They don't have any," she said as she studied the description at the bottom of the card. "That's the thing. But they have a powerful sense of smell, which is almost as good as being able to see. Maybe even better." She paused dramatically as she looked into each of their eyes.

"Go on," Max said impatiently, still a little shaken from his dream about the Slayer.

"It also says they can move between the faerie world and our world. I guess they are the only kind of faerie that can do that."

"Whadda you mean?" Ernie asked. "I thought we were talking about goblins. Not faeries."

"A goblin is a faerie," Natalia sighed as she picked up her bike and walked back to the sidewalk. "Don't you know anything? Just like a wolf is a type of dog. At any rate, according to legend, faeries live in a world of shadow that is connected to the earth by magical bridges called portals. These Slayers are one of the few creatures that can use the portals."

Harley paused a moment as he looked at the picture on the card. "That thing does kind of look like what I saw today," he concluded after giving it some thought. "But like I said, I didn't get a very good look."

"Not to mention faeries aren't real," added Max, more for his own comfort than anything else.

"Hey, what if it was a baboon that attacked Roscoe?" Ernie suggested on a wild tangent. "I bet there's a whole tribe of baboons living in the woods. Wouldn't that be cool?"

Everyone looked at Ernie as if he had worms crawling out of his ears.

"Ernest," cried Natalia in exasperation. "Baboons come from Africa, not Avalon, Minnesota."

"Maybe they migrated," continued Ernie, the idea of baboons loose in his hometown being too interesting to let go.

"The only thing that migrated is your common sense," Natalia replied.

"How do you know so much about baboons, anyway?" complained Ernie.

"Because I read books, you nincompoop," she replied. "In fact, my dad just bought me an encyclopedia set. . . ."

"I wouldn't talk about 'dads' in front of you know who," whispered Ernie, rather too loudly, as he pointed over at Max.

Max set his jaw. Ernie was right. He didn't like anyone mentioning his dad. The memory of the divorce was too fresh, and it didn't help that Max had only heard from him a couple times in the three months since he had left.

"I'm sorry," Natalia offered, not realizing she had brought up a sore subject.

"It isn't your fault," Max sighed, pushing his bike ahead of the others.

"Maybe we can all hang out at your place tonight," Ernie called after him. "We could stay up and watch TV all night."

"Can't," Max called back. "I'm sleeping at my grandma's." With that he hopped on his bike and tore off down the road, leaving his friends far behind.

2 How Max Found a Magic Book

HIGH ATOP A HILL that overlooked Mystic Bay on Lake Avalon, the Sumner estate sprawled for as far as the eye could see. It was nestled among acres of trees and a sea of lush grass, a true architectural marvel. The house looked like a medieval castle, with gargoyles, turrets, and a grand fountain in the front drive. In fact, it was actually hundreds of years old, imported from Scotland brick by brick and reconstructed on the Sumners' vast property. It was the envy of everyone in town, but Max didn't care. He would have traded it all to have his family back together.

"I'm home!" Max announced to no one in particular as he burst through the kitchen door out of breath.

"Hello, Max," Rosa greeted him with a cherubic smile and a rich Spanish accent. While his mom liked to say that Rosa only helped with the cleaning, the fact was that Annika Sumner was simply too busy with manicures, hair appointments, shopping sprees in Paris, and a calendar full of social events to bother with household duties. There were many servants—some for driving, some for cooking, some for pulling weeds out of the driveway. But Rosa, an expensive nanny from Toledo, Spain, with an impeccable résumé, served as Annika's "chief of staff" in her absence, and in many ways she was more of a mother to Max than his own mom.

"Hi, Rosa," Max said, digging into the cookie jar. "Where are Mom and Hannah?"

"Your sister is taking a nap," Rosa answered in her delightful Castilian accent. "And your mother has gone to Minneapolis for the day. She needed some new clothes for her trip tonight."

Max rolled his eyes as he stuffed a whole cookie in his mouth sideways. A former model, who even after two children could have graced the covers of fashion magazines, his mother needed new clothes like a zebra needed more stripes. Most of the shoes in her cavernous closet had never even been worn.

"What's this?" Max asked, walking over to the breakfast table where a giant package sat. Three feet tall and just as wide, it was wrapped in brown paper, and the return address showed that it had come all the way from Scotland. It was from his father, who had been spending time overseas managing Sumner Enterprises' European real-estate ventures. Max ripped open the package with fervor.

"I believe it's your birthday gift." Rosa smiled. "You see, your papá hasn't forgotten about you."

Max had been devastated when he hadn't heard from his father on his eleventh birthday, which had passed three weeks earlier. No card. No phone call. No gift. Nothing. Of course his mother reminded him of it every day, letting Max know what a louse his father really was. And though Max didn't want to believe her, his father's lack of interest had been demoralizing. Yet here it was—the gift he had been waiting for. It wasn't that he 'needed more stuff. He just needed to know his father cared. Maybe it had been held up in the mail?

Digging through the mess of packaging material, Max searched anxiously for his birthday card. Bingo. He pulled out the envelope, but his smile quickly faded. Scribbled on Sumner Enterprises stationery was a brief note that was obviously written by his father's assistant, Ursula, an emotionless, calculating German woman who wore pin-striped pantsuits and pulled her magenta-dyed hair back into a strict bun.

"Grayson, your father wishes you a happy birthday. He will call you as soon as he gets a chance," the note read. And not a single word more.

Max tore the note in half and threw it back in the box, closed the lid without a thought to what was inside, and promptly threw it out the back door.

"Grayson Maximillian Sumner, what's wrong with you?" Rosa demanded. "That's a terrible way to show gratitude for a gift."

"I'm going to pack, and then I want to go to my grandma's house right away," he huffed. "Call Logan and tell him to have the car ready." With that Max stomped away, his eyes downcast in frustration, though he felt guilty for snapping at Rosa. She was so sweet, and he didn't want to start treating the household staff like his mother generally did. But he was mad. That's why he failed to see, until it was too late, a silent figure standing in the shadows of the kitchen archway.

Like a Ping-Pong ball, Max bounced off the man, who felt as if he were made from stone, not flesh and blood like everyone else. Max looked up into piercing eyes set beneath a disapproving brow. The man's face seemed to be fixed in constant critical judgment, and a mysterious scar trailed down his chiseled cheekbone. Short-cropped raven hair parted to the right in military efficiency, his face covered in dark stubble.

"Oh . . . sorry, Logan. I didn't see you standing there," Max apologized to his driver, relaxing a bit as he rubbed his forehead.

"What have I told you about walking with your head down?" the man scolded in a brisk Scottish accent. It wasn't an acquiescing tone typically used by servants. Then again, Logan wasn't a typical servant.

"That if I keep my head down I could walk right into a trap," recited Max. "But there aren't any traps around here. The only thing I have to worry about in Avalon is dying from boredom."

Rosa laughed quietly. Logan didn't. "Whether you wanted it or not, Max, you were born into an important family," Logan said sternly, crossing his thick, hairy arms. "And there are more ruthless people in this world than you think. You'd make a nice prize for any one of them. It's my job to make sure that doesn't happen."

Why anyone would bother, especially when his own father didn't seem to care, was incomprehensible to Max. But he trusted Logan, who had never been wrong. Not even once. Logan also seemed to know things before they happened—which was why the Scotsman wasn't actually on the family payroll because of his driving skills (despite racing professionally in Italy for several years). In fact, Logan was the Sumner family bodyguard, and you would be hard-pressed to find a more qualified candidate in the civilized world.

He was a bit of a mystery and not much of a conversationalist, and Max had gathered from a handful of stories that Logan had been raised in an orphanage somewhere in the damp alleyways of Glasgow, Scotland. There were rumors that he had run away and survived as a street fighter in the underworld of Europe, and that eventually he stowed away on a cargo ship, sailed to China, and studied kung fu with a series of anonymous grand masters.

Max didn't know much more, other than that Logan spoke nearly as many languages as Iver and somehow was on a first-name basis with the queen of England. But why he always wore black and no smile ever crossed his lips Max could only guess.

"I believe you'll find everything in order," Logan said as he handed a fully loaded backpack to Max. "The car is waiting outside."

"Uh, thanks, Logan," Max said, amazed at how the driver always seemed to be one step ahead of him.

Logan dropped off Max at Grandma Caliburn's earlier than anticipated — not that it mattered. His mother had decided to go straight from the mall to the airport to catch her plane to New York. She didn't even bother saying good-bye. Hannah, Max's eighteen-month-old sister, was going to stay at the house with Rosa. The kids were always left behind.

"Thanks, Logan," Max said politely as he hopped out of the blacked-out Mercedes sedan. The car was one of Logan's latest projects and was in the midst of a supercharger overhaul. Heads of state didn't even have cars like that. Then again, heads of state didn't have Logan in their employ.

"No problem. Just remember to stay alert. I don't want to see all your training go to waste."

But Logan's warning fell on deaf ears as Max sprinted toward his grandmother, who was standing on the front steps, waving. She was the only thing in Max's world that hadn't turned upside down, and by the time he finished a delicious, homemade dinner later that night, Max had forgotten all about the divorce and was soon laughing with Grandma Caliburn over a plateful of cookies. Just being around this magical woman had a way of curing all of life's troubles. There was no one Max loved more.

"It's wonderful having you here, Max," she said in a soft voice, tucking him into bed after a night of old movies and card games. Like his mother, Max's grandma was beautiful, tall and regal with salt-and-pepper hair cropped in a stylish bob. But where his mother was nervous and demanding, Grandma Caliburn was gentle and kind. Her husband, Max's grandfather, had died two years before, and ever since then, Max had spent a great deal of time with her. She was lonely. But as he thought about it, maybe Max was really the lonely one.

"Do you miss Grandpa?" he asked, looking at a picture of his grandparents on the nightstand.

"Very much."

Max sighed. He remembered every detail of that tragic day

two years ago when the patrol car rolled up the gravel driveway with the news of his grandfather's death. The officer didn't have to say a word. Max's grandma already knew. She'd dreamed of it the night before.

"Who's that in the picture with Grandpa? I haven't seen it before," Max wondered, wanting to push away the dark memories. "It kind of looks like Iver."

Grandma Caliburn smiled, picking up the picture Max was looking at. Dressed in dapper suits with fancy sashes across their chests, Grandpa Caliburn held a rapier in his hand and Iver was gripping a staff. They looked to be in their early twenties.

"Yes. That is Iver with your grandfather," she said, smiling. "This was taken a long time ago, before the war. London, I think it was. Your grandfather asked me to marry him a few days later."

"Grandpa and Iver were friends?" asked Max, astonished at the thought.

"Yes, I suppose you could say they were." She paused thoughtfully. She seemed about ready to share something very important, but then decided against it and gave him a kiss on the forehead. "I'll see you bright and early for chores. Don't let the bedbugs bite—and be sure to say your prayers."

"Good night, Grandma. I love you."

"Sweet dreams, honey."

Later that night the serenade of crickets faded as a dark storm rolled across the sky. The stars were lost behind ominous clouds while the wind began to run its cool autumn fingers through the trees outside. A crack of thunder shook the house as flashes of lightning electrified the air. Max awoke with a start, unsure of where he was. And though it took several fuzzy moments, eventually his eyes adjusted to the strange strobe effect of lightning bursts that painted the familiar landscape of his mother's childhood bedroom.

Unable to settle back down, Max lay awake. He felt like an orphan. Maybe the divorce was his fault, he thought. Maybe if he had been a better son or showed more interest in his father's business, things wouldn't be the way they were.

His mother had sent him to counseling right after it happened — the most expensive she could find. Counseling seemed to be her answer to all of life's problems, but it wasn't working.

Tired of thinking about it, Max whipped off his covers and went in search of a midnight snack. A few chocolate chip cookies would hit the spot.

Half-asleep, Max shuffled down the hall toward the kitchen stairs, but stopped suddenly when he saw light seeping out from beneath the door to his grandfather's study. He hadn't been in that room since that fateful night of the car wreck, but curiosity got the better of Max. Slowly, he turned the knob and peeked inside. Nobody was in the room, but there was the strange feeling that someone had just left. Max thought he'd take a quick peek around before Grandma Caliburn decided to come back.

The desk lamp had been left on, washing the room in a soft emerald glow, allowing Max to see that everything was exactly as it had been. Shelves lined the walls behind the desk, with the books perfectly aligned, sorted alphabetically by author. Pictures and plaques decorated the walls in geometric precision. Even the pen and ruler on his grandfather's desk were exactly parallel. There was no wild clutter of bills, no haphazard pile of magazines, and the newspaper bin next to his reading chair was neatly stacked.

Max spied Grandpa Caliburn's familiar pipe atop the sprawling desk that occupied most of the room. The desktop was inlaid with pearl in the shape of a strange cross, the very same symbol that had been etched in many of the plaques, along with other foreign symbols that Max didn't understand. But Max had never got the chance to ask his grandfather about any of them.

Just then a cold wind blew in through an open window, sending the drapes dancing in the breeze.

Shivering, Max quickly walked over and shut it. Strange, he thought. He didn't think his grandmother would have left the window open. But then something even more bizarre caught his eye.

Behind the desk, Max could now see that a drawer had been left ajar, if only slightly. Yet in a sea of perfection, that open drawer stuck out like a neon light, especially since he remembered every drawer in the desk had always been locked.

Slowly, Max opened it, not sure what he might find. But it was empty. Maybe Grandma Caliburn was cleaning out the desk. He supposed she had to do that sooner or later. Yes, that had to be the answer, he reasoned.

Yawning, Max decided it was time to return to bed, forgetting about the cookies. As quietly as he could manage, he shut the door to the study and crept back to his room, where, unfortunately, the same cold breeze was blowing through the drapes. Strangely, it felt like there was frost on the floor under his toes, and he could see his breath in the air. With a frown, he pulled down the window and huddled under his covers.

For several minutes, Max lay there with only his head peeking out above the blankets. The covers were warm, but Max's feet were frozen, and even with the window shut, he could still see his breath rising from his mouth every time he breathed.

Then his sleepy eyes caught sight of movement. It was only for a fraction of a second, but something had moved beneath the old bureau across the room. Max wasn't alone. His nightmare had returned. Only this time, Max wasn't asleep. He gasped in terror.

Slowly, a dark silhouette crept toward his bed, keeping to the shadows as it inched across the room. It was the Slayer goblin. There was no doubt as the monster's deadly claws scraped the floor. It had come in through the window... maybe it had been in his grandfather's study as well. But what did it want?

Max rubbed his eyes, pinching himself to wake up. But this was no dream. And it was no game. If he didn't do something fast, the Slayer would have him.

Flinging off his covers, Max sprang to the door, but the Slayer leapt after him, hungry claws lashing out. Somehow Max was faster. As the tail of his pajama top tore from the monster's grasp, Max slammed the door, trapping the goblin on the other side.

Max's heart pounded as he gripped the doorknob tightly in his sweaty hands, expecting at any moment to be swept away under a torrent of claws and teeth. Nothing happened. After a moment, he wiped a small trickle of blood from his wrist. He was wounded, but it could have been worse.

Seconds crept by and still there wasn't a single sound from the other side of the door. Max started to wonder if he was dreaming. Curious, he fell to his knees and peeked through the crack.

Suddenly, a great howl ripped through the air as the Slayer smashed into the door, sending Max sprawling backward. Again, the monster hit the door, buckling the hinges. Cracks split the wood, and the screws began to pop out. It wouldn't last much longer.

Looking frantically up and down the hall, Max caught sight of a silver cord hanging from the ceiling. Where was Logan when Max needed him most? Unfortunately, wondering wasn't going to change anything, so like an arrow shot from a bow, Max lunged with his outstretched hand and pulled with all his might, releasing a set of old wooden stairs that slid out of the inky darkness above. Max had never seen the stairs before, but there was no time to ask questions. Up he ran, slamming shut the attic trapdoor once he reached the top.

Eyes adjusting to the pale attic light, Max bent down and slid a bolt across the trapdoor, locking it shut. He held his breath, waiting for the monster to try to break through and hoping the small bolt would hold. Max felt he had to get word to Logan, but how? There was no phone in the attic, and no other escape, save a storm window—and that was a thirty-foot drop to the ground below. It looked as if there was little Max could do but wait for morning and hope someone would come to his rescue.

But after about fifteen minutes, mostly spent holding his breath, no attack came. Max started to relax, but he had to make sure the coast was clear. Curious, though it might not have been the best idea, he unbolted the door to steal a quick peek.

The hallway was empty, and he could just spy the bedroom door, which was still closed. Max sighed in relief. But wait. It wasn't hanging off the hinges, and there were no splinters of wood littering the hallway. In fact, it looked as if nothing had happened at all. Did he imagine the attack?

Feeling rather strange and a bit unsure of himself, Max pulled the trapdoor back into place quietly and stood there in the half-light of the attic. The good news was that he and his grandma were safe. The bad news was that Max was starting to believe he was going crazy.

The attic was sparsely furnished with an old floral print sofa, a few boxes of assorted magazines, and a steamer trunk overflowing with dress-up clothes. There were tattered floor lamps with their shades askew and lots of milk crates jam-packed with hundreds of envelopes and letters. But the dust was so thick that every step Max took left a soft print. From the looks of it, no one had been up there for ages.

Then something caught his eye. Books. Hundreds of them lined the shelves along the far wall. All of them were bound in leather, looking old and mysterious—much like the books in Grandpa Caliburn's study. Then he saw a golden picture frame, almost as tall as he was, leaning next to the bookshelves. As Max approached, he could see an armored knight, tall and proud, with piercing eyes. The sky behind him was dark and cold, and upon his chest was painted a large red cross. In one hand, the knight held a card faceup—but it was too dark for Max to tell what it was. In the other hand, he held a shining blue ball of fire that seemed to flicker in the moonlight, illuminating the attic. All about the knight were stars, and on his armor were many strange symbols, oddly of the sort Max had seen in his grandfather's study.

As he leaned over to get a closer look, a soft glow coming from the far corner of the attic caught Max's attention. Taking one last glance at the painting, he slowly approached the source of the strange radiance and found a desk tucked away in the corner. As Max drew closer, the glow seemed to grow brighter. And it wasn't coming from a lamp or flashlight. Somehow the light was coming from an extraordinary book bound in rich leather. It sat upon the desk with an awe-inspiring majesty, its cover traced with intricate drawings and symbols, bound together by a golden lock. In the center of the cover, framed on either side by silver fittings, lay a curious slot, as if something of great import had once rested there but was now missing.

Slowly, carefully, unable to resist, Max reached out and touched the cover. The book flashed, and a golden trail of liquid snaked around the title like a flowing river of molten metal. It read:

CODEX SPIRITUS
THE SHADOWLANDES OF FAERIE

Mesmerized, Max slid his fingers over the strange letters. The book was warm, and though he could never say why, Max felt as though it was somehow looking right back at him. Tingling with excitement, Max scooped up the treasure and carried it over to a nearby couch.

"How am I supposed to open you?" Max mused, noticing there was no keyhole in the lock that held it shut. He looked for a trick release, latch, or button of some sort, and though he pushed, pulled, pried, and pressed, the book remained safely locked. Then Max grabbed a screwdriver he had found and tried to tear it open. It didn't even leave a scratch.

"Abracadabra!" Max called. It was the only magic word he knew. Unfortunately, that didn't work, either.

In frustration, Max schemed until he thought his head might explode. Then, in the quiet of his mind he heard a whisper—a word. He didn't understand what it meant or how it got there, but it seemed to be coming from the book.

"*Kienesara.*" He recited the word from his mind.

Immediately, something inside the lock sprang open, and the book unfurled before his eager eyes. Fully expecting to see magic spells, runes, or even recipes for potions, Max found instead an odd pair of eyes looking directly back at him. They belonged to the painting of a rumpled creature crouched atop a giant mushroom. At first, Max thought the beast resembled a cat, drenched and angry after an unwanted bath. It was the color of fireplace soot, which was perhaps why it appeared so scruffy. But as Max peered closer, he realized it was no cat at all. It wasn't even close.

Where a soft pink nose should have been there was a short jagged beak, and the fur atop the creature's head (if fur it was) shot out in a tangled mane of spikes. There was both intelligence and mischief captured in the giant eyes that shimmered like moons in a starless sky. Its hands and feet were long and oddly stretched, ending in grasping claws, and it had a scaled tail that coiled off the edge of the mushroom cap. In fact, Max could have sworn he saw it swish back and forth.

His eyes drifted slowly from the picture to the beautiful looping script in the margins, written in a language he couldn't read, though it somehow looked familiar all the same. The text started to sparkle then flash as it shot into the air with a swirl of golden light. The characters transformed into words and finally sentences that Max could actually read — though whether it was English or Max could suddenly understand a foreign language he didn't know for sure. But at the moment, amazingly, the entire page was floating in the air right before his eyes.

The first line read *Spriggan,* which was the name of the creature in the painting. Max was about to read the rest of the description, but his eyes were immediately drawn to the embossed seal at the bottom of the page. It was leafed in gold, surrounded by strange symbols. The seal itself had been crafted with intricate designs resembling a series of clockworks and gears overlaid one upon the other. Faintly, he heard the soft voice whispering words into his ear once more.

"Sprigga! Kai antare intexium!" Max called, this time with more assurance.

There was a brief flash of light followed by a deep rumbling sound, as though the heavy wheels of a steam train were slowly beginning to churn. Max watched in wonder as the seal turned and twisted by a series of gears and wheels. At first they remained on the page, spinning slowly back and forth like a combination lock trying to open. But then, with an audible click the gears shot out like a telescope, spinning in a spectacular display of light and sound.

Mist rose from the book, and the attic grew suddenly chill. Faster and faster the vapor swirled until, like a hurricane, it roared through the room. Max desperately grabbed hold of the couch, barely able to save himself from being blown out the window. As the gale-force winds grew, Max's fingers weakened. Yet despite the danger he was transfixed. In the eye of the storm there appeared a chasm, dark and deep, and out from the void shot a strange shadow hurtling toward him.

A loud crack of thunder shook the walls like a mighty wave, and everything went black.

3 Secrets Are Meant to Be Shared

WHEN MAX FINALLY opened his eyes and looked around, he expected to see the attic in ruins.

The attic hadn't changed at all.

He stood up, dusting himself off. The book was lying facedown nearby, and he carefully went to pick it up. Remarkably, the *Codex Spiritus* was still open to the page with the spriggan, yet the creature was missing from the painting. All that remained was a lonely mushroom.

Max stared at the picture in wonder until a creaking noise in the rafters above made him jump. Desperately, Max's eyes devoured the inky darkness, until he noticed two pale eyes gazing down at him. Max's heart leapt in terror. But just as suddenly, the eyes disappeared, replaced by a dark shadow that flitted across the rafters, appearing and disappearing as quickly as Max could blink.

Max jumped toward the trapdoor. A spark of light. A poof of smoke. And suddenly a strange creature was blocking Max from his escape. It was hanging upside down by its tail right in front of Max's nose. Complete with claws, scaly tail, hooked beak, and a matted mass of tangled spiky fur, it wasn't the Slayer goblin at all. Instead, it was the spriggan. How?

"Kairay?" asked a crackly voice. The spriggan's sweet breath was making Max feel a little dizzy. He didn't respond.

"*Salway?*" Whiskers arched in question. Then its beak broke into an odd smile as it fluttered its eyelashes at him. She was definitely female.

"Wha-what are you?" Max finally managed to stutter through parched lips.

"What are we?" she asked in perfect English.

"There are more of you?" asked Max, growing uncomfortable with his guest as he looked around the attic.

"No, no, no. Just us," the spriggan said as she yawned and stretched. The monster (if a monster she was) looked rather amusing as she hung upside down. "It's just that we were trapped in that wretched book for so long that we took to talking to ourselves."

Max nodded as he picked up the book and held it tightly to his chest, afraid of what might jump out of the pages next.

"Where did you find the book, we wonder?" the spriggan asked as she nervously stared at the *Codex Spiritus*.

"This book?" asked Max, raising it toward her.

"Yes!" the creature hissed, and protected her eyes. "Put it away! We hate it."

"Wait a minute," he said, trying to put the puzzle together. "But I thought this is where you came from. How can you hate it?"

"We don't remember," she said, crossing her furry arms. An awkward moment of silence fell over them, until Max reluctantly set the book aside and returned to the couch.

"What are you?" Max asked as he reached for a pillow. "I mean, you're a spriggan, right?"

"So we have been called," the little creature replied as she groomed herself absently. "But we wonder what you are?"

The question puzzled Max. "I guess you're asking if I'm a boy?"

In the blink of an eye she disappeared, instantly reappearing on the sofa beside him. "You are a human child! And it was you that set us free?" she mused with a whistle and a clicking sound.

"I guess," said Max, shrugging. "I don't know how I did it, but I suppose I did. How long did you live in there anyway?"

"We didn't live in there," she practically spit. "It wasn't living. It was death—miserable death."

The spriggan looked at him with narrow eyes, and Max tried to change the subject. "Do you have a name?"

She looked perplexed, scratching her chin in thought. "We haven't been asked our name for a very long time." She paused, struggling for an answer, but none came as she sighed in defeat. "We have forgotten."

"Well, I have to call you something," Max proclaimed. "My name is Max. Why don't I call you Sprig?"

The spriggan's eyes welled with tears. "Oh, thank you!" she said, throwing herself into Max's lap, wrapping him in a furry hug.

"Uh . . . you're welcome." Max cleared his throat as he pulled the spriggan's arms off his neck in embarrassment. "Hey, can you do magic?" He felt a little weird asking it, but what eleven-year-old boy in his situation wouldn't wonder?

Sprig smiled shyly as she jumped down to the floor with a playful glint in her eye. "Oh, young master, we can do many things."

She bowed reverently. "We can raise a sunken ship from the stormy sea, turn your enemies into frogs, or even make you the richest human child for miles."

Max already had the last offer covered, though having her turn his worst enemy into a frog sounded pretty good. But as he was about to ask for help with the Slayer goblin, he heard a knock and a familiar voice calling his name.

"Max?" the voice repeated. It was his grandmother.

Startled, Sprig burst into a cloud of vapor, out of which came a slender silver dragon, no longer than arm's length nose to tail. It shot out from the mist and flew past Max, through the attic window and into the night.

"One thing's certain," he said to himself as the wet wind from the storm outside burst through the open window. "Nobody's gonna believe this."

"Max?" the voice called once more. "Max, honey? It's time to get up."

"Time to get up?" Max pried open one eye and then the other. Slowly, he turned his head, and looked around the room. There was the antique yellow lamp, the imitation wood bureau, the old rocking chair. Yes, he realized. He was back in his grandmother's guest room, tucked snugly under the covers. Sunlight poured in through a crack in the shade and he groaned. Sunday morning had come far too quickly, and he hadn't slept well at all. Somehow every muscle in his body was aching, and a tangle of strange imagery—magic books, haunting eyes, and flying dragons—rushed in.

"Max?" came Grandma Caliburn's voice as she opened the

bedroom door, greeting him with a bright smile. "Oh good, you're awake. Did you have pleasant dreams last night?"

Max's eyes grew wide as he stopped short in midstretch. Could she have known? No, he thought as she smiled again, handing him a cup of orange juice. But at least she was safe.

"It's this room, you know. I honestly don't know why, but something about it brings the most wonderful dreams. Maybe it's the fresh air," she said as she threw open the bedroom window.

Max said nothing.

"Well," Grandma Caliburn continued as she turned to leave the room, "I imagine the horses are getting hungry. Why don't I meet you out in the barn after you finish getting dressed? Then we'll see about getting you some breakfast, too."

"Okay, Grandma. I'll be down in a minute," Max said, sliding out of the covers.

When his feet hit the floor, his left foot struck something hard, and as he crouched to massage his sore toe, he saw a strange object sticking out from under the bed.

"What's this?" he whispered. Glowing softly in the shadows was the book from his dream. As his eyes fell upon it, Max was overwhelmed with a mixture of excitement and fear.

After chores and a hearty breakfast, Max washed up and got ready for church. Most of the time Max sat in the pew thinking about the book that sat under his bed, replaying the entire night over and over again. But he put his worries aside on the ride home.

Grandma Caliburn had volunteered to host a special Sunday

dinner for Max and the other Grey Griffins. The four friends feasted on piles of mashed potatoes and gravy, heaps of honey ham, and an endless supply of creamed corn, fruit salad, and homemade bread slathered with rich butter and sweet raspberry preserves. And then there was dessert—ice-cream sundaes with all the fixings.

As Grandma Caliburn cleaned up, Harley and Ernie dozed off in front of the television, while Natalia sleepily thumbed through a magazine. Max, though, was wide awake, and his mind started to tingle. No one would notice if he just went to go have a peek at the *Codex*.

Max quietly snuck up to his room, peered under his bed, and reached for the book bag where he had safely hidden the book earlier that morning. The golden glow filled him with excitement as he opened the bag and smiled.

"What've you got there, Max?" came Natalia's curious voice from the doorway.

"Um, nothing," Max said as he quickly zipped the bag shut. Where had she come from?

"Well, what on earth is all the glowing about?" she persisted.

"Yeah, Max, what do you have in there?" Ernie echoed, who was now peering over Natalia's shoulder.

"Okay," Max said, angry but realizing he wasn't going to be able to hide the secret for long. "I just can't show you here."

Minutes later the kids made their way across the backyard, hurried into the old red barn, and climbed the rickety staircase that led to the cavernous loft. The towering ceilings were home to a multitude of ropes and pulleys that hung like giant strands of a spiderweb. In the murky darkness above, a noisy family of swallows dove and spun in the dusty light that filtered through a small glass window.

The loft had become a storage place for all sorts of half-forgotten treasures, like the old dollhouse that had belonged to Max's mother. Scattered here and there were piles of magazines that his grandfather had collected, an old radio, and an assortment of other junk. But the kids shuttled right past, making their way to a pyramid of hay bales that Max and Harley had fashioned into a fort. There was a small tunnel they had to crawl through to get inside, where they had even cut out a skylight.

"Wow, Max. This place is amazing! We should make it our headquarters," proclaimed Ernie as he jumped onto a bale, sending dust and hay flying everywhere. Max ignored him, quietly walking to the far corner where he sat down, clutching his bag nervously.

"We already have a headquarters," replied Natalia. "And besides, as Marshal of the Grey Griffins, I can tell you that this place doesn't meet regulatory standards. It's not private enough. Anyone could be downstairs listening."

Ernie sighed rather dramatically. To make their secret society official, Natalia had created an entire book of rules, along with assigning each member particular roles and responsibilities. Natalia's role of Marshal meant she was the Griffins' Treasurer (which was the role Ernie really wanted—he loved counting his money). To his dismay Ernie was chosen as Steward instead, which was little more than a fancy title for Secretary. He tried to argue that only girls were secretaries, but Natalia had pinched him into submission.

"The only thing downstairs is an old tractor and a litter of kittens," replied Ernie, crossing his arms. "Who's gonna hear us? Besides, you're not in charge."

"Well, neither are you," she shot back.

"Pipe down," commanded Harley, who was the Grey Griffins' Warden. What he said was law—and only Max, the Master of the Order, could overrule him. Max got that title because forming the Grey Griffins had been his idea, not that he really wanted it. Max rarely used his power to overrule anything. He trusted Harley more than he would a brother.

"Max, do you need to call the meeting to order or what?" continued Harley.

"Only if it's an official meeting," Natalia replied as she turned back to Max.

"Does that mean I have to take notes?" Ernie complained.

"Fine. Let's make it official," agreed Max offhandedly, for he was too deep in thought to pay much attention.

"Very good," Natalia said, handing a pen and a piece of paper to Ernie, making it painfully obvious he was to indeed take notes. "Then I call the meeting to order."

"I second," Harley said as Ernie slurped on a can of soda he had brought along.

"I call the Grey Griffins to order," Max concluded.

"I'll start," Natalia said, folding her freckled arms across her chest as she tapped her foot on the dusty floor. "You have a secret, Max. It's plain as the nose on your face, so out with it!"

Max looked at each of them in turn, wondering if they'd think he was crazy. He'd have thought so himself, dismissing the terrifying episode from last night as a bad dream, if it weren't for the book that sat in his bag.

"Look, what I'm about to tell you is pretty big," he said, a bit grudgingly. "You have to promise to keep it a secret," Max insisted. "Or I won't show you." Natalia and Ernie pledged their secrecy, and Max looked to Harley, who nodded.

"Fine," he said, taking a deep breath as he unzipped his bag. To everyone's astonishment, bright golden light streamed from the backpack as he reached in and pulled out the book.

"Whoa!" Ernie shouted. "What's making that thing glow?"

"Yeah, Max. How the heck are you doing that?" asked Harley, amazed.

"I don't know. I found it in my grandma's attic," Max began. Then he went on to tell them the entire story, about the Slayer goblin, Sprig, and everything. When he had finished, they sat staring at the book in silence. Ernie was chewing his fingernails as he imagined the Slayer lurking in every shadow of the barn—or worse. What if it was home under his bed waiting for him?

"So what's that slot in the cover for?" asked Natalia as she reached a curious finger toward the book. But Max pulled the *Codex* away protectively. He wasn't trying to be selfish; he just wasn't ready to let anyone else touch it.

"I don't know. Something must have fallen out."

"Maybe you should ask Sprig," mentioned Ernie, unconcerned by the missing piece. The fact that Max might have found a magic book was exhilarating.

"Speaking of Sprig, check this out. It came from those expansion decks Iver just got in," Max said, pulling a pile of Round Table cards from a pouch in his backpack. "It's a spriggan card—just like the one Iver had in his deck the other day, though this one isn't quite as powerful as his, but it looks just like Sprig."

"She's kind of cute," Ernie said, forgetting the Slayer for the moment. "It says here that spriggans are shape-shifters."

"Yeah, and she told me she can do magic, too," explained Max.

"You do realize this isn't the most believable story I've ever heard, don't you?" Natalia stated. She was torn between believing Max because he was one of her best friends and the facts at hand: Faeries and magic books just didn't exist.

"I know," Max agreed. "I'm having a hard time believing it myself. But when I woke up, the book was right there under my bed."

"Have you tried to use it again?" asked Harley.

"No."

"Good," Natalia said, jotting down some notes in her writing tablet. "Because the first thing you need to do is talk to your grandmother. The *Codex* was in her attic, so she has to know something about it. Second, we need to go down to Iver's and ask him what he thinks is going on. There seems to be some kind of weird connection between this book and the game of Round Table. At the very least we've seen spriggans in both, and I doubt it's simply a coincidence."

"Makes sense, I guess," Ernie agreed. "Iver does know just about everything."

Max wasn't so sure about talking to Grandma Caliburn—or Iver—at least not yet. Thankfully, Harley seemed to agree. "Hold on," he said. "Before we talk to anybody, what makes you think they're gonna believe a word we say?"

"I suppose that's a good point," Natalia conceded, giving it some thought. "We'll just have to prove it. Adults always like proof."

"How?" pressed Harley. "It's not like we can call Sprig to a witness stand."

"We could show 'em Max's book," offered Ernie. After all, it seemed like a perfectly logical step.

"That's true. And we could open it up and see if there're any Slayer goblins missing, too," Harley suggested.

"Who said anything about opening it up? What if we let out a bunch more monsters? That doesn't seem like such a good idea," Ernie gasped.

"Well, we can't just sit here and do nothing," Natalia argued. "Max, what do you suggest?"

In fact, Max hadn't opened the *Codex* for just the reason Ernie had suggested. He didn't want to risk letting anything even more dangerous than Sprig escape. Though he had no idea if the Slayer had come from the book or not. It had obviously been loose before Max read a single page. "I don't know...."

"If you're worried about any of us blabbing about what we see, we can make an official Pact of Secrecy."

"What official Pact of Secrecy? Where do you make this stuff up?" complained Ernie with a wave of his hand.

"It's in the *Grey Griffin Book of Rules*," Natalia replied. "If you ever bothered to read it, you'd know that." Of course, Max and Harley had read the book, but they didn't remember it, either.

Ernie looked over at Natalia suspiciously. "What exactly am I promising again?"

"To not tell anyone about Max's book," she replied. "And also that we are all in this together now. No more secrets."

Everyone agreed.

"We also can't open the book without full Grey Griffin approval," she added quickly.

Max was about to protest. He didn't like the idea of being restricted. After all, it was his book. But Natalia's stern look persuaded him otherwise. Besides, she was probably right. There was safety in numbers, and with things like that Slayer skulking about, Max needed all the help he could get.

"Okay then." Natalia held out her hand, and the others placed theirs on top. "Repeat after me."

And they did.

Darkness comes from hidden truths
Lines in sand point westward to
Blindfolded ones with ropes in hand
To take us to the secret land

If I take this oath today
It is bound on earth in every way.

"All right then." Natalia smiled in satisfaction. The strict observance of protocol gave her a feeling of contentment. "Let's take a look at this book."

The Griffins gathered around Max as he slid the book onto his lap, excitement filling the air. They were going to see real magic.

"Kids?" came Grandma Caliburn's voice from below at the most disappointing time. "There's a storm rolling in. Pack up your things. Your parents are on their way to pick you up."

"You have to be kidding," Natalia cried like a starving castaway who had just had her only meal ripped out from under her nose. But already their parents' cars had begun pulling into the driveway. "Hurry up, Max. Maybe we still have time to read a few pages."

"No way," Max replied as he returned the *Codex* to his backpack. "We can't let anyone see this book. Who knows what would happen."

As the kids descended from the loft in single file they did not notice that high above in the rafters, hidden in shadow, sat a tangled shape of fur with glowing eyes, wringing its clawed hands in worry and dismay.

4

Exploration,
an Accident,
and the Root of All Evil

LATER THAT DAY, Max watched in boredom as a torrent of rain-water washed across his grandmother's green lawn. Though the sky was still dark, the wind had actually lightened a bit. His face pressed heavily against the screen door as he stared out into the wetness, wishing he was anyplace but trapped inside. Then the telephone rang.

"Max?" came his grandmother's soft voice from the kitchen. "That was for you. Logan is on his way over right now. He says it's time for your karate lesson."

Actually, it was kung fu, not karate, but his grandma didn't know the difference. Logan had been teaching Max martial arts for almost a year now. Max enjoyed it, and Logan seemed to think he was a natural. Besides, Max didn't have anything else to do. After he had made the official pact with the Grey Griffins, Max certainly couldn't browse through his magic book whenever he felt like it — even though that was the one thing he wanted to do more than anything.

Not ten minutes later, the roar of Logan's 1969 Ferrari Dino 246 GT announced his arrival, the car ripping through the gravel drive-way like a crimson hurricane. Many drivers for the wealthy were paid handsomely, but how they were paid was vastly different. Some liked lump sums. Others liked weekly payments. Logan, who already had enough money, was paid in rare and hard-to-find automobiles. The Ferrari was the most recent.

Despite the gloom and wet, Logan was barefoot in his kung fu uniform—his signature sunglasses hiding piercing eyes even as the rain splashed his face, soaking his black hair. They looked at each other through the screen door—Max not-so-secretly hoping that the lessons might be inside instead of out. But Logan remained where he was. Apparently, he had no reluctance about Grayson Maximillian Sumner III getting a little wet. Not that he had ever treated Max gently, but Max wouldn't have it any other way. Everyone at school treated him like he was made of gold. It was refreshing to be with someone who treated Max like a human and not a rock star.

With a nod, Max walked out the screen door into the downpour.

"Hi, Logan," Max greeted him. "Nice day out."

The Scotsman remained silent as he reached into his backseat and grabbed two long poles, handing one to Max. Before Max had a clue as to what was happening, Logan attacked with his own staff, forcing the boy to defend himself. With hypnotic grace, Logan wielded the weapon as though it was merely an extension of his arms, twisting and turning with a fluidity that mesmerized his student.

Max's large gray eyes were locked wide in fear as the rain matted his hair to his forehead, blinding him slightly. Logan's staff might as well have been a helicopter propeller closing in, and it was all Max could do to keep from falling on his face as he tried to parry Logan's attacks, each stroke cracking loudly as he hit Max's staff. Certainly Logan could have ended the session quickly, but that wasn't the point of the exercise. He needed Max to be ready for anything—at any time, in any circumstance. Logan believed Max had to learn that the hard way. And he had this twisted idea that pain somehow helped Max remember better. He was right, though. Every time Max fell or his knuckles felt the crack of Logan's staff, Max learned exactly what was needed to avoid that pain.

The lesson went on for another hour without a single word of instruction outside of grunts, groans, and an occasional "keep your guard up" — as though Max weren't already trying to do just that. When it was over, Logan simply caught Max's attacking weapon in his hands and pulled it away effortlessly. He then walked over to his Ferrari, pulled out a soft rag, and wiped the dirt and grime carefully away from the weapons. Logan was meticulous. At almost any time of the day, Logan could be found waxing one of the Sumner automobiles, oiling his sword, or pruning one of his twenty-eight bonsai trees. The only thing he let go was the stubble on his face.

"Max, I know I can be a bit hard on you," the Scotsman said. The rain had lightened to a cool drizzle, and he motioned for Max to come over and sit next to him on the damp grass. "But I promise one day soon you'll understand why."

"I guess," Max said, shrugging. At least the sparring had taken his mind off the divorce that had cut him to the core.

"You're going through a tough time right now, and I wish there was another way, but these lessons are critical to your development. Take heart, though. Big things are in store for you, Grayson," Logan said, reading Max's thoughts, though it wasn't difficult to do.

Before the divorce, Max had been a happy-go-lucky kid, but since the breakup of his family, Max was heartbroken, and it was spreading through his body like poison. Logan had never met his own parents, so he understood the heartache that came with loneliness.

"What do you mean?"

Logan put his hand on Max's shoulder. "Each of us is born with a very important task we must fulfill, and I have a feeling the task you've been given is pretty important."

"What's your task?" Max asked the Scotsman, having no idea what his own was.

"To equip you to fulfill yours," Logan said solemnly.

Max didn't know what to say. He was touched but confused. What was Logan supposed to equip him to do? He couldn't have known about the *Codex*. . . .

Logan caught the questions in Max's eyes. "I can't say much now, but I will tell you this . . . ," he explained. "There aren't many things in this life that scare me, Max. Soon I will have to face at least one, but I want you to know that if I'm able, I will always be there to protect you. Should I fail . . ."

"You? No way," interjected Max.

"There is always someone stronger, smarter, faster," instructed Logan. "And you must never underestimate your adversary."

Max just stared at the Scotsman. He wasn't buying it. Logan was the toughest man on the planet, and Max would put his entire inheritance on that claim. Logan, fail? Impossible.

Logan smiled at Max, a rare occurrence for the stoic bodyguard. "Know that as long as I have breath, I'll do everything in my power to ensure no harm comes to you. Your training is a part of that. I want you to be equipped for any circumstance, for if my guess is right, those lessons will be put to the test sooner than you might think."

Logan left shortly after the kung fu lessons, and no sooner had the Ferrari disappeared around the corner than Max had thrown on his rain jacket, slung his backpack over his shoulder, and rushed out toward the forest—a vast woodland that fenced in Avalon from the north.

"I'll be back soon!" he shouted over his shoulder to his grandmother.

"Don't go too far!" she called from the kitchen window. "The woods can be dangerous this time of year—especially after a storm."

"I know, Grandma!" Max shouted, picking up speed.

"And stay away from the ravines. That water moves fast after a big rain, and I don't want you slipping in."

Max had heard it dozens of times before, but he didn't pay much attention. He knew the woods better than just about anyone, having explored every leaf, branch, twist, and turn since before he could remember.

Ducking underneath an arching honeysuckle bush, Max left the open sky and disappeared into the darkness of the woods beyond. It was still raining, but the leaves were so thick and the branches so intertwined that only a few raindrops found their way through the canopy. Even so, the ground was soaked and a bit slippery, sloping toward the ravine fifty feet below.

Grabbing a hairy root, Max started to lower himself down into the ravine. It wasn't easy. The leaves were slick with rain and dust, and the earth beneath had turned to mud pudding. But before long, having narrowly missed an encounter with an angry thornbush, Max was standing on the bottom ledge, the water below rushing by at an exhilarating rate.

Max loved excitement, and raging water drew him like a bee to honey. Picking up a long stick, he drove it into the water. The current was moving so fast that it nearly yanked the stick right out of Max's hand. He struggled to keep it straight, pushing it down as far as he could reach. There was no bottom.

Max sat on the edge of the cutting, dangling his legs over the ledge. He was content for the time to throw small stones and twigs into the current, mulling over the amazing things that had happened. Mostly his thoughts were focused on the magic book. Was he supposed to find it? Was the voice that told him what to say coming from the book? And was it safe?

Plus, after seeing that Slayer goblin again (dream or no), he was worried about what would show up next. Yet the Slayer had appeared before Max ever found the book, so maybe there was more going on outside of the *Codex.* Besides, Sprig didn't seem too scary. But what was a magic book doing in his grandmother's attic to begin with?

Max skipped a smooth stone across the water. Once, twice, five times it jumped, finally landing on the other side of the stream where Max noticed that the grass and leaves looked different. Gray and cracked, the vegetation was covered in a thin veil of frost.

A chill air rushed across the water, sweeping over him, as Max's eyes slowly raised in dread. To his horror, not more than ten feet across the rushing water was the Slayer, blindly peering out from the shadows of a fallen tree that was carpeted in rotten ice.

It was back.

Scrambling to his feet in terror, Max realized too late that the flooding water had undercut the ledge where he had been sitting, devouring his only support. Before he could cry out for help, the ledge crumbled. In a flash, Max was gone.

The rush of water hit Max like a freight train as he fell deep into the icy flow. Gripping him with unyielding fingers, the current crushed the breath from his lungs. Once or twice he managed to kick back to the surface, but he was weakening from the shock of the freezing waters.

Then, just as he was about to give up, something soft brushed up against him. It was his backpack, floating in the torrent. With what little strength remained, Max pulled it close and curled his arm around the bag. But it didn't matter.

That was the last thing he remembered.

Max was launched over the edge of a towering waterfall where murderous rocks awaited. Then the world exploded in a flash of light and heat.

Max was dead. Or so he thought. For when he opened his eyes, there was nothing but darkness.

"I thought heaven would be brighter," he murmured to himself.

"No," laughed a small, feminine voice. "You are not dead. We are inside a tree. It's always dark here."

"Sprig?" Max asked in disbelief.

"Yes." Her voice purred like a warm kitten's. "Max is safe now. No water. No rocks. No worries."

"We're in a tree?" Max shook his head.

"Of course. This is where Sprig lives," she laughed.

"I thought you lived in my book," said Max.

She growled but gave no response. Max decided to change the subject. "How did I get here?"

"Faerie magic," Sprig replied. "It can take you anywhere you want to go."

"Anywhere?"

"Anywhere," she answered.

"Can we go someplace else? I'm kind of claustrophobic," Max explained, though anything was better than dying. But he couldn't move, and Sprig's toothy smile was only inches from his nose. Her breath had grown rancid, and he wanted out of there.

Max suddenly found himself standing in the middle of an endless sea of ice, sleet stinging his face. The temperature was mind-numbing. His lungs burned with every breath as he weakly reached for Sprig. She was cleaning her fur, which had turned white like a polar bear's. Obviously, she wasn't the least bit bothered by the arctic blast. "Some ... place ... warmer ...," Max chattered. "P-p-p-p-lease ..."

"Does Max have somewhere specific in mind?" Sprig called over the howling wind.

"Home," he gasped weakly. It was the only thing he could think of.

In another explosion of light, Max found himself lying facedown under a gnarled tree back in the woods by his grandmother's house. The storm clouds had passed, and warm sunlight was shining down.

"Thanks for saving me, Sprig," Max said, brushing the remaining snow from his shoulders as he rubbed his numb hands to get warm. But then a thought occurred to him. "How did you know I was in trouble?"

"You rescued us," she replied quickly, turning to scratch an ear with her hind leg, her fur slowly fading back from white and fluffy to dark and spiky. "We are always watching now. We must keep you safe."

Always watching? Max was torn between thankfulness and discomfort. He settled with just being grateful to be alive, dismissing any thought of Sprig stalking him. "I just wish there was some way I could thank you."

The spriggan looked first right, then left, then glanced back at Max nervously. "There is something ... a favor, perhaps?"

"Anything, Sprig." Max smiled. "But I thought you were magic. Why would you need a favor from me?"

"There are things I cannot do." Sprig looked down sadly. "Things only Max is capable of."

"Like what?"

"We would never ask for it ourselves, but since Max has offered . . ."

"Anything," he repeated again. "Just tell me what it is."

"There is someone who helped us once. Someone who saved us just as we saved you. It is still locked inside the book, just as we were until you rescued us. It's very sad and very lonely. You must let it out," Sprig answered softly, slowly backing away.

Max went cold. "I don't know. . . ."

Sprig paused, and then crept closer. She was trembling. Was she afraid of something?

"We gave it our word that if we escaped, Sprig would help . . . just as Max gave us his word. We only want to keep our promise. It's the right thing to do, yes?"

"All right," Max conceded. He felt trapped. After all, she had just saved his life. "But who is it? Another spriggan?"

"Oh no, Max. It's almost nobody at all—just a harmless little Shadow. It doesn't even know how to speak."

"Well, I guess that doesn't sound so bad," replied Max with a shrug. A few moments later, Max closed his eyes and let the voice flow back into his mind . . . the words came and the *Codex* unlocked. It wasn't until after the book was open that he once again remembered his promise to the Grey Griffins. He'd be in trouble for sure.

Sprig had withdrawn as the book was opened, but edged a little closer as she directed Max to the back of the book. Max thought at first it was strange that she knew which way to turn, but he assumed that no one would know better where to look than a creature that had lived inside of it.

Shortly, he came to a dark page with two shining white eyes peering back at him. Max couldn't tell what it was, but what harm could it do? At least it wasn't a troll or a dragon.

"Letharaen!" he called aloud.

Much to his surprise, there was no great explosion as he spoke the words. No whirlwind. Nothing. The embossed seal simply fell away into the page, leaving a black hole in its place. Max stood there wondering if he had done something wrong.

"What happened?" he asked, puzzled. Then Max realized Sprig was gone. He was alone. And the air had grown suddenly cold—the same type of chill that had filled his bedroom right before the Slayer goblin . . .

It was then that Max noticed a dark shadow attached to his feet. But the Shadow wasn't his. In fact, it looked nothing like him at all.

Max stepped one way, then another. The Shadow mimicked him. Max jumped. It jumped as well. Then to his horror, Max noticed that every place the Shadow had fallen, the grass lay withered and brown. It was as if wintry death clung to everything it touched.

With morbid curiosity, Max reached toward the Shadow. As his finger passed through the darkness, a chill ran up his arm and coursed through his body, freezing him to the spot. Paralyzed, Max helplessly watched the Shadow rise from the ground until it stood directly in front of him, staring at Max with glowering eyes—eyes filled with sinister plots and dark secrets.

The Shadow moved closer, inch by silent inch, and Max's heart began to race. There was nowhere for him to go. He couldn't move; he couldn't even cry out for help. Besides, who would come to his rescue? Not Sprig. She had led him into the trap.

But just as the Shadow reached out with sinister fingers for Max's trembling heart, Max heard someone whistling a tune a short distance away. Evidently, the Shadow heard it as well. In a blur, the creature disappeared into the darkness of the trees beyond. Released from the spell, Max collapsed in the wet grass.

"Good afternoon, Master Sumner," came a familiar voice as Max looked up and saw Iver smiling broadly. He was smoking his pipe, holding a gnarled walking stick. "Stargazing in the middle of the day?"

Max rose unsteadily and dusted himself off when he caught sight of Iver studying the withered patch of grass where the Shadow had been only moments before. Ashamed at having opened the book without his friends, and unsure how to explain any of it to Iver, Max stepped between the old man and the dead grass, hoping somehow to distract Iver from any uncomfortable questions. "Ah . . . what are you doing here?"

Iver looked directly into Max's eyes. "Perhaps a better question would be what are you doing here," he suggested, taking a deep puff from his pipe.

But Iver's stern gaze melted into hearty laughter at the sight of

Max's worried face. "All right, young Master Sumner, you can keep your secrets. But if you must know, I come here often. All paths in the forest lead to this spot for those who know the way. But these woods can be unsafe," he continued, running his walking stick across the dead grass. "Particularly here. How you came to these parts I can only guess."

"I must have taken a wrong turn," Max replied, scooping the magic book into his backpack when he thought Iver might not be looking. "I don't remember ever being here before."

Iver's eyes glinted in the fading sun as he sent a parade of smoke rings into the air. "Yes, well, I imagine you wouldn't. Some places are not meant to be found."

For a moment neither said a word in the awkward silence. Iver had come to town not long after Max's grandfather passed away. It didn't take long for him and Max to hit it off. Max didn't know quite how to explain it, but whenever he was around Iver he felt completely at ease. Perhaps it was Iver's laugh, the twinkle in his eye, or the fact that he looked exactly like a giant St. Nicholas. But most likely it was because Iver reminded Max of his grandfather. They didn't look the same, of course. But they sort of felt the same—in a way only a grandson could describe.

Then Max turned to the old man. "Thanks, Iver."

"For what?" he questioned, a bit perplexed.

"You've always been there for me," Max explained. "I really miss my grandpa . . . and my dad, too, I guess. But whenever I have a problem, I can count on you."

If Max were looking closely, he might have seen Iver's eyes

mist over, if just a bit. "Master Sumner, you owe me no thanks, but rather it is I who should thank you, and your fellow Griffins, for spending time with this lonely old codger. If it weren't for you, I'd likely have taken to talking to myself, and from what I've heard, that isn't good for business."

Max laughed, but he knew better. If Iver spent half the time advertising his shop that he did playing Round Table or just listening to the stories of Max and his friends, he'd be a wealthy man. "You kinda remind me of him, you know."

"Who? Your grandfather? Well, that is high praise indeed," Iver said, smiling and offering a polite bow.

"It's true," Max said. "I can almost feel him here now."

"Odd weather we're having, wouldn't you say?" asked the old man, embarrassedly changing the subject as he tamped his pipe before hiding it inside his coat. "The cold wind, the sudden icing on the leaves—unnatural, some might say."

"Uh . . ." Max simply had no idea how to respond.

Iver's lips broke into a knowing smile as he removed his spectacles and wiped the frost onto a handkerchief. "Do you know why I came here to Avalon?"

"To open up your shop," Max ventured, glad to be changing the topic.

"No, Master Sumner. I came here to watch over you as a promise to your grandfather," he said, reaching into one of his deep pockets before revealing a thin gold chain in his enormous hand and presenting it to Max.

"What's this?" asked Max, taking the necklace from Iver. It

glittered, even in the half-light, as Max stood mesmerized. Hanging from the chain was a small crimson cross encompassed by a golden ring, just like the crosses in Grandpa Caliburn's study.

"It was your grandfather's. He wanted you to have it."

"Wow," was all Max could manage. "What is it?"

"It's your destiny, Max. Someday I'll tell you more about it when we have time."

"Cool."

"Cool indeed," Iver said, blowing into his hands to keep warm. "But it's getting late, and with school starting tomorrow, you'll no doubt have much to prepare."

"I guess," Max replied, slipping the necklace over his head and tucking it under his shirt.

"Why don't I walk along with you to ensure you find your way home?"

Max nodded, touching the cool metal of the cross now hanging from his neck.

"Wear it with pride," the old man said as they started to walk.

"I will," Max said as that pride spread from ear to ear.

"You're a fine boy, Max. As good as they come. But remember, one day you may find yourself lost again in a dark land, and who will rescue you then, I wonder?"

5   Malodorous Putrescence

KING'S ELEMENTARY SCHOOL stood tall and proud in the morning sunlight, its high stony walls decorated with a pageantry of red banners and balloons celebrating the first day of classes. From a bird's-eye view, the school was a series of castlelike buildings connected by an intricate system of pillared marble hallways, each more cavernous than the next. It was nestled into a green valley between three hills, fringed on all sides by crooked trees. Though no one really knew how old the school was, there were rumors it had been a monastery long, long ago. In fact, some went so far as to claim that the monks who once lived there now haunted the grounds.

Whether it was the fault of the ghosts or just plain bad luck, not five minutes into the first day of school, Ernie had plowed straight into the biggest bully King's Elementary had ever known, sending a shower of books, papers, and Round Table cards into the air.

"Oh . . . um . . . I'm sorry," stuttered Ernie apologetically, not fully realizing what he had done or whom he was apologizing to.

It really wasn't his fault—at least not directly. The culprit was a bulging backpack strapped over Ernie's skinny shoulders. When he wore it, Ernie resembled a nearsighted turtle shuffling down the hallway. Perhaps if he had installed rearview mirrors on his glasses, he might have seen the flock of children hurtling toward him. Unfortunately, he hadn't, so when the flood of students hit, he was tossed headlong into the hulking Dennis Stonebrow.

"Tweeny?" Dennis glared down for one awful moment of recognition, and then began to laugh. "Who put you up to this? Someone dare you?" He paused and looked around suspiciously, while letting Ernie squirm like a worm on the end of a hook.

Ernie only managed to squeak as he inched backward. Physical confrontation was not his specialty—that was Harley's business. All Ernie wanted to do was to run. Placing one foot behind the other, he began to inch away from Dennis's formidable shadow.

"Where do you think you're going?" asked Dennis with a laugh. He shot out a thick arm, catching Ernie by the shoulder strap of his bag, lifting his helpless prey right off the ground. Dennis was every bit as strong as he looked, which was regrettable for Ernie because Dennis was as big as a bull moose.

Every school typically had a student who was larger than the rest, but Dennis was different. He was a mutant—a freak of nature. As a sixth grader, he was bigger than all of the other students in school and most of the teachers, for that matter. He was a juggernaut of ill intentions and bad breath. And now Ernie was at his mercy, hanging there with his legs dangling, gasping for air.

"Aw, what's wrong?" mocked Dennis. Ernie's asthma was bad— a fact of which Dennis was well aware.

"Put him down, Dennis," a voice commanded from behind. It was Max, who had been watching the entire incident from his locker just a few feet away.

Max, like every other student in the school (with perhaps the exception of Harley on a very good day), would not have had a snowball's chance of confronting the giant. But like David facing Goliath, Max had always been a little short on fear. He figured the worst that could happen was that he'd end up with a black eye or bloody lip—an acceptable risk given the circumstances, he thought. Besides, Max was already in a bad mood. Another package had come from his father, and his mother had given him an impromptu speech about his father buying his love—all the while rushing to her weekly manicure. Max's life was upside down. He figured a fight, regardless of the odds, couldn't possibly make things any worse than they already were.

"What did you say, Sumner?" Dennis asked in disbelief as he continued to grip Ernie like a rag doll.

"I could repeat it more slowly if you think that would help." Max glared, taking a step forward. All the students who had gathered gasped as Max continued. "That is, unless you've somehow become as deaf as you are dumb."

Dennis stood there fuming, his eyes shifting rapidly as if they were trying to wind up the motor in his walnut-sized brain.

"So you wanna push your luck, Sumner? I'll smash the both of you like a couple of twigs," Dennis growled, clenching his fist, which was the size of a brick (and twice as hard).

"You mean 'snap you like a couple of twigs,' genius," Max corrected with a sarcastic smile. The growing audience of students broke out in laughter as Dennis simmered in dumbfounded silence above them. Almost everybody liked Max. Maybe for his money. Maybe not. But popularity had never been a problem.

Unfortunately, popularity could also be a bad thing. Especially when bullies the size of trucks ate popular kids for breakfast just because they could. If they couldn't be popular, they'd settle for feared.

"Stop!" shouted Ray Fisher, who had burst through the crowd, stepping in front of Dennis just before he plowed into Max.

Ray was Dennis's only friend, and twice as evil as the oaf, if that was possible. He was about the same size as Max, but he walked with his shoulders hunched and his knees bent. It made him seem smaller, but no less menacing. Ray had shining black eyes and a mop of thick, wheat-blond hair. While he was perhaps only a quarter of the size of Dennis, his quick mind, devouring intelligence, and acid tongue earned him far more fear and respect. All of those considerable talents were most often employed against Max and his family.

Ray hated Max, even though he had once been one of Max's closest friends. But over the last year, Ray had grown viciously jealous of Max—his money, his popularity, and the fact that everybody thought Max was perfect. It also didn't help that Ray's dad owned one of the handful of businesses in town that the Sumner family did not: the First Avalon Bank. It was more of an oversight by Sumner Enterprises than anything else—a curiosity that could be corrected should Max's father have even the slightest interest (which he didn't). But that undeniable fact kept Ray's family in constant anxiety.

"What do you mean?" complained Dennis, dropping Ernie to the ground in a heap. "We got 'em right where we want 'em. We can take care of these losers. Right here, right now."

"Let it go," snarled Ray. "This is too easy. Besides, knowing Max, he'd probably have his father kick your family out of town. They own everything—including the cops." He then turned back to Max and narrowed his eyes. "But then again, maybe not. Daddy Sumner already abandoned his family. I doubt he'd care if poor little Max was taught a lesson."

Max, overcome with anger, would have strangled Ray right then and there if it weren't for Natalia stepping in his way. "Grayson Maximillian, you stop this right now! Do you want to get suspended on your first day of school?"

"What a loser," Ray mocked. "Little Max needs a girl to protect him when his pet bodyguard isn't around. Too bad he can't take care of himself." Dennis snorted in laughter as he and Ray looked at Natalia in contempt.

But Natalia was not afraid of bullies or their little toady friends. In frosty defiance she turned and walked right up to Ray, nose to nose. "If you don't back off, everyone in this hall is gonna see you get the snot beat out of you by a girl. Then we'll see who's laughing."

"Whatever." Ray smirked. "You're all a bunch of losers. Let's get out of here, Dennis." The giant grunted a toothy grimace in reply as he turned to leave, his massive frame casting long shadows over the whispering students as the crowd pushed to get out of his way.

"Where's Mrs. Garvey?" whispered Natalia. As always, she was seated in the front row, her red hair tied back in bright ribbons for the first day of class.

Max shrugged as he slid into a desk nearby. He wasn't feeling very talkative after the scene back at the lockers with Ray and Dennis. It had happened before and would probably happen again. But Max had hoped that the summer would have cooled Ray off, and things would have gotten at least a little better. Unfortunately, Ray seemed to have grown even more sour.

As Max sat there in frustrated thought, he failed to notice a young girl standing next to his desk, waiting to be noticed.

"Hi, Max," she said shyly.

Max quickly forgot all about Ray when he looked up and saw Brooke Lundgren, a girl whom Max had asked to marry at the age of four. Of course, that was a long time ago. But time hadn't erased the fact that his heart seemed to jump whenever she spoke to him.

Everybody loved Brooke. Not only was she the most beautiful and popular girl in class, she was also the nicest and most thoughtful. With long chocolate hair and sparkling brown eyes framed by long lashes, Brooke could make any boy in school blush with a single wink. But the only boy she had ever winked at was Max. And he knew it. He just didn't know what to do about it.

Max smiled awkwardly, absently running nervous fingers through his hair. "Oh. Hi, Brooke," was all he could manage.

"Would you get ahold of yourself?" Natalia sighed. She was not a fan of Brooke, who Natalia believed was an annoying combination of too pretty and too sweet. And totally boring.

Just then, the door swung open, and an attractive young woman with long blond hair walked into the room. There was something different about her. Something powerful and warm. But whatever it was, Max was relieved that he wouldn't have to think of anything to say to Brooke.

"Good morning, class. I am sorry to inform you that Mrs. Garvey will not be with us this year," the woman said with a musical voice. She then walked over to a neatly kept desk, carrying a worn leather book and a picture of a black cat whose eyes seemed to be following Max.

"Are you a substitute?" Natalia asked matter-of-factly, not waiting to be called upon.

"Oh, I am much more than that," the woman said in a soft, kind voice. "But for the moment, I will be your homeroom teacher."

The students broke into excited whispers. Mrs. Garvey had been one of the most respected and influential teachers in the history of the school. Her sudden disappearance was sure to spark an avalanche of rumors.

"My name is Rhiannon," the new teacher explained as the classroom grew silent. "Now, before you laugh, I will admit it's a rather unusual name, but my father loved it, and that is enough for me. I hope it will be the same for you."

She was about to turn to write her name on the chalkboard, but stopped when she noticed the confused looks on her students' faces. It was obvious none of them had ever been allowed to call a teacher by a first name.

"Well . . . perhaps you should call me Ms. Heen instead. It seems to be the custom here to maintain formality. A terrible shame, but a matter of tradition it looks like we will need to observe." With that, she gave the class a wink.

"As you may already have noted from my accent, I'm not from Minnesota," she continued, writing her full name on the chalkboard. "In fact, I have only recently come to Avalon. Does anyone have a guess as to where I'm from?"

Just then, Ernie sneezed, which, despite the fact that he was hardly larger than a mouse, sounded alarmingly like an elephant's. The whole class laughed as Ernie raided his pockets for a handkerchief. Ernie was allergic to everything. This time, he could only assume it was Ms. Heen's perfume, but he wasn't going to complain. To Ernie, it was the nicest smell in the whole world.

When Max turned back to face the chalkboard, he found Ms. Heen staring right at him. He could feel his face flush. There was something strange about her—beyond the accent anyway—and Max couldn't put his finger on it.

"Do you have a guess, Max?" she asked, somehow knowing his name before he had ever given it. Max had a feeling that she knew everyone's name, and probably more.

"New York?" Max guessed. Compared with most kids his age, Max had traveled quite a bit, and he knew her accent sounded as if she had come from someplace out east.

She shook her head, giving Max a warm smile that made him blush. "Any other guesses?"

Only silence and a few giggles, followed by the sound of Ernie taking a shot from his inhaler.

"All right then, I'm from Salem, Massachusetts."

In a fevered excitement to raise her hand, Natalia nearly fell out of her seat. "Do you mean the same Salem where the witch trials were hold hundreds of years ago?"

Ernie suddenly looked worried. He didn't like the sound of that. What if his new teacher was secretly a witch? And now that he thought about it, the picture of the black cat on the desk was rather suspicious.

Ms. Heen nodded at Natalia. "Yes, Ms. Romanov, the very same town," she said as she walked to the front of the room. "But I am very pleased to report that Salem has come a long way since then. They no longer torture people—quite the opposite, actually. Now witches from all over the world move there, and the town loves them, though I believe it has more to do with tourism than anything. Either way, it's a beautiful place, and I suppose it reminds me a bit of Avalon."

"How?" asked Natalia, wondering how a town as dull as Avalon could be as exciting as a place like the legendary Salem.

"I don't know quite how to explain it," she said, wrinkling her nose as she thought a moment. "They're both earthy...raw. I would even say they have the same aura. In fact, a friend of mine owns a bookstore in Salem that reminds me a great deal of your Shoppe of Antiquities down on Main Street. Do any of you visit that delightful place?"

The Grey Griffins raised their hands just as the classroom door swung open. Principal Hamm, whose awkward first name was Gaspard, blustered into the room. Affectionately known to the student body as "Piggy," he was red-faced, out of breath, and still clutching a dripping cream doughnut in one of his round, piggy hands. He bustled to the front of the classroom, pausing long enough to realize that most of the cream filling was now spattered across his obnoxiously loud tie. Trying unsuccessfully to smear it out of existence, he puffed himself up for an announcement.

"Ahem! Pardon me!" he shouted over the bellow of his own breathing. He had a rather surprisingly high-pitched voice that contrasted decidedly with his tremendous girth (and bursting buttons). "All students are to form into lines and follow their teachers to the courtyard immediately. Something terrible has happened."

He had barely completed his sentence before the class erupted in chatter and a flurry of questions.

"There will be no talking. No laughing. Not a peep!" he commanded. "Everyone in line, now."

Like a herd, the students rushed to the front of the classroom, almost trampling the rotund principal. The first in line was, of course, Natalia. She was always first. Once, or perhaps twice, someone had tried to cut in front of her, but they learned the hard way that Natalia's pinches were vicious and her aim frighteningly precise.

Ms. Heen guided the jabbering students (who were blatantly ignoring Principal Hamm's "no talking" orders) through the labyrinth of stone hallways that led out to the central courtyard. There hundreds of other bewildered students crowded and clamored like chickens in a pen. They were all pointing and staring. Some laughed. Some squealed.

In the midst of what had once been a picturesque garden surrounding a white marble fountain with a stoic statue of the monk who had founded the school, there rested a spectacle that shredded all dignity and honor from the school and its proud history. For where clear bubbling water had flowed, there was now a thick spray of black clotted gelatin, more the consistency of snot than of water. It was burbling and spitting up out of the fountain, overflowing the basin, and oozing out onto the grass. No one knew what it was, but it was so gross and foul-smelling that in their shock, many of the students found themselves unable to even move, standing ankle-deep in the cold, gloppy goo.

But that wasn't the half of it. A grinning pumpkin head, half-rotten, was now resting on the shoulders of the statue. In one hand it held a moldy and distressed broomstick; in the other was a grinning skull.

Of course, the younger students suspected the ghosts that haunted the grounds were behind it all. The teachers, lacking imagination, didn't believe in magical nonsense and therefore immediately assumed a student was to blame—maybe more than one. If so, all the students knew there was a price to be paid, a heavy price.

Just then, Principal Hamm made his way through the crowd to stand on the edge of the fountain. How he managed to work his portly body up there without falling in was anyone's guess. And there, standing directly behind him, wearing a look of smoldering fury, was Dr. Diamonte Blackstone, the school's ill-tempered band instructor and acting assistant principal. Dr. Blackstone was abrasive, strict, exacting, and meticulously arrogant. He was also the school's chief disciplinarian, perhaps explaining why miscreant behavior was on the decline—the students were more afraid of him than of the ghosts. Rumor had it that he had been a child prodigy in the European classical music scene, but something very mysterious had happened, and for reasons unknown he had disappeared for many long years. It was only recently that he had resurfaced, strangely choosing to join the faculty at King's Elementary in obscure Avalon, Minnesota. No one knew why. Most people, especially his students, wished he had chosen to go someplace else—anywhere else. But the dislike was mutual. Blackstone hated the small town — referring to it often as a "cultureless sty of simple-minded pigs."

Principal Piggy cleared his throat many times, attempting to begin a speech from his precarious perch, but without success. His weak, tiny voice was overwhelmed by the commotion of the students below. And so, with some reservation, Principal Hamm turned to Dr. Blackstone and shrugged his shoulders. Dr. Blackstone nodded with a self-important smile, wearing his impeccable pin-striped suit, complete with handkerchief and pocket watch glistening in the sun, as he pulled forth a whistle. He immediately let go with a shrill blast that nearly deafened everyone nearby.

It was a horrible sound, but it worked. The courtyard fell completely silent, save for the disturbing burble of sludge in the fountain as it plopped onto the ground.

"Students of King's Elementary!" Blackstone began in his icy tone. "I am disappointed, very disappointed, to learn of this egregious effrontery. I am appalled at the notion that there are students among us to whom tradition, decency, reverence, and honor have very little significance. And yet," he continued, "I know there are many among you whose hearts are as pained as my own to see this foundational icon of our school shamed in such a cowardly act."

"Yeah right," Harley whispered to Max.

"Can't he talk like a normal person?" Ernie complained under his breath. "Who's he trying to impress?"

However, Dr. Blackstone's speech was far from finished. "To those loyal and obedient students possessing the knowledge of who it was that committed this appalling act, I ask simply this—come forward. Your loyalty will be rewarded."

"He's asking us to snitch." Harley shook his head. "He's got to be kidding."

A long pause followed, and Dr. Blackstone's eyes roved over the student body looking for a guilty face. But either no one knew who had done it or no one had any intention of telling.

"Very well," Blackstone growled, impatient with his reluctant audience. He then shot his long, bony index finger into the air. "Until someone comes forth and tells me who the perpetrators of this crime are, you will all remain here, every last one of you, until spring thaw . . . or the slime swallows you all—whichever comes first!"

As Dr. Blackstone bowed dramatically in conclusion, a great moan went up from the students and a flurry of complaints erupted all around the lawn. Even Principal Hamm looked disturbed at Dr. Blackstone's threat. His stomach rumbled just thinking about the possibility of missing his brunch, then lunch, and, worse yet, his afternoon snack.

"Whoever did this was good." Harley whistled in appreciation, while Ernie pinched his nose in disgust.

"I hope they get what they deserve," Natalia stated flatly, looking down at her new shoes and tights, ruined by the gooey mess. "This is awful, making us stand out here and get our clothes filthy. Honestly!"

"I just want to know how they did it," Max wondered, surveying the school grounds. "There wasn't enough time to pull this off, not between the first bell and now. That's only ten minutes."

"Tell that to the goop pouring into my new shoes," Natalia pointed out.

"That's not what I am saying," Max sighed, switching his weight to the drier foot. "What I mean is that to plan something like this, nobody else could have been in the courtyard or they would have seen the whole thing. You'd need at least four people, I think. There'd be one to dress up the statue, another to wreck the fountain, and at least two lookouts—one at the entrance from the bus stop over there by the hedge, and one at the courtyard gates."

"Hmmm...you might be on to something," Natalia offered, pulling out her pencil and paper to take notes. It was the perfect time to put her detective skills to work. "But look at those windows above the courtyard. That's where the third graders are. They would have seen everything."

Ernie shrugged. "Who cares? It's obvious who did it."

"Who?" demanded Natalia, thinking she had missed a clue.

"Ray and Dennis. Who else?" he responded casually. "Besides, Dennis is the only one tall enough to put the pumpkin on the statue's head."

"Please," replied Natalia with a roll of her eyes. "Dennis can't even tie his own shoelaces."

"Oh yeah? Then why aren't they out here with the rest of us?"

Max scanned the courtyard, taking in every face. He should have noticed it before, but Ernie was right. Dennis and Ray were nowhere to be seen. But as much as he wanted to believe they had done it, it didn't add up. It was simply too sophisticated a prank for a sixth grader. But if those two hadn't done it, then who?

"Sprig?" Max offered. However, since only Max had seen Sprig so far, Natalia wasn't quite ready to accept her as a possible suspect. But it didn't make any difference. If someone didn't come forward soon, they could all end up standing out in the courtyard until Christmas.

Looking for a sign of mercy, Natalia turned in the direction of the principal. Like a portly penguin in a sea of lumpy oil, Mr. Hamm remained standing on the edge of the fountain, shifting from one fat foot to the other, thinking the day could not possibly get any worse.

But he was about to be proven wrong. Grossly wrong.

At first, it was only a soft sound, barely perceptible. But then a deep rumbling resounded as rocks groaned beneath the courtyard with the clanking of iron poles being twisted and torn in the hands of an angry giant.

"The fountain's pipes!" Harley cried, causing a chain reaction of squeals and screams. "They're gonna blow!"

Brooke, who was standing close by, screamed as her foot broke through the soft earth. But that was only the beginning.

Nearby, a great fissure tore open in the lawn, and a disgusting spray shot high into the air like the blast of a fetid fire hose. Soon other explosions erupted all over the courtyard. Like a herd of gazelles that had stumbled upon a pack of hungry lions, everyone in the courtyard bolted in different directions, screaming.

Max and Harley launched into flight as Natalia hiked up her dress and followed as quickly as she could. A moment later the three of them had found safety behind an enormous hedge. Ernie was not so fortunate, for no sooner did he realize his shoes were cemented into the muck than the ground directly beneath him started to convulse.

"Oh no!" cried Natalia, peering out from behind the hedge. "He's stuck! We have to help him!"

Ernie's eyes grew wide as saucers as he realized his peril.

"Get out of there!" Harley shouted while Ernie frantically began tearing at his shoelaces, but it was far too late. A colossal blast of filth catapulted Ernie right out of his shoes, rocketing him into the sky. A second later, he plummeted back to earth with an enormous splash into a bubbling pool of slime, lying motionless in his rancid stockinged feet.

"He's dead!" cried Natalia, mortified.

Then, like a frozen fly slowly coming back to life, Ernie started to twitch, until finally he rolled over and began to slop on all fours toward Max and the others. He looked absolutely miserable, covered nose to toe in glutinous black goop. Luckily, he had managed to keep hold of his glasses, though his braces were crammed with nasty black slime.

"I don't feel so good," he sputtered as he dragged himself behind the hedge and collapsed.

While all the students and teachers in the courtyard were consumed with saving their own skin, they had forgotten about poor Piggy. He had been stranded on the fountain with no possibility of escape, beset on all sides by geysers of slime bursting into the air. Sweat beaded across his forehead as each explosion brought his impending doom closer and agonizingly closer. Then, like a capped volcano, the fountain began to rumble below. Principal Hamm looked down nervously, shaking his head. His fate sealed, Piggy drew in a breath of resolution and began to do something so peculiar that everyone watching immediately stopped and gaped in wonder.

"Why is he combing his hair?" shouted Natalia, horrified, but unable to pull her eyes away. Yet Piggy didn't stop at his hair. Next, he straightened his tie, then his shirt cuffs, and finally he made sure his pleats and the crease in his pants were fresh and sharp. It was one of the strangest things any of them had ever seen.

Then it was all over in one furious moment. The fountain collapsed into a heaving shower of inky pudding and debris. The liquid rose into the air, casting a shadow over the courtyard below. Poor Piggy only had enough time to let out one pitiful squeal before he was lost from sight under the mountain of slime that plummeted back to the earth like cold Vesuvian lava.

To no one's surprise, school was let out early that day and canceled for the rest of the week. No one had claimed responsibility, and luckily no real lasting damage had been done—at least nothing that a good fire hose and some nose plugs couldn't handle. That is, except for the fountain, which was little more than a pile of rubble and embarrassment.

Principal Hamm was able to return to his post with nothing more serious than a swollen thumb. But the story around the town took on a life of its own and quickly grew to paint Piggy as a hero who had braved the worst sort of calamity with dignity, while allowing the others to flee to safety. It was told at every barbershop and coffeehouse for three counties in every direction, and he relished every well-wishing card, fruit basket, and cradle of cookies that appeared on his desk each morning for a month and beyond.

6 Shoe-Eating Trees

FROM THE MAIN STREET CAFÉ to the Shear Magic Beauty Salon, the incident with the school's fountain had set the entire town abuzz. Had it been a student prank? A communist plot? An alien attack? No one knew. A handful of wishful thinkers who had not seen the black sludge firsthand suggested that King's Elementary School may have been sitting on an oil field. But their hopes were quickly dashed when county investigators confirmed the gooey material was nothing more than rotten mud—whatever that was.

Natalia and Harley came to agree with Ernie—Ray had to be the mastermind behind the plot. Max wasn't so sure. It wasn't that Ray or Dennis couldn't have played a part, mind you. He just couldn't get Sprig out of his mind. Certainly, she could have pulled off a prank of that magnitude. Max hadn't seen her in almost a week, not since the incident with the Shadow, and that made him suspicious. No word. Not even an apology for making him release the Shadow. For that matter, Max still hadn't told his friends about that creepy Shadow—or the fact that he had broken the pact. He wanted to tell them. It just never seemed to be the right time.

It was early Friday morning, and Max turned a brass knob, opening the green door to the Shoppe of Antiquities. Iver was sitting behind the counter reading and gave Max a nod and a smile.

Max waved back, then noticed a new painting hanging behind the display case. The canvas showed a group of knights seated around a table, perfectly round, and at the head was a regal knight with a neatly trimmed beard and a crown upon his head. It was King Arthur.

The figures in the painting resembled the mounted knight Max had found in his grandma's attic—the one with the strange symbols on his armor. But as he turned to ask Iver about it, he noticed that the book Iver was reading looked strangely familiar. In fact, it reminded Max of the *Codex Spiritus*—perhaps a little too much.

"Oh. Hello, Master Sumner. I was expecting to see you earlier with the others. They've been here nearly an hour already," Iver said, his eyes narrowing, which gave Max the weird feeling that the old man was reading his mind. He would do that from time to time, and it made Max uncomfortable.

"Um . . . well, I had to help my mom with Hannah," replied Max as his eyes remained locked on the book.

"And how is that sister of yours and your lovely mother?" Iver inquired. He closed the book and put it under the counter. Max watched it disappear with hungry eyes, determined to get a better look later.

"Okay, I guess," Max responded as he made his way to the plate of cookies that Iver kept near the register. Max's mother didn't care much for Iver or his store. She found the proprietor of the Shoppe of Antiquities to be overtly eccentric and more than a little suspicious. Of course, everyone was suspicious to Max's mom. She prided herself on being the highest class of skeptic. At any rate, while Iver was not blind to her criticism, he never once said an unkind word in return.

No. Unlike his mother, Max trusted Iver. Or at least he wanted to. But he really didn't have much of a choice. He had to talk to somebody.

"I found a picture of you with my grandpa the other night." It wasn't really a question, but Max wasn't sure where to begin.

"Did you now," Iver replied as he puffed on his pipe. "I'm quite surprised it took you this long to say so."

"How did you know him?"

Iver paused, then set down his pipe. "There are many things you don't know, Max. And many things you likely should. Perhaps it is time we had that talk, you and I."

"Umm . . . okay," Max replied, not prepared for Iver to instigate the conversation.

"But before we begin, a friend of yours stopped by to inquire about Round Table. I'd not met him before and didn't recognize him as one of your Grey Griffins. . . . Ray, I believe his name was."

Max dropped the cookie. "Really?" he asked, forgetting all about his grandfather. Ray had never set foot in the Shoppe of Antiquities before, but the strangest part was that Max was fairly certain the Grey Griffins were the only four kids in Avalon, Minnesota, who played Round Table. The only way Ray could have known anything was if he had been spying on them.

"Quite. Which I must say is a bit puzzling, for, you see, outside of the Grey Griffins, I've not advertised this game of Round Table to anyone. To my knowledge you are the only four in the entire town of Avalon—and perhaps the United States—who play. In fact, few who walk this world have seen these cards. They are a rare treat, indeed. Custom created for a chosen few... our VIP clientele, you might say."

"Really?" asked Max, thinking that was just about the coolest thing he'd ever heard—especially since it seemed to mean he and the Griffins were considered VIPs. "But you didn't sell Ray any cards, did you?"

"What kind of a proprietor would I be if I turned paying customers away?" Iver asked with a twinkle in his eye. Max's face sank. "But worry not," Iver said with assurance. "I had no cards to sell to the young man as my entire inventory had been bought out this morning before I was even able to turn on the light."

"I thought you said we were the only kids who played the game. Who bought them?" asked Max, growing strangely protective. He liked the idea that the Grey Griffins were the only kids around who played Round Table, and having Ray, or anyone else for that matter, horning in on *their* game really stunk.

"Your father," Iver said with a twinkle in his eye. "His office called this morning and wired payment not five minutes later. He requested I wrap them as a late birthday gift, but I'm afraid I have no wrapping paper—a frilly and nonsensical item in my opinion, gets in the way of the gift. So here you are, nonetheless," Iver said, handing Max a paper bag full of pack upon pack of Round Table cards—the new Goblin Wars expansion series.

"Cool," Max shouted, relieved, as he eyed the bag with excitement. "This is awesome."

"Indeed. Guard them well, Master Sumner. They are one of a kind."

"Really?"

"Of course. Why would I make up such a thing?" Iver asked, smiling proudly as he watched Max beam with excitement. Max needed to know his father loved him, and if Iver could help rebuild that relationship, he would do everything in his power to make sure that happened.

"Hey, Iver. My grandma wanted to know if you'd like to come over for Sunday dinner. She asked me to tell you she's making apple crisp."

Iver laughed. "Your grandmother is the finest baker I know, Master Sumner. And please tell her I'd be delighted, but I must postpone my attendance for a short time—as foolish as that is. My stomach will regret that decision for quite some time, but there are pressing matters I must attend to, and I really must be ready at a moment's notice. I would hate to be rude and have to cancel, so perhaps another time would be better."

Max's face dropped. He had been excited about the idea of sitting down at his grandmother's table, listening to story after story about his grandpa Caliburn (not to mention that his mouth was watering just thinking about that apple crisp). Besides, Iver was family as far as Max was concerned. And the more family Max had around, the better.

"Don't worry. If all works out according to plan, we won't have to put off the day for long," Iver said, noting Max's disappointment.

"Did I overhear you two talking about Ray Fisher snooping

around trying to play Round Table?" Natalia voiced with displeasure as she, Ernie, and Harley walked up. They had been upstairs sorting their own cards, working on a few practice scenarios. "We aren't letting him play, are we? He's such a beast, he'd wreck the whole thing."

Max shook his head. "He can't. My dad bought the last of the cards for my birthday. Check it out," he said, beaming, as he showed her the packs.

The other three rushed over to take a look.

"Sweet," Harley said, admiring the bounty.

"Yeah. Let's open 'em," pressed Ernie. "I wanna see what you got. Maybe we can trade."

Iver smiled. "You'll have plenty of time for that later," the old man said. "And you might be happy to know your friend Ray wasn't as interested in playing Round Table as you might think. He seemed a bit more fascinated with the knucklebone shipment that was supposed to arrive this morning. Of course, they hadn't come in yet, so he left in a rather sour mood. But they are here now. Would you like to see them?"

Carefully, Iver pulled out a wooden case from beneath the counter. It was loaded with row upon row of fantastically intricate knucklebone dice, each set different and more remarkable than the next. Some glittered like jewels. Others were as cold as iron. Still others had the grisly, cracked appearance of old bone, complete with numbers etched in what resembled dried blood.

"Ewwww," Natalia complained.

"How much for those, Iver?" Harley asked, walking over to the display and pointing at two black dice in the bottom row. They were neither shiny nor dull. In fact, they were wholly unremarkable to look at. Yet there was a mysterious draw to them that Harley couldn't explain.

Iver paused and a sparkle seemed to light in the depths of his eyes. "What do you think of them?" he asked.

"They're awesome!" Harley exclaimed with great enthusiasm.

"You know, these are a very special pair of dice," Iver said with a hint of mystery in his voice. "Would you like them?"

"I didn't bring enough money," Harley said. The truth, of course, was that even if he had wanted to, Harley couldn't afford them. He and his mother were agonizingly poor, scraping by each week with barely enough money to eat. However, despite their apparent destitution, they shared a love that was stronger than iron.

Iver just laughed. "These dice aren't for purchasing—or even bartering, for that matter. No, as I said, these are very special dice. They can't be chosen, but rather they do the choosing, and it seems they've chosen you, Harley. Would you have them?"

"Are you serious?" asked Harley in amazement. "For free?"

"I am quite serious. Gifts of this nature are no joking matter."

With great care, Harley picked them up, studying them. He held them to the lamp, admiring their detailed perfection, which had not been so apparent before. Every corner was cut and rounded without flaw. The numbers were etched across each face in shining silver. Harley closed his hand and smiled proudly before wandering into the depths of the shop to admire his new possession in solitude.

But Harley did not go alone. A Shadow had passed through the door of the Game Shoppe unnoticed, keeping to the corners, away from the light. It had been waiting, and when Harley walked past, it slithered up his pant leg, then his shirt, flying down his arm, and disappeared into the knucklebones.

"Ow!" shouted Harley, shaking his arm as if he had been stung by a bee.

"Something the matter, Mr. Eisenstein?" called Iver from the front of the store.

Behind a cabinet in a gloomy corner of the shop, Harley had frozen, darkness falling over his eyes. Like a cloud passing across the face of a full moon, his skin seemed to darken and lose color. Harley was no longer himself. His alien eyes were cast with sudden awareness and wicked intent, and a malicious sneer crossed his lips as he pulled the knucklebones close to his chest.

"Harley, are you all right?" hollered Max.

Just as quickly as it had come, the fit passed. Harley's skin and eyes returned to normal as he shook his head. "Yeah, I'm fine. Just a little dizzy, I guess."

"Maybe it's your sinuses," offered Natalia, looking up from a book she had picked up. "I know mine make me dizzy this time of year."

"Yeah," Harley mumbled. "Maybe."

Everyone turned as the doorbell rang. A cold wind blew through the entrance, sending a torrent of papers and leaves into the air, and standing there in the doorway was a mysterious raven-haired woman in a long black coat. She looked neither young nor old, but her dark eyes, impossibly deep, seemed ageless, and held within them a bitter ruthlessness that marked her as a powerful force to reckon with. She was beautiful in a cold and frightening way, and as the door closed behind her, a chill ran up Max's spine.

Iver nodded curtly, acknowledging the stranger. Generally jovial, the old shopkeeper seemed to suppress an undercurrent of anger, with an equal dose of begrudging respect. Whoever the woman was, Iver knew her. And he did not like her.

"Mr. Iverson." The mysterious woman spoke with a rich voice that seemed to contrast with her otherwise severe personality. She approached the register, stopping to study Max with a disapproving eyebrow. She was looking for something, Max could tell. And it felt as if she were peering into the depths of his mind.

"My name's Max," he offered, not knowing what to do or say under her oppressive analysis.

"Of course it is." She smiled knowingly, and then without another word, the odd woman walked to a small section in the back corner of the store where Iver kept his books on witchcraft and spells. Natalia, who was in her path, barely escaped being run over.

"How rude," Natalia said quietly, but not until the woman was safely out of earshot. "Who is she?"

Max said nothing. By the look on Iver's face, the old man knew something. But he wasn't talking.

After a long uncomfortable silence, Max decided to change the subject. "You didn't finish your story about Grandpa Caliburn," he reminded him.

"Right you are, Master Sumner," Iver agreed, speaking quietly as he kept a wary eye on the back of the store. "Your grandfather and I knew each other since we were just about your age," Iver mused, with a fleeting smile. "You remind me a great deal of him, in fact."

"I do?"

"Oh yes. Yes, indeed," Iver replied. And he might have gone on at length, which was exactly what Max was hoping for, but Natalia wasn't terribly interested in talking about family history. Instead, she pulled out her *Book of Clues* and cleared her throat, interrupting Iver with the rudeness of an alarm clock on a Saturday morning.

"What do you know about spriggans? I mean, aside from what the Round Table cards say."

Max was about to say something, but Iver patted him on the shoulder. "Hmm . . . ," the old man mused, looking at Natalia curiously over the top of his glasses. "A spriggan, you say? Now why is it you are asking?"

"I don't know," she said, shrugging, unprepared for the cross-examination. "We saw one in a book. . . ."

"May I inquire which book it was that you were reading?" Iver asked, turning to Max, much to Max's chagrin.

"Umm . . . I don't remember," Max stammered.

"You're a little young to be suffering memory loss, Master Sumner," remarked Iver, sniffing as he pulled down an oversized book from the top shelf behind the counter. It was dusty, its title written in gold, and it had a large red bookmark that rolled out from its middle.

"Ah yes," Iver started to read. "Spriggans . . . small, agile, and mischievous shape-shifters."

"That's it?" Natalia asked.

"Actually, it goes on and on in less than complimentary tones about the little faeries, discussing their inclination to lying, cheating, tricking, and even betraying the ones that trust them most. They are not all bad, but by and large they are a miserable lot. They trust no one, and no one trusts them." Max couldn't argue. Especially after Sprig had tricked him into releasing the Shadow. He knew the Shadow was evil from the moment he saw it. Max also had a feeling he hadn't seen the last of it.

"Are there any pictures?" Natalia pressed, desperately wanting a closer look.

"No, I'm afraid there aren't," Iver said, starting to put the book away. "This isn't that sort of book, you know."

"Does your book say anything about Shadows?" Max asked boldly.

"What did you say?" Iver responded, nearly dropping the book. "Shadows?"

"We read about those, too," Max replied matter-of-factly. It was only then that he remembered he still hadn't told his friends about his big mistake yet.

"No, we didn't," corrected Natalia, looking at Max suspiciously. "What are you talking about? I don't remember any shadow." Max didn't bother to explain just then. He was in trouble, and he knew it, but he'd just have to tell her about it later.

"Be warned," Iver said, his beard bristling in agitation. "I'm not sure which book it is that you've been reading, but Shadows are not creatures to be taken lightly or discussed over afternoon tea, for that matter. They are dangerous and wholly evil. If they get their hands on you, you'll wish you were dead. Forget you ever heard of them. I will speak no more about it. In the meantime, I suggest you—all of you—start being more careful. Not only in what you read but where you go. The world is not your sandbox. It's a wild and untamed land. Treat it as such—or you could find yourself in a desperate situation."

"I really wish Harley would beat up Ray," Ernie sighed as he and Max approached the woods on their bicycles later that evening. Ernie certainly wasn't brave enough to stand up to a bully himself, but he frequently encouraged others to do so. Safety first, he liked to say.

He and Max dismounted near an enormous maple tree, pushing their bikes under an overhanging branch. Their mothers had agreed to let them sleep over in Max's tree fort one last time before the cold set in. Harley was probably already there waiting for them.

"What would beating up Ray change?"

Ernie looked at Max in disbelief. "Are you serious? He needs somebody to teach him a lesson. If I weren't so small, I'd do it myself."

"It wouldn't change anything, Ernie. I don't think it will ever change."

Ernie disagreed, but Max didn't seem interested in talking about anything as they entered the woods and began their hike to the tree fort. They had taken this trail a hundred times and could probably have walked there blindfolded. But tonight was different. It started with the temperature dropping suddenly, and in no time Ernie was complaining that his glasses were frosting over.

"It's not your glasses, Ernie," explained Max as the forest grew dark. "It's fog."

Sure enough, a thick curtain of mist stood in front of them like a wall. Neither of the boys had seen anything like it before.

"We should probably hurry," said Max, remembering once again Iver's warning about the Shadow, which was probably still in the woods. Max shook his head. He felt like an idiot. Why would he come here? Logan would never approve of his lack of forethought.

Pulling their backpacks tight, the boys headed into the wall of mist.

The woods were cold and damp, the muddy trail covered with frost. That alone would have made the journey difficult, but the haze was impenetrable, so thick that Ernie had to hold on to Max's backpack strap just to keep from getting lost. But as long as the trail was under their feet, Max felt sure they were on the right track.

Like two blind mice, Max and Ernie wandered through the woods in silence, with the exception of the occasional sniffle from Ernie. His nose always ran when it was cold out.

"What's that?" whispered Ernie, dragging Max to a sudden stop.

"What's what?"

"That light up ahead."

"I don't see anything, Ernie." Max shook his head as his eyes peered out into the fog.

"Now it's over there," Ernie said nervously.

Finally, Max did see it, but he wasn't exactly sure what it was. Soft and hazy, it flittered between the thick trees like an old lantern or a flashlight. It wasn't far away.

"Max, what the heck is that?" Ernie pleaded, grabbing Max's sleeve.

Though he wasn't feeling any braver than Ernie, Max knew losing his wits wouldn't help the situation. "I bet it's Natalia," he answered. "She's probably trying to spy on us since she wasn't invited to stay over." It was a fair assumption. Natalia was a Grey Griffin and a great friend, but sometimes the boys just needed to be alone and do boy stuff. Natalia, however, was of a different opinion.

"Are you sure it's her?" Ernie asked. "I mean, what if it's not Natalia? What if it's the Slayer?"

"Trust me," Max assured Ernie, though he was secretly thinking the same thing. "If we cut across the creek bed, we could still beat her to the fort. Then the joke will be on her."

Ernie seemed to like the explanation, since a snoopish Natalia was better than a man-eating Slayer any day of the week.

Getting to the fort was no easy proposition. The bramble between them and the creek bed was thick—far thicker than either of them had remembered. With a nod, they agreed to burrow under it, shoveling the hard earth with bare hands. Ernie was the first to break through, as he slipped and rolled down the creek bank with a shout. Caked with mud, he sat alone, shivering as he waited for Max.

But Max never appeared.

"Max! Where are you?" Ernie called, not daring to raise his voice above a whisper.

There was no answer.

"Max, this isn't funny!"

Still, no answer.

Ernie's mind raced for an explanation. But whatever had happened to Max, he knew he didn't have a choice. Going backward was not an option. Not if there was a Slayer back there. No, his only choice was to keep going. The fort wasn't far off. If he got there fast enough, Harley would come and help him find Max.

Exposed and vulnerable, Ernie heaved himself up and began to run.

By the time Max had pulled himself through the bramble, Ernie was nowhere to be seen. "Where could he have gone?" Max murmured to himself, looking up and down the fog-choked creek bed. It was too dark to see footprints, but Max could hear rustling in the trees. It had come from the direction of the fort, and assuming it was Ernie, Max raced ahead.

But either the fort was farther than he remembered or Max wasn't actually where he thought he was. Stopping to catch his breath, he looked around and shuddered. The air was still cold, but the mist was disappearing, at least in this part of the woods.

But as he looked more closely, he saw something that set his heartbeat into overdrive. An icy carpeting of frost was sweeping over the floor of the woods. In seconds it had reached him, continuing into the darkness. The Shadow wasn't the only thing Max should have been worrying about. The Slayer was still alive and well—and probably nearby. Max shook his head. No, Logan would definitely have been disappointed in Max. Coming here had been a stupid idea.

"Ernie? Are you there?" Max's voice broke under panic.

"Here...," came a weak voice from the darkness beyond. Relieved he was no longer alone, Max found Ernie on his hands and knees searching for his glasses in the thick undergrowth.

"What happened?" Max demanded in a worried tone. "You were supposed to wait for me back at the creek bed."

"I did. But then you never showed up, so I started walking to the fort. Then somebody grabbed me!" Ernie squeaked as his probing hands landed upon their quarry. In a sigh of relief, he dusted off his glasses and set them back on his face.

"Who grabbed you?"

"This tree, that's who," said Ernie quietly, as if not wanting to be heard by the birch that towered above them. "It grabbed my foot. Then it started pulling me in. I picked up a rock and smashed it, and that's when it let go of me. But it still got my shoe! See?"

Sure enough, Ernie was missing a shoe, and in its place dangled a grimy sock.

"What are you talking about?" Max shook his head in confusion. With the temperature dropping, and the fear of Slayers, Shadows, and who knew what else wandering around in the night, Max didn't have time for games. But then he noticed Ernie's other sneaker being dragged underground by hungry tree roots. His jaw fell open in astonishment.

"We've got to get out of here!" Max exclaimed, dragging Ernie to his feet.

"You don't have to tell me twice," Ernie replied, limping along after his friend.

Wide-eyed and out of breath, Max and Ernie burst into the open glade where the tree house stood high above the fog. The supreme headquarters of the Order of the Grey Griffins. It was a fortress, at least by any eleven-year-old's standards, with three towers on three separate trees, all connected by hanging bridges. The boys scrambled up a spiral staircase circling up the center tree, which held the largest of the towers in its branches. At the very top of the stairs was a trapdoor with a large white sign nailed to it that read KEEP OUT. A warm glow seeped around the edges of the door, letting them know that someone was already inside.

"You'd better use the secret knock just in case," Ernie whispered in Max's ear.

"In case of what?" Max asked, anxious to get up and out of the woods.

"It might be a trap. What if it isn't Harley who's up there? What if it's something else?"

"You can't be serious. . . ." But Max's voice trailed off as he realized Ernie was very serious. "Fine."

Rap . . . rat-a-tat-tat . . . Rap . . . rat-a-tat-tat. Tat. Tat. Tat. Max knocked on the door, hoping Ernie was wrong.

Thud. Thud. Thud, boomed the familiar answer from above.

"Wait," Ernie pleaded, holding Max back as he tried to reach for the door.

Thud.

"There," sighed Ernie with relief. "There's always supposed to be four knocks on the answer. One for each of us. The Grey Griffins."

Suddenly, the bolt to the trapdoor slid aside and a shadowy hand reached down, yanking them inside.

Friends Are Friends
(Except When They're Not)

"ARE YOU SERIOUS?" Harley asked, sitting on the edge of his seat as Ernie finished recounting their adventure. Ernie made sure to paint himself as the hero, single-handedly fending off a shoe-eating tree, saving Max from certain death.

"Do you need more proof than this?" Ernie asked, holding up his muddy sock.

Soft candlelight illuminated the Grey Griffins' headquarters, which was stuffed with all sorts of odd and curious things: old books, homemade maps, fishing poles, movie posters, a dog skull (against Natalia's severe protestations), lots of candles—some scented (under Natalia's vigorous recommendation)—as well as boxes and boxes of comic books and Round Table cards with game boards and bags of assorted knucklebones.

Harley looked at Max to confirm Ernie's account, but Max wasn't paying any attention. That was until Harley threw a magazine at him.

"What?" Max grumbled.

"It sounds like you read the book again and let something loose," Harley joked.

Max's eyes shot wide. Harley and Ernie looked at him blankly. Max had been barely able to hold off Natalia's questions after she had overheard mention of the Shadow. He had hoped to bring it up later, once he had figured out a way to tell them.

"You didn't, did you?" Ernie asked in disbelief. Max still didn't answer. "But we had a pact! That's against the rules, Max."

"Ernie, would you pipe down a minute?" Harley said, motioning. "Max has a perfectly good explanation, don't you, Max?"

Max actually wasn't sure. Had he been tricked by Sprig, or had he just wanted to open the magic book again? Of course he'd wanted to tell them he had done it—that he broke their pact—it's just that he didn't know what to say. Max didn't want them mad at him. They were the best friends he had.

"Well," Max began slowly.

"And don't leave anything out. I want to hear every detail," Ernie said in excitement as he sat cross-legged near Max's feet. Ernie loved the very idea of magic, so long as he didn't think about any dangerous implications that came with it. And he was particularly happy that he got to be a part of it—despite the loss of his shoe.

Max recapped the entire episode. How Sprig saved his life, and how she had tricked him into opening the book, or at least that's what Max believed. But at the mention of the Shadow, Harley grew strangely silent, and a dark cloud crept over his eyes. At the same time, an icy wind blew through the shuttered window, nearly extinguishing the candles. It prompted Ernie to jump up and secure the window, his teeth chattering.

"You did a bad thing, Max," Harley said slowly, his voice slightly lower. "Breaking a pact with the Grey Griffins is almost unforgivable."

Max nodded. Even though he was Master of the Order, Max knew he had screwed up. As the Warden, Harley's job was to make sure everyone followed the rules. Max had broken them. Case closed.

"What do you think we should do to punish you?" Harley asked, a strange smile breaking across his lips. Max had never seen Harley act this way before.

"What's fair?" Max said nervously.

"Make him take out the trash," suggested Ernie, who wasn't really paying attention. "That's what my dad does to me."

"No." Harley shook his head. "I think Max needs to do something that will really prove he's sorry."

"Like what?" asked Max, eyeing Harley suspiciously. Something weird was going on.

"We want you to open the book again."

"We do?" Ernie gulped. "What about Natalia? Doesn't she have to be here? Otherwise we'd be breaking the pact, too. I don't want to be cursed."

Harley spun and glared at Ernie. "The pact is already broken. It doesn't have power anymore."

"Is that true, Max?" Ernie asked, oblivious to Harley's strange behavior.

What could Max say? Harley was right. The pact was broken, and Harley was obviously mad about it. Madder than Max had ever seen—and they had been best friends a long time. Yet if opening the book one more time would make his friend like him again, maybe it might be okay, Max reasoned. They'd just have to be careful.

"Fine," Max agreed, though with a great deal of reservation.

"But remember the Shadow. We don't want to make a mistake like that again."

Harley smiled.

"*Serann taech septonea.*" Max let the magic words flow as he held the book in front of him, though he noted the words were different from the first time he'd opened the *Codex*. Maybe it had a built-in security mechanism so people couldn't steal the password, he thought. How cool.

The lock clicked, but something was wrong. It hadn't opened. In fact, the whole book had suddenly grown cold in Max's hands. The lock seemed to be frozen shut. In pain, Max dropped the book and rubbed at his hands, stinging from frostbite.

"What happened, Max?" Ernie asked.

"I don't know. The book just froze up. Maybe I said the wrong words."

Suddenly, the window blasted open as the wind rushed into the room, devouring the candle flames. Darkness. But Ernie, this time with Max's help, managed to close the shutters and lock the window in place. Max relit the candles, bathing the clubhouse in a warm glow.

But something was different.

"Where's my book?" Max asked in panic, seeing that it was no longer where he had dropped it. A thousand thoughts flashed through his mind. Was it the Shadow? The Slayer? Sprig? Why would they want his book?

Harley smiled, a mist of cold breath issuing from his mouth.

"What's so funny?" Max asked.

"Calm down; I put it back in your bag," Harley said with a wink. "It's over there under the table. You shouldn't leave something like that just lying around. You never know what could happen."

Greedily, Max grabbed the bag, unzipping it a bit to make sure the *Codex* was safely inside.

"Satisfied?" asked Harley as he stood up. Max said nothing. "Good. I'm going to sleep." With that, Harley crawled over to his sleeping bag, and in seconds he was snoring.

"How does he do that?" asked Ernie. "How can he fall asleep so fast after everything that happened?"

"I don't know," Max said, his mind racing. He wanted to ask Harley why he'd moved the book. And now that he thought about it, how could Harley have even touched it without freezing his fingers off? He had a lot of questions, but he also knew how angry Harley had been about Max's breaking the pact. He didn't want to push his luck, at least not tonight.

So Max settled for rolling out his own sleeping bag and urged Ernie to do the same. He lay there awhile, unable to fall asleep as he twisted and turned trying to find a comfortable spot. Ernie's constant crunching and slurping wasn't helping much, so Max reached into his bag and grabbed a stack of his new Round Table cards, shuffling through them absently.

The first card that grabbed his attention held a picture of a band of goblins wrapped in black armor with wicked weapons in their hands. They were howling, screaming, and sniffing at the ground, madness in their eyes. *Hounds of Oberon,* it read across the top. At the sight of the Shadow King's name, a chill crept up Max's spine.

The Hounds of Oberon, he went on to read, were some of the most terrible and frightful hunters in the faerie world. They could track anything. And what they hunted, they killed.

Uncomfortable, Max kept on shuffling.

But when he drew the next card, his mouth dropped. On the face of the card was a painting of a woman that looked not similar to but exactly like the strange woman who had walked into Iver's shop earlier that day. Every detail of her hair, her eyes, and her expression was captured perfectly. Then Max saw the title and cringed. *The Black Witch.*

"Ernie?" Max whispered.

"Yeah?"

"I think things are going to get a whole lot worse."

Saturday morning came slowly as the first ray of sunlight peeked through the tree house window. Max lay bundled in a heap of sweaters and blankets. It had been a last-ditch attempt to fight off the night's frosty grasp.

He rolled over slowly only to find Ernie sleeping soundly in a bright orange ski mask with matching mittens. He was snoring away in a litter of candy wrappers, half-eaten corn chips, and empty soda cans. "Typical," Max sighed as he blindly reached behind his head for his backpack.

It was gone.

"Harley, have you . . . ," Max began, but Harley was nowhere to be seen.

"Wha-what's going on?" a groggy Ernie stammered, his voice muffled through his ski mask.

"It's gone!"

"What's gone?"

Max stopped and looked at Ernie, hysteria overwhelming him. "The *Codex*, that's what!"

"Huh?"

"My magic book!" Max shouted.

"Where's Harley?" Ernie asked as he hobbled over to the window, trying to get out of Max's way. "Did he have to go to the bathroom or something?"

"If I knew where Harley was, I'd have my book back, wouldn't I?" Max replied angrily.

Opening the trapdoor, Max stepped down to the stairs below. Unfortunately for Max, the stairs were no longer there.

Plummeting through the opening, Max grabbed hold of the ledge at the last second, struggling to hold on. It wouldn't take long before he started to lose his grip. . . .

"Ernie, help! Help!" Max screamed as his flashlight tumbled from his pocket, making an ominous splash far below.

A split second later Ernie was staring down at him in shock. Uncharacteristically heroic, Ernie managed to grab hold of Max's belt and pull him up. Breathing raggedly, both turned on their stomachs and peered out the trapdoor.

The ground was dizzyingly far away. Where had the stairs gone? The fort was now fifty feet in the air, surrounded by gigantic trees that, like colossal pillars, held aloft a great green canopy of leaves arching high above their heads. A faint emerald light filtered down upon the ground far below. The floor of the forest was decorated with mushrooms the size of houses and tree roots that tunneled into the earth, spiraling across the landscape.

"Where in the world are we?" whispered Ernie, taking a shot from his inhaler.

Stunned, Max couldn't say a thing. He was bewildered by the transformation of the woods—his woods. "I have a bad feeling about this."

Just then, a loud trumpet ripped through the air, startling them out of their wits. Rubbing their ears, they scrambled to the window in time to see a dark wave moving through the forest floor. As it approached, they could see it was a tangle of figures, hundreds of them, hopping, running, jumping, and burrowing with reckless abandon. They were heading right for the fort. Within moments, Ernie, with a rusty pair of binoculars, could discern razor teeth and rotten gray skin as the little beasts hooted and howled, tearing through the foliage. And from the long pointy spears they held in their gnarled hands, he could tell they were on a hunt.

"We're gonna die!" Ernie whimpered.

"Shhh . . . ," Max warned, taking the binoculars. The monsters hadn't seen them yet, and though Max was fairly sure they couldn't reach the boys in their treetop perch, he didn't want to risk it. "It's the Hounds of Oberon."

"What are you talking about?" breathed Ernie in amazement.

"From my Round Table cards. They work for the Shadow King," Max explained.

"Doing what?" Ernie asked, peeking over the window again.

"Hunting," Max replied, pulling Ernie back down.

"What kind of hunting?"

"Anyone Oberon wants dead."

A piercing cry woke Harley with a sudden jerk. The room was dark, cold, and full of the smell of decay. He could hardly see a thing as a thin strand of light filtered through the cracks of paneling on the wall where a branch had broken through.

"Where am I?" Harley murmured.

Something was terribly wrong. The walls of the fort around him were caved in as if they had been squeezed in the hand of a giant. The ceiling was on the verge of collapse, and the floor was littered with leaves and branches. Under the debris, Harley spotted a brass telescope, and it was then he knew he was in the east tower. But how had he gotten there?

Harley tried to stand, but knocked his head hard against an overhanging branch. Again, he struggled to his knees, disoriented as he noticed a soft glow coming from beneath his sleeping bag. When Harley pulled the sleeping bag away, Max's book erupted in light, filling the ruined room in a ghostly wash. Mesmerized, Harley watched as letters flew from the open page, forming the words *The Olde Forest*. The page across from the text was blank, and it was that instant when Harley felt a cold shiver creep over him.

"What have I done?" As if in answer, a cold and wicked voice from somewhere deep within his mind began to laugh. Harley was not alone. Something was wrong. . . . It was almost as if he wasn't alone in his body. Something was inside him. . . .

"Get out!" he commanded. "Get out of my head!"

"Never!" he heard the voice shout through his own mouth. A chill ran up his spine. His mind had been invaded.

But Harley was a fighter.

A battle began raging between Harley and the alien presence. Harley cried out, his body racked with pain as he threw himself against the wall, then to the floor—but he wouldn't give up. Inch by horrible inch, his willpower slowly forced out the darkness that fought to control him. Senseless and bruised, Harley finally collapsed, unaware of the shadow that seemed to drain from his body and crawl back into the dice that lay nearby.

"Harley, are you in there?" He heard Ernie's voice on the edge of his thoughts.

Harley groaned.

"He's in there. I can hear him."

"We've got to get Harley out of there," Ernie cried as he and Max stood on the branch that spanned the distance between the two towers. The goblins had disappeared, allowing Max and Ernie to formulate their plan to recover the *Codex*. Harley had to be in one of the two other towers, and as one was now impossible to reach, Max hoped that Harley was in the one that remained. Normally, they would have crossed the rope bridge. But today, the rope bridge was no longer an option, as it simply wasn't there. Instead, Max had found a thick tree branch that spanned the distance. They would have to be careful, though. Unfortunately, Ernie was afraid of heights, and even though the branch appeared to be big enough to park a truck on, he clung to Max nervously, eyeing the ground far below.

"I just want my book back," growled Max. "I can't believe Harley would do this to me."

"Aren't you worried he might be in trouble? I mean, you don't even know he took it."

"He took it," replied Max flatly as he forged ahead. "The forest didn't change on its own. This happened because Harley read from the *Codex*."

Ernie gulped. He had never seen Max so angry, not even after Ernie accidentally spilled orange soda in Max's aquarium, killing all his exotic (and terribly expensive) tropical fish.

"Come over here and help me," Max ordered impatiently. A branch thicker than a tractor tire had bored its way through the east tower, ripping through most of the wall and a good portion of the roof. There wasn't enough room between the branch and the paneling to squeeze through, so Max was trying to pry some boards loose.

"I could slip and fall. I'll kill myself," complained Ernie. "Have you seen how far down that is?"

"Don't look."

The two boys tugged and pulled until, with a loud crack, the board suddenly snapped. Falling back, they nearly slid off the branch. And as they tried to scramble for safety, Ernie's glasses fell from his face, bouncing over the ledge, and a second later they heard the discouraging plunk of his spectacles hitting water far below.

"My mom's gonna kill me," Ernie whined.

"Well, it could have been you instead," replied Max as he disappeared into the tower.

Max hopped over Harley's barely conscious form and snatched the *Codex* from the floor. It had been lying open, glowing brightly. Max thumbed through the pages, and to his horror, many of them were empty. What had been released from those pages was anyone's guess.

Harley only managed a groan as he looked up weakly. Max glared back.

"*Kaelan marae*," Max commanded, and the lock snapped shut. Max was too angry to realize that the voice from the book was now a part of him and the words he spoke came as naturally as his own thoughts.

"How could you do this to me?" he yelled as he turned back to Harley. "I thought we were friends!"

Harley was still in a daze. "I . . . I don't know," he mumbled in confusion. "I can't really remember anything. I . . . I hit my head on something."

"What happened?" Ernie wheezed as he made his way through the debris.

"Don't play stupid, Harley," Max continued. "You stole my book, and now everything is ruined. Have you even looked outside?"

"I didn't steal your book," Harley coughed, trying to get up. "Something happened—it wasn't me," he pleaded. "You're my best friend, Max. You know I wouldn't do that to you."

Max's eyes smoldered. "My 'best friend' wouldn't steal from me."

"Geez, Max, what's wrong with you?" Ernie asked, rushing over to Harley's side. "Take it easy. Can't you see there's something wrong?"

Suddenly, a strange scent of flowers and spice filled the room. The boys turned to discover two piercing eyes shining out from the darkness.

"Sprig . . . ," Max breathed in amazement.

"The Shadow . . ." She looked about the room nervously. "It's here. And it's betrayed us all. . . ."

"What do you mean? I thought the Shadow was your friend. It saved you."

"It tricked us," replied the spriggan in a hushed tone, wringing her hands in fear and desperation. "It wasn't supposed to hurt you. It wasn't supposed to be bad. And it wasn't supposed to take the *Codex.* It said it wouldn't. And we believed it. It's all our fault. It's always our fault." Sprig then started to cry and gnaw at her paw nervously. Max looked over at Harley, and now suddenly everything began to make sense. The Shadow had somehow taken control of Sprig, who had made Max open the book. But any relief he had in realizing Harley was still his best friend quickly vanished at Sprig's next words.

"And now it is too late. The Shadow has opened the dark portals," the spriggan cried, beginning to shake and looking out the window anxiously. "And now the bad ones—the nameless evils that sit behind the portals—have been released. Soon the way will be open and the Shadow King will return."

The Shadow King? Oberon? Slayers and Shadows were one thing, but the King of All Evil here in Avalon? "Why would he come here?" Max asked in disbelief.

"Oberon seeks revenge."

"R-r-revenge?" Ernie asked, stammering. "What are you talking about? I didn't do anything to him. Ask anyone!"

Sprig shook her head, her eyes wild with fear. "Too late. It doesn't matter now. Soon he'll have the Jewel and both of our worlds will die. Nothing will survive."

At that moment, the tower began to shake as howling erupted from far below.

"The goblins!" Max shouted frantically. "They're back."

A black arrow ripped through the window, rocketing into the wall with a loud twang just behind where Ernie was standing.

"Get down!" shouted Max as three more arrows rained in, followed by a nasty-looking spear. Harley, still bruised, chanced a look out the window and could see a pack of ugly-looking goblins scaling the tree toward them. Narrowly dodging another black-feathered missile, he dove for cover.

"Sprig, you gotta get us out of here!" Harley pleaded. "You've got to save Max."

Sprig remained motionless and said nothing; fear was surrounding her like a dark cloud.

"Please, Sprig!" Max begged. "Maybe we can find a way to make everything better again."

"We will try," the spriggan replied finally as the goblins drew close to the window, "but we cannot protect you from him."

Lifting up a furry paw, she pointed to a toy chest on the far side of the room.

"What are we supposed to do?" Max asked in confusion as the first of the goblins appeared at the window and another was about to break through the hole Max had created a few moments before. "Sprig! We're running out of time."

"Inside the box there is a portal—a doorway," she explained. "You must go through."

"Last one in is a rotten egg!" shouted Ernie, racing past Max toward the toy chest. He opened it and jumped through without another word, disappearing in a shimmer of light. Harley followed, and Max dove in last, barely escaping the flood of goblins that swarmed into the room just behind them.

8 Natalia's Favorite Wish

WITH A CRASH Max rolled out of his bedroom closet and onto the floor. Looking around, he found Harley nearby, rubbing his forehead. Ernie was already on the phone. "I'm calling Natalia," he said. "She's gotta hear this!"

Max nodded. "I don't believe it actually worked." As he walked to his closet, other than a monstrous pile of dirty clothes and baseball cards, there was nothing out of the ordinary. Not even a glimmer or hum. "Do you think the portal is still there?"

"It's still there?" Ernie nearly dropped the telephone as he envisioned a troop of goblins suddenly appearing in the room, roasting him for dinner. "Somebody nail the door shut!" he shouted frantically.

"Quiet down, Ernie," hushed Max. "Somebody might hear you." Max looked over to see the color draining from Harley's face. The cut on his head had stopped bleeding, but there was a deep bruise, purple and ugly. The wound had left Harley weak and unsteady, and before he could stand, his knees buckled as he fell face-first to the floor.

Max caught Harley just as he collapsed, dragging him over to the bed with a great deal of effort.

"We need to get him to a doctor," Max said as he turned to Ernie, who was already deep in an animated conversation with Natalia on the other end of the phone.

"Don't worry about me," Harley said as he rubbed at his wound. "I've had worse." Max nodded, feeling bad about how he had accused his friend of betrayal. He'd apologize later when they were alone.

Max walked over to his bedroom window and looked out. The forest, which lay all around his family's estate, looked alien now, like a lost jungle from an ancient world untouched by time. It might have been his imagination, but the trees seemed taller, a dark haze hanging over them like an ominous cloud. The situation had gone from bad to worse.

"Natalia says she doesn't believe us," Ernie reported as he set the phone back down, eyeing the closet suspiciously. "And she's not happy that we broke the pact and read the book without her."

"You shouldn't have told her over the phone," coughed Harley weakly.

"Now you tell me," Ernie squeaked. "Well, she's on her way over here right now."

"Great," replied Max, shaking his head. Natalia had a long memory, and forgiveness wasn't one of her better traits.

"Do you remember anything from last night?" Max asked.

Harley shook his head. "I remember Ernie showing me his sock. Then I think I blacked out after that." He paused for a moment, trying to remember more. "I don't know, but ever since we were at Iver's . . . I can't remember much at all . . . except a weird voice in my head. When I woke up this morning, it was still there. I tried to get it out, and then you showed up."

"Go on," Max prompted.

"That's it. That's all I can tell you. Honest."

Max sat silently, trying to make sense of it all. Something wasn't clicking. "If it's any consolation, I believe you."

"Those trees must be at least fifty feet tall, and is that fog I see?" Natalia chattered away as she peered out the window. "You three have some serious explaining to do, and you can start by telling me what exactly is going on. If any of this is true—any of it at all—I demand to know how it's happening. Is that book of yours behind all this craziness?"

"I already told you the whole story over the phone," replied Ernie. "There were goblins and mushrooms as big as a house and . . ." He paused in thought as he came upon an idea that just might get Natalia to forgive them.

"And what?"

"Unicorns," Ernie lied. Lying was a bad thing, which he had been told often by his mother. But it did the trick. Natalia was struck cold at the possibility of seeing her favorite creature of all time. Her eyes glazed over in delight, all anger disappearing.

"What are you talking about?" Max whispered to Ernie as Natalia turned back to the window and stared longingly.

"Shhh . . . ," Ernie replied. "I think it's working." Max had to agree, so he nodded, though he was not fond of lying, either. But it was only a little white lie, he told himself. What harm could it do?

Natalia turned back to them with a serious look on her face. It was the look Natalia always gave right before she announced an ingenious plan.

"Where's the portal?" she demanded. "The one you came out of when you landed here."

Ernie pointed at the closet proudly as if he were the owner of a newly discovered diamond mine.

In a flash, Natalia had swung open the closet door, but her eager smile quickly faded in disappointment. "Why, there's nothing in here but dirty clothes, which, by the way, you should wash soon. They're starting to smell."

"Fine," said Max, hoping she would give up the search. "I'll ask Rosa to clean it up."

"Now, what's this about the Shadow King, and what is he supposed to be so angry about?" asked Natalia. "Ernie was talking too fast on the phone, so I couldn't understand a word he was saying. Why does he want to destroy the world?"

Max shrugged.

"Is it the book?" asked Ernie, eyeing the *Codex* nervously. "Maybe Max's grandma stole it from him."

Natalia pinched him in the arm. "Why would Max's grandmother steal something? She's the nicest lady in the world."

Ernie flinched. "Well, people do stupid stuff. Harley did something stupid last night, and he couldn't help it."

"Good point," acknowledged Natalia as the Grey Griffins sat around in a circle and proceeded to discuss everything that had happened, from Sprig's saving Max's life to the release of the

Shadow. The conversation kept coming back to the topic of por-tals—after all, there might still be one in the room with them at that very moment. The idea of zooming across the planet instantly was amazing. Ernie had already begun to plan trips to amusement parks and toy stores all over the world.

"But Sprig said something about a dark portal," Harley reminded them.

"That's right," Max recalled. "She seemed to think that the por-tals would have something to do with the Shadow King destroying the world."

"And something about a jewel," added Ernie, but his mouth was so full of candy that no one heard exactly what he said.

"I thought the Round Table card said that only Slayers could use the portals," Harley commented as Ernie absently poured a suspiciously old bag of sunflower seeds into his mouth.

"That's supposed to be true," Natalia agreed. "But maybe the rules are changing." Natalia paused for a moment, turning to look at Max's closet curiously. "So you are saying there's really a portal in there right now?"

Ernie nodded.

"And you saw unicorns?"

Ernie nodded again, trying to hold back a smile.

Max gulped. He didn't like where she was heading.

"Let's test it." Natalia picked up a book, opened the closet door, and let fly. With a flash, it disappeared into thin air.

"Hey!" complained Max. "That was a first edition of *The Hobbit!*"

"Wow," whispered Natalia. "I wonder how long the portal will stay here."

"No," Max replied resolutely, reading her mind. "We're not going back. It's too dangerous. Don't forget about the goblins and the fact that they probably aren't even the scariest things in the woods."

Natalia was resolute. Jumping up from the bed, she grabbed her pink *Book of Clues* and marched back to the closet door, only to find Harley blocking her way, though he obviously was hurting.

"So, it's going to be like that?" she asked, shaking her head.

"That's right," replied Harley. "You'll have to get past me first. And that ain't happening."

Natalia smiled. "Suit yourself."

As quick as a wink, Natalia pushed Harley with all her strength. She was small, but using leverage, it was just enough for Harley to lose his balance and stumble into the closet. Just like the book, he disappeared in a spark of light.

"I'm going to see my unicorns now." Natalia smiled, batting her eyelashes at the other two as she turned and leapt into the closet, vanishing as Harley did.

Ernie turned to Max, his jaw hanging slack. "You're not thinking . . ."

"Sorry, Ernie. We don't have a choice now, as much as I hate to say it. We have to go in," Max replied. Determined, Max grabbed his backpack and pushed Ernie headfirst through the closet door, jumping in after.

The portal from Max's bedroom did not return them to the Grey Griffin tree house. Instead, they found themselves on the sandy bank of a stream somewhere, in what they assumed was the forest. This meant the portals could change destinations without warning—which was more than a little troubling. But for now, Natalia wanted to see her unicorns, and the others just wanted to get out of the woods alive. Not knowing what else to do, the Grey Griffins followed the stream for nearly an hour.

"Hey!" Natalia called. "Look at this!" She was leaning over a shining pool of water fed by the stream. "Have you ever seen fish like this?"

Max looked into the pool in amazement. Some of the fish were as round as a beach ball, others tinier than a speck of dust. A few were completely transparent, almost invisible. Some changed colors, while others flashed off and on like lightning bugs. And far beneath, giant shadows silently glided in the inky depths, their enormity unfathomable.

The friends stood mesmerized by the endless undersea world, completely lost in wonder until a brilliant streak of silver light launched over their heads. Like a rocket it flew, flames dissipating in its wake before disappearing back into forest. It had only been visible for an instant, but they all knew . . .

"A unicorn," Ernie proclaimed, nearly leaping out of his shoes.

"Follow me!" Harley shouted, hobbling through the trees as fast as he could manage.

In a daze, Natalia stumbled after him, and soon, after a couple of near-catastrophic wipeouts, all of the Grey Griffins were standing on the edge of a sunny clearing with luxurious grass and yellow daisies swaying in the breeze. Soft billowing clouds rolled through a warm blue sky—quite different from the twisted trees and foreboding gloom that dominated the rest of the woods.

"Oh my goodness!" Natalia exclaimed.

In the midst of the field stood a white unicorn, its majestic horn shimmering in the sunlight. Natalia was in heaven. Her whole life had been leading up to that very moment.

"It's so beautiful," she breathed, watching it from the shadows of the trees. Max agreed. In light of all the catastrophes that had happened recently, seeing the unicorn was like waking from a bad dream, and it filled Max with hope. Maybe the book wasn't such a bad thing.

Then a second unicorn of dappled silver burst into the meadow, racing along the tree line. It veered, bolting past the first, which in turn gave chase. Together they played, running back and forth, sometimes faster than the eye could follow, and at other times disappearing altogether, only to reappear somewhere else. The kids watched in silent wonder, fearing they might scare the unicorns if they made a single sound.

"*Ahhhhhchooooo.*" Ernie let go with an unmistakable elephant sneeze.

The unicorns stopped immediately, wheeling around to look at the Griffins. A chill crept over Max as he realized too late that there was nowhere to run or hide if things turned dangerous.

"Sorry," apologized Ernie as he rubbed his nose with the back of his hand.

The unicorns didn't seem interested in Ernie, Harley, or Max, though. Instead, they seemed only to watch Natalia, who was intently watching them in return. Yet too late the children learned that watching unicorns was unsafe. They were too wonderful, too beautiful, and Max knew the four of them were in trouble when Natalia stopped blinking. Her green eyes faded to black as she stepped from beneath the trees and walked slowly, hypnotically, toward the magical horses.

"Natalia!" Max cried. "What are you doing? You could get killed!"

She took another step toward them. Then another. And the unicorns approached her as well, their heads lowered and their horns shining like swords.

Harley, not knowing what else to do, wanted to run out and bring her back. But just as he launched forward, the temperature around the Grey Griffins seemed to drop, and a tree branch cracked, echoing ominously through the woods. Spooked, the unicorns bolted across the meadow, and the four friends were once again alone.

Ernie sighed in relief as Harley hauled Natalia back into the woods.

"They were so beautiful," she breathed in a dreamlike voice, oblivious to the fact that she was being carried like a sack of potatoes over Harley's shoulder.

"You need to be more careful," Harley complained, setting her back down. "You could have gotten us all killed."

"Uh, Max?" came Ernie's nervous voice. "The forest got really quiet all of a sudden."

"I know," replied Max. Ice was magically forming on the trees.

"This could be bad," Harley added, stepping protectively in front of the other three.

A low snarl came from the shadows above, and as one the Griffins looked up.

There in the lower branches of a decrepit tree, a monster clung, its bloodied claws tearing into the bark. The rest of its body was obscured by shadow, but Max knew what it was even before he saw it. The Slayer goblin had returned.

"Look at its eyes," Natalia whispered.

It was a terrible and gruesome sight as the dark goblin's empty sockets stared into nothingness. It was blind.

"Everybody run for it!" yelled Ernie.

Blind it might have been, but it was far from deaf. At the sound of Ernie's voice, the dreadful creature turned its lifeless eyes toward them and sniffed the air. The gash of teeth it had in place of a mouth opened in a ghastly smile. There was no chance of escape.

Natalia screamed.

It leapt.

Like a missile it drove straight into Max, slamming him to the ground. He tried to struggle, but the grip of the Slayer was like iron. Max was pinned, helpless, as the creature raised a single knifelike claw, preparing to strike.

Ernie and Natalia stood in horror, but Harley knew how to keep his head in desperate situations. He grabbed hold of a large, thorny tree branch and swung at the Slayer's head with all his might. *Crack!*

Harley's arm nearly broke under the collision as the branch shattered on impact. He had never hit anything that hard before. If the creature had been human, it would have fallen to the ground, stone dead. Unfortunately, it wasn't remotely human.

With a sinister, mocking smile and lifeless eyes, it turned toward Harley, then quickly spun back to face Max. It knew Harley wasn't a threat. No, the Slayer had a job to do. It would deal with the others once it had destroyed the boy with the book.

Natalia screamed again.

Unable to breathe, Ernie fumbled for his inhaler. Not finding it, he promptly passed out.

But just as all hope seemed to fade, a brilliant blaze of light shot through the trees and hammered into the side of the goblin. Hurtling through the air, the Slayer slammed like a meteor into a tree, shattering it on impact. Branches and bark exploded as the tree groaned and swayed before crashing to the earth, narrowly missing Ernie's unconscious form as smoke and debris rolled through the air.

Max slowly got to his shaky feet and looked around, bewildered and dazed. The goblin was gone. There was no sign of it anywhere, but it had left its mark. Looking down, Max could see that his T-shirt was shredded, and underneath it, three long, shallow cuts ran across his chest. The wounds were going to sting a little bit, but nothing serious. Yet if that Slayer had had only two seconds more, those small cuts would have been gaping holes. Max quickly zipped up his sweatshirt, concealing the wounds.

In the meantime, Natalia had gone to see if Ernie was all right, but her concern soon faded to annoyance when she found him curled up under a branch and snoring loudly. She rolled her eyes and prodded him in the ribs with her foot until he woke.

"Am I dead?" he asked, looking up at her, bleary-eyed.

"Not yet," Natalia sighed as she turned and walked back to Harley and Max. "And you missed the whole thing."

"What happened to the monster?" asked Max as he stood near the fallen tree.

"I don't know." Harley shrugged. "All I saw was a bright light, and the next thing I knew, that thing on top of you was blown away."

"Where'd the light come from?" asked Natalia.

Harley shook his head. "No idea. I couldn't see. But whatever or whoever did it . . . I hope they're on our side."

"I couldn't agree more," came a low voice from behind them.

Turning on their heels, the Grey Griffins found a dark figure looming ominously before them. It was a tall man wrapped in robes that seemed woven of fog and twilight. His face was shrouded in the darkness of a deep hood, but his eyes shone like brilliant diamonds in a night sky, and his gnarled fingers gripped a knotted walking stick that was still crackling with white light. This was the one responsible for saving them from the Slayer. They all knew it. But anyone who could destroy a Slayer could just as easily do whatever he wanted to the Grey Griffins—and they wouldn't stand a chance.

"It's an evil wizard!" cried Ernie. "Run!"

But just as he tried to leap away, an iron hand caught him and held him fast. The rest of the Griffins didn't have any better luck, and after a small commotion of flurry and shouts, they soon found themselves penned like frightened rabbits, held firmly in place by the power of the mysterious man.

"And where do you think you are going?" came his deep voice, laced with the hint of an unseen smile. "I came a long way to find you and can't have you running off like this."

"Who are you?" Natalia managed in an unsteady voice.

"Who am I, you ask?" said the old man with a laugh. "An excellent question. When you're my age, you sometimes manage to forget, but I think you know me well enough." With that, the shadowy figure drew back his hood and stepped into the light.

"Iver!" shouted Max.

9

Turtles and Dice and Everything (Not So) Nice

"AREN'T YOU SUPPOSED to be preparing for your Round Table battle?" Iver asked as the four friends tried to keep pace with his long strides.

"It's Natalia's fault," Ernie complained between puffs of air as he jogged along. "I didn't want to come here. Ask anybody."

"Passing blame is a rather unattractive quality, Master Tweeny," Iver replied as he ducked under the canopy of a giant purple mushroom. "Furthermore, it does little to answer my question."

"We could ask you the same," Natalia boldly commented.

Iver stopped and looked at her sternly. "Ms. Romanov, if I was back at my shop today, who would have rescued you?"

"How did you know where to find us?" Natalia pressed, unable to quell her curiosity. "You appeared out of nowhere."

Iver's eyebrow raised in question as he took to filling his pipe with tobacco. "Out of nowhere? Certainly not. I must have been somewhere."

"But you're not making any sense," Natalia complained with her hands on her hips. "Can't you see what's happening?"

"What I can see is four children who didn't give a second thought to my warning yesterday," Iver corrected in a reprimanding tone. "I've said this once already to Master Sumner, but I will say it again, and hope you all pay better attention this time. I cannot be expected to come to your rescue whenever you decide to go on a foolish errand. Strange and powerful things are in motion. Things you may think you understand, but trust me, what you are dealing with is beyond your comprehension. I just pray it's not too late."

"Too late for what?" Ernie shivered.

"I am afraid we don't have time for many more questions," Iver stated flatly, looking suspiciously at a nearby shadow. "We should be heading back to our homes. It will be dark soon."

Just what Iver was keeping from them, Max couldn't guess. But he knew Iver was right; they had to get out of there as soon as possible.

"But it's only a little after lunch," Harley pointed out. "How could it get dark so soon?"

"That's true," replied Iver as he stopped briefly to light his pipe. "At least, it's true anywhere but here. Thankfully, I found you when I did. Come along, now."

Silently, the five travelers fell in step as the light of day slowly melted into night.

Harley and Max sat quietly on the dock that stretched lazily over the green waters of Turtle Cove, their bare feet swishing across the surface. In the horizon, the tree line of the forest loomed menacingly, casting a long shadow over the lake; but so far the enchanted trees, mystical creatures, and horrible monsters seemed to be confined to the forest. Max just hoped they would stay there. Unfortunately, the Slayer didn't mind coming into town, so Max figured it would only be a matter of time before the rest of the creatures would pay Avalon a visit

"I'm sorry," Max said, skipping a stone across the water. It had only been a couple of days since the strange events in the forest, but Max's conscience had been eating at him to apologize to his best friend.

"For what?" Harley asked as he gave his fishing line a tug. Harley had always been a fast healer, and the bruise on his forehead had faded within hours of the incident with the Shadow.

"Getting you, Ernie, and Natalia wrapped up in this mess," Max explained. "It's all my fault. I never should have opened that stupid book."

"Wait a minute, Max," Harley said, putting down his pole on the dock as he turned to his friend. "It's not your fault. As far as I'm concerned, the book chose you for a reason. I mean, who knows what's going to happen? Anyway, the Grey Griffins stick together — no matter what. So don't say you're sorry. It doesn't matter what the problem is. We're in this together."

Max smiled and skipped another stone. Having friends like Harley made his parents' divorce a bit more bearable. Even when Max's own mother didn't believe in him, Harley did. And while they didn't have much in common on the outside, they were brothers on the inside. When Max's father had left, Harley understood, having never even met his own father.

Natalia and Ernie rode up on their bikes a bit later and were soon seated next to their friends. They asked one another how they were and commented on the beautiful autumn day. But they all knew why they were there. It was time to talk business.

"It's so cool that Iver's a wizard," Ernie said. "I always knew there was something about him." To Max's dismay, the old man had pulled away a bit, growing unusually testy since he had rescued them from the woods. He seemed completely consumed by who knew what, with barely time for a polite smile.

Max shook his head as he pulled out the *Codex*. "Well, I don't know if Iver's a wizard or not, but he was reading a book that looked a lot like this one the day Harley got his knucklebones."

"That's right," recalled Natalia. "But it was a slightly different color and maybe a little taller, too."

"And it wasn't quite as thick, but I'll put it this way: If those books were people, they'd be brothers," Max finished.

"Did it have a lock like yours?" asked Harley.

Max shook his head. "I didn't see one, but I didn't get much of a look."

"That's interesting," Natalia mused. "So instead of just one magic book, there might be two . . . or more? I mean, it's not impossible. He is a wizard, after all."

Max shrugged his shoulders. "Maybe."

"Which reminds me, Max," Natalia started. "Have you figured out where that voice inside your head is coming from, and why you're able to open that book of yours?"

"Shhh," Harley interrupted as he pointed toward the reeds near the shore.

"What is it?" Ernie asked in what he thought was a whisper. It was not.

"Just keep talking and pretend I'm still here," Harley instructed, sneaking down the dock.

Max nodded and winked at Natalia, who winked in return.

"Anyway, as I was saying," Natalia began twice as loud as before, "I think it is absolutely mean and horrible to use worms as bait for your fishing. They're living creatures, and they have feelings, too! Why do they have to die just because you get a kick out of throwing some string in the water and pulling it back in? It's beastly!"

"Who cares about worms?" complained Ernie loudly. "What about Max's magic book?"

Natalia shot Ernie a fierce glare that could have peeled the paint right off a house. "Ernest Tweeny," she snapped in a sharp whisper. "You'd better get with the program and play along," which she promptly followed with a pinch.

"Knock it off," Ernie cried out. But just then, Harley sprang into the deep thicket of reeds like a missile. Sounds of splashing and cursing carried over the water until Harley dragged his quarry to shore. He promptly threw the intruder down and pinned him with his knees.

"Get off me!" Ray Fisher shouted. Harley paid no attention. Though Ray struggled and kicked, Harley was nearly twice his size and at least three times as strong.

"Not until you tell me what you're doing here," Harley said as he tightened his grip.

"I was just looking for turtles, you big freak! Do you and your stupid group of Grey Gizzards own the whole lake now?"

"Grey Griffins," corrected Natalia. "And you're just jealous because you're not a member."

"Of what?" spit Ray. "A pathetic pack of losers that sit around all day and make up fairy tales about themselves?"

"What did you hear?" Max growled, fists clenched as he and the others joined Harley.

"Are you deaf or just stupid? I said I was looking for turtles. You want proof? Here, I've got one in my pocket."

Harley dragged Ray to his feet and held him by his neck as the spy scrounged in his pocket, trying to find the turtle. Then a curious expression fell over him as his fingers found something altogether different—something that had been waiting for him. All at once, Ray's body convulsed and his face grew deathly pale.

"What's wrong with you?" Harley asked. "You're as cold as a fish."

"Maybe he's faking," Ernie called from a safe distance.

But Ray wasn't faking. His face was cast in a cold shadow and dark circles framed his eyes. His breathing was erratic, and he looked as if he might be turning inside out. But after a few moments he seemed to grow calm. Lifting his eyes, he gazed at the Grey Griffins, unblinking, with his mouth pulled back into a creepy grin.

"Stop looking at me like that." Ernie shivered. "You're giving me the heebie-jeebies."

"No kidding," agreed Harley. "What the heck is wrong with you?"

"On the contrary, Harley, my old friend," Ray hissed in an unsettling tone. "For the first time in my life, everything is finally 'right' with me." At that moment, a bluish frost started creeping down the arm that Harley was holding on to.

Max's stomach sank as a feeling of dread spilled over him. Something had happened to Ray. Something bad. And now the tables had turned. Whereas before, Ray had been the one outnumbered and at their mercy, Max knew it was now the Grey Griffins who were in serious trouble.

He was about to warn Harley to let Ray go, but it was too late. With blinding speed, Ray's arm broke free from Harley's grip. Ray spun the larger boy around, and with a snap, sent Harley reeling into the water.

The rest of the Grey Griffins stood there with mouths wide open.

Like an actor on a stage, Ray smiled and bowed. "If you liked my first trick, just wait 'til you see what happens next," his raspy voice called as he turned swiftly and leapt high into the air. In the blink of an eye Ray disappeared over the hilltop.

"What was that?" asked Ernie a few awkward moments later.

"I'm not sure," Max said. "And I'm not sure I want to find out, either."

"Hey . . . ," Harley cried out from the water. "My dice are missing!"

"Oh no . . ." Natalia shook her head in sudden realization. "It was in the dice. That explains everything."

"What do you mean?" Max returned, looking over his shoulder nervously in case Ray had any other surprises.

"Don't you remember what happened to Harley in the tree fort? How he was taken over by the Shadow? That happened the same day he got the dice, right?"

Max nodded as Harley wrung out his sweatshirt in damp annoyance.

"So the dice are evil?" Ernie wondered. "Iver wouldn't give anything evil to us, would he?"

"I don't think so," replied Natalia with a shake of her head. The idea of Iver's being anything other than wonderful and kind was completely unthinkable. "But you have to admit . . . Harley didn't get weird until he was given the dice. And now the same thing is happening with Ray. The dice are dangerous—it's the only logical explanation."

"It's not the dice," Max called from where he stood overlooking a gray patch of dead grass where Ray had been standing only a moment before. He'd never forget the last time he saw that same sign in the woods, the day Sprig tricked him into opening the *Codex* for the second time. A chill swept over him at the implications of what that might mean.

"It's the Shadow." Max shook his head, feeling like such a fool for not seeing it before. "And it's been with us the whole time."

Tuesday morning dawned gray and wet. The clouds that hung over Avalon finally decided to burst, drenching the countryside. By the time the school bus rattled up to Max's house, there was more water inside his shoes than out, but as he squeezed into his seat, he was thinking about the encounter with Ray. One thing was for sure—his nemesis had heard more than he was letting on. Max had seen it in his eyes—and that creepy smile. When Ray didn't show up for the school's reopening on Monday, Max's suspicion had grown into a sinking certainty.

"Max?" called a familiar voice.

"Oh. Hi, Brooke. Feeling better?" Max tried to smile, though it was a bit forced. Brooke had been ill, missing school the day before, and he wanted to be polite.

"Yes. Thank you for asking," said Brooke, smiling brightly, touched by his concern. She was wearing a bright yellow dress, with a white cardigan. She looked beautiful, which made Max all the more uncomfortable. "Is this seat taken?"

Max shook his head and moved his backpack to clear space for her.

"Where have you been? After the fountain blew up, you disappeared. I don't think I've seen you for a week."

"Been busy," Max said, trying not to sound too interested.

"Oh." Brooke sat there looking nervously at the other kids before turning back to Max. "My birthday party is Friday night."

"I know," Max said, remembering how amazing her party was the year before. Birthdays seemed to be a very special occasion in the Lundgren house. "Are you excited?"

Ever since the invitations had gone out, it had been the central topic of conversation at school. Rumor had it that Brooke's dad was renting the entire movie theater for something very, very special. Even Brooke didn't know what was going to happen, and that made the secret even more tantalizing.

"I am. But only if you promise to come." Brooke smiled as butterflies began to flutter in Max's stomach. He looked down and blushed without knowing why. "You are coming, right?"

"I wouldn't miss it for the world."

King's Elementary had eased back into session after the near-catastrophic explosion of slime the week before. The courtyard, still a disaster zone, was blocked off with plastic yellow tape and orange pylons. Students who snuck close to get a better look were quickly accosted by a patrolling Dr. Blackstone, and then escorted, sometimes by their ears, back to class. Yet inside the classrooms, things continued in King's time-honored tradition—the relentless pursuit of good posture (no slouching permitted), good conduct (no talking allowed), and the memorizing of Latin verbs (no fun at all). By ten o'clock, some of the students were falling asleep behind their math books or drooling on their sleeves in social studies, while others doodled or daydreamed in art class—all but Natalia, of course, who continually exercised her right to a solid education.

However, in the few days Ms. Heen had been with them, her students had already come to expect something exciting each day, despite the fact that history class had been, before her arrival, something of a bore. The students had fallen in love with her—and none more so than Ernie. As she smoothed out her dress and rose to address the class, he sighed warmly.

"Well, students. As you know, it's time for your first history lesson of the school year. Most teachers will, of course, start from the beginning. But the beginning is really not the beginning, because there was always something that happened before it, now, wasn't there?"

Natalia nodded, curious where Ms. Heen was leading. But, of course, this was true. Before Natalia's dress was a dress, it was fabric on a bolt in some large warehouse. And before that, it was cloth woven on a busy loom. Even before that, it was cotton growing in some faraway field. But before that, well . . . who knew?

"So . . ." Ms. Heen smiled as she drew a cross on the board in chalk. It wasn't a regular cross, like a plus sign. Nor was it entirely like a cross one might find on a church. There was something different about it, the way the ends flattened to a curve. When looked at from a distance, it actually looked more like a circle or a wheel. "Who can tell me what this is?"

Harley raised his hand. "It's a cross."

The teacher nodded. "But it's a very special cross. Have any of you seen it before?" She looked around the room, her eyebrow raised in question. Max didn't raise his hand, though he had certainly seen it before. Lots of times, in fact. It was imprinted on all the books in his grandfather's study. It was also carved into Grandpa Caliburn's desk. And currently it hung from a chain around Max's neck.

"It's the cross on Christopher Columbus's boat," Natalia blurted aloud, not bothering to raise her hand. She'd read about it in the library just that summer.

"Excellent, Natalia. Thank you," Ms. Heen offered as Natalia radiated with pride. "Of course, you have all heard the story of how Christopher Columbus discovered America?"

"In 1492, Columbus sailed the ocean blue," Natalia repeated from memory. "He had three ships and left from Spain; he sailed through sunshine, wind, and rain." She knew the poem backward and forward. In fact, she had even put it to music once, playing it in her first piano recital, at the age of eight. The recital had been a disaster, and she had given up piano for the flute shortly thereafter. But the poem was still one of her favorites.

"Precisely," Ms. Heen said. "But I wonder if any of you has ever thought about how Columbus knew he was going in the right direction? Or even how far it was to where he thought he might be going?"

The students looked at one another blankly (even Natalia didn't know the answer).

Ms. Heen continued. "You see, there are all sorts of reasons to be sailing into the ocean to find America if you already know it's there. But if you don't, it seems dangerous and, well, a little daft."

"Daft?" asked Ernie.

"Silly," explained his teacher. Ernie nodded. It did seem silly. He could imagine what it might be like sailing across Lake Avalon, but if there were no shore on the other side . . . Well, the thought of that sent butterflies skittering around in his stomach.

"Why did he do it, then?" asked Max.

"Because he *knew* there was something on the other side and *exactly* how far it was."

"How did he know that?" asked Brooke, passing Max a quick smile as she caught his eye.

"Because he had a map," their teacher answered matter-of-factly.

"But how could he have a map if America hadn't been discovered yet?"

"You tell me." Ms. Heen smiled.

Again, the students returned only blank looks.

"He had no map," came a dark voice from the back of the room. All eyes turned to see Dr. Diamonte Blackstone standing near the door with a ruler in his hand, and as usual, a foul temper pulling his lips back into a sneer. "Of course this whole story about a map is just a fairy tale. Columbus sailed around the world, which he believed to be round, in order to find a faster trading route to the Orient. All the rest of this ridiculous tale is just conspiracy theory made up by people who have nothing better to do than discredit established traditions."

"Yes, of course." Ms. Heen smiled politely at Blackstone. "Thank you, Doctor, for bringing us back to the point: tradition and its proper place in education."

Dr. Blackstone narrowed his eyes as he gazed at the new teacher. He didn't like her. The students could see that well enough. And evidently he thought he had caught Ms. Heen in some sort of infraction.

"Tradition isn't just important," he replied with teeth bared and in a measured tone. "It's everything. King's Elementary has a reputation to maintain, and I would hate to see the careless mention of dangerous ideas bring about an unfortunate event. Wouldn't you?"

THE REVENGE OF THE SHADOW KING

"Oh yes," Ms. Heen replied, still with a polite, yet firm, tone. "And the children are most fortunate to have not only a school as renowned as King's, but also an instructor so well traveled, and with such a passion for proper education, as you."

"Quite so," Blackstone agreed with a nod, looking around the room to see if anyone might be admiring him. Despite his loathing for children in general, he was exceedingly vain and not too proud to gather up praise from the desks of his students. "A school such as King's Elementary employs the best methods, the highest curriculum, and the brightest minds. If we didn't, we wouldn't be the best."

"From what I hear, Dr. Blackstone, the school has flowered since your arrival. I find it invigorating to work with someone with such an established reputation for excellence. Thank you once again for joining us today, and we look forward to seeing you again in the future."

Blackstone stood there for several long seconds, not altogether sure whether he had been invited to join the class on a regular basis or asked to leave. And he didn't know which he disliked more. But with a slight bow of courtesy, he excused himself from the room. He had done his duty.

That afternoon found the Grey Griffins deep within the dark confines of the King's library instead of at recess. Ernie and Harley weren't very interested in the history of Christopher Columbus, but they all disliked Dr. Blackstone enough to find out why he was so worked up about the explorer. In her flare for the dramatic, Natalia had already named it the Columbus Conspiracy.

"Here it is!" Natalia exclaimed, bringing over a tower of books to the table where they were all sitting. "Everything we could ever want to know about Columbus."

Harley eyed the stack and rolled his eyes. Recess was starting to sound better all the time.

"It says here," Natalia began as she browsed through the first book, "that Columbus belonged to a secret order of knights—so secret, in fact, that no one knew about it for hundreds of years after the fact. But nowadays, everyone knows them as the Knights Templar."

Max had all sorts of books at home on knights, the Crusades, and castles, and he'd read a thing or two about the Templars. Mostly, they were known for being the most dangerous knights in the whole world, kind of a special forces unit like the Navy Seals. This was, Max recalled, because they had devoted their entire lives to warfare. They were said to be unstoppable. And they fought to the death. Max filled Harley and Ernie in on what he knew as Natalia perused through several more books.

"The cross on Columbus's sails was also the symbol of the Templars. There's a picture of it here," Natalia continued, pointing out the illustration to the others.

"What does any of this have to do with us?" complained Ernie, who had also begun to wish he had chosen the recess option. Geography was coming up next, and he was sure he needed some fresh air before diving into state capitals.

"I'm not sure," replied Max, shaking his head. "Maybe nothing. But that cross is everywhere in my grandparents' house—especially in Grandpa Caliburn's study. Look at this," he said, pulling out the chain and cross that Iver had given to him.

"Oh my," breathed Natalia, looking up from a dusty volume that had obviously never been checked out before. "Where did you get it?"

"It was my grandfather's."

She looked even closer, pulling out her tablet and a pen to sketch the necklace. "It looks like your grandpa was either a collector of Templar artifacts, or . . ."

"Or what?" Harley asked.

"Or nothing." Max didn't need to hear the "or what." Natalia was implying that his grandfather might have been a Templar—which was ridiculous. His grandfather liked to fish, hunt, and listen to baseball on the radio while he puttered about in his shed. Grandpa Caliburn wasn't exactly the picture of a knight in shining armor, but Max had to admit that the connection of the cross was a strange coincidence. And what was more, there were quite a few of those crosses in the attic near where he had found the *Codex*.

"What's this?" Ernie asked. He had pulled out an old book that didn't have a library stamp on it. It certainly didn't belong in the King's library, so how it had gotten there was anyone's guess. But all the same, the title, *The Templar Maps*, seemed promising.

"May I see it, Ernest?" Natalia asked politely. Ernie handed it to her right away. Natalia loved thick books. Ernie was afraid of them.

Natalia thumbed through the text before finding what she was looking for. "It says here that Columbus's secret society was one of the last surviving links to the great Templar Knights. Apparently, the Templars were more than just warriors. They were also classical scholars, advanced engineers, and the best sailors in the whole world. In fact, it says here they used ancient maps of Antarctica, Atlantis, and America to sail around the world hundreds of years before Magellan was even born. Oh, and they were also fabulously wealthy."

"Like Max," commented Ernie, patting his friend on the back. Max shook his head and sighed. Money was usually more embarrassing for him than the absence of it was to others less fortunate.

"Well, whatever the case, it didn't seem to help them. They were betrayed by a king who wanted all their money for himself. Before they knew what was happening, thousands of them were captured, tortured, and destroyed on Friday the thirteenth. That's why that date is considered unlucky."

"Wow, I never knew that." Harley whistled in amazement. "That's pretty cool."

"What's cool about being burned at the stake?" Natalia countered, with narrowed eyes. "It sounds awful to me."

"I was talking about Friday the thirteenth being unlucky." Harley glared back.

"So that was the end of them?" Max asked, scratching at his dark hair in puzzlement. "Then why would my grandfather have their symbol all over the place?"

"And what about Columbus?" added Ernie.

"Well"—Natalia returned to reading—"it says a few Templars managed to escape from France in their ships the night before. Someone had warned them, and they were last seen sailing out of the city of La Rochelle. I guess they took all of their money and secrets with them, because the king never got his hands on a single penny of it."

"Where did they go?" asked Ernie.

"It doesn't say." Natalia shook her head as she breezed through the remaining pages. "In fact, for almost two hundred years no one knew anything about them. Then, all of a sudden, Columbus rides out across the ocean to discover America with a big Templar cross on his sails."

"Using a Templar map to guide his way, I bet," Harley added.

"I wonder why the Templars wanted to go to America," Ernie murmured. "It's so boring here."

"Hmmm." Natalia's brow furrowed in thought. "If the Templars and the *Codex* are related somehow, this could be the biggest riddle of them all."

There's More than Bats
in the Belfry

"HEY, MAX!" Brooke called, joining him and Harley as they headed back to their lockers.

"Hi, Brooke," Max replied. Max had to admit that Brooke was definitely talking to him more often than usual. When they were little, they talked all the time, but somehow, in the last couple of years, it started to become kind of weird.

"You know my party? Well, I asked my parents, and if you want, we could pick you up. That way we could go together ... I mean, since we live so close. What do you think?" Brooke's eyes shone brightly, though she tried to act demure.

"Don't ... uh ... worry about it," Max stuttered slightly as he began working the combination to his locker. "I can just get my mom, or ... uh ... maybe even Logan, to drop me off."

Brooke leaned up against the neighboring locker and folded her arms. "It wouldn't be a bother," she said, smiling. "They'd love to pick you up. And I ... I ..." She paused.

"And what?" replied Max curiously. But before she could answer, his locker sprang open with a bang and a cloud of mist. When Max saw what was inside, he nearly dropped his books.

Sprig waved hello with a mischievous smile. Other than the fact that she was only a quarter of her usual size, she looked fairly normal—for a spriggan.

She was burrowed comfortably in Max's coat pocket, batting her eyelashes at him innocently. "We missed you. We are very glad you are still alive."

"Sprig!" he shouted in alarm. Max had been hoping to see her for some time, but not in the middle of school.

"What did you say?" asked Brooke, who couldn't see around the locker door. "What do you have in there, Max?"

"Oh, nothing," he lied. "I . . . uh . . . just kinda sneezed," he said as he closed the door a bit, waving away the smoke.

Brooke edged closer to get a peek. "Is there a radio in there or something?"

"Nope!" Max smiled nervously as he slammed the door shut and snapped the lock. "It's nothing."

"You're hiding something." Brooke laughed as the locker rattled.

"What makes you say that?"

"Come on, Max. Just show me."

"I don't think that would be a good idea. I . . . uh . . . It's your birthday present."

"Really?" Brooke blushed. "That's so sweet."

"Yeah, well . . ." Max offered an awkward glance. He hated lying, but he didn't know what else to do. Whatever he said did the trick, though. Brooke just stood there looking at him in a way that made him feel both good and bad all at the same time.

After an awkward silence, Brooke looked down at her feet and blushed. "I should probably get my books. The bell is going to ring soon." With a silly grin, Max watched Brooke turn and skip down the hallway. However, when he turned back to his locker, his smile faded. Ernie was working the combination to Max's locker.

"No, don't!" Max shouted in horror. Too late. The locker door fell open with a clang.

"Gee, whadda you yellin' for?" asked Ernie, taking a step back. "I just wanted to put my apple in your locker. Mine's full."

Fearfully, Max peered inside. But to his great relief, there was no longer any sign of the spriggan. "Sorry, Ernie," Max offered. "You can put your apple in here."

"This looks like a good spot," exclaimed Ernie as he reached inside, but as he did, his hand disappeared. With a yelp, he jerked it back.

"It's a portal," Max whispered, putting his hand over Ernie's mouth. Quickly, Max slammed the locker shut.

"In your locker?" mumbled Ernie, rubbing at his hand to make sure everything was in working order.

"I guess they can be anywhere," Max replied, looking over his shoulder to see if anyone was watching. "Sprig was in there a second ago. She must have disappeared through the portal when the locker was closed."

"Maybe she can control where they open up."

"Maybe," Max agreed as he and Ernie headed back to class. It was definitely a possibility. That would explain her ability to show up anywhere she wanted at any time. But that could also be a bad thing. Especially when Max desperately wanted to keep her a secret.

Over the course of the week, other portals would appear from time to time. On Wednesday, there was one in Max's lunchbox. On Thursday, a portal appeared in his desk, swallowing two baseball cards, a stick of cherry everlasting gum, and his milk money. On Friday, there was one in the boys' bathroom, causing a rather disturbing incident that left many students unable to eat for several days. The good news, although unexplainable, was that Max was starting to be able to predict where portals would show up from time to time. It was almost as if he had a sixth sense, seeing a rough outline, like a band of energy, when a portal would appear nearby. The bad news was that Sprig continued to appear at the most inconvenient times—and Max could never predict that.

At first, he tried to ignore her, but finally he had to order Sprig to leave him alone. That seemed to work, yet regrettably it seemed to have hurt her feelings. Still, Max hadn't gotten over his anger at Sprig's tricking him into letting out the Shadow, but each time he attempted to ask her about it, she'd vanish without a word. He didn't know if she was afraid to talk about it, felt guilty, or that's just what spriggans did. Faeries were strange, unpredictable creatures, and Max was still trying to get used to them.

Then there was the problem of Ray. He had shown back up at school after a few days. Everywhere Max went, Ray seemed to follow, watching him with malicious eyes. And each day, Ray looked sicker and sicker. Natalia seemed to think that the Shadow was eating him alive from the inside. And she may have been right. By Wednesday, Ray had stopped going to class altogether. Instead, he just hung out in the courtyard or playground, lurking and whispering to himself. Even Dennis, Ray's only friend on the entire planet, had stopped hanging out with him. Something was very wrong with that boy.

A sleek black Land Rover pulled alongside the movie theater the night of Brooke's party, and the passenger door was quickly pulled open by Logan, the Sumner driver, who was dressed in a stylish Italian suit with alligator shoes, along with his signature sunglasses, of course. Max jumped out and slung his book bag over his shoulder as the door closed behind him. With all the craziness, he didn't want to tag along with Brooke and her family and risk Sprig popping out of their glove compartment.

"Will that be all, sir?" came Logan's deep Scottish voice. It was far too formal to be taken seriously by Max. Logan was not the picture of propriety commonly expected of house servants for the wealthy when he and Max were alone. But when others were around, he was great at acting the part.

"Yeah, thanks," Max replied with a smile. "I'll call you when I'm ready to come home."

"Very good, sir." Logan winked and gave a formal bow before disappearing around the vehicle. Laughing to himself, Max turned and walked toward the movie theater, where a sizeable crowd had already gathered.

"This is so cool," began Ernie as he approached Max from the throng. "We have the entire place to ourselves. Do you think it cost a lot to rent?"

"I don't know. I guess," Max said with disinterest, the topic of money being his least favorite.

"Well, I bet it did," Ernie continued. "It probably cost a million dollars."

"I doubt it," said Max as he pushed his way through the crowd toward Harley, who was talking with Brooke near the theater's entrance. She was wearing a pink dress with lots of ruffles, and her hair was pulled back with a flower in it. Ernie followed Max, stopping every now and then to calculate the cost of Brooke's birthday extravaganza on his fingers. Just inside, they could see that the lobby of the Excalibur Theater was overflowing with gifts, pizza, soda, cake, and ice cream.

"Hey, Max," greeted Harley with a smile.

"Hey, Brooke," Max replied with more enthusiasm than intended. "Happy birthday." She blushed as Max handed her a small gift.

"I can't believe you kept it in your locker all week."

"You did?" Harley looked quizzically. "I thought Rosa just bought . . ."

"Um . . . so when are we going in?" Max interrupted, fumbling to change the topic.

Brooke stood on her tiptoes and looked across the street at the old clock tower. The minute hand had just reached seven o'clock, and the bells were echoing through the town. As the seventh bell chimed, the theater doors were thrown wide, and the kids began to pile inside.

"How about now?" laughed Brooke as they were nearly trampled by the exuberant partygoers.

Max started to follow her just as a hand reached out from behind and grabbed his coat.

"Uh, Max?" Ernie stammered behind him, looking like he had seen a ghost.

"What now, Ernie?" he asked in exasperation, watching Brooke disappear in the crowd.

"Something's up there."

"Up where?"

"On the clock tower. I think it might be Sprig."

Max turned and looked up to where Ernie was pointing, but he didn't see any sign of the spriggan.

"You sure?" he asked, not trusting Ernie's poor eyesight or his overactive imagination.

"I think so," replied Ernie.

"Hello, Ernest . . . Grayson." Natalia curtseyed in her ruffled lime and lavender dress. Natalia loved dressing up for almost any occasion, but parties were an especially nice reason to look her best. "Well?"

"Well, what?" Max sighed as he kept his eyes glued to the clock tower for any sign of the spriggan.

"How do I look?" Natalia tapped her foot impatiently.

"You look like you always do," Ernie said, a quizzical look on his face.

Wrong answer. Natalia crossed her arms and delivered a disapproving glare.

"You will never get it. I don't know why I even bother."

"Get what?"

"Honestly." Natalia crossed her arms and looked away. "Well, are you two going in or what?"

"Yeah," replied Max. "We'll be there in just a second. Ernie and I have to check something out first."

"What do you mean, 'check something out'?" exclaimed Ernie, once Natalia had gone back inside. "What are we checking out?"

"Sprig," Max said matter-of-factly. "It was your idea. Follow me."

"It was?" stammered Ernie, falling in behind as he looked nervously over his shoulder. The two boys headed down the dark street toward the clock tower. "But you said you wanted to go to the party. Besides, what if I'm wrong? What if it's the Slayer goblin instead of Sprig?"

Max stopped without a word, walked back to Ernie, took him by the collar, and began to pull him across the street. "The Slayer is dead, remember? Iver killed it. So it has to be Sprig. And I have to talk to her."

But as they marched along the damp street surface, doubt began to eat at Max. Maybe it was his imagination, but as soon as he saw the frost on the ground, and his breath misting in front of him, his heart began to thump loudly in his chest.

"Is it the Shadow?" Ernie asked, looking around fearfully.

"I don't think so," Max replied as a cold wind rushed past them. "I think . . . I think you were right, Ernie," Max whispered as they came to a halt, their shoes quickly freezing to the ground with a thousand tiny ice crystals. It was the Slayer.

"We're gonna die, aren't we?" Ernie's teeth chattered, out of both fear and the chill of the air.

At that moment, a dark bristling shape leapt from a high rooftop, landing behind them, cutting off their path of escape. Silently, it regarded the boys, sniffing at the air with hunger. Bubbling scars crisscrossed the creature's shoulder where it had been wounded by the lightning bolt, but it was certainly alive, and it wanted revenge.

"It's persistent," Max said, shaking his head in disbelief as the dark sky began to drizzle an icy rain. This just wasn't Max's day. Briefly, he pictured himself back at the movie theater, laughing with Brooke, warm and safe. But his daydream didn't last very long.

The Slayer spread its jaws, acrid saliva dripping from its fangs, sizzling as it hit the ground. Max closed his eyes, waiting for his sixth sense to kick in. There just had to be a portal close by. Nothing. Then the beast roared.

"The clock tower!" shouted Max. "Follow me!"

The two Griffins launched into a race for their lives down the rain-slicked street. They were fast, but the Slayer goblin was faster, moving like an evil wind. There was no way they would be able to make it to the clock tower in time. But just then, headlights flashed as a dark truck skidded recklessly around the corner, rocketing straight toward them. There was nowhere to go.

Luckily, the driver must have seen Max and Ernie, for he swerved at the last moment. Brakes screeched on wet pavement, sending up a jet of steam, as the mountain of metal hurtled directly into the Slayer's path. There was a terrible thud, followed by the sick sounds of grinding and crunching.

"Come on!" Max shouted, not bothering to look back. With a

surge of speed, they closed the remaining distance to the clock tower, bursting through the massive oak doors, then bolting them shut.

"I can't see a thing," whispered Ernie with his back against the door. "Why aren't the lights on?"

"I don't know," replied Max, who was trying to catch his breath.

"Do you think it's finally dead?"

"I doubt it," stated Max in frustration, thinking that if it had survived what Iver did to it in the forest, a truck wasn't going to kill it, either. In truth, Max doubted it would even slow the creature down.

"Is there a light in here?"

"I don't know," Max replied as his hand brushed over the wall in search of a switch. "Look, how certain are you that you saw Sprig?"

"I don't know," said Ernie, shrugging. "I thought I did. I wasn't lying."

"So she could still be in here?"

Ernie shrugged again as he kicked the frost off his shoes.

Max stood for a moment as his eyes adjusted to the darkness. "Is that the staircase?"

"You aren't thinking about going up in the tower, are you? You'd have to be crazy. Max, this place is haunted. I heard there was an old man with a long beard, a glass eye, and a limp who used to . . ."

"You can stay down here if you like. Either way, I'm going up," Max said. "If Sprig's not up there, at least we'll be farther away from the Slayer."

"Well, what about a portal or something? Isn't there another way? I mean, at least that way we'd have a quick escape."

"I already tried," Max said flatly. "There aren't any. Or at least I can't sense where they are."

"All right." Ernie sulked as he considered being left alone with a monster just on the other side of the door. "I'll come."

If the pale moonlight and bewildering shadows weren't creepy enough, the moaning of the stairs beneath their feet certainly was. Slowly, they crept up the stairwell, each step agonizingly uncomfortable as they imagined the evil things lurking in the darkness above.

In what seemed like an eternity, they came to the second floor landing where an arched window yawned in front of them. Max peered out and saw the theater in the distance. Then he looked down. The street was empty. No monster. Perhaps they weren't high enough yet to see anything.

The boys continued up the stairs, one flight after another. Four stories up, with just one more to go, they came to a sudden stop. There had been a noise above their heads. Something was up there waiting for them.

"Probably the wind," Max whispered, starting forward again. Ernie pulled him back.

"Are you out of your mind?" Ernie whispered through trembling lips. "That wasn't the wind. It sounds big!"

"I'm going up," Max said flatly. "If it's not the wind, then it's Sprig." Max really couldn't have explained his reasoning even if he had wanted to. He was just tired of running from things. After this latest attack by the Slayer, Max was getting angry. Somehow he almost wanted a fight.

Taking a breath for courage, Max chanced a look out a nearby window. Under the light of the moon he could see the woods in the distance. They rolled across the horizon like a great black shadow, swallowing the land in their grasp. Max knew the forest's power was growing. It would only be a matter of time. He needed answers. If he wasn't going to get them from Iver, then it was time to have a talk with Sprig.

With a warning to keep quiet, Max tore his arm from Ernie's fearful fingers and started up the final flight, into the darkness of the tower belfry. One stair, then two ... three ... five ... ten. Before he knew it, Max had passed through the attic door where a clockwork of gears, steel bars, and levers wrapped their way around a giant clock face. The room wasn't large, but there was no light, making it the perfect place for a goblin (or any monster for that matter) to hide. But on the other hand, goblins didn't seem the type to play hide-and-seek. No, they got right to the point, and if there were any up there waiting for him, Max knew he'd already be dead.

"Max?" echoed Ernie's unsteady voice from below. "Are you still alive?"

"Yes. I'm alive."

"How can I be sure? You could be a ghost."

"Well, I'm not."

"That's exactly what a ghost would say!"

"Why don't you just come up here and see for yourself?"

Against his better judgment, Ernie made the harrowing ascent to the top of the bell tower. A moment later, he was standing next to Max. Together the two of them slowly edged around the giant bell hanging like an iron vampire bat from the ceiling. On the other side, only a few feet away, Max thought he saw someone in a dark corner.

"What is it?" whispered Ernie.

"I can't tell. I think it's a person, and I think they're hurt."

"What makes you say that?" asked Ernie, inching his way behind Max.

"Look at the blood on the floor."

"Blood?" Ernie choked.

There was groaning as a dark form rocked on its knees in the shadows, rubbing its wrists and forehead in pain. Turning, Max thought he saw fear within a pair of glowing yellow eyes that seemed to plead for help. Just as quickly they filled with hate, and as a shriek ripped through the room, the figure launching itself directly into Max and Ernie. The impact sent them flying as Ernie's spare glasses rolled off into the darkness. He barely avoided hitting the gears of the clock face, but Max wasn't as lucky. He bounced off the heavy iron bell, falling to the floor in a heap.

An instant later their assailant was on top of Max, but instead of finishing him off, it coiled and sprang across the room, disappearing down the stairs.

"What in the world was that?" whispered Ernie as he crawled around looking for his lost glasses.

"Ray," Max answered matter-of-factly, rubbing his aching shoulder. "And he's changing."

The climb back down was a miserable one. They were both sore. Ernie had at least a dozen splinters rammed into his fingers and palms, but Max was even worse off. His shoulder felt as if it had been hit by a sledgehammer, and the taste of blood was in his mouth. The past few days had seen Max beat up and tossed around a little too much for his liking, and while his long-sleeved sweater hid the bruises on his arm from the Slayer, it wouldn't hide a bloody lip. It took a great deal of effort for them to struggle to the bottom of the stairs, where they rested a bit. Neither said a word.

"Well, we can't stay in here forever," Max sighed, realizing waiting wasn't going to change much. "I couldn't see the truck or the Slayer from the upstairs window, so we're probably safe." Ernie wasn't so sure, but he definitely wanted to be anywhere other than where he was.

Slinking out the tower door, the boys walked in silence, hugging the damp buildings along Main Street, staying in the shadows. There had been no sign of the Slayer or Ray. And Ernie had already admitted that he probably had been mistaken about seeing Sprig. But both boys knew things were getting worse, and tonight had taught them two things: that the Slayer was not going to give up until it had Max and that Ray had turned from a playground bully into a first-rate nightmare. The Grey Griffins were in trouble.

Just as they were about to cross the street to the theater, strange voices echoed from nearby. The sound was coming from an alley just around the corner of the building they were standing next to. There was no way to cross without being seen.

"Stay here and be quiet," Max whispered as he disappeared

under an awning. Max wasn't sure if it was safe to risk a look, but he felt compelled to find out. There were actually two voices, not just one, and whoever they were, they were arguing in hushed tones. He listened for a few moments, and then his jaw dropped.

"What is it, Max?" whispered Ernie, creeping up next to him.

"Shhh," Max whispered, frowning. "It's Iver—or at least I think it is."

"Who's he talking to?"

Max listened a bit more, but then shook his head. "I don't know. I can't really tell from here, but it doesn't even sound as if they're speaking English." Summoning his courage, Max peered cautiously around the corner. Not twenty feet away was a tall man with white hair and a beard—definitely Iver. But Max wasn't sure who the other person lurking in the alley was, although it was a woman; that much Max could tell. She was wearing a heavy cloak, and a hood kept her face covered. Behind her, in the shadows, stood a giant of a man with mountainous shoulders. His arms were folded as he watched the other two in silence.

Max stood quietly for a few moments, but his shoulder was throbbing, and he knew the longer he stayed, the greater he risked getting caught. The boys would have to find a way to get to the theater without being seen. The problem was that the only way to their destination was crossing in front of the alley.

"I'm gonna make a run for it," Max whispered. "When I give the signal, follow me. We've only got one chance."

Ernie didn't like Max's plan very much, but being left behind was even less appealing. Reluctantly, he nodded.

"One, two . . ." Max paused, waiting for the figures in the alley-way to turn away from him. "Three!"

Max covered the twenty-foot span of pavement in a flash, disap-pearing beneath the darkness of an awning on the other side. A moment later he peered cautiously around the corner and sighed in relief. Iver was still arguing with the stranger and hadn't noticed a thing.

Max motioned for Ernie to follow. Ernie nodded slowly and took a shot from his inhaler to give him courage. He then closed his eyes and took three deep breaths before bending down like a sprinter. Ernie was fast. Everyone knew it. Faster than any other kid in the class. Unfortunately, and much to the relief of the slower students, he was also cursed with the two clumsiest feet in the northern hemisphere.

Like a flailing newborn giraffe, Ernie launched himself into an awkward race against time. In a split second, he was already half-way across the gap. Momentum alone should have been enough to deliver him to safety. Unfortunately, he hadn't calculated how slick the pavement had become—nor the fact that not one but both of his shoes were untied. Ernie pitched dangerously forward, stum-bled, and then fell, crying out as he skidded onto the pavement in a tangle of limbs.

Iver and the mysterious figures spun around to see what had happened, and it was then that Max finally saw who was shrouded in darkness. It was the face he least expected to see, and one that he hoped he would never see again.

11

How Witches Came to Be a Nuisance

A THICK FOG had rolled in the day after Brooke Lundgren's party, casting an eerie light over the little town. All week (and beyond) the street lamps had to be lit morning, noon, and night, forcing people to drive with their headlights on, even in the middle of the day.

Perhaps the strangest thing of all was that Avalon seemed to be the only town in Minnesota perpetually plagued by bad weather week after week. Ten miles away in any direction, and you'd find sun and fluffy white clouds. People were starting to talk—and not just about the odd weather. At the beauty salon, Natalia overheard a woman claim an angry vine tried to attack her daughter on the jungle gym. The story would have likely been dismissed as just plain silly, but another lady had seen a mysterious figure climbing up the eaves of her neighbor's house. She shined a flashlight and banged some pots and pans together to scare off the burglar, but she said whoever, or whatever, it was hissed at her, jumped to the ground twenty feet below, and ran off down the street. Even city workers had reported seeing strange critters in the sewers, swearing that they weren't rats—rats didn't grow to be four feet tall.

The town was definitely growing nervous, especially with the continued disappearance of house pets and livestock. But a seemingly satisfactory explanation was quickly rolled out by local authorities that claimed Avalon was caught in a smog zone that had floated down from Minneapolis. As for the missing livestock and house pets, well, it had been determined that the local wolf population had become rather bold. Logical explanations, regardless of how outlandish, seemed to quell the fears of Avalon's citizenry and pave the way for the coming excitement.

Like New York City and its Thanksgiving Day Parade, Avalon was passionately tied to its Harvest Festival. It was an annual celebration when the farmers and townspeople alike gathered every September to give thanks for the year's bountiful harvest. The entire town would shut down for a gigantic carnival with block parties, bonfires, a farmers' market, and dancing—lots of dancing—all ending the next day with a grand costumed parade down Main Street. Nothing could stop the celebration, not even four-foot-tall sewer rats.

The Grey Griffins were piled into Ernie's tiny bedroom, where downstairs their mothers sewed, pinned, and stitched their costumes for the parade—well, everyone's except Max's mother, that was. Annika Sumner was conspicuously absent as usual. But the other mothers didn't seem to mind. If she had been there, she would likely have just stood in the midst of them, pointing this way and that, barking orders, and trying to act important. Instead, she just gave Max a credit card and sent him off with Logan to Minneapolis to buy his costume.

"Do we have to do this in my room?" complained Ernie as the Griffins sat around discussing the latest events. Ernie had a small bedroom, which was invariably strewn with books, toys, chocolate bar wrappers, and model airplanes. Even one person in the room was too many, but four made it impossible to move about.

"What's that stuff you're drinking?" Max asked as Ernie guzzled down his third bottle of a strange red drink that fizzled and popped as if it were radioactive. "It looks disgusting."

"It isn't so bad," Ernie answered, belching loudly. "It's called Plumples—Mom says it's good for me 'cuz it has plums and apples in it."

"Good for you?" Natalia asked suspiciously. Everyone knew Ernie was a die-hard candy-o-holic.

"I had a checkup last week, and the doctor said I had to start eating healthier. My dentist said the same thing the week before, so now my parents are making me eat a bunch of healthy stuff. At first, I hated it. But then, you know, when you get hungry enough, anything tastes good."

"Good for you," Natalia cheered. "A healthy diet is the only way to grow strong, have good teeth, and live a long satisfying life."

Ernie, obviously missing Natalia's point, reached for a bag of corn chips beneath his bed. Of course, he figured what better to make a fruit drink complete than a salty snack? Unfortunately, Natalia was quicker, snatching it away before Ernie could open the bag. With a hopeless sigh, he turned back to his Plumples, nursing it like a baby bottle.

Natalia then busied herself by reading a thick book about the history of the Templar Knights that she had borrowed from Max. Harley was thumbing through a stack of Ernie's comic books while Ernie moped over his lost snack. All the while Max's mind was reeling, trying to unravel the mystery of what had gone on in the alley the night of Brooke's party. His aching shoulder reminded him he hadn't been dreaming, though over the last couple of days it had started feeling better.

"Hey, Max," Ernie began. "How do you do it?"

Max look at him, a little bewildered. "What do you mean?"

"You know . . . like how do you use the book and know where the portals are? Do you think you can teach us how to do it?"

Max remained silent. The truth was that he had no idea what was going on, and it had really been bothering him. But the worst part was that Max was worried he was changing into some kind of freak like Ray.

"Well, I sure wish I had a magic book," complained Ernie. "I'd get it to do my homework. Now *that* would be real magic. Oh, and I'd have my own roller coaster, and my very own candy bar with my name on it."

Natalia rolled her eyes. "You should think about world hunger for once, instead of your own stomach. Besides, that's not what this book is about, is it, Max?"

Max shook his head. "I'm just as lost as you. I can open the *Codex*, but I don't know how or why. And the portals? No clue how I know where they are."

"I see. Well, don't worry about it," Natalia offered. "We're here to help." She then looked over at Ernie, who was in the corner looking at a candy bar wrapper and imagining his name written across it. "Well, some of us are . . . anyway, I have some interesting news about Ray," Natalia boasted, changing the topic. "It seems that Dennis hasn't seen him in quite some time."

"How the heck do you know that?" Harley asked, sitting up and setting aside his comic book. If Dennis, Ray's only friend, hadn't seen the little jerk, then it was doubtful anyone had, including Ray's parents.

"I talked to him yesterday."

"You what?" Ernie sputtered, spitting half a bottle of Plumples all over his bedspread. "And you're still alive?"

"Dennis isn't so tough—at least not when it comes to girls," Natalia said.

"So what if you talked to the tank? Why would you believe him, anyway?" Harley asked doubtfully.

"Well, I do believe him," she maintained, folding her arms. "I could see it in his eyes. Anyway, it seems that I'm the only one brave enough around here to get some answers. Have you got anything better?"

"Well, I know who the lady was in the alley with Iver," offered Max.

"Yeah," agreed Ernie.

"I think I already know," replied Natalia. "It was the lady from Iver's store. The one that nearly ran me over."

"That's right," admitted Max, impressed that Natalia had figured it out so quickly.

"Her name is Morgan," Ernie stated with great pride.

Natalia dropped her notepad. "How do you know that?"

Ernie just shrugged. "I read her mail."

"What? When?"

"Yesterday. Max and I followed her home from the coffee shop after school. It was raining pretty hard, so I don't think she saw us."

"Max! You were in on this and you didn't tell us?" Natalia complained. "How could you? Neither of you know a single thing about detective work. You two might have given yourselves away—or worse yet, missed an important clue."

"Yeah, well, anyway," Ernie continued, intent upon his story, "she lives in one of the old houses on the edge of town—the big one with no paint and dead trees."

"Do you mean the old Slaughter house?" breathed Natalia in wonder, forgetting her anger. The very name made everyone in the room shiver.

"Maybe. How would I know?"

Natalia peered out the window cautiously and then turned back. "You'd know it because the front door is black and the chimney's crooked."

"That's the one," said Max. "Ernie and I waited 'til she walked inside and we pulled a letter out of her mailbox. It wasn't that big a deal. Her name is Morgan La-something."

"LaFey," Ernie finished. "Morgan LaFey."

"What?" Natalia cried out in renewed agitation. "Are you putting me on?"

"Oh, here we go again." Harley rolled his eyes, turning back to his comic book.

Natalia stood and put her hands on her hips. "As if you don't know . . . as if everyone doesn't know who Morgan LaFey is."

"I'm lost," admitted Ernie.

"Morgan LaFey?" complained Natalia. "You don't know who she is?"

"Is she called the Black Witch?" Max asked as he pulled his Round Table card out of his pocket.

"Where did you get this?" Natalia gazed in amazement. "This is her? Oh my word. The woman in the shop was Morgan LaFey!"

"Why is she in our card deck?" asked Ernie.

"She was King Arthur's sister . . . well, half sister, anyway. That's the Round Table connection," began Natalia.

"Was she a good witch?" Ernie asked in hope. He had seen *The Wizard of Oz* at least twenty times and understood two things: Good witches grant wishes and bad witches send nasty-looking flying monkeys to get you. It was a fifty-fifty chance in his mind.

Natalia shook her head.

"A bad one?"

"The worst . . . ," Natalia replied solemnly. "Some say she killed King Arthur—and Merlin, too."

"But that was like a million years ago." Harley waved his hand as if the whole thing was crazy. "She'd be long dead by now."

"One thousand four hundred, actually," Natalia replied. "But that doesn't matter. She's immortal."

"What's that mean?" asked Ernie. "It doesn't sound good."

"It means she can live forever," Max explained.

"Oh, great." Harley rolled his eyes.

Max stared for a few moments at the card in disbelief. What was the half sister of King Arthur doing in a card deck with a bunch of monsters and faeries? Did she work for Oberon, too? Or was she an altogether different enemy? Whatever the case, the cards seemed to be telling them something. If they showed Morgan LaFey to be the Black Witch, then the Grey Griffins were in deep trouble.

"Maybe we should throw away the cards," offered Ernie. It seemed like a good idea at first glance, but Max quickly shook his head.

"The cards are the only way we know what we're dealing with. Besides, the cards aren't the real problem. It's my fault for opening the *Codex* in the first place."

"I agree," seconded Natalia as she pulled her own deck out from one of her pockets and started looking through it. "Not that it matters. What's done is done. Now, we have to deal with it. But we had better start taking these cards more seriously from here on out. They might save our lives."

Ernie folded his arms defiantly. "This town's getting too creepy. I'm moving to Iowa."

Max arrived at the Harvest Festival with his mother and his sister, fashionably late of course. Annika Sumner, a breathtaking beauty by almost everyone's standards, caused quite a stir wherever she went—a source of unending embarrassment to Max. That night she was dressed as a dark queen in a flowing velvet dress of black trimmed with glittering jewels. Max couldn't help but think about her resemblance to Morgan LaFey, though of late he wasn't sure which one would have been more difficult to deal with. Max's little sister, Hannah, was wrapped in a golden blanket with a jeweled tiara on her brow, and Max was dressed as a knight, complete with shining plastic armor and a shield emblazoned with his family crest. Because of his mother's paranoia about weapons (or anything that resembled fun to an eleven-year-old boy), he didn't have a sword to make his costume complete. Nevertheless, Max wasn't above begging.

"Don't even think about it," Max's mom warned. "It's too dangerous."

"Please?" he pleaded. "It's not like we can't afford it."

"Don't make a scene, Max," his mother snapped. "You're not getting a sword or anything of the sort, and that's that. And take off that silly backpack. It looks ridiculous with your costume. If you have so much homework, you should have stayed home."

"But . . . ," Max protested, worried about the magic book inside. Between the possibility of rain damage and outright theft, Max would have preferred to keep the book as close to him as possible. Unfortunately, his mother had other ideas.

"No 'buts,'" she interrupted. "Take it off right now and put it under the stroller so nobody can see that raggedy thing. Honestly, that bag is a tattered mess. It should have been thrown away years ago."

"Fine," he muttered under his breath. "But I bet Dad would buy a sword for me."

"What was that?" she asked, spinning around with fury in her eyes. "What did you say?"

Max looked at her and glared.

"Don't look at me like that," she commanded. "And don't you ever say that again." Tears welled in her eyes, sending Max's heart to the floor. "Leave me. Go find your friends."

That's all he needed to hear. Torn between regret and anger, Max jammed his backpack beneath Hannah's stroller and stomped off without so much as a good-bye.

Max wove in and out of the fantastically costumed crowd of townspeople, his eyes wide in curiosity. He wanted to drink in every delicious morsel he possibly could before it all disappeared. The Harvest Festival was the most amazing event to happen all year. Jugglers, fortune-tellers, and acrobats lined the streets. Everywhere Max looked was a treat to the eyes, and the smell of funnel cakes and turkey legs made his mouth water.

Then Max's heart stopped as cackling laughter filled the air. He looked over and couldn't believe his eyes. Pushing their way through the crowd were a dozen goblins, dancing and shaking their spears—and they were coming right toward him.

Max froze in terror, only to realize as the band of dark monsters approached that they weren't goblins at all. It was just a group of kids in their costumes.

Max closed his eyes and took a deep breath. He was growing paranoid and that worried him. He knew he couldn't afford to lose his wits, not with the forest growing darker every day. He needed a plan, a way to get rid of all the monsters that had been let out of the *Codex*—including Sprig.

"Whatchya doin', Max?" came Ernie's merry voice. "I've been looking all over for you."

Startled, Max turned to find Ernie wearing a ridiculously large jester's hat and a flamboyant pair of purple-and-canary-yellow silk pajamas. The clash of colors was only outdone by the tinkling of the bells sewn to every conceivable corner of his clothing. It was amazing Max hadn't heard him coming a mile away.

"Wow, you really look . . . interesting," Max said, trying not to laugh.

"Really?" Ernie asked in pride, brushing some lint from his sleeve. "I think so, too, but I was kinda worried people were gonna make fun of me."

Just as they were about to go off to find Harley, they ran right into Iver. He had a very serious look upon his face and his walking stick in his hand. Max hadn't seen Iver since the night of Brooke's party, and what he was doing in the alley with Morgan LaFey was still uncertain. At this point, it was hard to know who to trust.

"Hi, Iver," Max offered, hoping now might be a good time to get some answers.

"Mr. Sumner." Iver gave a slight bow in acknowledgment. "I feared I might find you here."

"What do you mean?" asked Ernie.

"Tonight is not a good night to be out alone. And it will get worse very soon. Is Logan nearby?"

"No," answered Max. "My mom gave him the night off. Why?"

"That is sore news. I recommend you turn yourselves around and go home as soon as possible."

"But why?"

"I've warned you thrice now, and unless I am very much mistaken, Master Sumner, the fact that your backpack is not on your shoulders indicates that you are not taking me seriously enough. The world is growing dark, my young friend. Darker than I first believed. I should have seen this coming. In any event, I am running out of time and must leave immediately while there is still a chance. But if I am not back when you need me most, go to the Catacombs. It will be your only chance. The Catacombs. Remember the word. It's important!"

"What catacombs?" asked Max as Iver turned and walked briskly away. But Iver either hadn't heard him or didn't have time to answer, for he had disappeared into the crowd without another word.

"Now that was weird," commented Ernie, taking a swig from his Plumples bottle and wiping his mouth on his costume sleeve.

Catching a commotion in the corner of his eye, Max turned to see Harley and Natalia racing toward them, Harley wearing a Viking helmet and Natalia in a fairy princess costume, complete with a hand-painted ceramic mask.

"Quick!" Harley shouted, barely stopping as he darted back into the crowd, with Natalia right behind. "Follow me!"

"What's going on?" Max called, racing after, Ernie trying to catch up.

"Ray," Harley replied. "He's back. And uglier than ever."

12

Of Dark Plots and Something Stolen

THE GREY GRIFFINS pushed their way down Main Street toward the orchard where Harley had seen Ray disappear. His fixation on getting even with Ray not only for throwing him into the lake, but for taking his prize knucklebones, was growing every day. But Ray had changed so much since then that catching him had become a dangerous proposition—even for someone as tough as Harley.

After a few minutes of weaving through stilt walkers, elephant dung, and fire-eaters, they arrived out of breath at the edge of an orchard lined with meandering rows of apple trees wrapped in yellow and red garlands. The tree boughs had been lit with small white lights, sparkling like stars that crept across the night sky. In the midst of the orchard, townsfolk had gathered around long wooden tables that were overflowing with every sort of food Ernie could have imagined. His mouth started to drool as he longed to devour as much pheasant, ham, sweet potatoes, and apple crisp as he could feasibly wedge into his mouth. They watched as people were laughing and dancing to a Renaissance band, raising their tankards to toast the year's fine crops, not in the least bit aware of the dangers that lurked in the darkness.

The Grey Griffins ran past the tables, straight toward Bonfire Hill. It wouldn't be long before the great fire would be ignited, climbing high into the sky, to be seen for miles in every direction.

"Where's Ray?" called Ernie, his bells jingling.

"Up there." Harley pointed toward a tower of timber.

"So what are we supposed to do?" Ernie asked.

"First, Ernie, you can take off that ridiculous costume," Natalia suggested. "Ray could hear those bells a mile away."

"My mom will kill me," whined Ernie. "After I lost my glasses, she told me the next time I lose something—anything at all—I'll be grounded until Christmas." Natalia looked over at Max and shook her head, but Max had an idea.

"That's it, Ernie!" he proclaimed. "You're brilliant. In fact, you're a genius!"

"I am?" Ernie was confused.

"Yeah," agreed Harley, trying to play along, although he really didn't know why Ernie had suddenly become a genius, either.

"You'll be our alarm," proclaimed Max. "All you have to do is stay here."

"Alarm?" Ernie's brow furrowed in confusion.

"Sure," explained Max. "If a monster eats you, your bells will warn us and give us a chance to escape. It's ingenious, really. And brave. Thanks, Ernie."

"Oh no. I'm not going to be the cheese in your mousetrap," Ernie countered. Two minutes later he was standing in his long underwear, shoeless and shivering.

"Let's go," whispered Harley. He didn't want to waste any time as he led the Griffins up the slippery hill.

"There's Ray," murmured Natalia, peering out over a fallen tree. She was out of breath and pointing toward a shadowy figure atop the timber pile. "I wonder why he's just standing there in plain view? That's stupid."

"Who cares?" replied Harley, punching his fist into his hand.

"He's waiting for us," Max said. "He probably saw us the whole time."

"Why's the ground shaking?" gulped Ernie. "Is he doing it?"

"I don't think so. Look . . . ," Natalia whispered.

Just then an old truck drove slowly past, stopping nearby. Its headlights lit up the woodpile, and the Grey Griffins gasped as the light fell upon their old classmate.

Ray's clothes were in tatters, his hair was disheveled, and somehow his skin had faded to a pale, sickened blue. Yet it was his eyes that were his most disturbing feature—two fiery disks that flickered in the twilight.

"Oh my," breathed Natalia. "What's happened to him?"

Three burly men in plaid shirts stepped out of the truck and started to unload firewood, completely unaware that Ray stood on the pile above them.

"This is our chance," Harley proclaimed. "He's got nowhere to go."

"You can't be serious," Natalia argued. "Look at him . . . he's . . ."

"He's a monster." Ernie shivered as panic welled inside him. "This is crazy. Look at him, Harley! Ray has horns."

Harley's eyes narrowed in anger. "I'm not scared of anybody, least of all that weasel, Ray," he spit. "And if you think I'm going to let him get away with what he did to you and Max at the clock tower, you're the crazy one."

As one, the four friends inched forward following Harley's

lead, hoping that Ray would be too distracted by the workers to notice them. But just as the Griffins closed in, Ray casually turned toward them and waved, taunting them.

Then, in a flash, Ray leapt high into the air, soaring over their heads before he landed twenty feet down the other side of the hill, disappearing into a cornfield.

"Tell me I'm dreaming," Ernie said, pinching himself.

"You're not dreaming," replied Harley, undaunted. "Follow me."

Harley took off, the other three right behind him, racing back down the slope toward the cornfield. Going up had been hard work, but going down was a mess. The grass, slippery from all the rain, sent Ernie skidding face-first to the bottom, nearly knocking over the other three as though they were bowling pins.

At the base of the hill stood a barbed-wire fence lining a vast sea of wilting cornstalks. "We can't go in there," stated Ernie. "There's a 'No Trespassing' sign."

"It's not the sign that bothers me," added Natalia, her voice trailing off in a sudden shiver.

The field was a part of the old Jacobson farm, a vast acreage of cropland that stretched for what seemed like miles. Amos Jacobson was a bad-tempered old man who lived alone with his two ferocious dogs. His wife had died years before in a mysterious accident that had never been solved, and the rumors around her death often led to fingers being pointed directly back at Amos.

"People say these fields are haunted," Natalia continued. "I heard Old Man Jacobson's wife was buried out there."

"That story is just a bunch of baloney," Max said, waving the idea off. "Everyone knows she was buried in a cemetery."

"Look here," Harley said, examining the fence a few feet away. He was studying a group of broken stalks at the edge of the field. "If the rest of his trail is as easy, we should be able to catch Ray in no time."

"This is a bad idea," Ernie complained as his jaw began to shake with the cold. "You saw Ray's eyes . . . and his skin—it's blue! Besides, did you see how far he jumped? He's like a supervillain from the comic books now. We're gonna get creamed."

"I'm not afraid," replied Harley.

"But Iver warned us not to do this stuff, like going into dark cornfields looking for ugly blue monsters," argued Ernie.

Harley turned to look at him. "This isn't just about Ray. It's a whole lot bigger. Sprig said so. And Iver did, too. Whatever's happening, this isn't going to stop after it gets to us. We have to think about our parents—and everybody else in Avalon. Who knows, maybe even the whole world." With that, Harley turned back and walked into the cornfield.

"We have to try, Ernie," Natalia echoed as she slipped into the corn behind Max. Ernie shook his head, grumbling as he followed.

Despite Ernie's reluctance, the Grey Griffins made good progress. Even in the dim moonlight, Ray's path could be plainly seen. Yet what they were going to do once they found him was another matter.

Max understood Ernie's fear. For all they knew, Ray was

working with the Slayer. And they were probably walking into a trap. But something terrible was going to happen, and Ray was their only lead. Harley was right. To protect their families, they had to do something.

Despite the possibility of an ambush, they continued moving at a fast pace deeper and deeper into the tall forest of dried cornstalks until they found themselves standing on the edge of a large clearing. Here the stalks had been flattened to the ground, as if something immense had fallen from the sky.

"It's a crop circle." Natalia whistled, leaning down to inspect the bent stalks. "I've read all about them. This is amazing."

"This isn't a crop circle." Harley shook his head. "It's not even round." In fact, instead of an intricate weave of stalks gracefully bent over, these were smashed, splintered, and in some places piled high, where other areas were bare. In fact, it looked a lot like a nest—but whatever had built it would have had to have been huge. Max just hoped it wasn't a dragon.

Harley wandered around the perimeter shaking his head. "There's no sign of Ray's trail anywhere. It's a dead end."

"What's that smell?" Natalia asked after a time, sniffing the air.

"It smells like a car," Ernie suggested.

"Not a car," corrected Harley. "It's gasoline."

"Where's it coming from?" Max asked.

"We've got company," Harley warned as the other three spun around. There at the edge of the clearing stood a ghostly silhouette silently watching them, yellow eyes shining in the night.

"Ray!" squealed Ernie. "And look what he's got."

"It's my book!" Max cried, his heart leaping into his throat. "Ray must have taken it from Hannah's stroller. I knew I shouldn't have listened to my mom!"

Harley's eyes narrowed in anger as he took a step toward Ray. "Give Max his bag or you'll be sorry."

Ray had always been scared of Harley. It was the whole reason he had befriended Dennis in the first place. But now with the Shadow, he no longer needed protection, making Harley's threat sound shallow and desperate.

Slowly, Ray set down Max's backpack and pulled a small box out of his tattered pocket, sliding it open.

"Oh no!" cried Natalia in sudden horror. "It's a match. He's gonna blow us up!"

Ray struck the match, sparking it to life. And as he did, the flickering flame exposed a haunting smile before he let the match fall to the gasoline-soaked ground below.

The clearing erupted in a cloud of fire.

Max barely had enough time to reach the ground before a wall of flame shot over his head. In one horrific instant, the serene cornfield had turned into a war zone. Fire leapt from stalk to stalk as black smoke choked out the night sky. A wave of heat sucked the air out of Max's lungs. Pulling his shirt over his mouth, he peered out. The field was in flames, but the clearing was relatively safe . . . save for the thick cloud of smoke overhead. "Guys!"

"What?" a voice called back, but Max couldn't see who it belonged to.

"You okay?"

"Not for long," Harley shouted, materializing from the smoke, his arm raised to shield his face from the heat.

Natalia limped into view with Ernie coughing and wheezing behind her. She looked completely a mess, her tangled hair shooting in all directions. Ernie was in worse shape, though. His face was black with soot, and his eyebrows had been burned right off.

"What are we going to do?" Natalia screamed.

"We're totally surrounded," explained Harley, pointing to the fire encroaching on all sides. "Ray's gonna kill us."

"No kidding," shouted Max as panic started to set in. "Did anyone see where he went?"

"Who cares?" yelled Natalia, pointing to Ernie, who had fallen to his knees, coughing. "Ernie's having an asthma attack. We have to get him out of here!"

"Where's your inhaler?" Harley shouted, but Ernie just shook his head, unable to answer. Max spun around, but soon realized there would be no escape for Ernie—or any of them. A feeling of hopelessness washed over him as his mind fell into darkness.

"Call Sprig!" Natalia cried to Max, but if he heard her, he made no sign, frozen as he peered into the inferno.

Ernie's cough had turned into ragged gasps. He was clutching his throat as tears streamed down his face.

Natalia rushed over. "Calm down, Ernie. You don't have to worry . . . you'll be safe soon." But she didn't believe her own words, and by the looks of it, neither did Ernie.

Max remained motionless.

"I hate this!" screamed Natalia. "I don't know what to do. Somebody save him   help!"

"Max!" Harley said as he shook his friend violently. "Wake up! You've got to get Sprig right now."

In a comalike trance, Max's mind shut down as his body gave way to a petrifying fear. Uncontrollably, and from deep within, raw emotions spilled over as Harley's hands released Max. A blue fire of crackling energy—almost like electricity—began to spark across Max's body. It began at his fingertips, spreading all around him before striking the ground and shooting up into the air. Harley had to step away to avoid getting struck.

"The fire's closing in!" Natalia cried out.

"There's something wrong with Max!" Harley yelled back over the roar of approaching flames, not knowing what to think about what he had seen. "Something's happening to him. You've got to help me."

Natalia's heart jumped as she felt Ernie's hand go limp. "He's passed out!" she called.

Harley didn't answer. A thick curtain of smoke had swept in, obscuring him from view.

"Harley?" Natalia cried out, stepping toward the spot she'd last seen him—a big mistake. In seconds the heat overwhelmed her.

With the last of her strength, Natalia crawled back over to Ernie's unmoving form, hoping to protect him from the fire. But as she lay there on the edge of a dream, waiting for the flames to take them both, an odd calm came over her and she smiled. "At least I got to see a unicorn," she murmured, before falling silent.

As the inferno was about to sweep over like a fiery wave, the wind miraculously shifted. The heat that had threatened to cook the Griffins was cast aside, and a cool breeze rushed over them as rain began to fall. Lightly at first, but within seconds a downpour opened, and the fire began to hiss and scream.

The last thing Natalia could remember was hearing the sound of muffled voices and feeling strong hands pick her up and carry her away.

13 It Was a Setup

MAX AWOKE to the sound of sirens and a blur of flashing lights. He was wrapped in a thick woolen blanket, lying on the damp ground. It was raining softly, and nearby he could hear his mother's sharp voice. Max blinked as he rolled over to see what was going on.

To his left, several fire engines were parked, their haunting lights flashing a cold blue that stung his eyes. To his right, his mother's black Land Rover stood with the door open, its engine humming as the exhaust slithered into the sky. She was yelling at a crowd of paramedics and firefighters, pointing toward a smoking hole in the middle of the field.

"There was another boy out there," he heard one firefighter say. "We found his footprints running out of the clearing, but they just disappeared into thin air."

"Thin air? How is that possible?"

"Hard to say, but Old Man Jacobson's dogs are on his trail, I hear. Whoever it was, if he survived, we'll know soon enough."

"Didn't you hear?" inquired his partner. "The little girl said she saw the missing Fisher boy start the fire."

"Little girls shouldn't always be trusted," said a dark, feminine voice just beyond Max's view. It was vaguely familiar, but Max couldn't quite place it. "Especially ones who are known for lying, like Ms. Romanov. Children are wont to get into mischief, and these four are nefarious. If it doesn't find them first, they'll find the mischief on their own. They probably snuck out here and were playing with fireworks, I shouldn't wonder. I believe the oldest of the urchins, Harley Eisenstein, has been warned about fireworks in the past? This seems like a reasonable explanation, doesn't it?"

"Yes, ma'am, it does," the firefighter replied in a rather hypnotic tone. "Thanks for your help."

It had to have been Morgan LaFey. Max was sure of it, and he was growing angry again. Things were completely out of control. And now, with Morgan convincing everyone that the Grey Griffins were responsible for the fire, who would believe them about anything else?

And then the image of Ray holding his book, the *Codex*, came rushing back to him. How that jerk had gotten his hands on the book was plain enough, but what he would do with it was another matter. Max knew he needed to get it back before Ray figured out some way to open it. If he did, who knew what would happen next?

"Grayson Maximillian Sumner!" Max heard his mother call. He turned to see her storming over.

"You're lucky to be alive," she began with a frown. "Look what you and your little friends did. What are people going to say? I wouldn't be surprised if it hasn't already been on the six o'clock news. Do you know what this is going to do to my reputation?"

"We didn't do it," argued Max, but his mother just held up her hand, cutting him off.

"I won't stand here and listen to you lie to my face, Grayson. I deserve more respect from you than that. You get into the car right now. I don't want to hear another word."

"I'm grounded," complained Max with the phone to his ear several days later. "Until Christmas break."

"Geez," replied Ernie from the other end of the line. "That's a long time."

"No kidding. I'm not even supposed to be talking on the telephone." Max was sitting on his windowsill, looking out through the steady stream of raindrops to the dark trees beyond.

"Well, if it means anything, I'm grounded, too," Ernie offered. "But Dad says I can still mow lawns if it ever quits raining." At the age of ten, Ernie already had his own lawn-mowing business, which he took very seriously, despite the fact that he looked preposterous mowing with a big white mask wrapped over his mouth and swimmer's goggles over his eyes to protect against his hyperactive allergies. He was good with money, though, and probably had more money in his piggy bank than kids twice his age. In fact, he'd already started saving for college, though if he had his own way, he'd rather skip school and open his own comic book shop.

"What about Harley?" Max asked.

"He's fine, I think. I haven't seen him for a couple days. He's mostly been fishing."

"In the rain?"

"You know Harley," replied Ernie.

"Natalia?"

"She grounded herself before her parents had a chance. Can you believe it? They actually told her they were just glad she wasn't hurt, but because you and I were grounded, she decided to punish herself, too."

"Is she crazy?" exclaimed Max. "That's ridiculous. How long did she ground herself for?"

"I'm not sure."

"Listen, Ernie. I want you to do me a favor. Can you call Natalia and get her to un-ground herself? We need to find out where Ray went with my book. I tried to call Iver at his shop, but nobody answered."

"Sure," Ernie replied. "But the cops are already looking for him. We told them it was Ray who set the fire, but I don't think they believed us. They can't find any trace of him. Natalia thinks he might have learned how to use the portals."

"Just tell her to do it anyway. She's our only hope. It's dangerous, but I don't know what else we can do."

"Hey, Max?"

"Yeah?"

"Harley said your body started to light up in a freaky blue light right before the rain started. What's going on? Did someone cast a spell on you?"

"I wish I knew, Ernie. I wish I knew."

The mud sloshed over the spokes of her wheels as Natalia pedaled her glittery pink bicycle down the dirt lane to Old Man Jacobson's field. Her white banana-styled seat, decorated with a smattering of unicorn stickers, was uninvitingly cold, and her handlebar streamers hung like soggy strings; but her pink unicorn flag, flying high over the tail of the bicycle, snapped proudly in the wind as she approached her destination. It was a long shot. The police had already inspected the field a hundred times, but Natalia had a hunch, and Natalia's hunches were almost always right.

There was a freezing chill in the air, and she could see her breath as she pedaled along in annoyed wretchedness. Natalia's mittens, meant to keep her hands warm, had turned out to be a bad idea. Within five minutes, they had become soaked from the fog and rain, and were now flopping damply from clips on her coat sleeves. Wet mittens were almost as miserable as wet socks. Natalia had both.

She would not give up, though. She knew the answer to where Ray was hiding rested in the cornfield. And considering the weather, she was certain there would be no interruptions while she looked for clues. Who else would be stupid enough to stand in the middle of a muddy cornfield in the rain?

When she spied fresh tire tracks on the road in front of her, Natalia quickly revised her previous expectations and decided to proceed with caution when she came to the base of a hill, right before the entrance to the cornfield. On the other side of the hill, just beyond her line of sight, she could hear the soft rumble of a car idling. She decided a closer look was in order.

Pulling her bike into the ditch, she covered it with weeds and followed the gully until she came alongside the mysterious car. It was unlike any other she had seen. The automobile was luxurious, black, and shiny, with white tires and a long, aggressive front end. The round headlights glowed eerily in the mist. The car was money, Natalia was sure. Every detail was finely crafted. Even the thin trail of exhaust that escaped its tailpipe held a certain elegance.

"It's a Rolls-Royce," Natalia said to herself, remembering seeing one similar to it in Max's family collection. But this one was more than an expensive collector's trophy. It was alive—or at least as alive as a car could be. Its engine purred like a kitten, and its headlights stared hungrily into the field as though it were a black panther waiting for its next kill. Natalia quickly decided that getting closer would be a bad idea.

There was only one family in Avalon with enough money to own a car like that—Max's (though Brooke's family wasn't far behind). Yet the license plate was from out of state—Massachusetts, to be exact.

Massachusetts? Natalia's mind sparked as she recalled the last time she had met someone from that state. Ms. Heen was from Salem, Massachusetts. A coincidence? Natalia didn't believe in coincidences.

Through the dark window tinting, Natalia could just make out a large man in a hat sitting behind the wheel. He was dressed in black, and despite the gloominess of the day, he was wearing dark sunglasses.

"He's waiting for someone," Natalia whispered to herself. "There's someone in that field, and whoever it is, is probably up to no good.

"Well, someone's going to have to go in there and find out what this is about," she told herself. "And I am just the person to do it."

With a satisfied smile, Natalia pulled her coat close around her and followed the damp ditch a little farther to where she could climb out, unseen, behind a rusty grain bin. Carefully, she poked out her head to make sure she hadn't been seen. The driver was evidently preoccupied. Perhaps he was working on a crossword puzzle? That's what she would be doing if she were him. Waiting in cars was a pet peeve for Natalia.

With only a few yards separating her from the first row of corn, Natalia knew she had to take a risk. She wouldn't be seen for much more than a second, and if she ran, she could blend in with the background. She had worn tan for that very reason. Natalia always thought of the most ingenious solutions.

"Well, this is it," she said under her breath.

Like a shot, Natalia hurried across the barren expanse between the grain bin and the field. A moment later, she was safely inside, and the driver hadn't so much as looked up. Natalia sighed and snuck along, crisscrossing, zigzagging, and jumping rows to hide her trail until she arrived at the center of the field.

In the midst of the burned-out clearing stood a tall woman in a long, black velvet cape fringed with white tufts of fur. She wore high boots of stylish leather and long gloves that glittered in the light. In fact, she was a dead ringer for the portrait on the Black Witch Round Table card.

Morgan LaFey.

Natalia knelt low to the ground, pulling her hat over her head, hoping Morgan hadn't seen her. And luck was on her side. Morgan was too preoccupied with something else. But what? And what was she doing in the middle of a muddy field?

As the witch walked back and forth, Natalia could see words form upon her lips, yet no sound escaped them.

Is it a spell? Natalia wondered. What's she saying?

Just then, Morgan, her back to Natalia, sank to her knees and pulled something from inside her cape. Natalia couldn't see it well, but it was small, black, and rectangular. Morgan dropped it onto the soft earth and sprinkled dirt over it.

Then Natalia heard Jacobson's dogs. Everyone knew they were the meanest canines in the whole state of Minnesota, and the barking was getting closer. Morgan apparently heard them as well, for she quickly rose, dusted off her gloves, and disappeared back into the corn.

Natalia knew she should escape as well while there was still time, but her curiosity wouldn't let her leave without knowing what Morgan had buried.

The barking grew louder.

Rising to her feet, Natalia tiptoed quickly across the empty clearing, pushed the dirt aside, and found a scorched matchbox.

Why would she leave an old matchbox in this cornfield? Natalia wondered as the barking miraculously faded. The dogs were probably chasing the car. Good riddance, Natalia thought.

When she opened the matchbox, Natalia's jaw dropped. Written on the inside of the bottom half was a single name, "Harley Davidson Eisenstein." What was worse was that it was Harley's handwriting. Natalia recognized it immediately. His penmanship was absolutely deplorable.

"Curiouser and curiouser," Natalia said to herself. Harley never carried matches, and he certainly wouldn't have written his name in a matchbox. What would be the point?

Then she knew. Harley was being framed.

Natalia put the matchbox in her coat pocket. She hadn't found any sign of Ray, but she knew Ray was no longer their biggest problem.

"The terrible thing about witches, is that witches are terrible things," she sang to herself as she made her way back to her bicycle.

Several wet days passed with no sign of the rain coming to an end. People had stopped having their lawns mowed altogether, much to Ernie's entrepreneurial disappointment. The grass was growing three inches a day, and the ground was so soggy that several mowers had already been lost to the sucking mud. Yet aside from the rain, everything else was business as usual. There were no goblins raiding convenience stores, and unicorns weren't grazing on anybody's lawn. But there were some notable changes, though less obvious. The moon always seemed to be full, and the trees were waking at night and moving about when no one was looking. At least that was Ernie's opinion. Ever since the night the shoe-eating tree had attacked him, he had made up his mind to keep them under watchful surveillance.

Farmers seemed to notice the changes more than anybody, and some of them were overheard at the Main Street Café claiming the town was cursed. "It's Jacobson's fault," his neighbor said. "He's done and brought a curse on us all. Look what happened to his field. It's no coincidence, I tell ya."

But restless trees, wet grass, and cursed farmers were hardly a deterrent to a seasoned detective like Natalia, who, fresh from her first success, had moved to the target she believed would lead them all to Ray: Dennis Stonebrow.

Natalia had tried tracking him down outside school on a number of occasions, but as she quickly found out, Dennis generally kept to himself. He lived in a cheap little house the church had handed over to his father, Avalon's minister, and Natalia could only assume Dennis spent the bulk of his off-hours penned up in a messy room, smelling of sweat socks, while listening to head-pounding hard rock music. That was, if he wasn't torturing some poor victim in the nearby junkyard, Dennis's home away from home.

But no amount of tailing her mammoth schoolmate had turned up any clues. Aside from being predictably brutish and smelly, Dennis was rather uninteresting. That was, until Wednesday morning.

As Natalia was weaving her bicycle through a line of rain-filled potholes in the school parking lot that morning, she caught sight of red lights flashing around the corner of the baseball field.

"Police," she murmured to herself. "Now what could they want here at King's Elementary?"

As casually as she dared, Natalia pedaled across the blacktop until she came to the dirt path that led to the bullpen. It was as close as she could get without drawing attention to herself, but it was just close enough to see that she had struck gold.

The cops were there, all right, and who did they have pushed up against their car?

"It's Dennis...." She smiled, leaning her bike against the bullpen as she peered around the corner. She could hear everything.

"Look, kid...," said one of the officers. "All we want is some information." There were actually three police cruisers lined up on the path and five officers surrounding Dennis, who despite the fact that he was only eleven years old was taller than most of them and probably weighed as much as all of them combined.

But Dennis didn't appear in the mood to talk. Instead he stood there defiantly with his arms crossed.

"We're gonna ask you one more time," continued another officer. "We know you were friends with Ray. Everyone does, so do yourself a favor and start talking."

"Or what?" replied Dennis, rolling his eyes.

"Your parents are fine, decent folk, Dennis. You'd do well to respect them and answer us."

"Whatever."

"If you're hiding him, Dennis, you could be in a lot of trouble—even for a tough guy like yourself." The other officers took a step closer, hemming in the student back toward the police car. But there was something very strange about these policemen. Natalia has seen them before around town. They were good men, but something in the way they were talking seemed, well, off, as if they were acting or reading lines. Or, as Natalia stumbled on the idea, like they were under a spell.

"Look, I don't know anything," Dennis maintained. "We just hung out sometimes."

Natalia frowned. "He's stalling. He knows something . . . ," she whispered to herself.

Just when it looked as if Dennis was about to be tackled and hauled to jail, a towering figure silently stepped out of the rearmost police cruiser, which raised at least six inches off the ground in the absence of his daunting form. He was huge, far larger than even Dennis, with shoulders as wide as a truck, enormous gloved hands, and smoked glasses. If he was wearing a uniform, it was hidden under a raincoat, and his boots, neatly shined, pressed deeply into the ground as he walked toward the other officers. Even Dennis, who perhaps had never known fear, began to edge away as the newcomer approached.

"Good afternoon, Mr. Stonebrow," said the man in a low voice, thick with a mysterious accent. "It is unfortunate that you are unwilling to help these officers today. They are, I think you'll agree, on a very important mission. You see, we need to find your friend Ray. He has something, and I would like to return it to its rightful owner."

"I don't know anything," stammered Dennis as he stepped behind a nearby officer. "You'd better get away from me." Natalia watched in amazement as Dennis began to shake in fear.

"Oh, I think you do," the huge officer continued with an intimidating smile. It was just the sort of smile a bear might flash before tearing apart a deer. "And I think you'd like to tell me," he said, placing his gloved hand on Dennis's shoulder.

"You aren't allowed to touch me. You can't. I'm just a kid. Why don't one of you help me?" he pleaded to the other police officers. But instead of helping him, the five officers backed away, leaving him alone under the heavy hand of the powerful stranger. Natalia doubted very much if this stranger was a policeman at all. No, there was something else going on here, and there was also something familiar about the man who had Dennis helpless under his power. She just couldn't place him yet.

"I can do whatever I wish, I'm afraid," replied Dennis's towering assailant, squeezing the back of the boy's meaty neck like a vice. There was no doubt in Natalia's mind that he could have snapped off Dennis's head if he had wanted to. "Now, I suggest we start at the beginning. Have you seen Ray since the night of the fire in the cornfield?"

Dennis groaned and reluctantly nodded.

"Good . . . ," growled the man, his shining eyes piercing through dark glasses. "Very good. And where is he now . . . ?"

Dennis, overpowered and outgunned, slowly raised his arm and pointed to the north.

"The forest?" the dark officer clarified. "He's in the forest?"

Again, Dennis nodded.

The man flung Dennis to the ground like a piece of trash, striding quickly back to his car. With a snap of his fingers, the other officers also got into their cruisers and started the engines, lights flashing and sirens screaming.

It wasn't until the line of police vehicles drove past that Natalia saw another figure sitting in the front seat of the last car—a woman, dark and terrible, dressed in fur. And then Natalia knew where she had seen the towering officer in dark glasses before. The corn-field. He was the driver of that Rolls-Royce.

"Morgan . . . ," breathed Natalia as she hid from view behind the water fountain. "So we meet again."

When the bell rang, Max was safely in his seat. Ernie, who was sit-ting next to him, chewed on his nails as he contemplated Natalia's disturbing news. It looked like Morgan was now a major concern. They couldn't afford to ignore her anymore—not after she tried to frame Harley for setting the field on fire. And now the Black Witch had Dennis Stonebrow questioned? She was after the *Codex*. That was the only answer Max could come up with.

But if she was working for the Shadow King, and so was Ray, then why would she still be after the book? She wouldn't. Max shook his head as the idea began to come clear in his mind. Morgan was an enemy. But she wasn't working for the same person Ray was.

Max didn't know if that was good news or not. Iver would know, but Iver had not been seen since the night of the Harvest Festival.

"I'm not going back into the woods, so don't even ask me," argued Ernie. "If you want your book, you're going to have to get it yourself," he continued, grabbing a second bottle of Plumples.

"You sure do drink a lot of that stuff," Harley mentioned as he sat down beside his friends and cast a suspicious eye at the numer-ous empty bottles squirreled away in Ernie's bag. "Maybe you should lay off it. It gives you gas."

"It does not!" Ernie jumped to his feet, red-faced with embar-rassment.

Max, still thinking about his stolen book, shook his head. "We can't let Ray open the *Codex*. It's too dangerous. And now that Morgan has wrecked any chance of our talking to the police and Iver's gone, we don't have any choice except to do this ourselves."

"Ray isn't gonna last five minutes in those woods," Natalia countered. "I don't care how fast he can run or how high he can jump in that blue skin of his."

"You survived longer than five minutes," Max pointed out.

"Yeah," replied Natalia. "But that was before. It's darker in there now."

"Well, you couldn't pay me a million dollars to go back there. No way," Ernie stated as he folded his skinny arms across his chest. "Besides, aren't you grounded?"

"Hey, what's that?" asked Harley as he suddenly stood up and walked over to the window.

"It looks like a cloud or something," Ernie suggested, following Harley's gaze.

"That's not a cloud," Natalia pointed out as she joined Harley.

"Is it a plane?" asked one of the other students.

"No," Natalia said as she squinted to get a better look. "But whatever it is, it's coming this way."

In a swarm of wonder and curiosity, the rest of the class rushed to the windows. They all made their guesses, but as usual it was Natalia who got it right. "Birds!" she shouted from the ledge, standing high above the other students. "It's a flock of birds."

"That's a mighty big flock," observed a short, blond kid who was jumping up and down to see over the others.

"Wow," said Ernie. "What do you think they're up to?"

"Hmmm," said Natalia, walking back and forth on the ledge, her mind working over the clues. "They appear to be very large. . . ."

"They're crows," Max answered slowly, without looking up from his desk. He didn't know how he knew it, but there was no doubt in his mind. They were crows. And they were coming for him. His stomach began to tie itself in knots.

"He's right," replied Brooke Lundgren, who had walked over to join the others. "They are crows, and they're definitely coming this way. Wow. I've never seen so many birds in my life."

Within seconds the storm of crows arrived, their numbers blotting out the sky, casting the classroom in shadow. Like a school of fish cutting through the atmosphere, they circled in a mass of chaos and feathers above the courtyard. Then a curious thing happened. A single crow, smaller than the others, broke away from the torrent and flew straight for their window. It hovered, flapping its wings as its head moved this way and that. It was looking for something.

Then its eyes landed on Max. Silently, they stared at each other, and in a flash, the bird shot back into the swirling blackness.

"That was weird," commented Brooke, her nose wrinkled in disgust.

"I have a bad feeling about this," Ernie whispered.

"What was that all about?" demanded Natalia, rushing over to Max.

"I don't know," Max replied. "But it looks as if we're about to find out."

At first the students thought it was an accident when a crow suddenly hit the window, bouncing off and spiraling down to the courtyard below. Most of the students jumped, though a few of the boys laughed nervously. Then it happened again. And again. Then two or three hit at a time. Soon the windows were barraged by a swarm of crows scratching, beating, and throwing themselves into the glass.

Then the windows began to crack.

"Everyone get away from the window," Natalia yelled. "It's gonna blow!"

Chaos broke as the students screamed, rushing for the door like rats on a sinking ship. Papers, pencils, and erasers flew into the air as several students tripped and fell to the floor, while others leapt over their comrades in a mad rush to escape.

"It's locked!" shouted Harley, first to the door.

"So unlock it!" Natalia yelled, her eyes wide with fear as she struggled to keep her place at the front of the crushing crowd of classmates.

"I can't. Somebody locked it from the outside."

"Max, do something," Brooke pleaded as she held tightly to his arm. Max was caught between his own fears and an overwhelming desire to play the part of a hero, but the students continued to scream as the window groaned under the onslaught of the murderous crows.

Harley slammed into the door with his shoulder, but to no avail. It wouldn't budge. They were trapped.

The glass splintered and shook. It wouldn't last more than a few more seconds.

Then, like an electric current, a strange energy seemed to fill the room, and the world seemed to shift into slow motion. Brilliant white light flared all around the classroom door, and like a bolt of thunder, it burst open. With deliberate steps, Ms. Heen walked into the room. Her dress was radiant, her eyes a bright blue fire. She strode purposefully to the windows and, as the students watched in silent anticipation, slowly lowered the blinds. One by one, as each fell, the clamor of the crows faded, until the room grew totally silent.

"Well, that was certainly exciting, wasn't it, children?" she asked, helping Natalia to her feet. Max had expected something more magical than just lowering the blinds, but whatever Ms. Heen had done, at least the students were no longer in danger.

Ms. Heen turned to the class. "I'm sorry I was late. I would have been here sooner, but I love coffee, and I left my favorite cup in the car." She laughed, holding the steaming mug for them to see.

"How'd you do that?" asked Natalia, her eyes full of wonder. "How'd you make them go away?"

Ms. Heen smiled and winked knowingly. "Now, Natalia, we women have to have our secrets, don't you agree? Besides, mysteries are only interesting if they remain mysteries."

Then, Ms. Heen walked back to her desk and gracefully sat down. As she opened the lesson for the day, she clearly indicated that the conversation was over. It was time for class to begin.

Ernie, who still had his inhaler between his teeth, stood frozen to the spot. It was definitely magic ... he just knew it was. There was no other explanation, and there was no doubt in his mind any longer. His homeroom teacher was a witch—just like Morgan LaFey.

The Game of Life

BEING GROUNDED wasn't really so terrible for someone like Max Sumner, who had an unlimited supply of video games, whole rooms of comic books and baseball cards, an arcade in his basement with all the latest games, and a television with more than a hundred channels that played just cartoons. The problem was that Max had no one to share it all with. Sure his mom was there from time to time, but she was still angry about the fire in the field, insisting that Max and his friends had committed the crime. And since his sister was only eighteen months old, she wasn't much of a companion when it came to playing with his superhero action figures.

Luckily, there was always Logan. When he wasn't busy escorting Annika Sumner around town or tuning the Sumner vehicles into high-performance road missiles, he could almost always be found out back in the Japanese garden working on his martial arts. Looking for company, Max found Logan sitting cross-legged in the rain beneath a red pagoda near the koi pond. He appeared to be unaware of Max, his eyes closed, and his shirt was off. Logan was built like a world-class athlete, but how many athletes had scars from bullet wounds and sword slashes?

Max noticed a Templar cross tattooed on Logan's shoulder. He'd never seen it before, but Max recognized it immediately as the same symbol on his grandfather's necklace that Iver had given him. Another coincidence?

"It's not polite to stare," came Logan's dark Scottish accent through the pouring rain. Still, the bodyguard remained motionless, his eyes closed.

"Do you have time to teach me more kung fu today?" asked Max. Ever since Ray's transformation, Max had spent more time with Logan than ever before. He knew Ray would be back. And if Max was to have a chance at survival, he'd have to get better at defending himself. Logan thought Max was a quick learner, but Max didn't think he was learning fast enough—not that anything short of a nuclear bomb seemed as if it would do much against Ray anymore.

"Not today, grasshopper," replied the Scotsman with a wry smile as he opened his eyes. "Today there is a different kind of training you must attend."

"What do you mean?" asked Max.

Slowly, Logan stood up and walked over to where Max was standing. There, on the bench beneath the bodyguard's shirt, lay an envelope. Without saying a word, he handed it to the boy. It was from Iver.

"But I thought Iver was missing," Max murmured as he looked the envelope over.

"That he is," replied Logan, in a surprisingly worried tone. Max didn't think worry was a part of Logan's vocabulary. "I was instructed to give this to you in the event he didn't . . . return."

"I don't understand," argued Max.

"It's time that changed, Max," Logan answered, pointing toward the envelope in Max's hands. "It's time you learned who you really are."

Max looked up and down the hallway, and then closed his bedroom door, assured that he was alone. Filled with curiosity, he studied the strange envelope, sealed with what appeared to be red candle wax that had been imprinted with the same cross that had become all too familiar. Quickly, Max grabbed a pocketknife from his dresser and broke the seal, dumping the contents onto his bed: two Round Table cards (which appeared much older than the cards in Max's collection) and a small, but ornate, iron key. What the key might be for, Max could not guess, for there were no instructions that came with it.

Max then flipped over the Round Table cards. The first was that of a glowing portal upon a hill, framed by two arching slabs of stone as it hungrily devoured the light. The title read *Oberon's Gate*. Max shivered. It was probably the gateway that the Shadow King would enter through with his dark faerie armies when he invaded earth.

Max then turned over the second card, and his mouth dropped open. It read *Codex Spiritus*, and the picture was a perfect match to the book Max had found in Grandma Caliburn's attic—the one Ray had stolen.

If ever there was any doubt that Iver was involved with the whole mystery, it was gone. Max just wished he had been able to talk with the old man before he disappeared. And from Logan's tone, it sounded as if Iver might be in trouble. Or worse.

Logan had said it was time for answers and that Max should learn who he truly was. But at the moment, Max was more confused than ever. Absently, but so as not to lose it, Max slid the key onto his necklace. Maybe he would know what to do with it later.

But the cards were another matter. The direct implication was leading Max down a road that seemed impossible: Were he and his friends somehow trapped in a giant game of Round Table?

Suddenly, Max's door swung open, and he found Logan dressed all in black: boots, pants, turtleneck, overcoat, driving gloves, and of course, sunglasses.

"It's time to go, Max," the Scotsman said.

As the Sumner limousine pulled up to Grandma Caliburn's old barn, the headlights cut through the drizzle, illuminating three small bicycles. It was then Max knew the other Grey Griffins were already there waiting for them. Logan must have invited them ahead of time, though how he had known that the loft had become the new meeting place of the Order of the Grey Griffins, Max couldn't even begin to guess. But at the moment, Max's driver remained completely silent as he opened the car door.

Just inside the window to the farmhouse, Max could see his grandmother standing in the kitchen's warm light, waving at him. Logan must have called her, as well. But whether she knew what was going on or not, Max had no idea. He doubted it. She was simply too nice and too proficient at baking cookies to be involved in anything this weird.

"So what's this all about?" Ernie asked as Max and Logan stepped from the stairs into the dusty loft. All three Griffins eyed Max's driver suspiciously, Ernie doubly so. "I'm still grounded, you know. I could get in a lot of trouble for this."

"Have another Plumples," replied Natalia with a sigh, handing him a fresh bottle.

"I took the liberty of gathering your team, Max," began Logan as he took off his glasses and tucked them away in his long dark overcoat.

"My team?"

"Yes, Max. You know . . . the Grey Griffins?" answered Natalia.

Logan nodded, offering a vague hint of a smile. "Though," he paused, "that name has been used before, I should tell you. And with God's grace, it will be used again someday."

"Cool," Ernie said, forgetting his suspicions as he hunkered down with his Plumples, hoping for a good story.

"I am here," the man began, "because Iver could not be—God help him. It really isn't my role to play tutor, but I no longer have a choice."

"What happened to Iver?" Natalia cried, fearing the worst.

Logan shook his head, offering little consolation. He didn't know. "Max, now that you've seen inside the envelope I gave you, you probably have a few questions that I'll try to answer as best I can. The story is a long one, but I'm afraid we don't have time. The abbreviated version will have to do."

"What envelope?" Harley asked. Max pulled out the envelope and handed it to his friend, making sure to mention the key.

Logan cleared his throat, not waiting for the actual questions. "First, you are probably wondering who I am and how I came to your family's service. The answer is that I work for the same people Iver does. His job was to teach you. My job is to protect you."

"Then, where were you when the Slayer attacked us at the clock tower?" asked Ernie, challenging Logan's claim with his knee-jerk response.

"Who do you think ran over the Slayer with that truck at your friend's birthday party?" Logan replied with a salute. "You've been saved more times than you know, and maybe more than you deserve."

Max and Harley looked at each other in wonder.

"Anyway," continued the Scotsman, "the next thing you'll want to know is, why the game? Why does everything that is happening seem to center on Round Table?"

"Exactly," Natalia replied. "Let's hear it." Logan smiled and nodded, amused at the girl's boldness.

"Iver probably told you that it's an old game. Well, that's true and it isn't. Old it is. But a game it is not."

"But King Arthur invented it, right?" asked Ernie.

"No." The Scotsman shook his head. "Arthur was long dead by then."

"If King Arthur didn't have anything to do with it, why is it called Round Table?" asked Harley, who was listening intently.

"I didn't say he had *nothing* to do with it," replied Logan. "I just said he didn't invent it. The truth is that King Arthur is only one piece in a very large puzzle." Logan paused for a moment, as if recalling some distant memory. Running his hands through his closely cropped hair, he sighed and sat down on a hay bale near the Griffins. "Arthur was a good king. I know you've heard that before, but it's true. Yet if he had any weakness, it was trusting people more than he should have."

"Isn't that a good thing?" interrupted Ernie.

"Not when people are trying to kill you," answered Logan as he cast an irritated glare in Ernie's direction. "As I was saying, Arthur came from a long line of kings, which the stories don't tell you about. Each king was a keeper of ancient secrets and treasures, which had been passed down from a far older world."

"Like the Templars," Max stated.

"Exactly, only older. Almost seven hundred years before the Templars, in fact. But when it came time for Arthur to pass on those secrets, he was betrayed by his son, Modred, and the Black Witch, Morgan LaFey."

Max's heart skipped a beat.

"That's right." Logan nodded as he gazed at Max. "The same Morgan LaFey who is after you."

"But I thought Morgan was only after the *Codex*," Natalia commented.

"Who do you think had the *Codex* before Max?" replied Logan. "Arthur. And when he was betrayed, Morgan stole it from him."

"Morgan had my book?" Max shook his head. "How long?"

"Five hundred years," replied Logan with a smile. "But she couldn't open it. Arthur died without telling anyone the secret— except one person."

"Who?" asked all the Griffins in unison.

"His true son, a son the stories don't talk about because he has been hidden from history—on purpose. It was this son who escaped with Arthur's secrets, and his treasures, forming a mysterious group of soldiers that would, hundreds of years later, become the Knights Templar. It took a long time before the knights were strong enough, but eventually they managed to break into Morgan's castle and recapture the *Codex*. It was a bold plan, but while they achieved their goal, they paid a heavy price, for it claimed most of their lives."

"But there was an army of Templars," countered Ernie. "How could one person defeat a whole army?"

"Betrayal," the Scotsman replied. "It worked to destroy Arthur, and it worked again seven hundred years later, nearly destroying the Templars. The surviving knights were forced into exile."

"I thought they were betrayed by a king," Max countered. At least, that's what they had read at the school library not so very long ago.

"Yeah," Natalia agreed. "On Friday the thirteenth."

"Philip, the king of France, betrayed them only because Morgan had poisoned his mind against the Templars. There was nothing she wanted more than revenge—perhaps even more than she wanted the book—and it's said that anyone who hears that witch's voice immediately falls under her spell."

"She's awful." Natalia's eyes narrowed in aggravation.

"You have no idea," Logan said. "She's evil to the core, that one. But she's nothing compared with the Shadow King, thankfully. Oberon's evil on a scale you can't even imagine."

The very mention of his name brought a chill through the loft, as, reflexively, the children huddled closer to Logan.

"I don't understand," Max said, his mind grasping for answers. "What does Morgan have to do with the Shadow King?"

"Hard to say what that witch wants. She may be in league with Oberon, or she may be up to something entirely different. That's the way evil is. Morgan would never trust the Shadow King, and he would never trust her. But they might work together if the conditions were right.

"You see," Logan continued as he took a deck of Round Table cards from his coat pocket and shuffled them, "the depth of this story is endless, each mystery spinning into another like a giant spiderweb. But I can tell you this—Morgan is not what she appears. Then again, neither am I. And that's what I need you to understand—all of you. You need to look past the surface and see the truth for what it is. And that's not fair, not at your age. But we have no choice any longer. Things have been set in motion that cannot be undone, and we must act before it's too late."

"What the heck are we supposed to do?" Max asked, the frustration welling up inside of him. "How are we supposed to fight against a thousand-year-old witch and a Shadow King, who wants to destroy the entire world? I'm only eleven years old! What do you want from me?"

Logan paused for a long moment, his eyes locking with Max's. There was understanding in his driver's gaze. And Max could somehow sense that the man felt just as much a pawn in this game as he did. Feeling a little awkward for his outburst, Max fell silent, and his gaze dropped to the rickety floorboards at his feet.

"These cards," Logan continued, holding up the deck for all four of them to see, "are the link to everything you need to know. They were invented by the Templars as a way to pass on our great secrets and the story of our struggle. It was Iver's task to teach you what they meant. But . . ."

"What do you mean 'our secrets' and 'our struggle'?" asked Natalia. "Are you claiming to be a Templar, too?"

Logan smiled.

"And Iver?" followed Harley.

Logan's smile remained as his eyes slowly turned back to Max. The heaviness of that gaze was almost overwhelming, as Max's mind collapsed around the one thought that had been closest to his heart for some time now.

"My grandfather," Max began slowly, almost as if saying it would make it not true, "he was a Templar, wasn't he?" He knew the answer even before he spoke.

"Your grandfather was one of the greatest of our order, Max," Logan replied quietly. "And it's time you should know his death was no accident."

"What?" Max cried. "But my grandma told me all about it. Everything."

Logan shook his head. "No, Max. She couldn't tell you the truth. It wasn't time, and if I may say so, you probably still aren't ready for what you're about to hear. But we don't have the luxury of time right now. There are things in motion that drive our haste. We have to do what we can."

"So what happened?" Natalia prompted, eyes wide.

Logan took a long breath and let it out slowly before he spoke. "It was Morgan," he confessed with a sad voice, but one equally laced with measured anger. "Just as Arthur was deceived, and later the Templars, your grandfather was betrayed by that Black Witch as well."

Max's throat seemed to narrow, and he choked in both surprise and sudden grief. Morgan had killed his grandfather? The implications were staggering.

"But that's not the end of the story." Logan waved his hand. "Your grandfather may have been a Templar, but he was even more. He was the Guardian of the *Codex*—the book that you found in your grandmother's attic, and the one that has now fallen into enemy hands."

Max gasped. How did Logan know that?

"Then Max is a direct descendent of King Arthur," Natalia proclaimed, writing vigorously in her notepad. The math worked, but it still seemed impossible to believe.

"He is," agreed Logan, turning once again to Max. "Your grandfather was to pass this responsibility on to you, Max. Sadly, he never got the chance."

For a long while, no one spoke. Logan's tale painted a picture none of them could have ever imagined. Then the Scotsman cleared his throat, pacing the floorboards as if he were waiting for something to happen, or perhaps for someone to arrive. "It was Iver's job to make sure you were prepared for what was coming," Logan added. "It was a promise he made to your grandfather the day he died. And I suppose that brings us back to where we started— Round Table and what it means to you. Iver had been using it to train you in the same way your grandfather was trained when he was your age. Something happened though, and things got out of control. You found the *Codex,* Max, well before you were supposed to." Logan scratched his head, obviously uncomfortable. "It's Iver who should be telling you this, but..." Logan paused, concern furrowed on his brow. "I knew him better than most, and that's what concerns me. He's a powerful man, more than you realize, but if something's happened to him..." For a long moment no one said a word, afraid to even think what Logan might mean.

Natalia wiped away a tear as she blew her nose. The rest of the Griffins looked just as dismal. They loved Iver like a grandfather.

"Where are the Templars now?" asked Max.

"In hiding," Logan replied flatly. "Yet we have not been idle, standing ever vigilant against the dark threat of Oberon, though we have done so from the shadows. It is better that way, for we do not seek vain glory. Our time is spent developing means to combat the dark magic of Oberon and Morgan LaFey, for without magic of our own, we must rely on technology and iron."

"That's so cool," Harley said, while Ernie sat open-mouthed and Natalia composed herself enough to scribble some words in her *Book of Clues.*

"Then you have to tell me what to do," Max stated, looking at his bodyguard. "I have no idea what I'm doing at all, and lately, everything I end up trying seems to go wrong. It's all because of that stupid book. I wish I'd never found it."

"Your path is clear, Grayson. You have to get the *Codex* back," Logan replied matter-of-factly. "And soon. The darkness must be captured."

"But how? Ray's in the woods. If the Slayer finds us there, we're dead."

"Yeah, can you help us?" Ernie asked. "Ray's pretty nasty, but I bet he'd still be scared of you. And if the Templar Knights are developing cool technology, maybe you could get us a plasma gun or something. They work awesome in the movies."

Logan was about to answer when suddenly the room grew cold and the lights flickered ominously. Max watched in horror as he caught sight of the darkly familiar frost creeping up the windows and across the floorboards.

Faster than Max could have thought possible, Logan ushered the kids down the loft stairs. Max felt sure his bodyguard could have handled the Slayer himself, but protecting four children at once was probably too risky. Soon all four kids and their bikes were stuffed into the limo and they were rocketing down the gravel road toward Avalon.

Presumed Thieves and Bicycles

THE NEXT MORNING when Max awoke, Logan was nowhere to be found. The Ferrari was in the driveway, and the Scotsman's apartment above the garage was locked. Logan wasn't answering. Then Max noticed a small sign hanging inside Logan's door window.

GONE WOLF HUNTING

"Wolf hunting?" repeated Max to himself. Was there even a wolf season? It just didn't make sense. Why would Logan leave Max alone to go on a stupid hunting trip? He was supposed to be protecting Max, not off on some ridiculous expedition to shoot a wolf. Besides, with Iver missing, Logan was the only one whom Max could rely on for any answers. He was the only adult who seemed remotely able to help them, let alone believe the stories of what they had seen. Not good. Max shook his head and walked back down the apartment stairs in frustration. He didn't have a choice. He would have to take matters into his own hands.

Fortunately, Max's mother had been called out of town, which meant that he was no longer grounded (and long before the original deadline). Ernie had also been let off early for good behavior (and healthy eating). Free to govern his own life again, Max wasted no time in organizing a plan to rescue the *Codex* from Ray. And they would have to move fast now that they appeared to be in some kind of a race against Morgan to reclaim the book. Then Max had to figure out how to put everything that had been released back inside. So within an hour of his mom's departure, Max had called the rest of the Grey Griffins and hatched a plan to sneak back into the forest that very night.

The last rays of murky sunlight dipped behind the trees as three of the Grey Griffins rode their bikes through the damp city streets. Visibility was low due to the fog that had rolled in like a sea against the shore—a perfect night for keeping out of sight.

"I sure hope Natalia isn't late," Ernie said, huffing and puffing as he got off his bike when they reached Leonardo's Pizza on Main Street. Ernie never had a good eye for fashion, but that night he had sunk to a new low, bordering on the visually excruciating. Instead of wearing camouflage, or even black as the other boys were, Ernie was wearing a thick, multilayered, canary-yellow sweatsuit, with red mittens taped around his skinny wrists, black safety pads lashed to his elbows and knees, and squishy rainbow moon boots. On his head sat a dented old football helmet, with his face awkwardly enveloped by a pair of sports goggles his dad used for racquetball.

"Hopefully, she's bringing you a change of clothes," replied Harley, smirking.

"I don't care what I look like," Ernie shot back. "I can't turn into lightning like Max, so I have to do something. I'm not going in there unprepared."

Max just rolled his eyes. He didn't remember turning into light-ning. In fact, he didn't remember much about the episode in the cornfield at all. As far as Max was concerned, being able to sense where a portal might pop up wasn't really going to be very handy if it came to a fight. It wasn't like he could fly or he had heat vision. He felt just as vulnerable as the others—whether he was the Guardian of the *Codex* or not.

"So what's with those?" Max asked, trying to change the subject as he pointed to a bunch of onions tied and dangling from Ernie's belt. Max was dressed more appropriately, covered from head to toe in black, with a dark ski mask pulled up like a stocking cap. He looked a bit like a junior version of Logan, though he wasn't wear-ing any sunglasses.

"It's for scaring stuff."

"Oh brother." Harley choked on the pungent smell. "That's sup-posed to be garlic, not onions, and it only works on vampires."

"Hey, what's this?" Max asked, walking up to a sheet of paper stapled to a telephone pole.

On the flier, which was nearly lost amid the slew of missing pet proclamations, was Ray Fisher's name in bold letters. There was also a rather unflattering picture of the sourpuss himself.

"A thousand-dollar reward for anyone who has information that leads to Ray's safe return?" asked Ernie. "That's a lot of money."

"I'm surprised his parents want him back," replied Harley with a snort. "The house probably smells better without him."

"Why are you always so mean?" Natalia scolded, appearing from the shadows beneath the awning. Unlike Ernie, she was dressed for the task at hand, clad in black winter boots with white fur trim and a matching hooded jacket with gloves. "I don't care how much of a jerk Ray is, I'm sure his parents miss him very much."

In fact, Ray's parents weren't the only people concerned about his disappearance. The whole town was in shock. The possibility of a child's abduction had rocked Avalon to its very foundations. Never had something so frightful happened, and they simply didn't know where to turn. Was anyone safe anymore? And what about all the disappearances of animals? Was it all related?

They'd even launched a countywide manhunt to search the surrounding fields, but nothing had come up. Then again, the Griffins knew why. Ray hadn't been abducted. He'd been devoured by dark magic. But who would believe that story? If they told anyone, they'd probably all be locked up in the loony bin and no one would be left to save the world.

"Put some of these in your pockets," ordered Natalia as she reached into a dirty cloth bag and pulled out a handful of nails.

"Nails?" exclaimed Ernie. "I thought you were going to bring us weapons or something."

"Iron nails," Natalia explained as she handed the first fistful to Harley. "We all know faeries hate iron. Even a tiny touch with iron will hurt them."

"What am I supposed to do with them?" complained Ernie as he shoved several of the nails into his jacket pockets. "Ask them to hold still while I go get a hammer?"

"Well, it's better than garlic, brainiac," Natalia shot back in annoyance, handing Max the last of the nails. "And it's all we have. So it will just have to do. If Logan has a better idea, then I'll listen."

"He's not coming," Max said flatly. He hadn't had the heart to tell them yet of the Templar's mysterious disappearance. Especially, Ernie, who had already declared that the only way he was going back into the forest was if Logan was there to protect them.

"What?" Natalia and Ernie cried simultaneously.

"He left a note saying he'd gone wolf hunting. And I can't find him anywhere."

"Wolf hunting?" Natalia repeated with a frown as she jotted down a note in her *Book of Clues*.

"Maybe the Slayer got him." Ernie's teeth began to chatter in fright.

"Nothing we can do about it now," Harley said in a matter-of-fact tone. Losing Logan was unexpected, but Harley was the type of kid who would have walked into the forest all by himself if he had to. And tonight would be no exception.

"That's right," Max echoed as he looked in the direction of the old woods. "Besides, if Logan were here, and one of us were missing, he'd do the same thing. We have to go on."

"I want to go home," Ernie muttered, his head slumped forward with the weight of the football helmet. He looked pathetic—which was exactly the look he was going for.

"Ah, don't worry, Ernie." Harley patted him on the shoulder confidently. "I won't let anything happen to you. Besides, I've got a little surprise, too," he said as he pulled off a dark glove and showed his fist to his friend. On his ring finger sat a heavy iron ring with a large Templar cross on its face.

"Where'd you get that, Harley?" Max exclaimed in wonder as he moved in for a closer look.

Harley shrugged with a sly smile. "Found it at a garage sale. I think it's a Freemason ring or something. Some old guy didn't want it anymore, I guess. But it has a cross on it just like your necklace, so I picked it up. Only a dollar. Totally cheap."

Max returned the smile. Not only did the Grey Griffins act like a team, but now they were starting to look the part. That was, everyone except Ernie and his rainbow moon boots.

"What do you plan on doing with that ring, Harley?" wondered Ernie.

"I'm going to punch Ray in the mouth," Harley said confidently, as if it were already written into the script for the night's exploits.

"Revenge is not attractive, Harley," chastised Natalia crisply. "At any rate, we'd better get moving. My parents think I'm sleeping over at a friend's house. If they see me out here, I'm in big trouble."

"So let's go, already," pushed Harley, whose mom was working the evening shift and wouldn't be home for hours.

"Ladies first," Natalia called as she rode her bike ahead of the others and back onto the street. "We just need to make one little stop first."

"What are you talking about?" complained Harley.

"Never you mind, Harley Eisenstein. Just follow me. And hurry."

It took at least three blocks of hard pedaling for the boys to catch up with Natalia's pink bicycle with the banana seat, but by the time they did, she had already skidded around the street corner and leaned it up against a slimy brick store wall.

"Why are we stopping here?" asked Ernie, who was nervously patting down his pockets in search of a candy bar.

"Because if you manage to keep your eyes open and your mouth shut, you just might see something. Look over there." She pointed in the direction of Iver's Shoppe of Antiquities, across the street.

"Is Iver back?" asked Max, hope welling.

"Shhh!" hushed Natalia. "Watch."

At first Max couldn't see a thing. All he could hear was Ernie's heavy breathing, but soon his eyes caught a flicker of movement behind the dark windows of Iver's store. A few moments later he heard the doorbell chime as the screen door swung open and a dark shape walked out. The shadowy figure looked right, then left, then turned and locked the door.

"I saw him going in as I was riding to meet you," Natalia said.

"Who is it?" wondered Ernie.

"I don't know," Natalia replied.

"What's he carrying?" asked Harley.

"Maybe it's a robber," Ernie gasped.

"A robber wouldn't lock the door on the way out," countered Max.

"Perhaps," Natalia mused. "Unless he was trying to cover his tracks. But it's not Iver—that much I know. One of us is going to have to go over there and find out."

"What?" squeaked Ernie.

"I'll do it," said Harley without pause. In a blur, he launched his bike from the alleyway, speeding full tilt at the shadowy figure.

"He's crazy," gasped Ernie. "He's completely lost his mind!"

With a squeal, Harley's dirt bike skidded, slid, and slammed right over the stranger's toes.

"Ouch!" the man cried as all the packages he was carrying flew into the air. At first, he reached for his wounded foot, but then thought better of it and made a quick snatch at the boy on the bicycle, but Harley was too fast for him and was halfway down the street before the man realized his fingers had only grasped air.

"Why don't you malcontent urchins watch where you're going!" he shouted, shaking his fist.

"Hey, that's Dr. Blackstone," Natalia gasped, recognizing the eccentric vocabulary immediately. The kids hadn't seen the Gestapo-like band instructor too much since that day the fountain had erupted in an explosion of slime. Whereas he was a usual fixture in the school passages, waiting to pounce upon anyone without a hall pass or sporting an improperly groomed head of hair, he was now seldom seen at school outside of his classes. Most of the students just thought it was a fortunate event—almost a holiday.

"What was he doing in the Shoppe of Antiquities?" asked Max.

"This mystery just got a whole lot more mysterious," Natalia murmured.

As they watched Blackstone pick up his packages, then limp away down the damp street, Harley rode up behind them. He was out of breath but had a huge smile on his face.

"Sweet, huh?" He grinned.

"You're insane," said Ernie. "But that was so cool. I can't believe you did it!"

"No big deal." Harley shrugged.

"Did you see what he was carrying?" asked Natalia.

Harley shook his head. "Not really. A couple books. Big books. And some rolled-up posters or something."

"Maps?" asked Max.

"Maybe, but the books reminded me a little of yours, Max."

Max looked at Natalia with wide eyes. "Remember? I told you Iver was reading a book just like mine. There might even be several books. I just hope Blackstone didn't get them all."

Natalia shook her head in disbelief. Blackstone, the most fearsome disciplinarian and perpetually sour teacher at King's Elementary, was now involved in the mystery. This meant that the children were no longer safe at school, either. Who could they trust? And where was Iver when they needed him most?

"What if Dr. Blackstone is really the Shadow King?" Ernie asked, wide-eyed. "He's sure mean enough."

"I'm gonna go into the shop and look around," said Max flatly, ignoring Ernie. "We need to find out what Blackstone took, and I'm the only one who knows what I'm looking for."

"I don't think so," Harley argued. "What if it's a trap?"

"I'll go, then," Natalia stated briskly as she edged her bike toward the street and looked both ways. Soon she was pedaling slowly but deliberately to the opposite alley, where she disappeared from view.

"What's she doing?" pestered Ernie. "I can't see."

"She's gonna look in the back window," replied Harley.

A few moments passed, and then a few more. The boys sat in silence, waiting for her to reappear, but when she finally did, it wasn't what they expected. Instead of sneaking back across the street in silence, she was pedaling as fast as her legs would carry her.

"What's wrong?" asked Harley as he grabbed hold of her. "Is it Ray?"

Natalia shook her head, her eyes wide in fear. "No," she huffed, "not Ray . . . and not Iver, either. I definitely saw someone, though . . . or something anyway."

"What was it?" asked Max anxiously.

"I . . . I think it might have been . . ." She paused as she looked back over her shoulder in fear. "I mean, it was dark inside. But, well, I think it might have been . . ."

"The Slayer," Max said, finishing her sentence. They all knew it would be back for them.

"I think so. It tried to attack me, but there was a window between us. Anyway, that's when I came back here."

"What about Iver?" asked Ernie in fright. "Do you think the Slayer got him?"

"I don't think the Slayer would have a chance against Iver," replied Max. "Not after what we saw back in the forest."

"What about Dr. Blackstone?" asked Harley. "How'd he get in there without being attacked?"

"He's working for someone," Max replied.

"If the Slayer is on the Shadow King's side, then Blackstone must be, too," offered Harley.

Natalia stamped her feet in the cold. "Unless Morgan gave him a magic necklace or something to protect him from the Slayer. Anyway," she continued, "it's getting late and we still have to break into an enchanted forest, find our way through an endless maze of giant trees, battle an army of goblins, find Ray, steal the book, figure out how to put everything that got out back inside, and get home before bedtime. We'd better get a move on."

The forest loomed ahead like a dark ship in the mist. Ernie was right—it was definitely getting worse. The trees were taller, the grass was longer, and vines were crisscrossing everywhere. The woods had actually devoured a good portion of the park. The swing set and the bike rack had long since disappeared under the approach of foliage. How long before the rest of Avalon disappeared?

The path leading into the woods was completely gone as well. Trees, ancient, tall, and twisted, had crowded together so closely that even a mosquito would have been hard-pressed to find a way through. Flashlights in hand, the four Grey Griffins walked up and down the tree line looking for any possible point of entry.

"Can you sense any portals, Max?" Natalia asked, not seeing any other way to get in.

Max just shook his head. Dejected, they had almost given up when Harley motioned them to come over.

"A tunnel," Harley said, out of breath, pointing just ahead of them. He had leaves on his shirt as he wiped the dirt from his hands onto his jeans. "I think it's an old water culvert. I crawled in a ways. It goes right under the trees to the other side."

Ernie eyed the dark hole suspiciously. "That doesn't look very inviting."

A moment later, they were inside. Just as Harley had explained, the tunnel was dark and damp, smelling of rotten leaves and animal decay. It was a rather gross and uncomfortable affair altogether, yet they made good progress until, as they reached the far end, they found they could go no farther. In front of them stood a rusty grate dripping with slime.

"How are we gonna get through that?" Ernie inquired with a tinge of hope as he looked at the roadblock. "Maybe we should go back. Ray obviously doesn't want us here."

Harley had other ideas. Lying down on his back and coiling his feet, he kicked with all his might. The gate shuddered, popped, then fell away from the opening.

"Last one in is a rotten egg," Harley said with a muddy grin.

Into the Woods

THE GREY GRIFFINS stepped out one by one into a wide hollow. The forest was immersed in a dim half-light that was neither night nor day, and the vegetation gave off an eerie glow, almost as if it were radioactive. Max turned off his flashlight. "Looks like we won't need these."

"Is it colder in here or is it just me?" complained Ernie, whose clothes were now smeared with mud.

"Hey, look!" Harley pointed. "A path."

Sure enough, on the other side of the hollow, the trees parted and arched like a cathedral ceiling over a grassy path. It was lined on both sides with neatly placed stones. Unlike the tunnel they had just emerged from, this definitely looked inviting.

"This is too obvious," Natalia said with suspicion. "It smells fishy to me."

"It is a little too perfect," Max agreed.

"What if it's a trap?" fretted Ernie. "You guys promised me I'd be home before my parents noticed I was gone."

"Follow me," Harley said as he sloshed through the ferns. "The sooner we get in, the sooner we can go home."

Together the Grey Griffins headed down the path under the canopy of trees. After a short time Natalia stopped and pulled a spray can from her backpack, painting a bright orange X on the path. "So we don't get lost on the way back," she explained. "A Griffin is always prepared."

"Not bad," Harley said.

"It beats bread crumbs." She smiled.

They continued to follow the path with little difficulty as it wound in and out of the massive trees. Lichen-covered boulders and thick-knotted roots created obstacles that forced them off the trail from time to time, but for the most part the going was smooth.

"Maybe Ernie's right," Max huffed, stopping to get his bearings. It wasn't as if they were lost—quite the opposite actually. The path clearly led into the heart of the forest, but that was exactly what Max was worried about. A normal woodland path would have had some twists or turns, or perhaps a fork to choose from, but oddly, their only option was to move ahead.

"We could always go back," Ernie pointed out.

"Nice try, Tweeny," Harley grunted.

"Well, I'm hungry," complained Ernie as he plopped down on the leaf-strewn ground, pulling out a chocolate bar before chomping away.

"Honestly, Ernest," huffed Natalia. "You know very well you aren't supposed to have any sweets. Now, hand it over."

"No."

"How can you just sit there and eat at time like this anyway? Why don't you try to do something useful for once?"

"I can't help it. I get hungry when I'm nervous."

"Why you don't weigh four hundred pounds is a mystery to me," she muttered, taking out her *Book of Clues* and jotting down some notes.

"What do you think, Max?" asked Harley. "Should we try breaking off the path?"

"What?" interrupted Natalia in frustration as she looked up from her tablet. "This path is leading exactly where we want to go. Why would we deliberately leave it and chance getting lost?"

"Because it might be a trap," replied Harley, irritated.

"It probably is," Max admitted. "But I don't think we have much of a choice. Let's just keep going—and keep an eye out. I have a feeling we're not alone." With that the Grey Griffins set off again, Ernie's paranoia growing with every step.

"The forest is still growing," Natalia said, looking over her shoulder nervously. Max had to agree. The air was growing considerably colder, and floating upon the rolling mist was the rotten smell of decay. Then they heard a twig snap.

"They're watching us," Ernie said, his eyes darting all about.

"Who's watching us?" Natalia replied with a frown.

"There's something up there," whispered Max, pointing to the branches above their heads. "It's trying to hide, but I think I saw it blink. Did you, Harley?"

Harley nodded and slowly reached his gloved hand into his pocket. A second later, he had scooped up a handful of the iron nails, pulled them out, and launched them into the shadows above.

There was a bloodcurdling screech from high above them, and then two or three nails, smoking as if they had been set on fire, fell back to the ground near Harley's feet. The eyes had disappeared.

"See," Harley said with a smile. "We can tackle anything. You just wait and . . ."

Unfortunately, Harley never got a chance to finish, for just at that instant a snarling monster materialized from the shadows, smashing Harley to the ground. The creature was as big as a truck, with a slavering mouth of broken teeth. Infuriated, the monster howled in pain as the smell of burned flesh seeped from its wound.

Ernie, still wearing his ridiculous football helmet, stood motionless, mouth agape, as the beast pinned Harley to the ground. Natalia was frozen to her spot as well. They were powerless against anything like this. Max had been a fool to think they could just sneak into the forest, steal the book, and walk back out alive. It had been Max's idea. And now his best friend was paying for Max's blunder.

In that moment, a flash of anger, like a lightning bolt, struck Max. Just as had happened in the cornfield, a blue field of electricity sparked and shot across his whole body, leaping from his hands and blazing from his eyes. The difference between now and that first time in the field was that now Max knew what was going on. Power. The desire to protect Harley consumed him, but just as the monster's misshapen hands wrapped around Harley's throat, Max noticed something odd. Where the iron nails had struck the monster, its skin was altogether different! Instead of a rocky hide like the rest of the beast, there sprang a smoking tangle of spiky fur—and the monster's eyes were strangely familiar.

"Sprig?" Max gasped, the electricity dissipating into the air instantly. He was in shock, his voice barely above a whisper as he remembered . . . spriggans could change their shape, just like that first night when Sprig had turned into a tiny dragon. "Sprig, is that you?"

The creature hesitantly loosened its grip and turned to regard Max with sad eyes and a single silver tear. Like ice melting away in a summer sun, the monster's form diminished, leaving only the spriggan standing on Harley's chest. Cradling her wounded paw, Sprig limped over and began to cry.

"Why did Max let him hurt us?" she whined pitifully, obviously in a great deal of pain. "Why? We trusted you. And you attacked us with iron."

"We didn't know it was you, Sprig," Max explained, kneeling down beside the wounded faerie. "Why didn't you say something?"

"And why were you following us?" Natalia demanded as she helped Harley to his feet. "That's very rude."

"To protect Max," the spriggan whimpered as she licked at her paw mournfully. Max felt awful. If he had only known it was her . . . "Max should not be here. Not in the forest. *He's* looking for you. You are in terrible danger. How can Sprig protect Max if he won't listen?"

"I'm sorry, Sprig," Max apologized. "Really, we didn't know it was you. I would never have hurt you. You saved my life, remember?" Instinctively, Max reached out to pet her on the head, trying to comfort the little faerie. But she shrank from his touch with a sharp hiss.

"We aren't giving up," Natalia said defiantly as she looked straight into Sprig's eyes. "We're going to rescue the *Codex* from Ray, and there's nothing that can stop us. So there!"

Sprig began to reply, then paused for a moment, listening. Suddenly, her eyes grew wide with fear and her tail curled tightly around her.

"It's too late. You should have listened!" Sprig cried as she disappeared in a puff of smoke.

"What was all that about?" asked Ernie in confusion. "Where did she go?"

"I don't know," Max replied as he scratched his head.

And then the forest started to shake around them.

"Let's get out of here!" Harley ordered, half dragging Ernie as he took off in a sprint after Max and Natalia. Goblins had appeared from nowhere and were uglier, meaner, and smellier than Harley had ever imagined, and they opened fire on the Grey Griffins with a hail of withering arrows and rocks. Hundreds of them swung from tree limb to tree limb, as others loped, hopped, ran, or leapt down the path—their awful snarls and wicked laughter echoing in the Grey Griffins' ears. And all about them, a frost seemed to spread.

The goblins were twisted and small with scaly green skin. Their bristly arms were long and powerful, with muscles stretched taut like steel cables. Jagged teeth littered their wicked mouths, popping out at odd angles, glinting like razors in the light. Some of the goblins wore armor, while others wore animal skins—but all of them carried weapons: wooden bows, notched daggers, and stone axes.

"They're gaining on us!" shouted Harley.

Then Max did something he knew he shouldn't have done—he

turned and looked back. And as he took his eyes off the path, a snarling goblin swung out of the trees and pinned him to the ground in a mighty grip of malice. Max looked up in horror as the hideous creature raised a stone ax above its head, preparing to make short work of him. But at that moment a softball-sized rock smashed into the goblin's face. The beast crumpled to the ground with a shudder as Natalia helped Max back to his feet.

"Thanks!" Max called between breaths as he rejoined the race.

"Don't . . . ," Natalia puffed, "mention . . . it." She then fumbled awkwardly through her pockets and pulled out a handful of nails. With a glance over her shoulder, she let them fall to the ground, where they bounced and scattered. The reaction was immediate. The goblins that were unfortunate enough to step on them fell to the earth shrieking in pain and anguish.

"Everyone!" Natalia called. "Throw your nails down on the ground. Now!"

And they did.

The plan was working marvelously, as the tangle of goblins that formed over the carpet of iron nails grew by the second. For the first time since the chase began, the Griffins felt as if they might actually have a chance to survive. They raced ahead.

A few moments later, not hearing the slightest sound of pursuit, Max chanced another look over his shoulder.

"Hey," he called to the others, out of breath. "Look."

The other Griffins skidded to a halt, looking back. Sure enough, the goblins had given up the chase. In the distance they were jumping up and down, waving their weapons in the air and beating their chests in anger. But they continued to shoot their black arrows, forcing the four to hide behind a tree for safety.

"Why aren't they following?" Harley wondered aloud as he tried to catch his breath. "I mean, we're out of nails, and they could just as easily go around them anyway. . . ."

"Maybe they're tired," wheezed Ernie as he patted his pockets looking for his inhaler. This was a little too much exercise for an asthmatic. He was just lucky he was still breathing.

"Um, guys?" said Natalia, tapping Max on the shoulder. "I think I know why."

"What are you talking about . . . ," began Harley as his words trailed into stunned silence. Standing before them was a withered gray hill steeped in mist. The top was crowned with a ring of hulking stone slabs pointing toward the sky like jagged teeth.

But that wasn't what the Grey Griffins were looking at.

In the midst of the stone circle, awash in a pale blue glow, a boy levitated in the air. He was lying on his back with his hands folded over his chest like a vampire, but this was no ordinary boy. Long spiraling horns rose from his forehead, and his skin was the deep blue of a winter's night, scaly and cold.

"Is that Ray?" gasped Ernie, his jaw dropping open in the realization.

"What's left of him," Max replied slowly.

17   A Narrow Escape

"ONLY MAX'S BOOK matters now. Ray's not important," reminded Natalia as the Grey Griffins huddled together in the shadow of a tree line. They were separated from the ghostly hill by a miniature forest of mushrooms, which seemed to surround the mound entirely. On the far side of the rise, like an ancient gravestone in the mist, loomed a stone altar that held upon it the missing *Codex*.

"So do we just run up there and grab it?" offered Harley, eyeing the distance. "I can get up there and back in twenty seconds. Time me."

"You're so hasty," Natalia scolded. "Don't you know anything about faerie hills?"

"What are you talking about?" asked Harley gruffly. As far as he was concerned it was time for action, not talk.

"Faerie hills are filled with gold and magical secrets, as everyone knows. They're some of the most revered places in the whole world. They are supposed to be protected by armies of faeries and horrible curses. I don't think we should go up there."

"How does she know stuff like that?" complained Ernie, though he secretly hoped Natalia's news might keep them from having to go any farther.

"It's called reading, Ernest Tweeny. You'd be surprised what you find out," Natalia answered sharply.

"Unfortunately, we don't have much of a choice," Max said.

"So what are we waiting for?" asked Harley, raring to go.

"Well, if you run into a faerie, and they offer you food, don't take it," Natalia continued, looking directly at Ernie. "You'd better turn it down. If you take just one bite, you'll end up as a slave to the faeries forever."

"Anything else?" Harley asked, rolling his eyes. He obviously wasn't taking Natalia's warnings terribly seriously, though, from the look on Ernie's face, he certainly was.

"Maybe I should just go," Max said, not wanting to put his friends in any more danger than he already had. Faerie hills didn't sound like the safest of places—whether Ray was there or not.

"I think it's best we go together," noted Natalia as she took a cautious step into the sea of toadstools. Satisfied, she turned and waved for the other three to follow. "I know everything there is to know about faeries. Just follow me. Come on. It's safe."

Unfortunately, Natalia was wrong—dead wrong—for just at that moment the glade flooded with a rush of tiny figures flying, walking, skipping, and floating. They were faeries—thousands of them. Too late Natalia realized she had made a costly mistake, for when she looked down she realized she was standing smack in the middle of a toadstool ring—always a bad move. Toadstool rings were one of the most powerful traps in the entire faerie world. How could she have been so careless?

"Uh-oh," she murmured, suddenly unable to move. Helplessly, she watched as a strange procession of faeries entered the toadstool ring. They were led by a diminutive creature no higher than Natalia's waist. He was playing a flute made of green willow reeds and had long pointy ears, a bare chest, and the legs of a goat. Slowly at first, dozens of faeries joined into a bizarre dance, dressed in everything from spiderwebs and mushroom caps to fantastic gowns of lace with small shimmering jewels that flickered in the twilight. Male and female, grotesque and beautiful, the faeries formed a circle of light and song as they danced about the ring with an eerie grace.

While faerie toadstool rings were hazardous, the music played within was even more dangerous. The rhythm was hypnotic to humans, and even though Natalia knew she shouldn't, within seconds she was spellbound and found herself joining the wild faerie dance. She quickly forgot all about her quest to rescue the book and the friends she had sworn to help.

Luckily, Max and Harley had not entered the toadstool ring, because, if for no other reason, Ernie had refused to budge from the safety of the trees. But even from outside the ring, the music was powerful, and it slowly gnawed away at their willpower.

Unable to jump in and rescue her themselves, they watched helplessly as Natalia spun around and around, her flowing red braids shimmering in the strange misty light. With an enchanted grace, she pirouetted and leapt through the air, all with an odd yet satisfied glee mirrored in her vacant eyes. A small winged faerie had climbed on her back, taking a piggyback ride as it grasped her braids like reins. Others tugged at her coat sleeves, leading her around the circle of enchantment faster and faster, until it threatened to become a circle of pure light.

Max began to panic. He had no way to rescue his friend, but he couldn't leave her there, either. If he didn't do something fast, there was a good chance Natalia would disappear forever. If only he had the book, then he might be able to save her. Without it, he felt powerless.

"We've got to get Natalia out of there," Max shouted to Harley, who nodded in return. Together, they cautiously approached the circle where the faeries were moving faster and faster. As Natalia flashed by, she gazed blankly at her friends without the slightest sign of recognition.

Max knew the time for thinking was over. When Natalia came back around, he cinched his arms around her waist, careful not to step inside the ring. But she was moving too fast. Like the wind, she was ripped from his arms. Max wasn't strong enough, and the way the faeries in the ring were looking at him, they wouldn't tolerate another attempt.

"Harley, help me!" Max shouted as the larger boy wrapped his arm around a nearby tree and placed his other arm around Max. Ernie just stood there in amazement, his mouth hanging open.

"I've got you," Harley called over the music as he kicked at a nearby faerie that was crawling up his leg. "Do it!"

"Don't make them mad," Max yelled, hoping the faeries wouldn't retaliate. "Let's just get her out of there. Ready?"

Harley nodded.

"One . . . two . . . three!"

Yanking Natalia out of the ring with all their might, the three friends came crashing down on one another in a pile of elbows and knees. Immediately, the glade fell under a shadow of impenetrable darkness and eerie silence. As Max had suspected, it had been a trap. Maybe Ray hadn't built it, but hiding the book on an enchanted faerie hill surrounded by toadstool rings was a very effective way to keep visitors away.

"What happened?" Natalia mumbled sleepily as she regained her ability to think.

"Faerie ring," replied Max from somewhere nearby as the light slowly returned. "You walked right into the middle of it."

"Oh, that's right," she murmured as if waking from a dream. Fortunately for her pride, she was too dazed to realize that she had been the only Griffin to not pay attention to her own warning about faerie hills.

"Okay, what's the plan?" Harley asked, surveying the surroundings as Natalia continued to collect her wits. Faerie magic, as they were discovering, was powerful—even deadly. "I think we can get across the mushroom patch without a problem; we just need to be careful where we step."

"I don't know," Max said, looking up the grassy hill toward Ray. Their old schoolmate looked fiendish in the eerie light. And while he may have appeared to be sleeping or perhaps even dead, Max knew better. "I don't think it's as easy as grabbing the book and running. Not after what just happened. Ray's probably got something worse up there, just waiting for us to touch the book."

"As I see it, there are two possibilities," Natalia answered, seemingly back from the trance as she browsed through her notes. "I've seen a movie like this once."

"You've got to be kidding." Harley rolled his eyes in exasperation. "Well, this isn't a movie."

Natalia just ignored him and kept on reading. "The first possibility is that moving the book, even an inch, may trigger a defense mechanism of some sort—possibly a giant man-crushing boulder or bottomless pit."

Ernie shivered.

"And the second possibility?" Max sighed, hoping this one might be a little better.

"The book is just an illusion. It isn't really there at all."

"How about number three?" Harley shook his head in annoyance. "I just grab the book and nothing happens? Because that's what I think."

"It's possible," Natalia admitted, biting her lip. "But it isn't likely. Ray isn't stupid, you know."

"We don't have much of a choice," Max sighed in frustration. He didn't like their odds. Even if they were able to escape with the *Codex*, there was an army of goblins waiting for them back down the only path that led out of the forest.

"Well . . ." Harley looked at Max expectantly. While the rest of the Griffins would have preferred to avoid the encounter, Harley was perfectly willing to go up there and do the whole thing himself. Especially if it meant getting a chance to even the score with Ray. "Are you going to let me go up there or not?"

"No," Max said, shaking his head. "This is something I have to do. But . . ." He paused as he looked up at Ray hesitantly. "Get ready, because we may need to make a run for it."

"Good luck," offered Ernie, relieved to not be going along. He would have, of course, but he was awfully glad to not have been asked.

When Max cleared the mushroom barrier, careful to avoid stepping in any more toadstool rings, he began his steady ascent up the faerie hill toward the *Codex*, keeping a wary eye out for any gravestones or strange faeries offering him food. On his right, he could see Ray, who lay floating eerily in the fog with a weird icy light flashing around him like a protective shield. Max could see Ray's blue-skinned chest heave up and down in apparent sleep. He was also able to see the black horns and his razor-sharp claws up close. If Ray woke up, Max would be in big trouble.

But he forgot all about that when his eyes fell upon the stone slab that lay in front of him. There rested his magic book. Once again within reach, the *Codex Spiritus* flared with golden light as Max approached. It was no illusion.

"Hi," Max whispered as the warm glow washed over his body. If what Logan had told him was true, then the book did belong to Max, or at least its safety was his responsibility. The more he learned, the more his heart accepted the possibility of his role. Cautiously, he stooped over to get a better look.

The lock was still intact. "So," he whispered in relief. "Ray wasn't able to open you after all." But if Ray hadn't opened it, then where did the crows that attacked the school come from?

Morgan LaFey.

It had to be her, Max realized. After Logan's story, that seemed like just the sort of thing she'd do. But Max couldn't dwell on it—not when he was this close to rescuing the book. So licking his lips in nervous anticipation, he stepped closer to the stone altar. Max's hands trembled in fear as he began to reach for the *Codex*. What if Natalia was right? What if touching the *Codex* triggered a terrible trap? Max's mind spun in a thousand directions as his fingers grew ever closer to their goal. With only a few inches left, Max closed his eyes, not wanting to witness his own death.

Just before he reached it, sparks of blue fire flew into the air as a burning sensation shot up Max's arm. In seething pain, he screamed. Only then could Max see a barrier of cold blue magic surrounding the *Codex*. A series of silver symbols etched like fire upon a glowing wheel hovered over the book. There were at least a hundred of the ethereal disks spinning one direction, then the other, each to its own rhythm and purpose. Max felt as if he were gazing upon a magical safecracker, hammering away at the lock on the *Codex*. How long could the book hold out?

"Max!" Harley shouted as he and the others raced up the hill. "Are you all right?"

Just then, laughter, deep and menacing, echoed behind Max. "Welcome to my new home," Ray said in a hollow voice dripping with malice and hate. The hair on Max's neck stood on end as he turned slowly to face his archenemy. "I was wondering when you would finally get here. Do you like what I've done with the place?"

Ray seemed to have grown in stature as his sickly blue skin glistened in the light radiating from Max's book.

"We can help you, Ray," Max offered, though he wasn't sure how. "Just let me have the *Codex* back, and I promise I will find a way to fix what's happened to you."

Ray laughed once more as he flexed his powerful arms in obvious pride. "Help me?" he said scornfully. "I have everything I've ever dreamed of. Life has never been better."

"What about your parents?" Natalia protested as she stepped protectively in front of Max. "They have the whole town looking for you."

"You're messing with things you don't understand, Ray," Max pleaded. "You have to trust us."

"Trust you? The boy who has had everything handed to him on a silver platter? No, I won't trust you. Instead, I'm going to make you pay for all the times you've tried to humiliate me."

"Ray . . . ," argued Max, "we used to be friends. Don't you remember?"

"Things change, Max," replied the monster as his yellow eyes smoldered. With that, he slapped Natalia violently, sending her rolling to the ground. "You're mine, Sumner!"

As Ray reached out for Max's throat, Logan's kung fu training kicked in. Reflexively, Max deflected Ray's lunge, sending the monster sprawling. With a frustrated growl, Ray rolled back to his feet. But this time, he didn't look as confident. Max had surprised him. Ray might have been more powerful, but he was unsure how to take advantage of that power.

"Guess you underestimated us, eh, Ray?" Harley jeered, stepping again between Max and the blue boy.

"I beat you at the Turtle Cove already, trailer trash. You want me to do it again?"

"I've been looking forward to this for a long time. Let's see if you've got what it takes to do it again."

Ray spit and let out a howl as he launched into the air, flying toward the Griffin in rage.

Ray was fast. But Harley was smarter. As the wretched beast-boy was about to land outstretched claws on his enemy's neck, Harley ducked, squared his shoulders, and drove his elbow into Ray's ribs, as Ray flew overhead. Ray plummeted to the ground in a tumble. Harley was on him in an instant, pressing his advantage. As Ray struggled to his feet, Harley's gloved fist caught him on the jaw, spraying spit and yellow blood into the air. Ray fell under Harley's flurry of fists. Max looked on with hope. No matter what he looked like, Ray was apparently no match for Harley Davidson Eisenstein.

But Ray was growing stronger by the moment; with an unexpected twist, he managed to kick out his legs and topple Harley, pinning him to the ground with his wicked hands.

"Now who's stronger?" Ray asked with a playful sneer as Harley struggled to get free. Ray opened a hand and dropped Harley's missing knucklebones to the ground, smoking as if they were on fire. "Looking for these, Harley? Well, guess what? Finders keepers!" Then, just as Max was about to shout out a warning to his friend, Ray violently head-butted Harley.

"Oh my goodness!" Natalia shouted in horror as she watched

Harley's body go limp. Without thinking about the consequences, she sprang to her feet and rushed at Ray, hitting him as fast and as hard as she could. For a brief instant, Ray backed away, confused. That was all the distraction Max needed. With a burst of speed, he tackled Ray around the middle, sending both of them to the ground. Natalia, in righteous fury, dove into the fight, followed closely by Ernie, whose courage had been reinvigorated at the sight of his friends' tenacity. Quickly, they helped Max pin their enemy to the ground. Ray might have been able to get out from under Harley, but toppling three Griffins at the same time was another matter altogether.

"All right, Ray," Max shouted as he pressed his knee against Ray's shoulder, trying to use leverage as Logan had taught him. "Do you give up?"

"You're dead," Ray spit. "You and your pathetic little friends."

Max smiled down at him. "How are you gonna do that when you're lying on your back?"

"Oh, I've got a few tricks of my own." Ray smiled back, and before Max knew what had happened, Ray spit hissing slime from his blue lips directly into Max's face. With a cry, Max rolled off. He was blind.

Ray threw off Natalia and Ernie, jumping to his feet. With a look of glee, he walked over to where Max was struggling and raised a clawed fist in the air. They all knew it—Ray was going to kill Max right there on the faerie hill.

"You know, Max," Ray said with a laugh, "it's too bad you're blind. You're going to miss your own death."

"Eat iron," came Harley's voice, appearing from out of nowhere. Ray barely had enough time to realize his danger when Harley's fist, the glove now removed and the iron ring shining in the moonlight, crashed into his jaw. As the metal came into contact with his new faerie skin, there was an explosion of heat and smoke. Ray cried out in pain, falling to the earth as he screamed and convulsed.

"What have you done to me?" he shrieked at Harley, clawing desperately at his smoking wound.

"Iron," Harley replied as he held up his fist so Ray could see the steam rising off the ring. "Faeries hate it. And now that you're one, I thought you'd hate it, too. Want some more?"

Ray shrieked as Harley drew near, scrambling to his unsteady feet. With a cry of anguish, he launched into the air and disappeared into the darkness of the woods. The Griffins were alone on the hilltop.

"Are you all right?" Natalia shouted, running over to Max, who was struggling to his feet.

"I think so," Max answered, wiping the remainder of Ray's yellow spit from his face. "I can see a little bit now, even though it's fuzzy."

Harley, on the other hand, had taken a beating. Ray's head butt had left its mark, and a trickle of dark blood was running down from Harley's brow.

"Don't worry about me." Harley smiled as he wiped the blood away from his eye. "It looks worse than it really is. Besides, I finally got my Christmas wish."

"What's that?" asked Max.

"To punch that jerk right in the mouth."

"Max," called Ernie, pointing back at the stone where the *Codex* lay. "The shield is down. I bet you can get your book now."

The book! Max spun around, and sure enough, the protective blue field had dissipated. Fearing it might reappear, Max ran over and scooped up the *Codex*, sliding it quickly into his backpack.

They had done it. Ray had failed, and the Griffins managed to defeat him on his own turf—with their own ingenuity and strength. The victory had given them hope.

That was until a black arrow shot over their heads.

"The goblins!" Harley shouted as he looked down the hill. "They made it past the mushrooms, and they're headed this way."

"What?" Ernie exclaimed. "They're still after us?"

"Where are we gonna go?" Natalia asked, looking around the hilltop in panic.

The air around Max seemed to spark with electricity. "I think I know a way out," he cried.

"What? Where?" Harley shouted.

"This way," Max called as he ran down the far side of the faerie hill and disappeared into the thick canopy of trees. In a furious chase, his friends followed. Soon they had found another path and were moving along it at a great speed, zigzagging in the darkness. But the goblins had found it, too. And with every second, they were gaining.

"Where are we going?" Ernie called in fright.

"A portal," Max shouted back over his shoulder. "It should be close now. I can feel . . ." But before he could finish, Max had vanished.

"Hurry up, Ernie!" Harley shouted as he disappeared into the portal. Natalia vanished a second later.

Unfortunately, Ernie, trying to duck under an overhanging branch, failed to see a mossy stone lying rather inconveniently in front of his foot. With a yelp, he stumbled over and landed face-first. But while his football helmet had saved his nose from being smashed, Ernie was far from out of danger.

He was within inches of the portal, but it might as well have been a mile. Alone and utterly hopeless, Ernie rose to his feet and slowly turned to face the ferocious horde of goblins that had swiftly surrounded him. As one, the ugly monsters pulled back their bow-strings, aiming a hundred black arrows at Ernie's heart.

A large goblin, uglier than the rest, stepped forward and pointed a nasty finger at Ernie. He would never forget that dry gasping voice as it warned: "Now you will die. . . ."

The twang of a thousand bowstrings sounded, and Ernie closed his eyes in horror.

But before the arrows could strike, a firm pair of hands reached out of midair, grabbed Ernie by the collar, and pulled him through the portal.

Ernie Rolls Up His Sleeves

HARLEY HAD YANKED Ernie through the portal in the nick of time, just as a barbed arrow shot through, plunging into the wall with a twang. Then, with a *pop*, the rift disappeared, and the Griffins were alone in the dark.

"Where are we?" Ernie asked as he pulled off his football helmet and rubbed his eyes.

"I'm not sure," Natalia answered, shining her flashlight around. "It looks like some kind of basement or cellar."

"That portal trick is pretty handy," Harley said from the darkness beyond. "That was awesome."

"Yeah, thanks, guys," Ernie said. "I thought I was a goner."

"Don't mention it," Harley said. "It wasn't a big deal."

"Yes, it was," Ernie disagreed. "And so was the way you knocked Ray around. That was awesome. Do you think he's dead?"

"No," Natalia reprimanded Ernie. "And don't say things like that. What an awful thought. Ray needs our help."

Whether Ray needed help or not, Max wasn't so sure Ray wanted help. He had changed, and from all accounts, it seemed that Ray liked the changes. But Max was changing, too. That energy he had felt when Sprig attacked Harley was kind of scary. Was he in the early stages of changing into some kind of freakish monster like Ray? Max couldn't bring himself to tell the others, fearing their reaction, were it true.

"How did you know where to find the portal, Max?" asked Harley, wiping away some blood that had run down his cheek.

Max shrugged. "I just did. I really wish I could tell you guys how I know where they are, but I just can't explain it. . . ." His voice trailed off.

"We'll find the answers, Max. We're with you all the way," Natalia assured him.

"What's this?" Harley asked, stepping over an old wooden bench toward a tall rack of shelves. Row upon row of dusty old bottles lay upon them, their noses pointing slightly downward.

"It's a wine cellar," Max said in a depressed tone. "We have one at our house, too. My dad is . . . was a collector."

"I'm taking this arrow with me," announced Ernie, spying his intended trophy in the wall nearby.

"Why would you want to even touch that nasty thing?" Natalia complained.

"Because"—Ernie smiled as he pried it loose—"if anyone ever calls me a scaredy-cat at recess again, I can show them this arrow."

"Lots of spiders down here . . . ," Harley noted. His head was pounding, and one of his eyes had swelled completely shut.

"Spiders? Where?" Ernie squealed, dropping his lucky arrow. He was afraid of everything, but some things worse than others. Spiders, as a general rule, topped the list. Size didn't matter. The small ones that snuck into your bedsheets at night were just as horrific as the fifty-foot-tall variety that squashed houses in the movies.

"Let me see your cut," ordered Natalia, shining the light right in Harley's eyes.

"I'm fine," Harley protested as he pushed the flashlight away.

"Do you guys hear that?" Ernie asked, looking up at the ceiling. The Griffins stood in the dank basement, listening as footsteps raced by above them. Back and forth, to and fro they went, and soon the room above was full of chatter and the clanging of plates and silverware.

"We're below a restaurant!" Natalia exclaimed. "With all this wine, it has to be the Café Boa. My parents always come here for their anniversary. It's the only decent restaurant in town."

Up a rickety old stairwell they crept, but just as Harley was about to turn the knob of the door, Max grabbed hold of his shoulder. "Slowly," Max whispered. "We don't know who's out there. . . ."

"Yeah," Ernie whispered, putting his football helmet back on. "Be careful. It could be a trap."

"Oh, come on. It's a restaurant." Harley rolled his eyes as he cracked open the door. "Unless you're allergic to garlic, I don't think you're in any danger."

Sure enough, it was the Café Boa. The early dinner crowd was just warming up as waiters in black tuxedos with crisp white aprons hustled by carrying trays of pasta and veal shanks. Nobody noticed the four children gazing out from the darkness of the cellar stairs.

"There." Harley pointed across the walkway. "It's the door to the patio. We should be able to sneak out."

Like marching ants, the Grey Griffins streamed out in a single file, hurrying out the patio door. But they hadn't gotten far before Max's hair stood on end. "Wait!" He motioned, crouching behind one of the potted cypress trees flanking the entrance.

"What is it?" asked Natalia. "We can't stay here, you know."

"Trouble. Look."

Sitting at an intimate table for two were Morgan LaFey and Dr. Diamonte Blackstone. Both dressed in black from head to toe, they were sipping coffee beneath a glowing heat lamp, quietly talking. Blackstone's eyes kept darting about as though he were concerned someone might overhear their conversation, and just as a waiter came over to freshen their cups, the pompous musician waved him away without so much as a thank-you.

"What are they talking about?" Harley asked, trying to peer over Max's shoulder through a swollen eye.

"I can't tell," answered Max. "But they look nervous about something." Seeing Morgan for the first time since Logan had told him about his grandfather's death was a strange experience for Max. On the one hand, he wanted to run away from the Black Witch. On the other, he wanted to make her pay.

"Can we please get out of here?" Ernie pleaded. "It's getting cold. Besides, I'm starving, and this food is making me hungry."

"When aren't you hungry?" Natalia huffed. "Put a sock in it, will you? This is important."

Max shook his head. "I wish we could hear what they're talking about. We have to find out what they are up to," he stated firmly.

"We can't all go," Natalia pointed out. "They'll see us for sure."

"I'll do it," volunteered Harley.

"No way." Max stopped. "You're in no condition to do anything."

"Then who?" asked Ernie.

"Then you," Natalia replied. "That's who."

"What?" gasped Ernie. "You aren't serious? I can't do it. I'm not a detective—you said so yourself—and I have asthma. I'd probably have an attack right there in the middle of the restaurant and blow the whole thing. I can't go."

Natalia glared back at him and shook her head. "Everyone else has been pulling their weight around here. It's about time you tried rolling up your sleeves and pitching in."

"But what if I get caught? What if they see me? I mean, you know how clumsy I am. That Morgan's a witch; you said so yourself. She'll turn me into a toad . . . or worse!"

"No, she won't," replied Max, hoping he was right. "Not in the middle of town. This is the safest place you could hope for. Trust me, she's not gonna do anything to you with all those people watching."

"All those people? They're the only two people stupid enough to sit on a patio in the freezing cold," Ernie whined.

"Just sneak up behind them by the water fountain," instructed Natalia. "It won't be that difficult. I could do it with my eyes closed."

"Then you do it."

"That's not the point, Ernest. Now, get going, and when you find out what they're talking about, come back and tell us what you heard."

"But . . . ," Ernie protested until Natalia began pinching him. So it was, like a bear being chased by an angry bumblebee, Ernie disappeared back through the restaurant. Several minutes later, Max could see Ernie's thick-rimmed glasses peering around the water fountain that sat near an ivy-covered wall.

"What the heck is he doing?" Harley asked, frowning.

"It looks like he's waving at us," explained Max, hoping that whatever it was, Ernie would stop doing it.

"That nitwit is going to give us away," Natalia complained.

"Wait," Harley said, straining to see. "I think he's trying to tell us something. I don't think he can hear what they're saying. The fountain is drowning out their voices."

"Oh no." Natalia's heart sank as she watched Ernie. "He's climbing up the wall to get a closer look. He's insane, that's what, and he's going to get us caught. I should have gone myself."

"No. Wait!" Max instructed, pulling Natalia back behind the cypress. "He's doing it."

Sure enough, despite gravity (and a legacy of clumsiness), Ernie was actually pulling himself up from the slippery fountain, inching his way up the wet ivied brick near Dr. Blackstone and Morgan LaFey.

"Yes!" Natalia cheered quietly.

"Way to go," Harley joined.

Ernie had a solid grip on the base of the railing and a decent foothold on a moldy brick outcropping. A smile spread wide as the glare of his braces flashed brightly.

"It's not over yet," Max cautioned. "Keep your fingers crossed."

"...quite surprised you managed it, Diamonte." Ernie heard Morgan's icy voice filter over the railing. "Nevertheless, I suppose a man of your obvious ambition can be unusually resourceful when required."

"You're too kind, Madame LaFey," came the band instructor's cool and measured tone. But Ernie heard something new in the teacher's voice—fear. "I have to ask," Blackstone continued, his voice cracking slightly. "What do you intend to do now that you have them in your possession?"

"That is none of your concern," replied Morgan coldly. "Even were I to tell you, I doubt your stunted mind would grasp the elegance of a design a thousand years in the making. No. And let us be clear with each other—I am using your services and paying generously for them. While you are in my employ, I expect obedience, not questions. Should the terms of our agreement no longer suit you, I am sure I can find someone else...."

"That is not necessary, my love," Blackstone countered quickly. "The terms are agreeable."

"Excellent," Morgan replied.

Then the two conspirators fell silent for a long while as Ernie could hear Blackstone anxiously sip at his coffee.

"Still...," Morgan continued, breaking the quiet. "There is another insignificant task you may perform, another service through which you can at last show your quality."

"You need but ask," Blackstone offered, his voice lowering to a whisper. "I am forever in your service, as you know."

Ernie edged closer, holding his leg over the ledge to keep his balance.

"Time is short, and every moment that passes is more precious than the next," Morgan said slowly.

"I understand," replied Blackstone, still whispering.

"I doubt it." Morgan laughed.

"Yes, my dear . . . ." Blackstone said obediently.

Ernie's face puckered. The terms of endearment Blackstone kept lavishing upon Morgan were disgusting.

"In ten days' time the Shadow . . . ," Morgan began, but before she could complete the sentence, Ernie's luck abruptly ran out. The brick outcropping beneath him crumbled. With a yelp, Ernie fell headfirst into the fountain, sending a surge of water high into the air. The splash doused the two dinner companions, and they cursed and rose to find the culprit.

Ernie didn't stick around long enough to be identified. He shot out of the fountain and ran across the busy street, disappearing into an alley on the other side. By the time the other Grey Griffins caught up with him, he had run all the way to the back door of Iver's Shoppe of Antiquities, where a broken light flickered eerily.

"Do you think they saw us?" Ernie's teeth chattered as he peered over his shoulder nervously. His clothes were dripping wet, and every time he took a step his shoes squeaked like little mice. Once he had recounted Morgan and Blackstone's full conversation to his friends, he looked down at the group in dejection. "I'm sorry. I guess I messed up everything."

"Are you kidding?" replied Max, patting his friend on the back.

"You did great." But the news was far from good. Blackstone was definitely working for Morgan. And Morgan wanted Max's book for some evil purpose. She had killed Max's grandfather, and she probably wouldn't think twice about taking care of Max in the same way.

"Except that you came here," complained Natalia as she kicked absently at Iver's door. "This is the first place she'd look, by the way. And that Slayer might still be here, too."

"Yeah, why did you come here anyway?" asked Harley. "Iver's gone, remember? Logan said so."

"What do you think happened to Iver?" Natalia asked sadly, for they still had no answers.

"I don't know," replied Max. "When Ernie and I last saw him, he said some weird things. It's almost like he knew he wouldn't be coming back. And the last thing he said was something about catacombs. But I have no idea what he meant."

"You never said anything about the catacombs before," Natalia complained. "How can I keep my notes straight if you aren't telling me everything?"

"What's a catacomb?" asked Ernie.

"It's kind of like an old underground tunnel filled with tombs," she offered. "In books and movies, they have things like dead bodies and giant rats in them."

Ernie's eyes widened in distress. That was clearly not what he hoped to hear. As he backed away from Iver's door, Ernie stumbled into a pile of rickety wooden crates, behind which, in the shadows, lay Iver's walking stick . . . and a crimson stain.

"Blood!" Max gasped as he ran over.

"He's dead." Natalia broke into full-blown tears. "Iver's really dead. Oh my goodness, I knew it."

By the look on Max's and Ernie's faces, they seemed to agree. But Harley wasn't as convinced. Ignoring Natalia's sobbing, he touched the substance, rubbed it between his fingers, and sniffed at it like a bloodhound.

"This isn't blood," Harley said calmly, brushing the red stain on his jeans. "It's candle wax."

"Candle wax?" asked Natalia in a great sigh of relief. "Are you sure?"

"Pretty sure," replied Harley as he handed the walking stick over to her. "Anyway, it's time we had a look inside Iver's shop. Maybe we can solve this mystery right now." With that, Harley led them down the alley toward the front of the building, making sure no one was following. "Act natural," he whispered, sauntering to the doorway. "We don't want to look suspicious." As he approached the door, he dug into his pocket and pulled out a small but sturdy piece of metal.

"What's that supposed to be?" asked Ernie.

"I'm going to pick the lock. What's it look like?"

"We're breaking in?" Natalia asked. "You can't be serious."

"Just be quiet and make a wall in front of me," Harley said. "Act like you're having a conversation or something."

"Hurry up," Max urged. "I don't have a very good feeling about this."

Harley tested the knob. To his surprise it turned freely, which was good, since he was having trouble seeing out of his bad eye.

Picking locks was no easy proposition. "It's. . . . " But before he could finish pointing out that the door was unlocked, Ernie grabbed him by the cuff. "Someone's coming," he whispered through chattering teeth.

"I don't hear anything," Natalia said.

"Shhh," Max whispered. "I think he's right. Harley, get away from the door. Someone is coming."

Sure enough, a moment later a soft and cheerful whistle rang through the night air.

"It's a woman," Natalia pointed out.

"Morgan!" Ernie hissed, ready to bolt.

"Stand still," Max said, holding on to Ernie's soggy sleeve. "It isn't Morgan. It's Ms. Heen."

"Remember, act natural," reminded Harley as he let go of the doorknob.

"Is this natural enough?" asked Ernie, sticking out his tongue.

"What a charming expression, Ernie," Ms. Heen said, smiling as she strode up the walkway toward them. She was wearing a casual blue skirt and a white sweater with a matching hat and gloves. In her hands she carried colored shopping bags filled to the top with glittering packages—where she came about them in Avalon was anyone's guess. It certainly wasn't the dime store.

Ernie mumbled a self-conscious "thank you" as he stepped behind Max, hoping she wouldn't notice that he was soaking wet.

"And what are you children doing here on such a beautiful evening?"

"We just came by to see if Iver was still here," replied Natalia with an innocent smile as Harley turned his swollen eye away from view. He wasn't in the mood to answer questions.

Ms. Heen studied Natalia for a moment and then smiled warmly. "I'm sorry," she said. "Iver didn't tell you he would be away on business this week?" The four friends shook their heads, looking at one another in surprise. Away on business?

"In fact," Ms. Heen continued, "that's the very reason I am here. He asked me to make sure his door was locked. Iver was telling me how he'd been a bit absentminded lately."

Natalia's eyes followed Rhiannon Heen's hand as she reached into her purse and pulled forth a golden key. With a twist and click she had locked the door behind Harley.

"There we go," Ms. Heen said with a smile as she placed the key back into her purse. "Safe and sound." Then she reached over and took Iver's walking stick from Natalia's hands. "And thank you for finding this. I know he's been terribly worried about it. Why don't I just keep it safe until he returns? Now . . . ," she began as she turned back to the Griffins. "What shall we do with you?"

"What do you mean?" asked Natalia suspiciously.

"Well, it would appear as if you four have been left with nothing to do this evening. It just so happens that I am free as well." She glanced at her watch and smiled brightly. "Why don't you come over to my house? I'm sure we have lots to talk about."

"Like what?" Natalia narrowed her eyes.

"Like cookies," Ms. Heen replied.

"Cookies?" asked Ernie, stepping back out from behind Max and rubbing his stomach.

"Yes. I baked several dozen this afternoon ... chocolate chip, macadamia nut, peanut butter, sugar, oatmeal raisin, and snickerdoodle—which I believe are your favorite, aren't they, Natalia?"

"Why would you bake so many cookies if you live alone?" replied Natalia, more than a bit wary.

"I was expecting guests." Rhiannon smiled.

"Who?" Natalia pressed.

Ms. Heen looked at Natalia in puzzlement. "Why, you, of course."

With the exception of Ernie, who was almost floating in anticipation of the gooey chocolate chips, the friends froze. The fact that Ms. Heen had shown up when she did and just happened to have a key to Iver's door was strange enough. But how could she have been expecting them? Could she read the future? Was it a trap? What did she want with them?

"Thanks, Ms. Heen, but we can't," Max replied, pushing Ernie behind him. "We actually do have plans."

"What?" cried Ernie, who was wringing water out of his shirt. "What plans? C'mon, Max, I'm starving—and cold."

"Thanks, anyway, Ms. Heen," Max maintained as Natalia gave Ernie a solid pinch to keep him quiet. "Maybe next time?"

"I'll look forward to it," Ms. Heen said with a wink as she turned to walk away, but not before pausing and turning back around. "In the meantime, I suggest you keep Harley out of sight until his eye heals. People may start asking uncomfortable questions about where you've been spending your time."

19

Unlocking Both Windows and Secrets

THE ALARM CLOCK rang sharply at six thirty in the morning as rain poured down Max's bedroom window. Slowly he rolled out of bed, his hair tousled from a rough night's sleep. Too many bad dreams. But bad dreams were a holiday compared with what he'd encountered in the forest the night before. The goblins, despite their deadly intentions, were really only an annoyance. Ray was the real problem. Or was it Morgan LaFey that was the threat? No matter how nasty, blue, and smelly Ray had become, the witch was probably a thousand times more dangerous. Max was in way over his head.

If only Iver and Logan were here, Max wished as he stretched and yawned. But there was no sense wasting time wishing for something that wasn't going to happen. They were gone, and as far as Max could tell, they weren't coming back.

Absently he leafed through a thick book that lay next to him. It had been a gift from his father—a history about the knights of the great Crusades. Max had only rediscovered it a few days before, and when he looked through it, he found a large section completely devoted to the Knights Templar. Max hadn't had enough time to read everything yet, but the more he learned, the more he doubted that he, or anyone in his family, could ever have been a Templar—despite Logan's story. And where was Logan, anyway? Max found the idea of wolf hunting preposterous.

Listlessly, he approached his window and looked out, his breath fogging the landscape in front of him. It must have been cold out, he thought—a lot colder than normal. Then he heard a soft scratching sound outside his window—the same sound he had heard at his grandmother's house the night he had discovered the *Codex*, the night he had first seen ... the Slayer.

It was back.

"Grayson, are you up yet? You're going to be late for school," his mother called, back from her trip with a vengeance. She burst through his bedroom door with Hannah in her arms. Both were looking tired.

Max looked back at the window. The Slayer had not yet appeared. Maybe, with his mom in the room, it had decided to leave? Max hoped that might be true.

"Max, why do you continue to play me for a fool?" she scolded him in an icy tone. "Rosa told me last night that you've been coming in past curfew lately. And that you've been hanging out with those friends of yours. Did you not learn anything from being grounded?" The streaked makeup around her eyes told Max she had spent another sleepless night crying. At least she never cried in front of him, no matter how much the divorce had affected her. She was too strong for that—or so she wanted everyone to believe.

"I ... uh ..." Max's mind spun, searching for a way to keep the two situations—the Slayer outside his window and his angry mom—from getting worse.

"Never mind the explanation you're about to concoct. I don't even want to know why you refuse to listen to me. You're becoming more like your father every day. . . ."

"What?" Max shouted in sudden anger. "That's not fair!"

Hannah then began to cry.

"Now look what you've done, Max," Annika said in exasperation as she cradled Max's little sister in her arms. "This is what happens when you hang around with children like Harley Eisenstein. If you keep up this behavior, I will call that boarding school in Switzerland. Don't think I won't." With that, she turned and walked back out, leaving Max alone with an anger that was quickly forgotten when he remembered what was just outside the window waiting for him.

No sooner had the door closed than a clawed hand reappeared on the window ledge. Hollow eyes turned in Max's direction as the beast pressed its nostril slits to the glass and sniffed. There was no one to save Max now, and the monster knew it. Pulling its tortured body onto the ledge, the Slayer smiled wickedly.

Max panicked, his chest constricting as his breathing grew shallow. Then his body started to tingle again and the world slowed around him. The *Codex* was lying at his feet, shimmering in golden light. Without thinking, the magic words escaped his lips:

"Kai entare kelenasiem mora soluntaria."

In response, the book rose into the air, its pages flipping by in a blur. Max feared the Slayer was about to burst through the glass. "Come on . . . ," he pleaded to the book. "Show me what to do."

The *Codex* came to rest on a blank page just as the hideous goblin pounded its fist against the windowpane. Max's heart jumped.

He hoped desperately that the glass would at least slow down the monster, but then the window slid open, the Slayer's long fingers snaking through. Why had he left the window unlocked? An instant later, the Slayer's hideous head popped inside, sniffing the air, as its nostrils oozed with slime.

That was when the open pages of the *Codex* began to change, folding in on themselves as they wrapped into a ball of energy that crackled with blue fire. Slowly, the fireball rose, spinning wildly into the air. Then, like clouds parting to reveal the sun, Max realized what he had to do. He was the Guardian of the *Codex*, and with that title came a power that he was just beginning to realize.

"Come on in. I'm not afraid of you anymore," Max, the Guardian, said through gritted teeth.

The beast didn't need an invitation. With a furious howl, the Slayer burst through the window and into the room. In the blink of an eye, it had closed the distance between itself and the boy, but Max knew that was as close as the monster would ever get.

The Slayer realized its danger too late. In one fluid motion Max caught the book's swirling globe of brilliant blue fire and wound up like a pitcher. "Catch!" he shouted, hurling the fireball with all his might.

The impact sent the monster hurtling through the air as the sphere of light expanded, overwhelming and engulfing the Slayer. It howled, flailing to break free from its magical cage, but there was no escape. And suddenly, the orb collapsed like a dying star around the goblin, and in a blur of blue energy it crashed into the *Codex* with an explosion of light.

The book fell to the ground.

Max stood in disbelief, his heart pounding wildly. He had done it. The creature from his nightmares was finally gone. Cautiously, Max walked over to the *Codex* as colors swirled on the page before his eyes, forming an image of a shadowy monster crouching in the branches of a tree. It sat there motionless, staring out with those empty eyes Max knew so well, its mouth pulled into a savage grimace of malice. Then words formed atop the page: *Slayer Goblin.*

Max slammed the book shut only to notice that the open slot in the book's cover, which he had not paid much attention to, was now beginning to glow with a soft blue light.

"Well, that's new," Max said with curiosity as he rushed to get ready for school.

Despite the relentless storm, Ms. Heen's sixth grade class marched onto the yellow school bus that would be taking them on their long-expected field trip. It was a bit of a surprise the trip hadn't been canceled. Ray's disappearance had caused such a state of alarm that most parents were even reluctant to let their kids step out the front door. But Ms. Heen had been able to charm the parents into conceding by arguing that it would do the kids a bit of good to get outside and forget about all the unpleasantness that had enshrouded Avalon. Still, there were no less than twelve chaperones clucking about the bus like mother hens. No one could blame them.

Yet the obsessive behavior of the parents was putting the students on edge—not that a trip to an archaic church crammed full of creepy paintings and dusty statues wasn't bad enough. It wasn't exactly a visit to the candy store or the toy factory, which would have been more to their liking.

"This stinks," Ernie complained, watching the rain pour as the countryside slowly passed by. "I haven't been dry in a week. Couldn't we have gone someplace else?"

"Oh, I think you'll find our trip today is exactly what you are looking for," Ms. Heen replied with a warm smile, walking to the back of the bus where the Grey Griffins were seated. "The Chapel of Mist is one of a kind, unique in the whole world. The people of Avalon are lucky to have such an amazing wonder in their backyard, don't you think?"

"I suppose," Max said, shrugging. He'd been to the Chapel of Mist lots of times before. In fact, his dad used to take him from time to time and tell him about a similar chapel in Scotland. But Max had his mind on other things. Primarily, what he would do when Morgan came looking for his book. He had a feeling that the book wouldn't work on her like it had on the Slayer. Then there was Sprig. He hadn't seen her since the forest when Harley had accidentally hurt her. As he recalled her dreadful wound and the way she was crying so pitifully, his stomach tied itself in knots. It had been an accident, but he didn't know if Sprig believed that.

Ms. Heen continued talking with some of the other students, but soon everyone fell silent. Outside the rain-splattered windows the scenery forcefully reminded them with every passing tree that the world around them was changing. The grassy lawns of the farmhouses swayed like a green ocean, thick and deep, and tree lines towered like wooden giants on the horizon. In some places they blotted out the sun altogether. Everyone knew something was happening, but no one really knew what. Except the Griffins.

"My mother thinks it's the end of the world," Scottie Johnson claimed; his bowl-cut hair lay hidden under a greasy John Deere tractor cap.

"Is that so?" Ms. Heen asked inquisitively.

"Yeah. She says that this weather is a sign that the world is coming to an end. Dad doesn't believe her, but I know the poplar tree in our front yard has grown over ten feet in the last week. And that's not normal."

"Well, we have had quite a bit of rain," Ms. Heen pointed out.

"Our entire house is covered in vines," Brooke added, who was sitting across from Max. "Every morning our gardener has to go out with clippers just to get the garage door open. He tried burning the roots with gasoline, but I think it just made the plant mad, because the next morning there was twice as many vines as before."

"I don't think it's the rain," commented Scottie. "Anyway, some of our cows went missing, too. There's no sign of them. No broken fence and no hoofprints leading down the road. They're just plain gone. How do you explain that?"

Max sat silently as the conversation murmured around him. He had a sinking suspicion that the goblins were getting hungry. All the houses and farms near the forest seemed to be affected now, and it wouldn't be long before the slavering monsters found their way into the sleepy town. Then the trouble would really begin.

The old bus rattled up the winding dirt road toward their destination. Located on the northernmost shore of Lake Avalon, the Chapel of Mist got its name from the mist that rose off the water every morning, covering the small church in a sea of fog. The ancient Gothic structure was made of gray stone and black iron. Menacing gargoyles perched high above the entry, and the windows were all stained glass. Yet unlike the rest of the town the chapel seemed to be unaffected by the overgrowth of vegetation, and the rain seemed to fall less heavy there.

"This place gives me the creeps," Ernie said as he unloaded, opening a bright orange umbrella emblazoned with a giant yellow duck. The Chapel's keeper, Mr. Thorvald, was waiting for them as they stepped out onto the muddy lot. An emaciated man with a scraggly beard and a menacing look in his eye, he strode past them in the downpour with his giant growling canine, Loki, loping by his side. The dog was immense, ill-tempered, and his neck was strapped with a bloodred collar studded with threatening-looking spikes.

"Ma'am." Mr. Thorvald nodded, tipping his hat as Ms. Heen approached.

"How do you do, Mr. Thorvald?" asked Ms. Heen politely. "It's good to see you again. It's been a long time, hasn't it?"

"T'ain't been long enough," he replied in a sour tone. "Meaning you no disrespect, ma'am."

"None taken." Ms. Heen smiled warmly as the rain fell around her. "Are you ready for us today?"

"I reckon I'm as ready as I'll ever be with this dratted weather," he said, looking hopelessly at the sky as rain skated down the deep crevices of his old face.

"Very well, then. I'll take it from here if you don't mind."

"You know your business." He nodded as he turned away. "Just keep an eye on the rascally ones. We don't need them mixed up in the business of their betters."

To someone who had never seen the inside of the Chapel of Mist before, the building was breathtaking, and much larger than one would ever have imagined looking at it from outside. The ceilings disappeared high above the swarm of damp students in the dark expanse, with arches and domes tracing intricate patterns in the shadows. Tapestries and paintings lined the cold walls, and flickering torches offered a meager light.

"With all these shadows," Ernie fretted, grabbing Harley's sleeve, "there could be an army of goblins hiding in here. Or worse. What if Ray . . ."

Harley punched his fist into his hand, remembering how much he loathed his old classmate. After their fight in the forest, Ray seemed to have disappeared. Maybe Harley had hurt him worse than he had thought. Luckily, Harley's own wound had healed up fairly well since Ray's head butt. Explaining it to his mom had been tricky, but he had managed to brush it off as an accident, which she could easily believe: Harley was an adventurous boy, constantly falling out of trees, scraping his elbows, and cutting himself on thornbushes.

"Ray's not here," replied Max as he ran his hand along an old stone sidebar lining the foyer. "I don't think he could ever come here. This place feels different. It's scary. But a different kind of scary."

"Max," Natalia whispered, pulling her friend aside. "The *Codex* is glowing bright blue. You'd better shut your backpack or you're going to get caught." Max nodded and did as he was advised. He didn't know what was going on with the book, but something had definitely changed, that was for sure.

As Ms. Heen led the students on, the Grey Griffins fell in line. The building was magnificent. All throughout were strange and wonderful works of art, mostly comprised of intricate carvings on the pillars and ceilings. Stony leaves and branches seemed to sway in the breeze of eternity as the students looked on in wonder. And behind the rocky foliage peeked mysterious faces and symbols, each more curious than the next.

"No one seems to know who built the Chapel of Mist," Ms. Heen remarked as she led the students and their overly attentive parents past two massive pillars. "It is, of course, of the European Gothic style. The problem, I hope you realize, is that if this place were truly Gothic, it would mean that it's older than Christopher Columbus."

Natalia looked over at Max and winked. Another clue to the unraveling of the mystery of the Templars? First, Ms. Heen's lecture had led them to the library, where they had found out about the link between Columbus and the Templars and America. Then, Logan's revelation that Max was a descendent of the Templars as well. And now this. Max's heart raced at the thought that he might be standing in a structure that had actually been built by one of his ancestors. But why would they have traveled all the way to Minnesota a thousand years ago just to build a chapel? It didn't make much sense.

"And this painting is called *King of Camelot*," noted Ms. Heen as they all stopped to admire a magnificent oil painting that hung in a long, lonely corridor. It depicted a very sad-looking King Arthur standing in a beautiful room, pointing downward at a table by his side, upon which sat a book that looked very much like Max's *Codex*. Behind him was an open window through which seven stars shone, and to his right was a desk with a golden pyramid and a silver compass upon it. In his left hand was what appeared to be a Round Table card, depicting the Black Witch, and on the floor lay a severed silver cord, which, as Max traced it, led back to a very dark corner of the painting where he noticed a creature hiding in the shadows. Max felt the hairs on the back of his neck begin to tingle. It was the Slayer.

"Oh my gosh . . . ," Ernie started, his eyes nearly bugging out of his head. "It's that . . . that . . . that thing!"

"I had no idea there was a picture of King Arthur here," stated Max, scratching his head in wonder as the rest of the students disappeared around the corner. The Slayer was definitely not what he had expected to see, but right here in front of his own two eyes was painted the truth behind Logan's story. Morgan was behind the death of King Arthur. But if the greatest king in all history couldn't stop her, how could Max have even the slightest hope?

"It gets worse," interrupted Harley. "Look up there."

Max found himself looking at a mural painted across the ceiling. It was a scene of a great battle between two armies. One army appeared to be made of medieval knights, red griffins emblazoned on their chests, sitting atop armored warhorses. In their hands were held white flags with the same red cross that was tattooed on Logan's shoulder.

The other army was awash in a dark shadow, but as Max looked more closely, he could see the frightening forms of countless goblins and other horrible monsters hidden within the darkness.

"Look what's sitting there between the two armies," Harley whispered.

Max saw it even before Harley had opened his mouth. There, sitting atop a golden altar, was a book, above which were written two words—*Codex Spiritus*. Suspended in midair above the book was a jewel that shimmered like a star.

"I wonder what that jewel is all about," marveled Ernie as his eyes devoured the scene before him.

The rest of the tour was rather uneventful, as was the ride back to school. Exhausted with a thousand thoughts and possibilities, Max went home right after school and spent the rest of the afternoon and early evening looking out his bedroom window deep in thought. He was in danger. The Slayer had tried to kill him. Ray had, too— twice! And by now, Morgan and Blackstone were probably devising their own plans to deal with Max. But there was a darker shadow that loomed on the distant horizon of his dreams, the Shadow King. Max knew it was Oberon, the Shadow King, who was ultimately behind everything that was happening. Max had been warned he was coming. He wasn't looking forward to that day.

With a sigh, Max pushed away his cold dinner tray, turned off his lamp, and crawled into bed. But just before he closed his eyes, a flash of light flared at the foot of Max's bed, nearly blinding him.

"Are you awake?" asked Sprig in a low whisper as she crawled out of a portal and onto his bed. She looked terrible. Her fur was disheveled, her eyes seemed distant, and the wounds that the iron nails had left on her looked horribly painful.

"Sprig! Oh gosh, I'm so sorry. It really was an accident. I would never hurt you on purpose. You have to believe me," he said in shame.

Sprig took no notice of his apology and crept closer, trembling with each step. "Did Max see it?" Sprig began, looking around nervously. What was she looking for? His book?

"See what?" Max replied in confusion.

"In the chapel today . . . ," Sprig continued.

"You were there?"

Sprig shook her head. "It is holy ground. Faeries are not permitted." Max sat there in silence for a moment, trying to sort out what she was talking about.

"The Jewel," she said softly, looking intently at Max.

"What jewel? I don't know what you mean."

"Titania's Jewel." Sprig lowered her eyes. "The Shadow King wants it back."

As if in a dream, Max recalled the painting in the Chapel of Mist, and the shining jewel hovering in the air between the crashing waves of two great armies. He also remembered that day, which now seemed a lifetime ago, when Sprig had mentioned the jewel back at the tree house. He had forgotten all about that. Putting the facts together in his head, Max quickly realized that he'd made a big mistake. He should have taken the jewel more seriously.

"Oberon is looking for it. He needs Titania's Jewel to open the Gate."

"What do you want me to do?"

"You must find it first," Sprig replied as her eyes darted to the window nervously. "It's the only way," she continued, her voice dropping to an eerie whisper. "You must find the door to the Catacombs."

Max's heart raced as he recalled Iver's last words the night he disappeared. The old shopkeeper had also mentioned the Catacombs. The pieces of the puzzle were starting to come together.

"But what if I can't find it?"

"Then Max Sumner will die."

20   The Good News and the Bad

"I THINK IT'S TIME we split up," Max began as Ernie looked at him in disbelief. Once again, the Grey Griffins tried to make themselves comfortable in Ernie's bedroom. The friends were quickly running out of places to organize their plans. And no one was more annoyed about this than Ernie, who hadn't even been consulted. Harley's trailer home was too close to the woods, almost within a stone's throw by now. Natalia's house was off-limits because her sister had the chicken pox. And Max's house, now that their tree fort had been destroyed, was off-limits to children in general, thanks to his mom. She wasn't a big fan of "urchins." Besides, Max had no intention of making her mad again and getting sent off to boarding school.

"No, seriously," Max continued. "Sprig said that we don't have much time. So if we're going to find out where the Catacombs are, we'd better start looking now."

"But why would we split up?" Ernie questioned. "Isn't that what happens in the horror movies right before everyone gets eaten by a brain-sucking zombie?"

"I've got a feeling that the answer to the Catacombs is in one of the books Iver had on his back shelf," Max replied. "The ones that look kind of like the *Codex*."

"That doesn't answer my question," Ernie maintained. "Why do we need to split up?"

"Yes, it does," Natalia countered as she pulled a compulsively gnawed apple from Ernie's sticky hands. "You just aren't paying attention. If the answer to the catacombs is in the books, then we have two places to look for them: Iver's shop and Blackstone's house."

"What?" choked Ernie. "Why Blackstone?"

"Because he was carrying a bunch of books when we saw him leaving Iver's shop the other night, that's why. Don't you remember?"

"Oh . . ." Ernie's voice trailed off as he tried to piece the puzzle together. But then his eyes shot wide open when he remembered the conversation he had overheard at the Café Boa. "I'm not going to Dr. Blackstone's. Morgan will be there. You'd have to be crazy to do that."

"Good," replied Max. "Natalia and Harley can check out Blackstone. Ernie, you can come with me. We start when it gets dark out."

"It's always dark nowadays," Natalia pointed out. "But I agree. Anyway, bring your raincoats. It's starting to drizzle."

"Do you think there will be more monsters in Iver's shop?" asked Ernie as Max turned to leave.

"Definitely." Max smiled as he patted his book bag. "But this time I've got a secret weapon."

"Did you hear that?" Ernie asked for the fifth time since they had opened the door to Iver's Shoppe of Antiquities. Max tried the key Iver had left in the envelope, but it didn't work. So the other two joined them just long enough for Harley to pick the door lock; then he and Natalia raced off in the direction of Blackstone's residence. Max and Ernie were all alone.

"No, I told you I didn't hear anything," Max whispered sharply as a bolt of lightning illuminated the room from outside the front window. The weather was only getting worse. "If you keep saying that, then I'm not going to believe you when you really do hear something."

Max shook his head in exasperation as they crept over the threshold. The door chime rang unexpectedly, announcing their presence to whoever or whatever was inside. Max bit his lip. He had forgotten about the bell. Mistakes like that could be deadly.

They waited together, hoping the sound hadn't given them away.

"This way," Max whispered after a few moments, edging by a stack of old books and a shelf full of pewter figurines. "The book I'm looking for should be over behind the counter." Ernie nodded as he unzipped the duffel bag he had brought along to hold the book once they found it.

When they arrived at the front counter, Max ducked through the opening and snuck behind the glass case holding the knucklebones. His palms were sweating as he quickly scanned the shelves for his prize. Max had never stolen anything before, but if he had to find the Catacombs, he didn't know any other way.

"Do you see it yet?" Ernie asked, chewing his fingernails.

"No," Max whispered. "I need a second to let my eyes adjust. It's dark back here. Besides, I . . ."

But before he could finish, a mysterious rattling echoed from the far corner of the room. Maybe they weren't as alone as they had hoped.

"Hurry," pleaded Ernie. "Something's in here with us."

Harley and Natalia stood under the shadow of a giant elm, staring down Rosewood Lane at Dr. Blackstone's creepy home. It was a large brick house with oddly shaped windows and a thick covering of ivy. At the moment, a soft glow was emanating from an upstairs window while the rest of the house was wrapped in a blanket of darkness.

"Now what?" Harley asked, his hands tucked in the pouch of a sweatshirt. His clothing was soaked, another example of bad planning. Natalia, on the other hand, smartly wore her bright pink rain slicker buttoned to the top with her hood pulled tight, as well as a pair of lamb's wool-lined rain boots. There was no doubt she was warm and comfortable, while Harley was wet and miserable, but he liked making things hard on himself. If everything was comfortable, he reasoned, what would the challenge be? Besides, it kept him on his toes.

"We need a closer look," Natalia said. "If Iver's books are in there, they might be locked away upstairs, maybe even in the attic. That might be where they are keeping Iver, too."

"What makes you think Iver's up there?" Harley replied incredulously. "That would be stupid to kidnap someone, and then keep them in your own house. That's the first place the police would look."

"They won't look if they don't think he's missing," replied Natalia. "Everyone but the four of us seems to think he's on a business trip, remember?"

"Just Ms. Heen. And I wouldn't call her everyone."

"We're wasting time," prodded Natalia, in no mood to argue.

With stealth they made their way down the lane, hiding behind cars and sneaking between houses until they were standing near Diamonte Blackstone's mailbox. Together the two Griffins gazed up at the house, each trying to come up with a plan.

"I have two choices," Harley offered. "I can jimmy open the lock and sneak upstairs...."

"I don't particularly like that one," noted Natalia. "Especially if Blackstone is in there. What else do you have?"

"I can try to climb the tree and look through the window," Harley replied, peering through the rain as he pointed at the twisted oak enveloping Blackstone's front yard. "But we did just break into Iver's."

"That's different." Natalia frowned. "But climbing that tree doesn't look terribly safe. What if you get struck by lightning?"

"Do I have a choice?" Harley sighed as he rolled up his sleeves. "We need answers."

Natalia nodded. "And if Iver is up there, we might be his only hope."

"He's not up there. I'm telling you. Blackstone wouldn't be that stupid." Leaving Natalia behind a hedge, Harley waded across the sea of grass toward the old tree.

The first branch was fairly high, and it took every inch of vertical jump that he could muster just to reach it. When he did, he found the rain-soaked bark slippery, making the climb treacherous.

"This better be worth it," Harley muttered under his breath, ascending the slick maze of branches. Hugging the tree as close as he could, Harley slithered up like a snake. It was messy, the bark tore at his fingers, and green moss on the limbs made the footing treacherous.

A few minutes later, with iron determination and extraordinary physical effort, Harley finally pulled himself up to the branch where he could see inside Blackstone's window. He immediately wished he hadn't.

There, standing with its back to the pane, was some kind of strange faerie. It was about the same size as a goblin, though it stood more upright, with ashen skin, gray and coarse, covering its body. A bizarre tattoo was branded onto its shoulder, and the creature was wearing armor—iron armor. Bad news.

If these monsters were immune to iron, that meant the puny weapons the Grey Griffins were carrying wouldn't do a lick of damage. Unlike the knights of old, the Griffins didn't have any swords or battle axes at their disposal—as if they could wield them even if they did. But they did have Max's magical book, and that was something. Unfortunately, Max wasn't there just now.

Harley then realized what the creature was. There was only one monster in the game of Round Table that was immune to iron. In fact, it dug deep into the heart of mountains searching for the ore. It was a kobold.

While not as vile as goblins, kobolds were far more intelligent and, consequently, more dangerous. And this kobold wasn't alone. Harley could make out two others standing guard in the tiny room, with broad shoulders and nasty teeth, each of the despicable beasts uglier than the next. Yet somehow the kobolds seemed civilized, if that was the right word, not like a wild pack of slavering animals. Much different than feral goblins, these kobolds were working as a single unit, standing watch. But over what?

From where Harley was sitting, he couldn't see the entire room, but he had to get a closer look. Cautiously, Harley inched his way out onto the rain-soaked limb, and when his eyes finally caught sight of what the kobolds were guarding, his blood froze.

"Oh no," Harley mouthed. "It's Iver!"

There, shackled to a doorway with magical bonds of red fire, was the tortured and beaten form of the Griffins' mentor. One arm, torn and bruised, was pulled high over Iver's head, fastened to the top of the door. His other arm was stretched out to the side, tied to the frame, and his feet were suspended over the floor, one atop the other. Iver's head hung limply from his shoulders, and his hair, matted and stained, clung to his face, which was cast in a sorrowful shadow. The old man didn't appear to be breathing.

A profound sadness fell over Harley as the rain fell like tears down the window in front of him. Then a fire started to burn, and anger rose. Right there, Harley vowed retribution for Iver's death, immediately starting to survey Blackstone's room for a heroic, if not foolhardy, act of vengeance. Pulling out his ring, Harley slipped it on his finger. If he could get past the kobolds, Harley's next move would be to wrap his hands around Blackstone's scrawny neck, teaching him a lesson that was long overdue.

Scattered about inside were open books, shredded notes, and old yellowed maps. Harley recognized many things from Iver's Shoppe of Antiquities, yet many others were unfamiliar: strange mechanical devices, drawings of mysterious symbols, and over-turned bottles of brightly colored liquid. It was clear enough that Iver had been kidnapped because of something he knew. But what did Blackstone and the kobolds want? And had they succeeded?

A door on the far side of the room swung open, and the dark form of Dr. Diamonte Blackstone walked in, followed by another armored kobold—this one with a long knife gripped in its hand. Smiling, Harley whispered, "You're mine."

He couldn't hear what was being said, but Harley watched with venom in his eyes as Blackstone seemed to bark orders at the dark faeries. Seconds later, Iver's body fell from the doorway and crashed to the ground. The kobolds laughed, slapping one another on the back in pride. Then as one, they huddled around Iver's motionless form, heaving him up on their shoulders before carrying him from the room like cartoon ants marching off with a picnic basket.

Blackstone made ready to follow, but just as he was about to leave, he stopped and grew very still, his back to the window. Then Harley felt the hair on his neck tingle.

Slowly, Blackstone turned to face the window, his dark eyes lit with the fires of suspicion. He seemed to know he was being watched.

Harley, suddenly losing his bravado, started to inch backward, trying to hide in the branches as Blackstone approached in slow, deliberate steps. There was nowhere for him to go, and if Blackstone drew any closer, Harley would be discovered. Panicking, Harley scrambled and tried to swing down to a lower limb, but the rain betrayed him. With a cry, he lost his footing and plummeted to the ground.

"They're only garden faeries." Max sighed in relief, shining a flashlight across the room. "Not much bigger than your finger." He knew they were garden faeries, for unlike Ernie, who lately had been too scared of his Round Table cards to look at them, Max had spent the better part of the last few evenings trying to memorize everything he could from his own deck. Luckily, he had a garden faerie card—actually two. Even more luckily, they were virtually harmless, or so the card had said.

"Oh, thank goodness," Ernie said, recovering his composure. "I thought for sure it was that Slayer back from the dead." He stood up and looked around, feeling a bit braver. "I wonder what they're doing here. There's no garden."

"I don't know," admitted Max.

"Maybe Iver put them here to protect his store?"

Max shook his head. "I don't think so. If they were for protection, then how did Blackstone get in and out of here safely?" Ernie nodded as one particular green faerie darted past his nose, sending a shower of faerie dust onto his glasses.

"Then maybe Dr. Blackstone put them here?"

Max ignored the question as he began his search in earnest. "If I were a magic book, where would I hide?"

"I'll stand watch while you look," offered Ernie, waving at another faerie that had landed on the glass counter. She seemed rather pretty, with lustrous eyes, glittering wings, and a sparkling yellow dress. It was just the sort of faerie one might expect to find on the petal of a tulip.

Max started to poke around the bookcases behind the front counter. He was feeling for hidden drawers or cubbies as more faeries flew into the room, studying the boys.

"Wait a second!" Max exclaimed. Scattered haphazardly across the glass counter was a handful of bullets. Thirteen to be exact. Each was polished to a brilliant shine, and as Max picked one up to study it more closely, he could see the words *100% Troy Silver*. Beneath them lay a folded note written in hasty script that read, *For Logan*.

Silver bullets? he thought. Why would Logan need silver bullets? Unfortunately, Max didn't have time to put the puzzle together.

As the minutes went by, the room began to fill with hundreds, if not thousands, of the dainty faeries. With silken butterfly wings and clothes made of leaves and flower petals, some of the faeries peered out of bookshelves, while others hung from the chandeliers.

"Uh, Max?" Ernie's voice wavered as he started to feel outnumbered.

"I found it!" Max shouted, pulling out the exact book he had been looking for. It had been under a pile of invoices next to the cash register, hidden in plain sight. But as he went to place the book in the bag hanging from Ernie's shoulder, the army of faeries turned and let out a great hissing sound, like a room full of snakes. The air around the boys started to hum with electricity as Max froze and looked around in astonishment at the scene he had up until now been oblivious to. As he moved the book closer to the duffel bag, the hissing grew louder, and the look on the faerie faces changed from inquisitive to wicked. This was a trap. But who had set it? Certainly not Iver.

Max gently put the book back down on the counter.

The humming stopped. The faeries grew silent.

"This isn't going to be easy," he muttered under his breath.

Harley crashed through the branches, falling like a stone into a pile of leaves.

"Are you dead?" Natalia asked as she ran over.

"I don't know," Harley replied, coughing. "Maybe you should ask me tomorrow."

"You sure are lucky this pile of leaves was here," she replied as she helped her friend to his feet.

"If I was lucky, I wouldn't have fallen," Harley retorted, trying to catch his breath as he brushed himself off. Then, as his memories came back about what he had seen in the upstairs window, he turned to Natalia and shook his head in sadness. "I have some bad news. . . ."

But before he could complete his thought, the porch light flickered on, and Blackstone shot through the front door like a rocket, scanning the yard with his wild eyes. "All right! Who's out here?"

he bellowed from the crumbling concrete steps. "Show yourself this instant!"

Just then a pair of headlights flashed as a large black automobile came screeching to a halt in front of Dr. Blackstone's house. Natalia had seen the car before, and once she was assured Harley was all right, she crept behind a bush to get a closer look.

The front door of Morgan LaFey's sleek Rolls-Royce opened as the mountainous man with shoulders as wide as a house stepped out into the rain. He was dressed in a black suit covered by a fashionable full-length raincoat. His shoes were made of the finest leather, or at least Natalia imagined they were, and his driver's cap was pulled over his eyes. But Natalia knew him well enough. It was the same man who had been waiting for Morgan at the cornfield, and it was also the same man who had threatened Dennis Stonebrow at school a few days ago.

Silently, the driver strode to the back of the car and opened Morgan's door, popping open an umbrella for her. The Black Witch snatched it out of his hands.

"Wait here," she commanded, marching through the rain to where Blackstone was waiting.

"And why are you standing out here in the rain, Dr. Blackstone?"

"I heard something," Dr. Blackstone replied, still glancing about his yard with suspicious eyes. "Something was outside my window."

"Indeed?" she asked in a tone rather short of humor. "Your lack of wits astounds me. I suggest you have your curtains drawn next time."

"But the kobolds should have given warning," Blackstone countered. "I don't understand. . . ."

"Silence, you dolt. Get inside," she ordered, storming through the front door past the band instructor.

"But, Morgan, my dear . . . ," he pleaded as he followed after her like a whipped dog. The front door slammed shut behind them. If only Blackstone had bothered to turn at that moment, he might have seen two small shadows running down his driveway and into the night.

"On the count of three, we're going to make for the door," Max whispered to Ernie.

"What about the book?" Ernie replied.

"That's why we've got to do it fast. As soon as they see me take it, they're gonna attack. So when I get to three, I'm going to grab it and run."

"What's supposed to stop them from following us right out into the street?" worried Ernie.

"Do you have a better idea?"

"Yeah," replied Ernie. "We could leave the book and walk out. Seems reasonable."

"One . . . ," Max began his countdown.

"I don't know, Max."

"Two . . ."

"I have to go to the bathroom."

"Three . . ."

As Max scooped up the book and slid it into the duffel bag, a flood of faeries shot into the air and dove straight for him—faster than he could have imagined. He barely had enough time to shove Ernie to the ground before dozens of the airborne assailants rocketed over him. If Ernie had still been standing, he would have lost his head.

Max dove for a large shield lying next to a suit of armor near the desk and swung it around for protection. Like the sound of hailstones on the roof of a car, a swarm of faeries pummeled the shield, the force rattling Max's teeth.

Then Max had an idea. "Ernie!" he called from behind the shield. "Open the door and get out." Not surprisingly, Ernie was already crawling on his belly toward the exit. The faeries apparently had lost interest in him. All that mattered to the flying fiends was the duffel bag Max held under his arm.

"I'm trying," Ernie whined as he crept along.

"When you get outside, open the door as wide as you can. I'm going to throw the book to you." Max didn't know if it would work. And Ernie might very well be right that the garden faeries—if that's what they really were—might just follow the book out into the street.

"What?" exclaimed Ernie. "You have to have a better idea than that. They're gonna kill me."

"We have to have this book!" shouted Max, the weight of the shield and the pounding faeries slowly sapping his strength. "If it wasn't important, they wouldn't want it so bad. So when you catch it, kick the door shut."

"What about you?" Ernie complained. "You'll be trapped inside."

"Never mind me!" Max yelled as his arms began to weaken. "Are you there yet?"

Ernie had just crossed the threshold and was opening the door. "I'm ready . . . I think."

"Here it comes!" shouted Max.

With the shield in one hand and Iver's book in the other, Max launched himself into the storm of faeries with his last burst of energy, knocking them backward in a confused tangle of wings. It was just the break he needed. With a mighty throw, the book rocketed through the air.

Unfortunately, as the book sailed over Ernie's head, his fingers completely missed their target. In horror, he froze, not sure what to do.

"Max! I missed!"

"It doesn't matter. Shut the door!" Max yelled as the faeries realized what had happened. They instantly changed direction, heading straight for Ernie.

"Do it!" Max yelled again. With a heave, Ernie slammed the door shut, smashing a dozen faeries on the glass like bugs on a windshield. Hundreds more threw themselves against the door, as it began to shake under the onslaught. It wouldn't last long. Not knowing what else to do, Ernie took off as fast as he could down the street, the duffel bag in his hand. But after about a block, he realized he wasn't being chased. And then he remembered his friend, still trapped in Iver's shop. He couldn't just leave him there.

Ernie slammed on the brakes and ran back to rescue Max. He

didn't know how or what he could do. But that didn't matter. Ernie was a Grey Griffin, and Grey Griffins didn't abandon their own.

Even before he reached the store, he saw that the windows were flashing with an eerie blue light. Something very strange and powerful was happening inside. As he raced along, he could feel the hair on his head and arms start to rise, and he could feel waves of magic rolling over him, like bursts of static electricity. It was just as he reached for the door that a great explosion of light and magic blew it open, sending Ernie sprawling to the sidewalk.

When Ernie opened his eyes again, Max was standing over him with a smile as he slid Iver's book into his satchel, right next to the *Codex.*

"But how did you . . . ?" began Ernie, who was a bit shaken.

"Things are changing," replied Max as he helped his friend back to his feet. "Follow me."

Pulling Ernie after him, Max raced along Main Street, dodging through alleys. Finally, they came to the grassy shadows of Patriot's Park. That's where they found Natalia with Harley limping beside her.

"We've got the book," Ernie cheered.

"I wish our news was as good," Natalia said, unable to look at them, her eyes full of tears. "They killed Iver. Harley saw the body." Then she began to sob.

21

NATALIA'S WORDS hung over them like a storm cloud, and Max wondered if it could be possible. *Iver? Dead?* Logan had warned them of just such a fate, but dealing with the reality was something altogether different. None of the Griffins had been prepared—least of all Natalia, who was solemnly guiding them down an alleyway choked with fog. They were quickly moving toward the safety of a nearby church.

"Why a church?" Ernie asked, jogging along behind the group. "Is there iron there?"

Harley shook his head. "Iron won't work. At least not with the kobolds."

"What?" Ernie cried out. "But I thought . . ."

"They were wearing iron armor, Ernie," Harley answered, exasperated. "And they're working for Morgan. With our luck, they're already on our trail."

"She's certainly not taking any chances," commented Natalia. "This is one witch who knows what she's doing."

"How can we stop faeries if they don't have a weakness?" Ernie asked in frustration.

"That's why we're going to the church!" exclaimed Natalia, her nerves overwrought by Iver's death. "Kobolds might be resistant to iron, but there's no faerie alive that can walk on holy ground. Sprig said so, remember? We'll be safe there."

"Why do we always have to go through dark alleys?" Ernie complained, pulling his coat closer. Avalon was an old town, and old towns had alleys. Some alleys went somewhere, while others appeared to go nowhere, but if you knew what you were doing, they would eventually lead just about anywhere you needed to go. They were also excellent places to have private conversations while on the move.

As they followed Natalia through the misty back corners of the city, the two groups were able to share what had happened and what they had seen since they had split up earlier in the evening. Max was glad to have the book and was growing more and more confident of his abilities. But the news about Iver gripped their hearts like a vice, and they moved silently, lost in despair.

A few minutes later, the Grey Griffins came to a halt at the end of a long, damp passageway. Across the street from where they stood was the church. Usually it was quite warm and friendly-looking. However, with the fog rolling all around, it took on an unearthly appearance, eerie beneath the darkened sky. Towering above them, its pale steeple soared into the mists, disappearing from sight.

"It looks kinda creepy," Ernie noted. Yet the doors, heavy and old, stood wide open, just as they did every day of the year, welcoming anyone who sought sanctuary. That was exactly what the four of them needed. But while faeries wouldn't be able to follow them inside, Blackstone and Morgan were another matter.

"All we need to do is get across this road and up the steps, right?" Natalia tried to assure herself, her voice laced with uncertainty.

Max nodded as he placed one foot cautiously onto the sidewalk, looking up and down the damp street.

"Wait." Natalia grabbed at his sleeve in fright. "Did you hear that?"

"Hear what?" Ernie's eyes widened.

"I don't know. It sounded like rock scraping on rock, or something like that, anyway. It came from up there," Natalia explained, pointing overhead. Max looked up and squinted into the rain. They were standing near the library, one of the oldest buildings in town.

"Have you ever been up on that roof?" Max asked Harley.

"Sure. Lots of times."

"Anything up there?"

"Nah, on a night like this? The only thing up there is a bunch of gargoyles."

"Gargoyles?" gulped Ernie, remembering his Round Table. "Aren't they related to . . . to goblins?"

"Don't worry, Ernie." Max patted him on the shoulder. "They're just statues. They aren't real."

"Yeah," replied Harley. "There's some really cool ones up there. Wings. Claws. Fangs. The works."

Ernie looked as if he might be getting sick.

Again, the mysterious sound filtered down. However, this time a shower of dust and small rocks accompanied it.

"I'm not sure what it is, but something's definitely up there,"

Max said, brushing the dust from his jacket. "I think we'd better keep moving."

But as they made to move forward, a bolt of jagged light tore through the sky as a shadow fell from the rooftop.

"It's a gargoyle!" Ernie cried, diving to the sidewalk. "They're alive. Everybody duck!"

Max dropped to the ground as a rush of wind passed overhead. Stone claws tore through the air where he had been standing. Ernie was right. It was a gargoyle, gray and grotesque, hewed from living stone. Its eyes burned a haunting green, and long hooked wings spread from its body as it circled for another pass. Max knew it was one of the dark servants of the Shadow King and it had one mission—to kill him.

"Run!" he heard Natalia cry. "Go to the church!"

Max struggled to his feet, but the church seemed miles away. He'd never make it before the winged monster picked him off. Already the gargoyle was rocketing back toward him, boxes and newspapers flying in its wake. Summoning all his resolve, Max pulled his book bag close and ran as fast as his legs would carry him. He leapt off the sidewalk, over a rain gutter, hitting the wet street at a dead run. The church loomed ahead. Safety.

Then Max heard Natalia scream, and the blood froze in his veins. Fearing the worst, he turned as he ran, only to find the extended claws of the gargoyle swooping down on him. As Max frantically dove for safety, the gargoyle struck with the force of a freight train, sending him flying into the air.

The gargoyle stayed on its prey with frightening speed, striking Max again before he had a chance to hit the ground. Its claws ripped open his coat, severing the straps of his backpack. Too late, Max realized that the gargoyle wasn't trying to kill him at all. The monster's claws yanked his precious cargo away. It wanted his book bag.

Max was dragged through the street helplessly, his arm still caught in the straps of his bag. Not able to bear his weight, the straps broke, and Max tumbled to the ground, rolling over again and again. Triumphantly, the gargoyle rose into the night, its prize clutched in its long talons.

But just then, a second winged shadow leapt from the library roof, ripping into the first gargoyle.

"Another one!" Max heard Ernie shouting. But why were they fighting each other? Max had read many times, both in books and in his Round Table cards, that faeries were unpredictable and often attacked one another for no apparent reason. Sometimes it was for territorial reasons; other times it was over food; still other fights were more mysterious and just seemed to happen for the fun of it. But this time, it seemed both gargoyles desperately wanted Max's backpack. And they were willing to kill each other to get it.

Like two eagles fighting over a fish, the monsters battled with chiseled fangs and greedy claws, ripping Max's backpack from each other's covetous grasp. Deep gashes were torn into their stony hides, sending showers of dust and rock down to the street.

A terrible rending sound echoed as one of the gargoyle's wings was completely shorn off. With a shriek, the wounded creature plummeted toward the Griffins, crashing onto the road and exploding into a thousand pieces. When Max opened his eyes, he saw his backpack fall, hit the ground, and bounce once, then twice, until it slid right to his feet.

Once again, luck had found him.

Max scooped up the bag and turned to race for the church doors. He'd only have a few seconds before the second gargoyle would be on him. "Come on!" he cried as the four of them ran madly from the winged fiend.

Hitting the church steps with a bounce, Max was the first one through the doors. Harley and Natalia rushed in after. Ernie dove in last, eyes wide in fear, the gargoyle right behind, deadly claws outstretched.

But now the Grey Griffins had nowhere to go. They had thought once they were inside the church, they would be safe. But the gargoyle wasn't showing any signs of giving up. Frozen to the spot, they looked on helplessly as the gargoyle screamed toward the doors, rocketing toward them with great stony claws.

Ernie whimpered.

However, just as the monster crossed the threshold of the church, and the warm light of the vestibule touched its rocky skin, the gargoyle let out a great scream and disintegrated in an explosion of sparkling white dust.

"I think I wet my pants," Ernie whispered as Max, Natalia, and Harley brushed away the powdery remains of the gargoyle. Natalia, grossed out, took a few steps away from Ernest. Luckily, it was a false alarm.

"We can't stay right here, in the doorway," complained Harley, survival instincts kicking in. "That explosion is going to draw attention."

"Know any good hiding places, Natalia?" asked Max, looking over at his teary-eyed friend with a reassuring smile. Natalia's family had attended that church for years, and considering her penchant for snooping, there was little doubt in Max's mind that Natalia knew the place inside out.

"Of course, I do," she answered, though she did not return his smile. The news of Iver's death was still gnawing at her. "The organ pipe room. It probably has a real name, but I just call it that. No one ever goes in there."

"No one except you, that is," Harley pointed out.

"Never mind," Natalia said testily. "Follow me."

The Grey Griffins rushed down the aisle behind Natalia, passing pew after wooden pew as the three of them followed her through a hidden door on the right side of the altar. Just as she had claimed, columns of towering brass organ pipes filled the tiny room, leaving little space for four kids. But at least they felt safe.

"How come you never told us about this place?" Harley inquired, looking up in awe.

"You didn't ask," Natalia replied as she blew her nose into a lacy handkerchief.

"Let's take a look at Iver's book," Max said, pulling it from his mangled backpack. It didn't glow or hum like the *Codex*, yet they could sense something strangely inspiring about it. Also, to their relief, it didn't have a lock.

"Here it goes," Max breathed, opening the cover. As they gazed down at the contents, they could see that the pages were hand-written in a dark blue ink. But the language was unfamiliar. It certainly wasn't the magical language of the *Codex*.

"I think it's Greek," offered Natalia.

"I can't read Greek," Max muttered in disappointment. He was pretty talented with Latin (especially after his father had hired a relentless tutor from Oxford), but Greek was a lot harder, with a whole different alphabet. "What are we supposed to do now?"

Then they heard footsteps coming toward them just outside the door.

"They've found us," gasped Ernie. "We're done for." The Griffins only had enough time to get to their feet before the door slowly opened with an ominous creak.

There in the door's frame was none other than Ms. Heen smiling at them.

"What a wonderful hiding place you have," she said, looking around. Her eyes glittered as Max took a step back, hoping to hide the book from view. To say the least, the Griffins were shocked to see her standing there. How had she known they were in the church to begin with? This was the second time she had shown up unexpectedly, almost as if she knew exactly where to find them.

"Oh," Ms. Heen said as her eyes lit upon Iver's book. "Is that what you've been doing on this stormy night? Reading? How delicious."

"No." Max shook his head. "Not really."

"But what are you doing here?" asked Natalia protectively, stepping in front of Max.

Ms. Heen smiled, motioning toward the sanctuary. "It's a church. People come here when they have no place else to go. Isn't that why you're here?"

"Nope," lied Ernie.

"Perhaps I've guessed more closely than you are willing to admit," Ms. Heen said, smiling and turning to Ernie. "But what is this that you're reading?" Max never knew how it happened, but one moment the book was firmly in his hands, the next, Ms. Heen was leafing through the pages. The Grey Griffins exchanged bewildered glances. None of them had even seen her move.

"Oh, I love this story," she laughed as she read along.

"You can read Greek?" asked Ernie in wonder.

"Oh, this isn't Greek," Ms. Heen replied as her eyes sped along the page. "It is much older than that. But in my line of work, I have to know quite a bit about many things. Anyway, it's a very old story. A fairy tale, I suppose you could say, and it begins in the Shadowlands of Faerie, though it doesn't end there. In fact, to my knowledge, it has no ending at all—at least not yet."

"Sounds interesting," Ernie said as he took a seat, pulled out a package of smashed jelly beans, and proceeded to pour them into his mouth. Ernie loved a good story.

"Hey, I thought you were supposed to stop eating junk food," Natalia whispered.

Ernie just turned to her and smiled impishly, the jelly beans stuck to his braces. Natalia rolled her eyes.

"It all started long ago when the world was still quite young," Ms. Heen began. "You see, Titania, Queen of the Shadowlands of Faerie, had been given a marvelous gift, a Jewel that glittered more brightly than any star in the sky. And within it was a power far greater than any other on earth. What that power might be, no one now can say—not even Oberon, her husband, King of the Shadowlands, who was wise beyond measure."

At the name of the Shadow King, the Griffins stirred. His very name sent shivers down their spine. But what was most shocking to Natalia was that Oberon was married, and then she wondered if he had children, too, and what they might be like. Hopefully, they were better behaved.

Ms. Heen continued, "Yet despite his wisdom and preeminence in Faerie, Oberon was given no gift. And as the ages passed, his desire for the Jewel and its power consumed him with jealousy. Hoping to appease her husband and prevent a terrible war, Titania locked the Jewel away, so that neither of them would possess it. When this was done, Oberon's anger faded, bringing peace back to the Shadowlands of Faerie.

"And so it might have remained, and we might all be happy still, were it not for the curiosity of one insignificant creature—a hand-maiden of the queen. For one day, when Titania was distracted, this creature captured and escaped with the Jewel."

Ernie raised his hand. "But why would the creature want it? Was it worth a lot of money?"

Ms. Heen shook her head. "The Jewel was extremely power-ful—some say within it was the power of creation as well as death—but on a scale far beyond your wildest imagination, Ernie. Yet the Jewel was also indescribably beautiful, and it was this radiant beauty that overcame the simple little creature. It wasn't out of greed or desire for power that she felt compelled to steal the Jewel—it was simply out of the single-minded desire to feast her eyes upon it and never, ever look away."

"So what happened next?" Natalia prompted.

"Oberon knew of the theft the moment it happened. Such was his power. Immediately, he unleashed a mighty army of goblins to ravage the land in search of the great Jewel and its thief. But the handmaiden had a special power that made her elusive. She was a shape-shifter, and her race was that of the spriggans."

Max's eyes grew wide as Ms. Heen read. Was his Sprig the very same spriggan that had stolen the Jewel thousands of years ago? Was she just using Max all this time to get to Titania's Jewel?

"And so," Ms. Heen continued, "the spriggan escaped through a mystical portal that led from the Shadowlands of Faerie into the world of humans—our world. But the Shadow King, as Oberon was sometimes called, had portals of his own, and soon his armies poured into the strange lands searching for the spriggan, destroying everything in their path. No force on earth could stop them."

Ms. Heen closed the book.

"Is that all there is?" asked Ernie, disappointed.

Ms. Heen shook her head before closing her eyes with a hint of sadness. "No, I'm just remembering."

"You have the whole story memorized?" wondered Natalia.

"In a sense," Ms. Heen replied quietly. "The story is quite long, and I fear I might be boring you."

"You might be surprised," Max responded.

"Well, in that case." Ms. Heen smiled as she set down the book. "Things didn't go well for the spriggan. Of course, her kind is very good at hiding, but when the Shadow King is hunting after you, changing shapes can only get you so far."

"Was she caught?" asked Ernie, looking over at Max, who was lost in thought.

"No," answered Ms. Heen. "Not by the Shadow King, anyway. The spriggan's fate was to stumble into a trap set by the Knights of the West who discovered both her and the treasure that she carried. Their great king, wise and powerful, understood immediately the danger of keeping the Jewel for himself and the even greater danger of allowing it to fall into the hands of the Shadow King. He knew he would have to find some way to repel Oberon back into the Shadowlands and close all the portals.

"Calling upon every resource across his empire, the king and his knights had constructed a book of tremendous power, which was called the *Codex Spiritus*. And upon its cover was placed Titania's Jewel, which acted as the key to the book's great power. When the Jewel and the *Codex* were combined, nothing could withstand its power. Not even Oberon."

Max had forgotten all about the missing piece in the cover of the *Codex*. It must have been meant for the Jewel. So that was why it had started glowing. The book knew that the Jewel was near.

"The story goes that as long as the king had the *Codex* and

Titania's Jewel in his hands, he was invincible. But, alas, the king was betrayed, and the book slipped from his possession at the wrong moment. That was all it took. A terrible tragedy, I am sure you can imagine—for both his family and his kingdom."

"So what happened? The goblins won?"

"Thankfully, no," replied Ms. Heen. "As the king lay dying, he spied the *Codex* laying only a hand's reach away, the Jewel glittering brightly upon its face. With his last breath, he called to it and unleashed its terrible power. In an explosion of unimaginable force, the wicked armies of the Shadow King were swept away under the onslaught of potent magic. Oberon himself only barely managed to escape back to his kingdom before every faerie, small or large, fierce or friendly, was captured within the pages of the *Codex Spiritus*. There they were to remain, passed down from king to prince, father to son, generation after generation, to this very day."

Harley looked over at Max apologetically and shook his head, but Max knew it was his fault that the faeries had escaped. It wasn't Harley's.

"One more thing," Ms. Heen cautioned. "After the king's death, the *Codex* was disassembled—the Jewel and the book never again to be locked together. That was the only way to keep the Shadow King trapped on the other side. But if he were to find a way to bring them together again, under his power, the world would fall into unimaginable darkness."

"Well, if the *Codex* was passed down through the family," reasoned Natalia, "then what happened to the Jewel?"

"No one knows," replied Ms. Heen. "From that point on, it was always kept separate from the *Codex*. Although it's said that the Jewel was last seen in the possession of the Knights Templar six hundred years ago."

Max's heart leapt. The Templars. Here again was another clue to his destiny.

"Although . . ." She paused thoughtfully, picking up the book again as she leafed through the pages. "This particular book seems to have a little more about the story. Yes, here it is. It tells us that the Knights Templar brought Titania's Jewel across the Western Sea, hid it deep within their secret Catacombs, building an extraordinary stone monument over it — and there it remains to this day."

Max looked over at Natalia with wide eyes. Here was their first clue to where the Catacombs might lie!

"What sort of monument would the Knights Templar build?" Natalia asked, trying to act as nonchalant as she could.

"Oh." Ms. Heen's eyes sparkled. "Just about anything. They were masters of building and architecture, but they generally built castles and chapels more often than not."

The Chapel of Mist? Max knew it. The Catacombs had to be there. He was such a fool not to have thought of it before.

"Does the book you're reading have a happy ending?" Ernie asked fearfully.

"If I told you that, it would spoil the whole story, wouldn't it?" Ms. Heen replied with a wink. "But I think right now the most important thing is to get you home. The storm is picking up, and the temperature has dropped quite unexpectedly, I'm afraid.

307

Luckily, my car just happens to be right outside. May I offer you a ride?"

"You have a phone call," Max's mom said sharply after barging into his room the next morning. "It's Natalia, and we've talked about this before. I don't like it when girls call on boys. It's not proper."

"Okay, Mom," he said as he slid out of bed, stumbling past her to take the receiver.

"What's up?" Max asked, covering his mouth as he spoke, trying to keep his voice down.

"It's Harley," she said on the other end, almost in tears. "Dr. Blackstone has him."

"What?" Max almost dropped the phone, causing his mother to look at him disapprovingly. "How?"

"Harley and I went back to the church to get our bikes an hour ago."

"Go on," Max urged.

"When we got there, Blackstone was waiting. He wasn't interested in me; he just pulled Harley into his car and drove off before I could do anything."

"Where'd he take him?

"I think he took him to King's Elementary."

"Call Ernie," Max ordered. "I'll meet you there in fifteen minutes."

By the time the Grey Griffins arrived at the King's Elementary School grounds they found Harley walking toward them, head down.

"Harley, are you all right?" Ernie called from his bike. "Did he torture you?"

Harley only shook his head, glaring back at the school in anger. "He asked me a bunch of questions, but he couldn't prove anything."

"I can't believe he just hauled you off like that. Your mom should complain to the school board," added Natalia. "That's kidnapping!"

"Did you find out anything?" Max jumped in. "Did he mention Morgan?"

Harley shook his head again. "No, but I grabbed this when he wasn't looking." Harley pulled out a folded piece of paper from his pocket.

"What is it?" Natalia asked, yanking the paper from his hands before reading it. A moment later all the color drained from her face. "Oh no," she breathed.

"What's wrong?" asked Max.

"The Chapel of Mist," she replied, handing the note over to Max. "This is a permit for an archaeological survey of the chapel grounds. Blackstone's and Morgan's names are on the order, along with the mayor's and the governor's, too."

"So?" Ernie shrugged.

"So?" replied Natalia. "Didn't you listen to anything Ms. Heen said last night? That's where the Catacombs are — where Titania's Jewel is. And you can bet that's what those creeps are looking for. They're going to dig it up."

"If we don't do something to stop them," Harley continued the line of thought, "they'll get the Jewel first. . . ."

Ernie scratched his head. "But why does Morgan want the Jewel if she's not working for the Shadow King? I thought she was only working for herself."

Max shook his head. He didn't know. It was a mystery. Sometimes, he thought Morgan was working for the Shadow King. Other times, she seemed to be working for herself. But one thing was for sure: Morgan was up to something evil. And the Griffins were in deep trouble.

"But wouldn't they need Max's book?" argued Harley. "I mean, if they don't have that, then they won't be able to use the Jewel, right?"

Natalia nodded. If Morgan had the Jewel, Max and his friends would be on the menu next. "We have to prevent her from getting the Jewel. That's all there is to it."

"How are we going to stop an evil witch from doing anything?" complained Ernie.

"Great question. We need a plan and we need one now. According to this work order, the excavation began an hour ago."

22

Into the Catacombs

As it turned out, the plan was simple. All the Grey Griffins had to do was steal Titania's Jewel before Morgan and Blackstone got to it, figure out what to do with it, close the portals, and save the world—all without being caught, or worse... killed. Simple? Maybe. Easy? Not even close.

Unfortunately, they got off to a rather dismal start. The bike ride to the Chapel of Mist had been an uphill battle in the driving rain. By the time they arrived, the backhoes and bulldozers had already been abandoned, and Morgan LaFey's Rolls-Royce Phantom was peeling out of the gravel parking lot, spitting up slime and stone as it nearly ran over the Griffins, roaring out onto the road.

"Why is she heading toward the forest?" Natalia glared at the car fading into the distance. "She still needs the book."

Max shook his head in confusion and relief. "I don't know. It doesn't make any sense. I'm sure she saw us."

"Now what are we supposed to do? The world's probably gonna end and I haven't even kissed a girl yet," complained Ernie, his eyes suddenly darting about in embarrassment once he realized what he had said.

"Maybe Natalia could help you," Harley snickered.

Natalia offered an icy glare. "And maybe I could punch you in the . . . Wait! Do you guys hear that?" Natalia asked, cupping her soggy mitten to her ear. "It sounds like a dog crying."

Without bothering to see if the others were following, Natalia ran toward the creepy old cemetery. A moment later, the Grey Griffins found Mr. Thorvald, the old keeper of the Chapel, lying motionless in the wet grass near a broken tombstone. His monstrous dog, Loki, stood over him protectively, the poor animal bleeding from a multitude of cuts and wounds.

Cautiously, Natalia tried to approach to see if she could help, but Loki bared his teeth viciously, warning her to stay back. Natalia knew a wounded animal was a dangerous thing, so she froze.

"Don't move, Natalia," Harley warned as he stepped in front of her cautiously. Waving for Max and Ernie to stay put, Harley started gingerly toward the big dog. Loki growled deeply, but the growl gave way to a whine as he licked one of his many wounds.

Harley stopped, putting his hands in the air to show he meant no harm. "It's okay, boy," he assured the animal. "I don't want to hurt you." If Harley knew anything, he knew how to handle big, mean dogs. But this dog was different. Without warning, Loki lunged at him ferociously, pinning Harley to the ground.

"Do something!" Natalia screamed as Ernie turned and ran back to the bikes. With Mr. Thorvald unconscious, or worse, there was no one there to stop the animal from finishing Harley off.

In a panic, Max rushed in, hoping to save Harley's life. As he moved, electricity shook the ground like thunder. Natalia's mouth dropped as she once again watched blue lightning crackle over Max's body, like a thousand explosions of energy.

Evidently, Loki had seen it as well, whimpering in fear as he leapt off Harley's chest before slinking back to his master.

"Max!" cried Natalia. "What's happening to you?"

Max shook his head as the waves of light faded away as quickly as they had come. "I . . . I don't know," he stammered in astonishment. "I don't even know what's happening. I thought the book was making me do that. But now . . ."

"That wasn't the *Codex*," Natalia pointed out. "It's still in your bag."

"Holy cow, Max!" Ernie exclaimed in excitement. "You're magic."

Perhaps he was. And that gave him a little encouragement. But he didn't have time to think about it just then. "Are you okay, Harley?"

Harley nodded. However, Mr. Thorvald wasn't so fortunate. Max approached cautiously, not wanting to frighten Loki, who remained with his head on his master's chest. "We aren't going to hurt you," Max said as he held out his hand for Loki to sniff. The dog seemed to perk up just a bit at the gesture. But Mr. Thorvald was still in critical condition. The gash on his forehead was bleeding horribly.

Natalia quietly made her way over and knelt down, taking out a handkerchief and gently applying it to Mr. Thorvald's head.

Mr. Thorvald stirred. "What's going on here?" he muttered in a feeble voice.

"You're injured, Mr. Thorvald," Natalia said as softly and calmly as she could.

"What happened?" asked Max, kneeling beside the old man.

When Mr. Thorvald's eyes caught hold of Max, a spark of recognition was lit. He struggled to sit up, but the loss of blood had made him weak and he quickly lay back down. "So it's you, is it?" the grave keeper croaked under the driving rain. "Well, I shouldn't wonder now how things got the way they are. Should have seen it coming."

"What do you mean?" asked Max, fearing that somehow his secret was out.

"You know right well what I mean, boy. Your grandfather trusted me once and now it's your turn. The time for secrecy is over." With that he carefully pulled something out from beneath his undershirt. It was a chain with a worn cross swinging in his feeble hand. Mr. Thorvald was a Templar.

"Not quite what you thought a knight would look like, eh?" he asked, a haggard smile briefly crossing his grizzled face. "Well, don't look so surprised. Iver told you there were people looking out for your scrawny hide, didn't he?"

"Was it Morgan LaFey?" Natalia interrupted.

"Yes, girl. LaFey, and that monster she keeps by her side. They surprised us, that's all. We should have been more watchful. But then . . ." He paused as if remembering something horrible. "They had Iver with them. Beaten and broken, he was. Poor soul. I never thought I'd see the day. . . ." His voice trailed off as he seemed to be losing consciousness.

"Iver's alive?" Natalia shouted in sudden hope.

"The Catacombs," Mr. Thorvald whispered hoarsely, his eyes closing as the life started to drain from his broken body. "Once you are in the Chapel, you'll know what to do." Max didn't know what to say as the old man started coughing up blood, his face growing deathly pale. "My time's just about over, Max, but your time has come. We'll meet again, though. We always do."

Mr. Thorvald drew one last breath, and then his eyes closed forever.

Natalia began to cry as the boys turned their sad faces to the ground in grief and despair.

The Grey Griffins stood on the cold expanse of stone that paved the cavernous sanctuary of the Chapel of Mist. It was just as they remembered, except that now the entire chapel was bathed in darkness. The storm must have knocked out the power.

"Anyone got a match?" asked Max, his voice echoing amid the stone columns.

"You have to ask?" answered Harley as Natalia handed him the matchbox she had kept in her pocket since the day she'd uncovered Morgan's evil plan in the cornfield. Lighting the first match, Harley read his own forged name on the inside of the matchbox and smirked. Morgan's plan to frame him had not only failed but had provided the Grey Griffins with a useful tool. Quickly, Harley lit a nearby candle and handed it to Natalia, and immediately the two of them split up to either side of the sanctuary, lighting all the candles within reach. Soon, the whole room was bathed in a warm, almost comforting, glow.

"I'm probably not the only one who noticed," Natalia began as she looked about the room in worry, "but only Morgan and her driver were in that car. Iver wasn't with them."

"I know," replied Max, clenching his jaw. "He's got to be in the Catacombs somewhere."

"I'm sure he's still alive," Harley added, patting Natalia on the shoulder. She was trying not to cry.

The Grey Griffins split up and began canvassing the Chapel's interior with their roving eyes for the door to the Catacombs. Natalia chose the back, Harley the left, Ernie the right, and Max made his way toward the front where two massive pillars stretched to the vast ceiling.

"Why aren't we just checking the normal doors?" offered Ernie. "There can't be that many."

Natalia rolled her eyes. "Honestly, Ernie. Does it have to be spelled out for you?"

"What?" complained Ernie.

"It can't be a door like any old door. It has to be a secret door—otherwise anybody could have found the Jewel by now."

"Look," Max said. "Do you see the carving here on the pillar in front of me?"

"Which carving? The place is covered with them," Natalia pointed out as she squinted in the half-light that shrouded the Chapel.

"The one below the pyramid with the eye. It looks just like the lock on the *Codex*. And look here . . . it has a keyhole."

"Hmmm." Natalia studied it for a moment. "You're right. Harley, think you could pick the lock?"

"But it's magic. How's he gonna do that?" Ernie asked.

Then Max pulled the iron key from under his shirt—the very key Iver had left with Logan. It hadn't worked at Iver's shop, but maybe , , ,

Max pulled off the necklace and inserted the key. It was a perfect fit.

Without hesitation, Max turned it.

Nothing happened for a long while as the four friends looked at one another nervously. Then, just as they were about to give up, a low rumbling far beneath their feet shook the floor. Before their very eyes, the pillar began to turn in different directions as if it were made of stone clockwork gears—each section spinning and crunching like a monolithic combination lock.

"I think s-something's h-happening," stammered Ernie. "Maybe we should get out of here."

Perhaps they should have, but no one was listening to him. Instead, their eyes were glued as one gear, then another, locked into place with a thud. Then, as the last section spun to rest, a deep cracking sound echoed from below. That's when Natalia noticed something they had all failed to spot before. They were standing on an intricate circular design carved into the floor. It was a spiral, like a snail's shell with the strange pillar in the exact center. But shooting out from the base of the pillar was a series of deep scoring lines, like rays of the sun. But where each ray intersected the line of the spiral, the pieces, like a jigsaw puzzle, broke apart and they slowly lowered into the darkness, forming a spooky spiral staircase that led far below.

"Look out," Natalia warned, grabbing Ernie by the shirt collar as she sidestepped a moving stone. Harley and Max followed, scrambling out of the way just in time.

"Whoa, that was freaky." Ernie shook his head as he peered down the stony stairs. "I wonder where it goes."

"Down," replied Max grimly, patting his friend on the shoulder. It was exactly what he was looking for, and with a little luck they might even be able to find a way to stop Morgan, find the Jewel, and save Iver.

The Griffins followed Max as he disappeared into the Catacombs.

The staircase seemed to go on forever, spiraling tightly around the outer wall of a deep and narrow shaft. Water echoed eerily in the distance as flickering oil lamps lit the pathway downward. It was peculiar to say the least. The stairs themselves seemed suspended in the air, attached to nothing more than the mortar on the walls, and more than a few stones had fallen away in their old age, leaving gaps that the kids had to jump over.

"We're gonna get ourselves killed," complained Ernie, who had slipped more than once already, saved only by Harley's quick reflexes. Ernie liked to blame his poor coordination on his recent growing spurt (which went unnoticed by all save Ernie).

"I wonder who lit all these lamps?" Harley asked.

"I smell Morgan's perfume," Natalia informed them as she ran her finger across a slimy wall. "She was definitely here. Maybe she did it."

"Good," replied Max as he pushed on. "At least we know we're on the right track." The other Griffins watched him in wonder as he leapt over a large gap in the stone, continuing on without a word. What they had seen at the cemetery just couldn't be explained. Max was no longer the same person they once knew. He was changing.

One by one, the other Griffins followed, continuing their arduous descent.

The crumbling staircase finally spilled out like a great rocky wave onto an old stone floor littered with the remains of centuries of decay and fallen stairs. As the four friends peered down at it from above, they could just make out that under a thick carpet of dust lay a bloodred Templar cross in the center of the room.

"I guess we're on the right track, huh?" Harley noted as Natalia took the opportunity to scribble the design down in her *Book of Clues*.

"X marks the spot," she repeated absently as she clipped her pen back in its place.

In the center of the cross stood an old stone well covered in grime and moss. It looked ancient, its decrepit walls crumbling and broken. Worse yet, as the Griffins approached, they could hear the creepy sound of countless insects and other horrible things biting and scratching deep within its black throat. They backed away slowly, not caring to disturb whatever was down there.

But there were more items of interest in the room than just a slimy hole in the ground. Against the far wall, set within a shallow niche, was a solitary wood table that was richly carved, its feet dressed in gold. Even under a thick layer of dust, the kids could see that it had once been an amazing work of art. But even more amazing was the large golden box that sat on top of it, intricately decorated with signs and symbols of the Templars. The lid was hinged, and no lock held it closed.

"I bet the Jewel's in there," Ernie breathed in wonder, his eyes devouring the scene.

"What do we do, Max?" asked Harley. "Should we open it and see if Ernie's right?"

"Not so fast," Natalia said, stepping in front of him. "This could be a trap."

"What are you talking about?" Harley was agitated.

But Max hadn't really been paying attention. Instead, he was still looking back at the crumbling well. He felt drawn to the abyss, somehow, though he didn't know why.

Then he saw something written on the side of it, hidden beneath a thick layer of moss. Max moved in for a closer look. "Hey, look at this." He waved for his friends to join him. Once Harley had rubbed away the grime with his shirt sleeve, they all stepped back to look at what he had uncovered:

THE ROAD TO HEAVEN OR THE ROAD TO HELL,
TRUST THE VOWS AND DESCEND THE WELL.

"What?" exclaimed Ernie, backing away as he eyed the well in horror. Thoughts of dangling worms, bristling centipedes, giant beetles, and a carpet of maggots made him sick to his stomach. He just knew they were down there waiting for him. "I'm not going down that hole. Forget it. Besides, I'm telling you the Jewel is right here."

"Then why didn't Morgan grab it?" countered Natalia sharply. "It's a trap."

"We have a choice," Max pointed out. "We can open the box and take our chances, or we can climb down the well like the sign says."

"The box is a trap," restated Natalia, completely sold on the idea. She didn't like bugs any more than Ernie, but she liked being wrong even less.

"Harley?" asked Max, looking over at his friend, who was staring down the well. "What do you think?"

"I say we go down," Harley replied after a few moments of uncomfortable silence. Ernie had been holding his breath, hoping for a different answer.

"I guess that settles it. We go down." Max looked at each of the Griffins in turn.

"No way," Ernie stalled. "Why doesn't my vote ever count? I have good ideas sometimes. Not all the time ... but sometimes I do. I'm telling you that going down that stinky hole is going to be a big mistake."

"Look, Ernie," replied Max as he put his hand on his friend's shoulder. "We're a team, and each of our votes counts the same. Sometimes you win. Sometimes you don't, but we vowed to stick by one another no matter what."

"We don't want to go down there any more than you do," Harley added. "But we have to. For Iver."

"Yes," agreed Natalia. "For Iver."

Ernie shuffled his feet uncomfortably. "But what about the box?"

"I think Natalia might be right," Max said, giving their predicament more thought. "Besides, the sign says to go down. I think we need to do what it says."

Ernie shrugged in defeat and laid his forehead against the cold wall, banging it once or twice in frustration. "If I die down there, you guys have to promise to carry me back out. I don't want to be left there to be eaten by bugs. Promise?"

"Promise," answered Max, echoed by Natalia.

"Promise." Harley nodded with a smile. "But if I can help it, I won't let anything happen to you."

As the Grey Griffins made ready for their descent, Harley caught sight of a ladder leading down into the darkness from which he brushed away a thick crusting of insects and slime. Unlike the other three, Harley couldn't care less about insects. They were interesting to collect from time to time, but he couldn't imagine a reason to be scared of something so ridiculously small. "I'll go first."

"Be my guest." Natalia waved.

Harley lowered himself down, clearing each rung of the ladder with his shoes. Each step he took was greeted with a rather disturbing series of squishing and hissing sounds that brought Ernie to the point of turning green. Within a few minutes, Harley had cleared enough space for Max to go next.

"Your turn, Ernie," Natalia said after Max had disappeared into the mouth of the well.

"I'll go last."

"No, you won't. You're going next. That's the only way I know for sure that you're coming with us."

Ernie glared sourly at Natalia. "Fine." He pouted and walked over to the well as he looked down at his friends below. They were completely covered in beetles and sticky cobwebs. "I won't forget this." With that, he took a shot from his asthma inhaler and began his descent, complaining loudly with each rung of the ladder. Natalia was not far behind.

The climb was just as nasty as Max had imagined. Within seconds, he was covered with bugs, and his hands were coated in the slime of those he'd already trampled. But other than worms occasionally dripping from the walls onto his face, it really wasn't that difficult. The hardest part was managing to keep Ernie moving. If it weren't for Natalia constantly threatening to step on his head, Ernie would have still been glued to the top of the ladder.

A short time later, Harley had reached the slimy end of the well.

"Stay up there, Max," whispered Harley. "I think there's one of those oil lamps next to me on the wall. I'll try lighting it." With that, he struck a matchstick against the box, igniting the tip and bathing the tunnel in light. Immediately, Harley wished he hadn't.

Thousands of sleepy eyes opened at once, staring back at Harley. "Uh-oh," he murmured under his breath.

"Uh-oh, what?" Natalia called back down.

But if Harley answered, no one knew for sure. His match had ignited far more than he had bargained for. At once, a swarm of screeching, crying, clawing bats, numberless and louder than a jet engine, shot toward him. Frantically, he dove for the ground, narrowly escaping the beating wings and gnashing teeth. But the other Griffins weren't so lucky. Like a dark cloud rising out of some horrible dream, the swarm of bats rocketed up the well. Max clutched the ladder tightly as the bats rolled over him like an ocean wave, threatening to yank him away.

Ernie screamed. It seemed appropriate. No one blamed him.

Natalia, unfortunately, had it the worst. The bats, anxious to escape the well, locked themselves in a frenzy all about her, nearly ripping her from her perch. Dozens of the winged creatures were caught in her hair, pulling and twisting it. It was all she could do to hold on.

But just as quickly as it had begun, the storm of bats disappeared, leaving the Griffins alone in the well with the slimy insects—which, after what had just happened, didn't seem so bad. One by one, the friends descended the ladder, joining Harley at the bottom. He had managed to light the oil lamp and was holding it in front of him, illuminating the tunnel ahead.

"I hate bats," Natalia growled through clenched teeth as she tried to pull her tangled hair back into a respectable ponytail. "And I probably won't be able to get this smell out of my hair for a week." Many girls might have been traumatized by the experience. But not Natalia. No, she got angry. Any bat that dared cross her path after that day would need to think twice.

Ernie, on the other hand, who was busily wiping off his slimy hands on his pants, was just grateful to be alive.

"Still no sign of Iver," Harley noted as he looked around. "Is that good or bad?"

"I don't know," replied Max gravely. "But I have a feeling Morgan needed him alive."

"I hope so," Natalia added. "If she's smart, she probably used him to find the Jewel. That's probably why the trap wasn't sprung upstairs."

"You don't know it was a trap," countered Ernie. But Natalia wasn't in the mood to argue anymore. Not when Iver's life was on the line.

"Whoa!" shouted Harley as the Grey Griffins neared the far end of the tunnel. There were two tall figures that seemed to be running toward them, though in actuality they weren't moving at all. They were golden statues of two knights, their faces frozen in horror as they appeared to be running away from something. The Grey Griffins looked closer, amazed at the detail that illustrated the ghastly fear in their eyes.

"How awful." Natalia whistled. "Who would've carved such a thing?"

"Well, if they're supposed to frighten us off, it's working," Ernie said, standing safely behind Harley and Max.

"Speak for yourself," Harley replied as he rushed past the statues and peered out over the horizon. "Check it out."

Harley was pointing beyond the statues, far out across a rocky grotto toward a great mountain of golden coins and glittering gemstones, all piled high like an island in the midst of a silvery pool. Upon the island, as if it had run adrift, rested a ship with tattered white sails and cannons pointing out over ancient rails.

"A pirate ship," Ernie breathed.

Sure enough, a black flag bearing the skull and crossbones hung from its mast, but on its sail was emblazoned a fiery red cross—the sign of the Templar Knights.

"The Templars were pirates?" Natalia asked, confused, as they all looked at the ship in wonder.

"Who cares?" Harley replied. "It's the most incredible thing I've ever seen." With that he was off.

"Wait! It could be another trap," Max called in warning, but Harley was already too far away to hear. The Griffins watched in trepidation as Harley shot down the rock slope, jumped onto the narrow suspension bridge that wavered over the silvery waters, and made his way across. Nodding, Max and the other two followed. Soon, they were standing next to their friend, who was staring at an open treasure chest, flowing over with jewels of every imaginable sort. On the inside of its lid was written another message:

A MILLSTONE HEAVY OR A NEEDLE'S EYE,
REMEMBER YOUR VOW OR YOU WILL DIE.

"That doesn't sound good," Ernie commented.

"What does it mean?" wondered Harley. "I don't get it."

Luckily, Natalia was up to the task, or so she thought. "It's a combination of two old sayings," she began, as if remembering a story she had once heard. "The first is what they would do to a thief who was caught stealing was to tie a millstone around his neck and throw him in the water."

"Yikes!" exclaimed Ernie, who was deathly afraid of water.

Swimming lessons had been a waste ever since a catastrophe involving a pink pair of water wings and a bully with a bottle of glue.

"I heard the second saying in Sunday school, though I don't remember it very well. It has something to do with a rich man fitting through the eye of a needle . . . or something like that."

"I don't know." Ernie was worried, noticing several other gold statues, each with a horrified expression on its face. "It doesn't make sense to me."

Max was studying the boat, looking for any clue to help them solve the puzzle. Then he saw something on the side of the ship's bow: *La Rochelle.*

"*La Rochelle*? That's French," mused Natalia, walking closer to the words. "Now where do I remember hearing that name before?"

"That book we found in the library," Max replied. "Remember that's where the Templar Knights were last seen before they disappeared from France. Their ships were supposed to be full of treasure."

"This is the most amazing thing I have ever seen!" Harley shook his head with excitement, admiring the boat. "I'll be right back. Just want to take a look around."

"Harley. We don't have time," Max called. His nerves were unraveling as he thought of Iver.

"Wait, Max. I think I figured it out," shouted Natalia as Harley wandered off, ignoring Max completely. She had been puzzling out the riddle, scribbling furiously in her notebook for the last several minutes. "It's like the last test, where we had to do what the sign said, no matter how good the box on the table looked. Except this time, the sign is telling us to not be greedy. So my guess is, and I am hardly every wrong, that we are supposed to take only one thing—something that we need and not something that we want."

"Well, I need a new bike," Ernie replied as he reached for a golden crown. But Max yanked him back roughly before Ernie grabbed hold of the treasure.

"We'd better not touch anything until we know for sure."

"But our shoes are already touching it," Ernie countered.

"Grabbing something with your hands is totally different."

"How do you know?" Ernie argued. Max ignored him.

"Oh my goodness," called Natalia as she tiptoed over to the side of the boat. "You have to take a look at this. I've never seen anything like it in my whole life."

Max and Ernie had to agree. When they reached the spot where Natalia was standing, they found a statue of a beautiful woman, captured by the sculptor just at the moment she seemed to be reaching for something. The look in her eyes was haunting and desperate. It made Max feel uncomfortable.

Natalia took a step back. "It's amazing. This could have been made by Michelangelo."

Ernie nodded, not that he knew who Michelangelo was, but it sounded good.

"Her eyes . . . ," Max observed. "They're looking at something."

"It's just a statue, Max," Natalia reminded him. But her jaw dropped as she followed the gaze of the golden figure. There seemed to be something just below the surface of the coins, not a few feet away. Something big.

This was it. This was the one thing they needed. Natalia knew it. She raced over and rolled up her sleeves, ready to dig. "Help me, Ernie."

Ernie, eyes wide with wonder, stuffed a bag of corn chips back into his pocket. But just as they were about to plunge into the treasure, Harley appeared from behind the ship, waving his hands and shouting, "Don't touch anything!" A moment later, he was standing next to them looking pale.

"Don't worry." Natalia waved him away. "I already solved the riddle. It's right here." Natalia pointed in the direction where she and Ernie were about to dig.

"I wouldn't touch anything if I were you." Harley shook his head. "The statues?" He pointed to the figure of the woman that had inspired Natalia's revelation. "They aren't statues. They're people."

"What?" Ernie recoiled from a nearby figure. "You mean they're alive?"

"No," countered Harley. "That's the point. I wouldn't have even noticed if some poor guy hadn't carved a message into the side of the ship right before he turned to gold."

"What are you talking about?" Natalia folded her arms crossly. As far as she was concerned, the case was solved.

"I'm saying anyone who touches anything turns into gold. Why do you think these statues look so real? It's because they are."

"He's right," Max admitted in horror as he studied the statue of the beautiful woman. The details were simply too perfect, right down to her delicate eyelashes and the individual strands of hair that framed her face. But it was the single golden tear frozen to her cheek that was most haunting. The process of turning to gold didn't look like it had been instantaneous, and judging from the facial expressions of the statues, it was the kind of experience Max wanted to avoid.

"I told you this place is creepy," Ernie reminded them.

"Greed," Harley stated flatly as he kicked at a large diamond near his feet. "The treasure's cursed. We should get out of here."

"What about the test?" Natalia asked. "We can't just quit now."

"That was the test," Max answered.

"What do you mean?"

"The sign said that we were only supposed to take what we need," Max repeated.

"So?"

"Well? We're trying to stop Morgan LaFey, right?"

"Go on."

"Do we need gold to do that?"

"You're right," admitted Natalia, a bit ashamed by her haste. "Besides, it all makes perfect sense. It's the only possible solution."

"What do you mean?" asked Ernie, confused.

"It means," began Natalia, "that if you take anything, you're dead. Just like all these people here who were turned into gold."

Ernie's face grew pale as he looked down at all the gold at his feet. He hoped it wasn't already too late. He had no interest in becoming a statue.

"So when we're told to take only what we need," Natalia

continued, "the answer is that we don't need anything. We could have skipped this whole test and walked straight through to the archway at the other end of this dreadful cave."

"What if you're wrong?" Ernie countered. "Then what happens?"

"Oh, please. I'm hardly ever wrong," replied Natalia, though a bit sheepishly given her little mistake that had nearly cost her her life (and Ernie's). The other three just stared at her. "Well, I'm certainly not wrong now."

A few moments later, the Grey Griffins quickly crossed over the next bridge and marched through another gateway. Lying next to the threshold were several golden statues in various states of pain and agony. But they weren't all knights. One was different. As Natalia looked closely, she recognized him as one of the police officers who had been working with Morgan. His hand was outstretched toward the open hallway, almost as if he were pleading for someone to come back and save him. No one had. Natalia shuddered.

"This ought to be interesting." Harley shook his head.

As they passed through the crumbling archway, they were met with a strange sight at the far end. At one time, perhaps even only hours before, a mighty portcullis had barred the way. But now a great tangle of iron bars and shattered stone lay at their feet, as if the gate had been hit by a train.

"Morgan," Natalia breathed with a hiss. "She was here." Just imagining Morgan LaFey had been there already was bad enough. When Max saw the gate, his heart sank. The portcullis had been strong enough to stop an army, and by the looks of things, it hadn't slowed down Morgan one bit.

"What's this?" Harley called as he pulled something small from the wreckage.

"It's a Round Table card," Max said as he took it from Harley and held it up to the light. "It's the Wise Man."

"Oh my gosh," cried Ernie as he stood on his tiptoes to get a better look. "That looks a lot like Iver."

"You're right," Harley agreed in amazement. "It totally looks like him."

"It's a sign!" Natalia exclaimed with a broad smile. "He's still alive. He must have left this for us to find."

"I hope you're right," called Max as he picked his way across the rubble. "We don't have any time to lose."

A few moments later, they had stepped into a long, perfectly square hallway of sand-colored stone blocks. The ceiling was low, but with the exception of Harley, they were in no danger of hitting their heads. The way was lit with strange oil lamps, and despite there being a lake just a few hundred feet away, the tunnel was dry and dusty.

"This place feels like a grave," Ernie whispered as his eyes darted nervously about.

"Let's go," Max pressed, undeterred. "Iver needs us." The other three followed as Max led them down the gently sloping hallway. Looking to either side, there were no other tunnels or passageways, and the ground was as clean as Ernie's plate after dinner. Yet an oppressive weight, intangible but ever present, pressed in on them from all sides.

"What's that?" Harley asked, after a good ways down.

"What?" wondered Max.

"Up there. It looks like a gap in the ceiling. I bet we could climb through."

"I don't know. Look at all this rubble," Natalia pointed out as they got closer. "It looks like someone blew the hole open with dynamite."

Morgan. She'd been there as well.

"Well, which is it? Up or down?"

Then, all four of them froze as a spine-chilling, inhuman-sounding shriek rang out from the tunnel below, and the lamplight shuddered ominously.

"Up is good," Ernie offered. The others agreed.

Pulling themselves through the hole in the ceiling, the Griffins dusted the sand from their knees and turned to see a very similar passageway to the one they had just left—only this one led upward. Up they marched, each step more wearisome than the last. They were all growing frustrated; the thought of the Jewel and Iver's safety hung heavily over them like a dark cloud. None, save Ernie of course, had thought of bringing any food, and they were getting hungry. Natalia had brought a canteen full of water, but they had finished it off long ago. Not that it did much good. The canteen tasted of rusty metal and was about as refreshing as licking a chalkboard.

The final leg of the journey led them to the entrance of a great room. Its floor was hewn from the same sandy stone, but the ceiling, if there even was one, was so high they couldn't guess its height. There were no other doors, in or out, and except for a single chair squarely in the middle of the room, there were no furnishings.

Yet scattered about the cavernous space were piles of rock strewn across the floor.

"They were statues," commented Natalia as she knelt beside a giant stone hand that gripped the hilt of a broken sword.

"And here's a head," called Harley, kicking at the rubble. "They must have been huge. Twenty feet tall, I bet, or bigger."

After closer inspection they found the remains of four statues in all, each a knight with what was strange and wonderful armor. Three of them wore helms, each shaped to resemble a different animal. One was that of a lion roaring, another, a mighty bull with horns now shattered into dust. The third looked like an eagle, wings swept upward. But the fourth knight was plain and unadorned, his carved eyes staring blankly into the darkness of his eternal tomb.

"Why would Morgan bother destroying statues?" asked Ernie as he pulled a stick of gum from his pocket. After catching Natalia's stern look, he held the gum toward her and put on an indignant face. "What? It's sugarless."

"I don't care about the gum, you ninny," replied Natalia. "The point is that it should be obvious what happened here."

"Not to me." Ernie shook his head as he popped the gum into his mouth. "I'm just glad Morgan's not here waiting for us."

"She was here," Max stated flatly. "That's for sure. This was the final test. My guess is that she failed, but she got through the others awfully quick. Maybe these stone knights were the punishment. If it was anybody other than Morgan, I bet they'd have been dead in a second."

"Geez." Ernie's eyes widened. "How are we gonna stop her?"

"We'll figure it out when we get there," replied Max, "if we get there."

"So what's the deal with this chair?" Harley mused. "Seems kinda out of place, doesn't it?"

It was one of the strangest, but most beautiful, chairs any of them had ever seen. The high back was carved with symbols and signs, reminiscent of those in the Chapel they had left far above, while the arms of the chair were sculpted to resemble eagles launching into flight, their mouths open in a mighty cry. But they were no ordinary eagles. They were griffins: mythical animals with the head, wings, and front talons of an eagle and the torso and tail of a lion.

Max circled around it a few times, wondering if there was any coincidence between the name of their secret club and the odd, though beautiful, chair. Logan had mentioned that the Grey Griffins existed long before Max and his friends. Yet coincidence or not, that chair was obviously the final test, and it filled Max with dread.

"Look." Natalia pointed. Two words were inscribed on the back:

SIEGE PERILOUS

"I don't know what it means, but it doesn't sound good," noted Ernie.

"I know." Natalia sighed. "And if you'd do a little research, you would, too. It comes from the story of King Arthur and his Round Table."

"But this is a chair," Ernie pointed out, trying to be helpful.

"It is one of the chairs, actually. One of twelve. And the most famous of all." She pulled out her notebook, fishing through the pages, until after a moment, she found what she was looking for. "It was created by Arthur's wizard, Merlin, who placed a spell on it. Anyone who sat on the chair would die a horrible death. Anyone, that is, except the one."

"Who?" asked Max.

"Just like in the story of King Arthur, this chair was made only for the knight whose heart was the most pure."

"So all you have to be is good?" asked Ernie.

"It's a bit trickier than that," Natalia continued. "I think it also has a lot to do with humility. Knights that were pure of heart had to be the best at what they did, but at the same time they had to believe they were really the worst. It's very complicated."

"Wait!" exclaimed Max suddenly. "I get it now. The tests. It all makes sense."

"What are you talking about?" questioned Natalia, her brow furrowed.

"The tests," Max repeated. "This one is purity, right?"

"Right." Natalia nodded. "So?"

"Well, I was reading the other day in my book about the Knights Templar. There were three vows they had to take before they could join the Order: obedience, poverty, and purity."

"You're right!" exclaimed Natalia as she pulled out her notepad and began scribbling down the discovery. "That's it. The first test told you to do something you didn't want to do like climbing down that nasty well, but you obeyed and passed. The second test was about poverty, so in order to pass, you couldn't touch any of the gold. And now here's the last test. Purity."

"It doesn't sound so tough," Harley commented as he looked at the chair skeptically.

"It's tougher than you think," Natalia countered. "For one thing, you won't know you're right until after it's too late to change your mind. And if you are wrong, the chair will destroy you—or worse."

"Worse?" Ernie mumbled to himself incredulously. "What's worse than death?"

Natalia shook her head. "I don't know. That's just what the books say."

"Well, I'm not sitting in the chair," proclaimed Ernie.

"No one was asking you to," replied Harley.

"I'm doing it," stated Max.

"But, Max," argued Natalia, "maybe we should think about this a little more. You can't just rush into something like this." Max's mind was set. This was his test. He was just glad he had friends like the Grey Griffins to stand by his side, even when things looked their worst.

"Stand back," he cautioned as he approached the Siege Perilous. He knew it was waiting for him, hungrily. It was scarier than anything he had experienced so far. Including the Slayer. Much worse.

As Max turned to sit down, he closed his eyes and took a breath. In those seconds, a flood of thoughts rushed through his head. He remembered the words he had told his father—that he never wanted to see him again. Max recalled how he had told his mother he hated her. There was his anger against Ray, and the happiness he felt seeing Harley beating him up. And more, much more. He remembered stealing cookies from his grandmother's jar, cheating on a math test. There was also the time he had not let an unpopular kid sit next to him on the bus.

But it didn't really matter. Even if he passed the test, who was he trying to kid? Max didn't feel he stood a chance against Morgan. He'd only found the *Codex* by accident, he reasoned. Iver must have been wrong about his role as the book's Guardian. It must have been meant for someone else. Yes, it was an accident. Maybe his whole life had been an accident. Then he knew. He was going to die.

Closing his eyes, Max prayed under his breath, and slowly, cautiously, walked to the chair, turned around, and sat down. His last thoughts were of Iver, helpless and beaten by the Black Witch. . . .

One Last Chance

AT FIRST, nothing happened. Then the sound of stone scraping against stone echoed through the room.

Natalia screamed. "The statues!" she cried as she pointed to her feet. "They're alive." The others looked, and sure enough, the eyes of the dismembered heads were lit with a ghastly light and the wreckage of their bodies began to glow and vibrate. Then a hand started to pull itself across the floor, with other broken pieces of stone following after.

Natalia screamed again. Even Ernie screamed. But Max remained where he was, frozen upon the Siege Perilous. He wasn't moving. He wasn't even blinking.

"Quick," Harley ordered. "Everyone gather around Max."

Before their frightened eyes, the stone hand joined an arm. Fingers, once shattered, reached out for a nearby sword.

"The knights are putting themselves back together!" Natalia shrieked as she backed up against the chair, protecting Max, even in her despair. "We failed the last test!"

"What are we supposed to do?" whimpered Ernie, his teeth chattering. Helplessly, they watched as the stone goliaths that surrounded them pulled themselves back together. When the transformation was complete, the knights towered over all four

Griffins. Each held a different weapon. The knight with the lion's helm carried a wicked mace. The bull held a giant war hammer, and the eagle knight gripped a sword in each hand. The knight that wore no helm held a single mighty spear. How anything could have survived, let alone defeated, these enchanted giants was impossible to imagine. But Morgan had.

For what seemed like an eternity, the giant knights remained frozen, their eyes oppressively gazing down at the tiny Griffins who seemed like ants in comparison. But then the colossi began to move.

"I'm doomed," Ernie cried as the knights raised their weapons. All of the children expected to be smashed into oblivion, except Max, who remained completely motionless. Yet to their great relief, the stone giants did not attack. Instead, in an odd twist they turned so their backs were facing the Griffins. In three long strides, the knights arrived at the four walls that lined the chamber, each knight facing its own wall.

"What are they doing?" Ernie asked, his teeth still chattering. "Does this mean I'm not going to die?"

As one, the giants slammed their weapons into holes bored into each wall, each a perfect fit, and with clockwork timing, the knights turned their weapons like keys in a giant lock.

Without warning, light spilled forth and flooded the room in a great wave, blinding the Griffins. On all sides of the Siege Perilous, strange symbols could be seen etched across the floor, glowing with a yellow fire. Then, ominously, a loud boom echoed underfoot, followed by another overhead.

The Griffins' eyes raised as the light from the symbols on the floor was suddenly reflected upward in a brilliant display that was answered by a similar pattern in the ceiling. All at once the four friends found themselves standing in the midst of the great pillar of light with Max in the center of it all. Shuddering, the platform they were standing on broke free from the floor and lurched the Grey Griffins slowly upward like a mighty elevator.

"You did it." Harley smiled at Max. "You passed the test."

But Max didn't move. His eyes didn't even blink. His mind was still lost in the magic. It wasn't over yet.

Ever higher the platform climbed as Ernie peered over the side, queasy. What was pushing them upward was anyone's guess. Perhaps elaborate gears or pulleys. Maybe magic. But whatever it was, they were now far too high to consider jumping off. In fact, the stone giants that had once towered over them menacingly were now only dark specks far below.

As they neared the never-ending ceiling, they could see a gaping hole in the center, directly where they were heading. But it wasn't supposed to be there, they could tell. The rock was blackened with fire and smoke. It must have been blown open by the same magic that had destroyed the knights. As they passed through the wreckage, they could see at last that they were entering an enormous circular room lit by the light of a thousand lamps. The platform came to rest, locking into place with a thud. Max seemed to wake from his dream, rubbing his eyes to get a better look at his surroundings.

"That was amazing, Max!" Ernie shouted in relief. "I thought we were gonna die for sure down there."

"I knew you could do it," said Harley, helping his friend up out of the chair.

Natalia had even managed a smile, despite her growing concern for Iver. Max had come through for all of them, triumphing over his own fears. But as he stood there, trying to get his bearings, he noticed they now found themselves standing in the strangest of rooms: Surrounding them were walls of black hammered iron. Even the floors and ceilings were made of it. Of course, where Morgan had blasted her way through, the iron was torn and shredded. Save for the devastation she had caused, the Griffins were standing in a virtual fortress.

"The iron is to keep the faeries out," surmised Natalia as she began looking around. "It's like a giant safe. This must be where the Jewel is kept."

"Too bad Morgan isn't a faerie," replied Harley. "Maybe they should have sprayed it with some 'witch-be-gone.'"

As Max stepped off the platform, he found himself looking down a dark hallway where breathtaking paintings and tapestries covered the walls. He found himself drawn to the hallway like a bee to honey. There was something very familiar about this place.

"They look like the images from the *Codex*," Natalia pointed out.

Just like Max's magical book, the paintings seemed to be alive. Each brushstroke held limitless dimension. Tall mountains, endless seas, and impenetrable forests shone in vast scenes, with a story behind each just waiting to be told. Max walked from one masterpiece to another, and it felt as if he were watching the entire history of a forgotten land.

"They're kind of creepy, if you ask me," Ernie said as Harley walked over to join him.

Spellbound, Max found himself standing open-mouthed in front of a mural framed by human bone. It captured the image of an army of dreadful power and evil. In its midst stood a dark and terrible figure. It looked like a man with raven hair, wrapped in a black cloak, yet he was nothing like a man. His features were far more beautiful and infinitely cruel, for in his eyes flashed a wickedness that leapt off the canvas, tearing into Max's heart. He stumbled backward.

"The Shadow King," he whispered.

"Max!" Natalia screamed as she ran to the far side of the room as fast as she could propel herself. "Max, come here. It's Iver!"

There, lying on the floor like a discarded bag of laundry, was the body of the old shopkeeper. His beard was torn and his face bruised. And lying not far from him, toppled on its side, was a small iron jewelry box. Its lid was open, yet whatever had been inside was no longer there.

"Iver, are you all right?" Natalia cried. She ran to him, brushing back the matted hair from his bloody face as tears ran down her own. "Please be alive. Oh, please tell me you're alive."

"Alive?" replied the old man they once thought to be a mighty wizard. "I should say I am." He coughed. "Though I've been in better shape, I daresay."

Trying to pull himself back to full consciousness, Iver smiled, though it hurt his face, and looked into the eyes of the four children who hovered nervously above him. "Ah . . . the Grey Griffins. I am certainly glad to see you. And Master Sumner." He paused, studying Max. "I see you've passed the tests, though I knew you would. I never had a doubt."

"Are you dying?" asked Natalia. After what had happened with Mr. Thorvald, she wasn't able to handle death again—especially not Iver's.

"No," Iver said weakly. "Though I am afraid my ego is a bit bruised." He then struggled and, with Harley's help, sat up. For a while none of them said a word as Iver rubbed at his bruised wrists, wincing uncomfortably when he tried to move his shoulder.

"I thought you were dead," Harley stated. "I saw you tied up at Dr. Blackstone's house. It looked like you weren't breathing."

"Yes." Iver nodded. "I was there, though as you can see, I am breathing. And I am sorry you had to see such a thing," noted Iver with regret. "It's not a sight for someone so young. But you are a brave lad, and I was glad to see you."

"You knew I was there?"

"Of course. Though the kobolds, luckily enough, did not."

"Why not?" Ernie asked.

"Kobolds have unique talents," Iver explained. "Torture not least among them," the old man said as he rubbed at his ankles, black and swollen. "It's their eyes—those black tunnel-dwelling eyes."

"You mean they can see in the dark?" Natalia interrupted.

"Beyond that, they can see through walls," Iver corrected. "Those creatures weren't there to stand guard over me, as you may have suspected. They were placed there by the Black Witch herself, to keep an eye out for you. She knew you'd come, as did I—though I wish you wouldn't have risked your lives for me. I do apologize."

"You'd have done the same for us," Harley said.

Iver grinned wryly. "Luckily, I had enough wits left about me to keep you from being discovered. Though I fear that was the last miracle I could offer. After that point, I was powerless against Morgan."

Natalia, overcome with emotion, threw her small arms around Iver, sobbing in relief.

"There, there," Iver comforted, patting her shoulder. "There's no need for tears. We've too much to do before this night ends. The fate of the world may well depend on us."

"We found your card." Max smiled as he held up the Wise Man card from Round Table.

"Did you?" Iver returned the smile. "Good. And I am glad to have it back," he said as he took the card from Max's hand and placed it into one of his inner pockets. "They are irreplaceable, you know."

"Did Morgan get the Jewel?" asked Max after hugging the old man in relief.

A look of sadness passed over Iver's face as he looked down at the overturned box at his feet. "I was not able to stop her."

"But you're a wizard!" Ernie exclaimed. "We saw what you did to the Slayer back in the woods."

Iver shook his head. "I am no wizard—at least, not in the way you seem to think. And you must remember that there are always bigger fish. Morgan is one of the biggest. And regretfully, I was no match for her. Few are, as no doubt Thorvald discovered."

"He's dead, you know." Natalia sniffed.

"Yes." Iver nodded sadly. "But that would be his wish, I am sure. To die in battle with the Black Witch herself. Which reminds me," he began as he struggled to his feet, using Harley as a crutch. Whatever had happened to him had damaged one of his legs so that he could not walk without their support. "We don't have much time. As you can see, Morgan has what she came for. All she needs now is Max's book."

Max shook his head. "But she could have taken it from me outside the Chapel. She had the chance. And she didn't. She just kept driving."

Iver growled and his eyes narrowed. "This is what I was most afraid of." If his leg weren't wounded, Max could imagine Iver would have been pacing back and forth in deep thought at this moment.

"What do you mean?" asked Natalia.

"There is a chance she may not require the *Codex*. We've always known it was a possibility. The Jewel is far more powerful than the book, though certainly the book holds power enough. It may be possible Morgan has found a way to use Titania's Jewel alone to open Oberon's Gate."

"That's not fair," Ernie complained, realizing all the bravery he had (arguably) shown in the past few weeks wasn't going to pay off. "That's cheating."

Iver smiled down at the littlest Griffin. "True, Master Tweeny. But that's the way it is sometimes. Good is always constrained by rules that evil never observes. Terribly inconvenient. For that reason, the Jewel has remained hidden and separate from the *Codex* all this time. Still, Morgan LaFey has not yet opened Oberon's Gate, I believe. If she had, we'd know by now. So take heart. There is still hope. Are you ready?"

"To do what?" asked Max cautiously.

"To steal the Jewel from the Black Witch and for the first time in thousands of years reunite it with the *Codex*." Max's eyes widened. "That's the only way Oberon can be defeated, and that is the only chance we have. You, as the Guardian, are the chosen one. Only you can do this, Master Sumner."

"But if I put the Jewel and book together, isn't that what the Shadow King wants?"

"No longer, I think," replied Iver. "The Shadow King now wants the *Codex* destroyed. It appears he used it to release the portals where his servants had been trapped. Now he must destroy the threat that it still represents."

"What do you mean?" asked Max.

"Oberon wanted the Jewel for himself, as he has since the beginning of time. He will stop at nothing to get it. No doubt to his displeasure, Morgan found it first. Why she wants it remains to be seen. We can only assume that some terrible bargain is about to take place in the forest tonight—a bargain between two forces of evil that could only mean that our world is about to come to an end."

"But what can we do?" asked Natalia in desperation.

Iver offered a weary smile. "Max must follow the path of the great King of the West—he must unite the Jewel with the *Codex*. Only then does the book have the power to defeat Oberon and close the portals."

"But once they are put together . . . what then?" Max argued. "I don't know what to do!"

"The *Codex* will know what to do. As its Guardian, so will you."

Max stood in stunned silence.

"But what if Morgan just squishes us and takes the *Codex*?" Ernie pointed out. "Then she'll have the Jewel and the book. Wouldn't that be worse?"

Iver nodded. "It is a risk. The greatest risk of all, perhaps. You will have to be careful."

"Careful?" replied Ernie incredulously. Careful was not stepping on a sidewalk crack. This was something altogether different.

"But what about the rest of the Templars?" asked Natalia. "Shouldn't there be an army of them to help us?"

Iver shook his head. "Perhaps once there might have been. But time can be as cruel as any witch. There are no more glorious armies, though we are far from powerless, I assure you. You are never alone."

None of the kids seemed overly convinced, but they were bound together as one. So it was that Natalia, Ernie, and Harley stepped beside Max. Whatever he chose, they would follow.

"Ready?" Iver asked.

They were the Grey Griffins, and they would stick together to the end.

"Very good. Then, follow me."

Max nodded.

Iver swung his arm around Harley for balance, and the Grey Griffins fell silently in line behind him like small soldiers marching to battle. He limped slowly across the room weaving in and around white pedestals that held tall, brooding statues with menacing eyes. "Stay close. No dawdling," Iver warned as they walked under the shadow of a monstrous dragon made of stone. Its mouth lay open, with the beginnings of a firestorm forming just behind its murderous teeth.

"That's amazing." Harley whistled. "Who made it?"

"Made? I should say no one," replied Iver. "Making living things is not man's providence. That dragon is quite real, and should it manage to break loose, we'd certainly have our hands full."

"He's alive?" gawked Ernie.

"She. And yes, quite alive," replied Iver. "No more questions please. Follow along."

Soon they found themselves standing in front of a painting cast in mysterious blues and greens. It was of a forest, large and ominous.

"Why does that look so familiar?" Ernie asked, chewing a piece of dried pineapple he'd found in one of his pockets.

"It's the old woods," added Natalia, proud that she was the first to notice.

"Keep looking," commanded the old proprietor.

As Max's eyes pored over the canvas, the dark forest spread across the land like a heavy blanket. It overwhelmed him. And in the corner of the picture, on the verge of being engulfed by the darkness, was a small town. Its streetlights were dim, but Max knew it well enough. It was Avalon. In fact, he could see his house . . . and King's Elementary . . . and Turtle Cove. Then his eyes fell on a gray hill that stood in the midst of the great wood, and upon it were stones placed vertically, resembling teeth biting up at the sky.

"Hey!" exclaimed Natalia. "It's the faerie hill where we fought Ray." Max looked closely to discover she was right. But it was more than that. This wasn't just a painting. As Max gazed into it, he could see movement—shapes walking across the hill. A bright light flashed brilliantly nearby.

"It's the Jewel!" Ernie cried.

"This painting," began Iver, clearing his throat, "is quite different than you might imagine: It is a window into the *now*. I won't go into the details, but suffice to say that it will allow you to step through the frame and into the scene you see before you. Some paintings could take you to Africa, others to nearby planets. This one takes you to your forest, and the faerie hill upon which rests Titania's Jewel."

"You mean it will take us straight to the hill?" asked Harley.

Natalia nodded in understanding. "So it's like a portal."

Iver smiled proudly, brushing aside a stray hair from Natalia's forehead. "Quite so. These paintings are, in fact, related to portals. Only in this case you can actually see where you are going. Which, in my opinion, makes traveling much more agreeable."

"Morgan is there," Max noted as he looked more closely. He could even see her driver standing nearby. In the air, not far from the Jewel, an opening was being made that seemed to bend the paint strangely. Then Max knew what it was.

"Oberon's Gate," he breathed. "She's done it. She knows how to use the Jewel. It's too late."

"Not yet," Iver maintained. "But if you wait much longer, it will be."

"I don't wanna go back," Ernie cried as he backed away from the painting. "No way."

"Are you coming with us?" inquired Max as he looked up at the old Templar.

"I am afraid I cannot." Iver shook his head and wiped away a trickle of blood from his forehead. "Morgan's magic has broken me. I am afraid I would only be a hindrance to you now. And, anyway, this is something only you can do. You and your Grey Griffins."

"So how do we do it?" asked Harley, popping his knuckles. "The sooner we go, the sooner we can get this over with."

"Just step into the painting. It will take care of the rest."

24 The End – or the Beginning?

AS THEY STEPPED into the painting, all color washed away into a sea of white fog, and their bodies began to tingle, crackling with energy, causing their hair to stand on end. Then a great wind rushed past them, and the sound of a roaring train shook their brains and teeth. Finally, with a *pop*, they broke through the barrier. Iver's words were true, and the picture had delivered as promised. All at once, they found themselves standing again in the lush forest under a canopy of dark and ominous trees. Ernie checked immediately to see if he was missing any important body parts, like a nose or a finger.

"Home sweet home." Harley shook his head, his sarcasm bringing a wry smile to Max's face.

"I wonder where we are, though," asked Natalia, rubbing her arms to warm her from the bitter wind that seemed to circle about them.

"Closer than you think," replied Max, pulling off his book bag, from which light began to blaze forth like a fire.

"What's going on?" asked Ernie unsteadily as he backed away.

"The Jewel," Max replied flatly. "The *Codex* knows that it's close."

"That's not all that's close," Natalia noted as she pointed at the frost-covered ground at her feet. "Something big and bad. The temperature is dropping fast."

Harley nodded as he followed the ever-thickening line of frost into the nearby undergrowth. A moment later he returned and waved for his friends to follow.

"We're at the bottom of Ray's hill," Harley pointed out as they took cover behind a large boulder at the base of the incline. The portal had brought them exactly where they needed to go. Unfortunately, their destination didn't look terribly inviting.

"Morgan's up there, all right," Natalia noted, squinting in the half-light of the encroaching darkness. "I can see her standing in front of the stone altar."

"Does she have Titania's Jewel?" Ernie asked, unable to see from where he was hiding.

"I think so," answered Natalia. "Either that or she's carrying a star in her hands—it's really amazing. So bright and so beautiful. Wow . . . I never imagined . . ."

"I don't see Blackstone," Harley interrupted. "Or anybody else."

"What about Sprig?" Ernie asked, looking nervously into the trees.

Max was feeling a little unsure about the spriggan as well. He hadn't seen her in a while, and though he did care about her very much, he knew quite well that she wanted the Jewel just as much as, if not more than, Morgan did. Sprig had stolen it before, long ago, and she'd do it again. And if the Jewel fell into her possession, there would be no way to find her, though eventually the Shadow King would. And then things would get really bad. They'd have to keep their eye out for her.

"Wait. Morgan's driver is standing guard over there," Harley pointed out.

"Holy cow," breathed Ernie, gawking at the dark tower of muscle squeezed into a black tuxedo. Ernie had never seen the man before, and immediately wished he could have avoided the experience altogether.

"He's going to be a problem," Harley noted. Harley always preferred the direct approach . . . to muscle his way through issues by relying on his size. But Harley wasn't nearly as large as Dennis Stonebrow, and this man had made Dennis look frail by comparison.

"Just Morgan and her driver?" asked Max. "Are you sure there's no one else up there? I thought I saw more shadows in the picture before we jumped through."

"Yes," replied Natalia. "But Blackstone is still unaccounted for, and we don't know where Sprig is."

"What about Ray?" Harley asked. "He's still out there somewhere."

"That means we have three wild cards," sighed Natalia. "I don't like the odds."

They all turned to Max, who seemed lost in thought. "All right," he finally said. "We're gonna have to wing it. Let's concentrate on Morgan and her bodyguard."

"I think we're too late," Harley whispered.

Through the low-hanging branches, the Grey Griffins could see Morgan chanting an incantation. She was standing with her arms stretched high as she placed Titania's Jewel in a brilliant column of light that suspended the gem in the air. An electric current stirred, rushing through the forest like a tidal wave. The Griffins were in awe as red fire hung in the air before Morgan. Oberon's Gate was like no portal they had seen before, as a hail of lightning shot out of it in all directions. Whether it was devouring the warmth of the air or vomiting icy blasts of wind onto the hill, Max could not tell. But the grass and stones nearby were encased in ice; the numbing air was swirling about like the brew in a witch's cauldron. Even a fleeting glance into the portal's depths, terrible to gaze upon, drained all hope from the four who had come so far and endured so much.

Morgan continued to chant, calling forth a mighty storm.

"He's there," cried Natalia, her voice barely audible over the roaring wind. "I can see Oberon through the portal!"

Max saw him, too—piercing eyes against a fathomless face—Oberon, the mighty Shadow King, husband of Titania, and Wrecker of Worlds, radiated unrelenting anger and merciless hate. The Gate was almost complete, and soon the world would fall into darkness as he marched with an army as numberless as the stars in the sky. They were too late.

"No!" Max shouted as he charged toward the hill in sudden anger. Without thinking, the Grey Griffins followed, yelling as they raced to meet an enemy they could never hope to defeat. Yet no sooner had they reached the foot of the hill than they ran headfirst into an invisible wall. With cries of pain and frustration, they tumbled backward.

"A force field," Ernie called over the gale, rubbing the burn mark on his forehead. "Just like in the movies. How do we get through that?"

"She's too powerful," answered Max, slowly rising from the ground and glaring up at the portal that continued to grow.

Harley threw a rock at the magical barrier with all his might, but it ricocheted off even faster than it had struck—whizzing over his head like a missile. There was no way through. The Grey Griffins' hopes were shattered. They had come so far, only to find out that there had probably never been any chance of success to begin with. Morgan LaFey could defeat kings and destroy armies. Four little kids from Minnesota were nothing to her.

"But why would Iver send us all the way back here just to fail?" argued Natalia. "It doesn't make any sense."

"Unless he knew something we didn't," replied Max.

"Like what?"

"Uh, guys?" Harley interrupted as his eyes locked onto something in the night sky. "I think the cavalry is coming."

"What are you talking about . . . ?" Natalia's voice trailed into stunned silence as her eyes fell upon the same strange sight.

Just at the moment when everything seemed lost, a shining light, like a star, flew down from the sky and broke through the invisible barrier, sending sparks of errant light and scorching heat in all directions. The force field had been shattered, and yet the light continued to descend. As it slowed, the Griffins could see that it was an angel—or something very much like one. Hovering above the hill, the figure was clad in a long dress of ethereal light, with golden hair and shining eyes. It was a woman of dreamlike beauty that reflected both mercy and terrible power. She smiled in a businesslike fashion as she turned to face Morgan LaFey.

"Ms. Heen!" gasped Natalia. "I knew it."

Morgan did not smile back. She spun with her hands outstretched, a fury of red fire leaping from her fingertips. The sheer power of the attack would have leveled a skyscraper, but Ms. Heen merely waved it away. Flames fell to the ground, sizzling and spitting until they were extinguished in the rain.

In reply, Ms. Heen raised her hand and the ground caved under Morgan's feet, forming a bottomless pit. Yet instead of falling, the witch leapt to the sky, levitating within a ball of crackling energy.

The two looked at each other and their eyes narrowed. Then things got serious.

With a flash, the hilltop exploded under a rain of fire and rock as they set upon each other with renewed fury.

"Holy cow!" Ernie shouted over the noise. "Are you watching this?"

"Look!" Natalia cried. "The portal—it stopped growing! Now that the force field is down, we might have a chance, but we'd better move while Morgan's distracted."

"What about the bodyguard?" Harley reminded them, pointing to the motionless figure on the crest of the hill. He stood like a watchtower, his silhouette backlit by the explosions of light behind him on the icy hill. The mountainous man ignored the battle, his hands folded behind his back as he stared into the night, unmoved by the storm.

"How are we gonna get past him?" worried Ernie. "He looks more dangerous than a whole army of goblins."

"We need a diversion," stated Natalia.

357

Strangely, and at an impossible moment, Max smiled. "Griffins, gather around. I have a plan."

Blinding flashes illuminated the dark summit as three small shadows crept up the far slope. One of the shadows was clearly a girl, for her pigtails and dress were fluttering madly under the pull of the brutal wind. The other two were boys, one much larger than the other. The smaller carried what looked to be a large book, which he held before him like a sword.

When the shadowy figures reached the top, peering over the crest, they could see the imposing figure of Morgan's bodyguard. As they had hoped, his back was turned to them.

The battle between Rhiannon Heen and Morgan LaFey continued to rage with great fury. Ms. Heen sent cobalt shafts hurtling toward Morgan. But the blasts sizzled and cracked as they were deflected by a fiery wall. Morgan returned the volley with a wave of her hand, causing the ground to shake as great stones broke from the earth and struck like battering rams against the defenses of their angelic teacher. Neither, so far, had gained the upper hand.

"It's time," the young girl wrapped in shadow called over the gale.

The two boys nodded.

A bolt of lightning shot across the sky as the three silhouettes hurtled forth. The larger boy and the girl raced headlong toward the massive driver, while the smaller boy with the book made directly for the Jewel of Titania, which hung suspended in the column of light.

Hoping to take the witch's servant by surprise (and push him off the ledge), Harley and Natalia poured on the speed. Five seconds 'til impact. Four seconds. Three seconds. Two. One . . .

And then they found themselves in the most awkward of positions, passing right through the dark form of the bodyguard, tumbling over the snowy crest.

The man had dematerialized into mist, and a moment later, as his body solidified, ghostly eyes flickered in amusement. Then, with a snarl, he turned his attention to the boy racing toward the Jewel.

All that mattered to the boy carrying the book was the Jewel. He was completely devoured by that single thought, which was most unfortunate, for he failed to see the witch's servant leap into the air, arcing high over the battle, and land directly in his path. Yet no longer did the driver appear as an impeccably dressed chauffeur. Instead, what stood before the boy was a black wolf with a mouthful of jagged teeth. With sadistic amusement, the giant beast looked down at its prey and smiled.

"Looking for something, human?" growled the werewolf, its acidic saliva dripping to the ground, burning and hissing.

With a frightened cry, the boy nearly dropped the precious book as he faked left, then right, finally running straight toward a towering stone close by. The werewolf followed with a hungry smile, knowing the boy had nowhere to go.

But just as the boy reached the rock face, a flash of light flickered—a portal.

Ernie jumped in.

In another instant, the portal disappeared. Unable to stop in time, the werewolf flew into the air, passing right through the place Ernie had been only a split second before. For a brief moment, the monster was airborne and vulnerable, but that's all the time that was needed. A crack of thunder was heard, and with a howl of pain, the werewolf's lifeless body tumbled down the side of the icy hill where it came to rest at the feet of a well-dressed man in sunglasses holding a short-nosed gun with a smoking barrel.

Logan had returned with Iver's silver bullets.

And he wasn't alone. From behind the trees stepped other men in dark suits. The Templars were here to protect their own.

In answer to their charge, hundreds, if not thousands, of shadowy monsters shot out from the forest straight toward the knights—the Hounds of Oberon. Like the roar of a mighty wave, they crashed into their opponents. Spears flew, teeth shredded, and a blaze of gunfire lit the forest floor in a haunting light.

Max stepped out from behind a tall stone where he had been watching the entire scene. So far the plan had worked. Morgan's driver had thought Ernie was actually Max. Now that the driver was out of the way, only Morgan remained. He couldn't defeat her, but the hope was she wouldn't notice him until it was too late.

Max sprang into action, racing toward the Jewel. In his periphery he could feel the eyes of the Shadow King upon him, the hatred burning with physical heat. Yet still Max pushed on, running toward the pillar of light where Titania's Jewel awaited, suspended in the air like a radiant island. Struck by its overwhelming beauty,

Max felt a connection with the precious stone. "This is it," he said, taking a deep breath to calm his nerves. He shook his fingers, let out a breath, and slowly raised his arms toward the hovering Jewel. Trembling, his anxious fingers reached into the light. . . .

Just then, a scaly blue hand wrapped like an iron cable around Max's wrist.

"Hiya, Max," a dark voice greeted him. "Miss me?" The next thing Max knew, he was thrown to the frost-covered ground as Ray leapt onto his chest.

"Get off me, you freak!" Max screamed. "You don't know what you're doing. We have to close the portal!"

"Now why would I want to do that?" Ray's lidless eyes flashed brightly. Imprinted on his cheek was the outline of a small Templar cross: the telltale white scar left behind by Harley's ring. It looked painful. "It's you who doesn't understand what's going on. The Shadow King offered you everything, but you were too weak to take it."

"What are you talking about?" Max yelled as an explosion from below the hill lit the sky in a plume of fire. The Templars had evidently brought the heavy weapons, and though they may have been no match for Morgan, the knights were ripping through the goblins like a hot knife through butter. Unfortunately, the Hounds of Oberon were numberless. Eventually, the knights would run out of ammunition. Then they would turn to blade and bolt.

Ray's blue skin sparkled in the glare of the battle that raged behind them. "You're a pathetic wimp. No wonder he found someone better—someone like me. "

"Ray, it's the Shadow talking. You have to fight it," Max choked as Ray's fingers squeezed around his throat. His evil strength had at least doubled since the last time they had met, and Max was held down so tightly that he could barely manage to stay conscious.

"Is it?" Ray laughed. "Don't you realize who you are talking to? The Shadow and the Shadow King are one and the same, Max. When you released the Shadow, *you* doomed the entire world."

Max gaped at Ray in confusion.

"That's right, rich boy. All along you've been played for a fool. It was the Shadow King who sent his Slayer to help you find the *Codex* in the first place. He knew you were just stupid enough to open the book. He used you because you're weak."

"He's using you, too," Max cried, though his voice cracked under Ray's unrelenting grip. "You have to fight it."

"The pathetic child you once tormented is gone. Only I remain now—the Shadow. And trust me, I hate you even more than Ray ever did. Good-bye, Max. Killing you will be a pleasure."

So consumed with his revenge, Ray failed to see Harley's boot before it smashed into his face. Ray toppled as Max lay gasping for air, but the victory was fleeting. In an instant, Ray was back on his feet, wiping yellow blood from his mouth with a smile. Things had changed since they had last tangled. Ray was now stronger than ever.

Snarling, he leapt at Harley.

While everyone was busy trying to stay alive, no one noticed an insignificant flash of light or the furry figure that stepped from a portal near the far corner of the hilltop. The creature looked this way and that to see if she had been spotted.

She hadn't.

So it was with caution that the faerie skittered and hopped across the snowy hilltop, keeping to the shadows and out of the way of the errant blasts between the two warring women. Quietly and quickly, she approached the Jewel she had stolen so long ago, and for which she had spent thousands of years imprisoned. Her desire for it had not diminished.

She looked at Max, who was safe for the moment; the shadow monster that had attacked him was now fighting with Harley, the boy who had wounded her so terribly. That fight was none of her concern. She then looked at Morgan LaFey, locked in deadly combat with Rhiannon Heen's angelic form. Even the Templars with their high-powered scopes and infrared imaging systems had not been alerted to her presence. Nothing could stop her now. And she knew it.

Harley had just enough time to blink before Ray was on top of him. He had hoped his attack would at least buy Max enough time to get the Jewel, but Harley had greatly underestimated Ray. With one crushing blow, the monster sent Harley's body reeling through the air as it crashed in a heap. Then Ray launched himself at Max, who had just spotted Sprig reaching for the Jewel. At that moment, Max knew everything was about to fall apart, and that it was probably his fault. If he hadn't hurt Sprig, she might be protecting him right then instead of betraying him.

"Sprig! Don't do it!" Max shouted as Ray smashed into him again. Within an instant, he was pinned back to the ground. And Harley was nowhere to be seen. If Ray had known what was happening behind his back, he might have had a chance to protect the Jewel. But his rage was all-consuming, and all his burning eyes could see was Max — his greatest enemy.

"Looks like it's just you and me, Sumner," Ray spit.

"Sprig," Max's weak voice called again, blood trickling from a gash on his head. "Help . . ."

In sudden indecision, the spriggan froze, turning to see the boy who had rescued her from the book. He had always treated her kindly and with respect — something she had never known before Max. This poor boy's life was now about to end at the hands of the shadow creature. She knew it was her fault. If she hadn't talked Max into letting the Shadow out, then this wouldn't be happening. But she had had no choice. She had a destiny, too. And it was right in front of her. Titania's Jewel was so close — so beautiful. She had loved it for so long. And her plan was foolproof; a portal awaited her perfect escape only a little distance away. But she did not move. Why was she hesitating?

Ray, who hadn't noticed the little creature or perhaps didn't care, smiled. "Time to die, little boy."

"Do what you have to do," Max coughed, wincing in pain. It was over, and he knew it. With Ray about to kill him, Harley probably dead, and Sprig within seconds of capturing the Jewel, hope drained from him. "Just get it over with."

"My pleasure," replied Ray. Reveling in his growing power, Ray raised his hand. Whether illusion or magic, it seemed to melt and transform into a long, wicked blade, dripping with a toxic green liquid. With an evil glimmer, Ray drove it down at Max like a missile.

Max closed his eyes, waiting for the end to come.

It never did.

Instead, Max heard a horrible cry. Sprig had abandoned the Jewel and thrown herself in front of Max. The blade had struck her.

"Sprig, no!" Max cried out as the faerie crashed to the ground with a cry of pain. Max's heart broke.

"Nice try," Ray snarled in frustration. "But you're running out of friends now. This time, it won't be so easy."

"No . . . ," growled Sprig as she slowly rose to her feet, blood dripping down her leg. She turned to face Ray as he towered over her. "Max is good. He saved us. *You* are the bad one. *You* are nothing but a lie. Sprig will make you go away."

Before Ray had a chance to react, Sprig leapt straight at him, transforming instantly into a winged griffin, furious in its might. In a fury of claws, they hit the ground like a meteor, sending up a shower of ice and rocketing through a portal that had mysteriously opened just at that moment.

With a flash, they were gone.

"Get the Jewel, Max!" Natalia yelled over the roar of the wind.

Max didn't need coaxing, though from where his strength came he could never recall. Dizzy from loss of blood, he leapt at Titania's

Jewel, yanking it out from the pillar of light. As he hit the ground, he yanked the *Codex* free of his backpack and slammed the Jewel into its waiting slot.

A thunderous explosion of light shattered the hilltop, and like a mighty wave, the blast overtook Morgan and Ms. Heen, who were instantly lost from sight as the destruction swept over them, illuminating the forest in the ghostly wash. Oberon's Gate, robbed of the very power that kept it alive, slammed shut with a scream of anguish and desperation.

That was the last thing Max saw.

When he awoke, Max was seated atop the same grassy hill. The night sky was dusted with sparkling stars as a loon called in the distance. The clouds were gone, and so was the rain. In fact, everything had changed. No longer did the trees tower into the sky, or the flowers softly glow in the dimness of the wood. The enchantment was gone. It was once again the woods Max had grown up with. Then his eyes fell on the *Codex* that lay at his feet, the Jewel of Titania shining brightly upon its face, and Max knew that it had not been a dream. Carefully, almost in reverence, he lifted it up and clutched it tightly to his chest.

"Hey, Max!" Ernie called out, followed by Natalia and Harley. They were cresting the top of the hill, waving.

"Are you okay?"

Max smiled and nodded. "How about you guys?"

Harley's lip was still bleeding, but like the others, he was smiling broadly.

"We found Dr. Blackstone down at the foot of the hill." Natalia pointed. "Logan has him tied to a tree. I guess he was trying to get away."

"Where are the other Templars?" Max asked, his mind just beginning to wake up.

Harley shrugged. "They left. Took their guns and disappeared into the forest, but Iver is still down there talking to Logan, I think."

Ernie nodded in excitement as if he had just survived the world's tallest roller coaster. "Yeah, and Iver's been busy. He's the one who opened the portal and saved me from the werewolf. And he used another portal to bring all the Templar Knights here so they could fight off the goblins." Ernie paused for a second to catch his breath, his eyes lost in a wondrous memory. "Oh, Max, you should have seen them. Templar Knights, just like in the books. Only they are even more powerful now. And there was this really big knight that had a Grey Griffins patch on his jacket. He watched out for me while the rest of them were fighting the goblins. It was so awesome!"

"Well, Ernest," Natalia said, smiling, "you'll be happy to know you missed Ray."

"Ray?" Ernie gasped, looking around nervously.

"He's gone now," Max said quietly. "Sprig sacrificed herself to save me from him, and now they're both gone—maybe forever."

"Sprig saved all of us," added Natalia, taking out a kerchief and dabbing her watering eyes. She loved melodrama, though Sprig's sacrifice had touched her deeply. "I can't believe it; if it wasn't for that spriggan, we'd have been finished. I just wish I had been nicer. . . ."

"What a wonderful wish," came a bright and cheerful voice.

The Grey Griffins turned to find Ms. Heen standing behind them. She didn't look like an angel anymore. She was dressed as she would have been for a day at school, complete with a warm cup of coffee in her hands.

"Ms. Heen!" exclaimed Natalia, wiping away her tears. "It's so good to see you!"

"It's good to see you, too," their teacher replied with a smile. "Although I think you can finally call me Rhiannon. No more of this stuffy 'Ms. Heen' business."

"What happened to Morgan?" Ernie asked, looking to make sure the Black Witch wasn't going to appear out of thin air. "Is she dead?"

"Oh heavens, no." Rhiannon shook her head. "She is far too powerful to go down that quietly."

"You call that quietly?" Harley asked in amazement. "That light show didn't seem so quiet to me." Rhiannon tousled Harley's hair—a sign of affection he wasn't used to (or so his blushing face seemed to indicate). "Um . . . what about Ray and Sprig?" Harley asked, changing the topic.

Rhiannon only shook her head. "I am afraid I do not know, nor, sadly, do I have the time to answer all your very important questions. Unfortunately, it's time for me to leave."

"What?" cried Natalia. "What do you mean? We have school tomorrow."

"You have school tomorrow," she replied with a kindly smile. "I have another assignment for which I cannot be late."

"Will we ever see you again?" Ernie asked, his voice breaking.

"I think that would be nice, don't you?" Ms. Heen replied with a wink. Ernie nodded, the lump in his throat nearing unbearable proportions as he looked at his feet to hide any tears.

"But," she continued with a look of warning toward Max, "you must realize that the Shadow King is far from defeated. He will be back, and he will not underestimate you a second time, I think. In the meantime, you have a great responsibility, Max. You now know your family history, and a little of the connection between yourself and the Shadowlands of Faerie. You are the Guardian of the *Codex*, and it is up to you to keep this secret safe. Guard it well, and know that your role will become clearer to you every day. Unless I am greatly mistaken, I'll be hearing many things about you in the future. You have proved yourself worthy. Your grandfather would be very proud."

"You knew my grandfather, too?" asked Max in wonder. "How?"

"Oh, you might say that I still do," Ms. Heen said with a mysterious laugh as she turned and began to walk away.

"But . . . ," Max started, his voice trailing off. "If you can't tell me anything about him, can you at least tell me what we're supposed to do now?" he asked.

"That is for you to decide," said Rhiannon as she turned and smiled, waving at them. With a parting wink she seemed to dissolve into a shining light, disappearing into the stars above.

The Grey Griffins were left standing alone on the windswept hill under a starry sky.

A Round Table Glossary

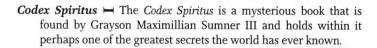

Codex Spiritus ⊢ The *Codex Spiritus* is a mysterious book that is found by Grayson Maximillian Sumner III and holds within it perhaps one of the greatest secrets the world has ever known.

Faerie Hill ⊢ Faerie hills are hollow mounds of earth where the faeries live, though they have also been used as both burial mounds and safe havens to hide faerie gold. They are heavily guarded, and to loot a faerie hill brings certain death and oftentimes something even worse.

Garden Faerie ⊢ Garden faeries are a unique species of the magical folk who are most often found tending to gardens and various fields of wildflowers. Diminutive and beautiful beyond compare, these tiny faeries have pointed ears, translucent wings, and wear petals and leaves for clothes. Often harmless, when riled, or particularly when their gardens are threatened, these faeries can be fierce protectors.

Gargoyle ⊢ Gruesome statues carved from stone, gargoyles stand guard upon cathedral rooftops, warding against evil spirits that would threaten both the church and the surrounding village. Legend claims gargoyles would come to life at night when the villagers were most vulnerable, only to return to their resting places before the sun rose.

Goblin ⊢ Twisted faeries, black of heart with sinister intentions, goblins make up the bulk of the dark armies of Oberon, the Shadow King. Though there are many subspecies of goblins, most are about the height of an average eleven-year-old, with long apelike arms, scaly hides, jagged teeth, and crooked noses that ooze with disgustingly slimy snot. Limited in faerie magic, goblins rely on crude weapons and their overwhelming numbers to defeat their foes.

Hounds of Oberon ⊨ The Shadow King's vast armies are powerful and sinister — but few are as frightfully efficient as his Hounds, a contingent of the most horrible and wicked goblins ever to walk the Shadowlands. The king uses them to track down and find anything fortunate enough to have escaped from his dark grasp. There is nothing and no one they cannot find.

Kobolds ⊨ The hired soldiers of the faerie underworld, kobolds were originally miners. Unique skills, such as seeing through walls and being immune to iron, made them ideal candidates for the employ of the Black Witch, Morgan LaFey.

Jewel of Titania ⊨ The Great Jewel of Titania was given to the Queen of Faerie as a gift, by the god of heaven. It is said to hold within it the power of life and death, and about it shines a light more brilliant than a thousand suns. While the Jewel was meant to bring light into the world, the desire for it, by Oberon and others, has brought with it a far more powerful darkness.

Morgan LaFey ⊨ Morgan LaFey is the half sister of King Arthur of Camelot. Sorceress. Immortal. Beautiful. Rich. Her dark motives are known only to herself.

Oberon's Gate ⊨ The Land of Faerie is separated from our world by a great Sea of Mist, impassable and desolate. In order to cross this great emptiness, Oberon requires the help of the greatest of portals, which he personally created and attended to every detail.

Order of the Grey Griffins ⊨ A secret society with four official members: Grayson Maximillian Sumner III; Natalia Felicia Anastasia Romanov; Harley Davidson Eisenstein; and Ernest Bartholomew Tweeny, the Order of the Grey Griffins formed shortly after the members banded together to rescue Ernie from the kindergarten class bully.

Portals ⊨ Like Oberon's Gate, portals are doorways that permit transportation from one place to another, usually in a very unpredictable and sometimes dangerous fashion.

Round Table ⊨ An ancient game of high adventure, heart-thumping battles, and careful strategy, Round Table is played with a deck of oversized trading cards and a pair of ten-sided dice called knucklebones. The Grey Griffins are the only kids in Avalon to play the game, but these cards hold more secrets than Max and his friends had ever begun to guess.

Shadowlands of Faerie ⊷ With dark corners and dreamlike edges, the Land of Faerie holds glistening towers of goodness and kingdoms of light. But there are also places where evil dwells and attends to its dark purpose. It is here, within the Shadowlands of Faerie, that Oberon, the Shadow King, rules over a world of nightmares and horrors.

Slayer Goblin ⊷ The assassins of the faerie underworld, Slayers are employed by the Shadow King for one reason: to kill his enemies.

Spriggan ⊷ Spriggans are small but surprisingly dangerous faeries left with the thankless task of guarding the treasures of faerie hills. Easily bored, spriggans are notorious thieves and troublemakers. As shape-shifters, they can take the form of any living creature.

Templar Knights ⊷ An ancient order of knights, once the most beloved and respected soldiers in the Old World, the Templar Knights were betrayed and murdered on Friday, October 13, 1307, and those that survived went into hiding — taking with them their mysterious secrets and legendary gold.

Titania ⊷ Queen of the Land of Faerie, Titania is the wife of Oberon, the Shadow King. While she rules over the Kingdom of Light and has often come to war against her husband's evil, she is still a fearsome queen with almost limitless power. It is said that even looking upon her unsurpassed beauty could drive a human to insanity and despair.

Toadstool Ring ⊷ Lovers of both music and foolishness, faeries often join in an enchanting dance about a circle of toadstools that can be deadly to any human. Once both feet cross the path of toadstools, any human becomes a slave to the faeries for life, caught in a musical web of madness, never to return. Only a rescuer who manages to fend off the faerie enchantment while keeping one foot outside the ring of mushrooms can snatch the captive, freeing them from their doom.

Unicorn ⊢ Pure and good, unicorns are magical beasts that closely resemble horses, snowy white with flowing manes and a spiraled horn growing from their foreheads.

Werewolf ⊢ Not born of the faerie world, werewolves are cursed mortals who take the shape of giant wolves during a full moon. It is said that men strong of will have been able to master the art of morphing between man and wolf at their whim, even in the daylight, but such power is extremely rare. Though holy water may slow them down, the only way to kill a werewolf is to pierce its heart with a bullet of pure silver.